LET THE DEAD ALONE

The Complete

Cases of Luther McGavock

1942–43

MERLE CONSTINER

---

introduction by Evan Lewis

illustrations by Peter Kuhlhoff

cover by Rafael de Soto

BLACK MASK

2020

Table of Contents

Introduction

NOTE: Precious little was known of this author's life until Peter Ruber's "The Hunt for Merle Constiner" was published in the September 1999 issue of Pulpdom. *Mr. Ruber went the whole hog, seeking out friends, relatives, acquaintances and historians from Constiner's home town and tracking down snippets of info from various newspaper articles and interviews. A revised version of this piece was posted on Duane Spurlock's* Pulp Rack *in December 2002. For much of the biographical information below, I am greatly in his debt. I am also indebted to the writings of Mike Grost, and input from my fellow Constiner fans Richard Moore and Sai Shankar.*

THIS BOOK IS the first in what promises to be a long series of collections featuring well-known and lesser-known series characters from the thirty-one-year history of *Black Mask*. Most critical attention has focused on the years 1926–1936 under editor Joseph T. "Cap" Shaw, when the mainstays of the magazine included such names as Dashiell Hammett, Frederick Nebel, Raoul Whitfield, Carroll John Daly, Erle Stanley Gardner and Raymond Chandler. But that was not the end of the story. During her tenure from 1936-1940, Fanny Ellsworth brought forth Cornell Woolrich, Frank Gruber, Donald Wandrei, Steve Fisher, Max Brand and others. When Popular Publications acquired the title in 1940, editor Kenneth White added folks like D.L. Champion, Cleve F. Adams, Robert Reeves, Julius Long, Robert Martin, Robert C. Dennis, John D. MacDonald, William Campbell Gault, and the man of the hour, Merle Constiner.

Stylistically, Constiner was one of the more gifted members of that Popular crew. His writing is vivid, his characters complex, and his mysteries deep. Though the stories are all novelettes, there's so much going on that each is as richly satisfying as a novel. The result is so damn good you'll want to read each tale again just to savor it.

On my own first reading, I'd have sworn Constiner was a deep-rooted son of the South. So I was a bit surprised to learn he was born and died in Monroe, Ohio. Further investigation, though, revealed that Monroe lies not much more than two hundred miles north of Tennessee, and the author apparently spent much of his young life south of that border before returning to Monroe sometime in his thirties.

The McGavock stories, you see, are not your garden variety hardboiled detective yarns. They're so rich in place and detail that they almost seem a travelogue of small-town life in the Deep South. To a northern boy reading them some eighty years later, it's like visiting a foreign country. It seems almost fantastic that places like this existed. Do they still exist today? I've no idea, but it makes me want to trek on down there and see.

The South is present in almost every line: the quirky characters, the poetic language, the haunting landscape, the quaint customs, the outrageous attitudes, the long-cherished beliefs and the mouth-watering cuisine. Its presence is so strong that it makes McGavock's missions to solve mysteries seem almost incidental. Actually, though, the mysteries are as deeply rooted and complex as the society. Clues are hard to come by. Motives are cloudy, and further obscured by lies and deception. McGavock must dig deep into the local culture to untangle complex relationships before getting a sniff of what's really going on.

LUTHER McGAVOCK, AS you'll learn, works out of the Atherton Browne Agency in Memphis. He's described as small, wiry and tough, with a deeply-lined face. His coarse black hair is worn in a short pompadour, with a bit of gray at the temples. Hardly the typical image of a hardboiled dick. Having bounced around to just about every major agency in the country, he's finally settled in the South. The reason for this transience, we are led to believe, is that his jeering, taunting personality is so repellent that one else could stand him. We're repeatedly told that he arouses instant animal antagonism in complete strangers. Despite all this lip-service, though, most people seem to take to him. The characters he meets tell him he's unlikable, then proceed to treat him like a friend.

McGavock's boss, Atherton Browne himself, is a somewhat more benign version of the Continental Op's Old Man. Browne is "the old man" in lower case. While clever and manipulative, he exhibits genuine emotion, finding particular glee in getting the best of his ace detective. "Luther McGavock is the best man who ever drew my pay," he tells his secretary, "But he's dangerous, touchy. You have to handle him like a black panther—with an electric prod." In doing so, Browne goes to great lengths to trick or shame McGavock into taking peculiar cases. And he's not above withholding vital information, just to make McGavock work harder.

These cases take him to small towns in the Tennessee hill-country. As an outsider, McGavock is our tour guide to this odd world of the Deep South. As Peter Ruber noted, though the stories are set in the 1940s, these backwoods towns are "still entrenched in an early 20th century lifestyle—where everybody in town is a character and hatreds run deep." McGavock finds them populated by mountain men, snooty women, hound dogs, mules, bobcats, and the proud descendants of a faded aristocracy. Buildings are old, vine-covered and dripping with character. There are revival meetings, cotton gins, shanties, and a swampy landscape that brings to mind an "eerie goblin world." Constiner describes a typical town as "One of those little secluded kingdoms of the deep south, lethargic, amiable—and explosive." "Like a sleepy bobcat," McGavock thinks. "It looks so cozy you want to tickle it under the chin."

And the food! Calling for dinner at his hotel, McGavock gazes in awe:

> There was a glass of buttermilk and a glass of sweet milk and a cup of steaming coffee, there was green-tomato pie and yellow-tomato jam and pear butter, there was fried beef heart, hog jowl and mustard, saddle of rabbit and marble cake. There were five vegetables and a family-size crockery bowl of golden spoonbread. The roomclerk bent over and inspected it. "It's pretty sorry, isn't it. My apologies. You caught us off guard."
>
> McGavock said gravely: "It'll do until the main meal comes along."

Though McGavock rarely carries a gun, he's capable of swift, brutal violence when threatened. He sometimes plants, and even *manufactures* evidence to ferret out his prey, and often calls—in the best tradition of Charlie Chan and Thin Man movies—for a gathering of suspects before revealing the guilty party.

Constiner delivers lines you'll rarely find in detective fiction. McGavock encounters a man who's "drunker than a shoat in a silo." He reads a report that's "as full of holes as a second-hand snood." He meets a man who complains, "My old lady is making me delouse her henhouse." And as for the heat: "I don't know about you gentlemen, but I'm sweating like a blue mule at a weight-pulling contest."

Constiner wrote a total of eleven McGavock stories, all of them appearing in *Black Mask* between 1942 and 1948. (You'll see the rest in future volumes of this series.) His sole non-McGavock tale for the magazine, "The Witch of Birdfoot Ranch," was also set in a small Tennessee town.

FRANCIS MERLE CONSTINER hailed from a family with deep roots in the area of Monroe, Ohio. His grandfather was a Methodist minister and his father a strict school teacher who later became principal of the high school. Born in Monroe in 1902, Constiner claimed to have left town at age four, eventually studying at four colleges. One of those schools is known to be Wittenberg College in Springfield, and the other Vanderbilt University in Nashville, where he earned a Master's degree in medieval history.

Despite Peter Ruber's extensive research, there are large gaps in Constiner's own history. A man who knew him told Ruber he was "secretive" about his own life. In 1949, the author told *Blue Book* readers he had "spent a year on coffee freighters in the South American trade," but whether that was before or after college is unknown. He also claimed to have spent "a good half" of his life (meaning more than twenty years) in Tennessee.

His first story, Constiner once told a reporter, was published in 1929. That story has not been located, but one of his poems appeared as early as May 1926 in the New Orleans-based magazine *The Double Dealer,* self-proclaimed as *The National Magazine of the South.* He was in good company. In its five-year run (1921–26), the magazine also featured work by William Faulkner, Ernest Hemingway, Thornton Wilder and Robert Penn Warren. "Witches' Dance," attributed to "F. Merle Constiner," celebrates moonlight passing through a grove of trees, which he envisions as "Beelzebub's chargers." It was an interesting window into his imagination, which would only get stranger in the years to come.

While at Vanderbilt, he collaborated with English professor Jack Boone on a 1931 story for the literary magazine *Prairie Schooner,* and two in *The Household Magazine* in 1932 and '33. "Big Singing," in the Jan. 1932 issue, earned a nomination for an O. Henry Award. These tales foreshadowed the McGavock series in that they, too, were set in the Tennessee hills. Another story, under Constiner's name alone, appeared in *Fiction Parade* in 1935.

In 1934, Constiner married a Southern belle named Susannah, and they settled for a spell in Akron, Ohio. Several years later they relocated to his home town of Monroe, living first in his father's house, then moving into a tiny three-room cottage. While he wrote, drinking cold black coffee and chain-smoking, Susannah bused to work at a Cincinnati department store, and later ran a nursery school in their front parlor. By 1949, they had a 150-pound Newfoundland named Lancelot du Lac, and by 1958 occupied a 130-year old house (The same three-room cottage? I don't know.)

Folks who knew him described Merle as a kindly man, but shy and reclusive. "If I ever had to go on a lecture tour, I'd die," he once told a reporter. "I just shudder to think of it." One of Mr. Ruber's correspondents said he was seldom seen except for "trips to the barbershop for a haircut and to meet the Bookmobile." When he spoke, it was not about himself, but about his writing and research. A 1964 newspaper article described Constiner as "slightly bent from his years, heavy of build with a slight mustache, and wearing shell-rimmed spectacles."

Susannah, on the other hand, was considered elegant, extravagant and socially active, and even organized the town's first Little Theater group.

Constiner was a dedicated writer. His daily quota was 2,000 words, he told a reporter in 1958, which often meant eight hours at the typewriter. "A professional writer writes every day whether he feels like it or not," he said. This sentiment was echoed in a quote noted in his obituary: "It's a punishment the author must learn to adjust to. There were times I'd rather find something else to do, but I had to make myself go back there and write—just like any other business, I hold daily office hours, and during those times, I write. But I can't turn my brain off when I finish writing, I'm always thinking, thinking."

CONSTINER ONCE SAID he had turned to writing fiction full time in 1939. That may well be, because his first known pulp story appeared in the August, 1940 issue of *Dime Detective.*

With that story, "Strangler's Kill," Constiner gave notice that his heroes would not be run-of-the-mill pulp detectives. Wardlow Rock, nicknamed "the Dean," sidelines as a fortune teller, and his cases delve into arcane subjects, often bordering on the bizarre. As a "consulting" hardboiled detective, he has much in common with Sherlock Holmes: an assistant and raconteur, Ben Mathews—with whom he shares a room; a fastidious landlady, Mrs. Duffy; a police detective, Lieutenant Bill Mallory, who needs help on weird cases; and a boatload of knowledge on strange on obscure subjects.

But Wardlow Rock is no Holmes clone. While his dialogue is sometimes formal, he often mixes it with slang. He's a classical and hardboiled detective rolled into one. A typical introduction by Mathews runs like this:

> The Dean uses a mixture of technics *(sic)* and all them 24-carat crackpot. Strangers write him off as an amiable crank. Actually, he reads six or eight Eastern languages, can do anything from cloisonne to gunshot surgery and totes a Magnum shoulder job that drives like an eight-pound sledge. Pursuit of criminals is his trade. His real interest is divination—he has a knowledge of black magic that would spell down a medieval alchemist.

Constiner contributed nineteen Dean adventures to *Dime Detective* between 1940 and 1945. Several titles reflect their fantastic elements: "The Riddle of the Phantom Mummy," "The Riddle of the Bashful Ghost," "The Affair of the Four Skeletons" and "The Riddle of the Monster Bat."

Though the Dean and Mathews inhabit a cockeyed world, with humor lurking around every corner, the comedy is more subdued than in the work of Norbert Davis, whose stories appeared in some of the same issues. The tone of Constiner's work is jovial, but never rises to the level of slapstick. In that sense, his use of humor is somewhat more in line with that of another contemporary, Robert Reeves.

The characters, the clues, the methods, and often the solutions in the Dean stories border on the bizarre, all of which adds to the fun. And as you'll discover in this volume, that could also be said of the adventures of Luther McGavock,

(And, you'll be pleased to note, Volume 1 of *The Complete Cases of the Dean, Volume 1* was released in 2016.)

WHILE THE DEAN stories contain only hints of a Southern setting, the McGavock series jumps into the Deep South with both feet, giving the author free reign with his vast knowledge of Southern life.

While writing the Dean and McGavock series, Constiner made brief appearances in *Popular Detective, Mammoth Detective* and *Ten Detective Aces,* and more substantial contributions to adventure magazines. There he began experimenting with longer stories, penning a three-part serial for *Adventure,* and a four-part mystery for *Argosy.* A *Blue Book* novella, "The Rhebavile Murder," was a contemporary detective story set in McGavock territory—a sleepy southern town with the usual complement of social misfits. Surprisingly, based on the direction his career took in later years, he apparently did *not* submit to Western pulps.

Constiner's only hobby was researching the history, customs and language of the neighboring states of Ohio and Tennessee in the early 1800s, which he did at nearby libraries, sometimes with the help of his wife. This research is reflected in the *Adventure* serial "Where Nests the Water-Snake" (featuring a group of rogues riding the Southern backroads of the 1840s), a *Country Gentleman* serial of the antebellum South called "Dusty Empire," and a short juvenile novel called *Meeting at the Merry Fifer* (1966).

As pulp markets began to fade, Constiner transitioned to slicks like *The Saturday Evening Post, Collier's, The American Magazine, Woman's Day, Cosmopolitan,* and *Argosy,* which had become a "men's" magazine. Most of these stories, too, revolved around Midwest life of the 1800s.

Constiner's first book—and only mystery novel—was *Hearse of a Different Color.* Published in 1952, it was based on the 1946 *Argosy* serial "Death on a Party Line." The hero visits a McGavock-style Tennessee town to study the quaint and wondrous colloquialisms, and gets caught up in murder.

Constiner then shifted his focus to Westerns. The first of these novels, *Last Stand at Anvil Pass,* appeared in 1957, and he wrote at least fourteen more, many of which appeared in Ace Doubles. The total remains hazy because it's rumored that a small number of the sixty-odd books attributed to "Tom West" (whom James Reasoner has identified as Fred East) may have been penned by Constiner.

Last Stand at Anvil Pass, like many of the novels to come, was based in history, and features a non-conventional hero. The protagonist owns the hotel, the general store and part of the stage line, a position usually reserved for the villain of the piece. In *The Fourth Gunman* (1958), a saloon keeper dishes out justice because the town sheriff is corrupt. *Outrage at Bearskin Forks* (1966) finds a peaceful cattle dealer riding out for revenge. *Rain of Fire* (1966) stars a storekeeper who—despite being a gun collector—just might be the slowest draw in the West. The tracker hero of *The Action at Redstone Creek* (1967) is an ugly, big-nosed shrimp. And in *Two Pistols South of Deadwood* (1967) a trapper impoverished by bank robbers sets out to catch them himself.

Most of Constiner's Westerns contains mystery elements, and several are mystery-western hybrids. *Short-Trigger Man* (1964) features an ex-gunfighter who acts like a private eye. In *Guns at Q Cross* (1965), a Texas cattleman solves a mystery on the trail to Idaho. A drunk turns detective to dodge a murder frame in *Wolf on Horseback* (1965). A sheriff solves a mystery puzzle in *The Four from Gila Bend* (1968). And in *Killer's Corral* (1968), the mystery is who hired the murderers—and why.

These Westerns have much in common with the adventures of Luther McGavock and the Dean. The prose is sharp, tough, fresh and loaded with wry humor. The plots are fast-moving, intricate, and full of unexpected twists. The language is sprinkled with cool colloquialisms. The settings come to life with poetic descriptions of food, clothing, buildings and landscapes. His heroes are clever, violent when necessary, and easy for readers to identify with. Correspondents informed Mike Grost that Constiner spent his last years writing in a room decorated with covers of his Western paperbacks. It's comforting to picture him there.

During this period, he also wrote two juvenile novels set during the Revolutionary War. These are *The Rebel Courier and the Redcoats* (1968) and *Sumatra Alley* (1971).

Constiner suffered a stroke in 1970, and his wife died of illness the following year. Peter Ruber discovered a newspaper article stating that before the stroke, he'd been working on a history of the American West, which he was forced to abandon. That, no doubt, would have been a *great* book. His last novel, the Western *Steel-Jacket,* was published in 1972.

He died quietly in a Monroe nursing home on September 24, 1979, and his belongings were auctioned off to pay taxes and medical bills. He left no will, had no children, and whatever papers he had at the time have not been located.

Thankfully, though, Merle Constiner left us an impressive and consistently entertaining body of work, of which the Luther McGavock stories are an integral part.

Evan Lewis has written stories for Ellery Queen *and* Alfred Hitchcock *mystery magazines. His first, "Skyler Hobbs and the Rabbit Man," received the 2011 Robert L. Fish Award from the Mystery Writers of America. "The Continental Opposite," an homage to Dashiell Hammett, was selected for* The Best American Mystery Stories 2016, *and nominated for a Shamus Award. His blog,* Davy Crockett's Almanack of Mystery, Adventure and the Wild West, *infests the Internet at evanlewis.com.*

Let the Dead Alone

"I don't know a snowshoe rabbit from a horned owl," Luther McGavock admitted when asked if he was a hunting man. What he neglected to add was that he knew two-footed killers very well indeed—and had come to murder-ridden Bartonville for the express purpose of potting one on the wing or any other way that seemed handy, using the help of native beaters, if necessary.

1

The Roofing Nail

THE FIRST THING McGavock noticed when he entered the chief's office was that the old man was wearing a clean collar. "I see you've freshened up your neckwear," McGavock said. "Are you anticipating early burial?"

The old man glared at him with salty, inflamed eyes. "I've got on my traveling clothes. For the first time in twenty years I'm going to leave my desk and go out on a case. This thing is too important to me to sublet to any slipshod hired help. I'm handling it myself and I'm taking you along with me. We're leaving immediately. You can buy a toothbrush at a drugstore."

McGavock was small, sinewy, tough. His coarse black hair was cut in a short pompadour and there was a dusting of tweedy gray at his temples. He had a selfish, taunting quality about him that aroused instant animal antagonism in total strangers. He'd worked for every major agency in the country. A genius at getting results, he was a hard man to take.

McGavock flushed. "I work alone and you know it. I came here to Memphis and you gave me a berth. You like what I bring in but you don't want to know about my methods. I work on a roving license, one that you cooked up yourself, a contract that you can repudiate if things get too hot. What is this big-time job?"

The chief corrected him. "It's not big-time, it's just personal. A cousin of mine, a second cousin, had a little trouble with a

friend of his—he wouldn't stay alive. Cousin Malcom lives at a place called Bartonville, a hill-town back by the Tennessee-Mississippi line. He just telephoned me. He's in some sort of a hole. He says that blood is thicker than water and that he thinks I can handle the affair with greater delicacy than the local law enforcement. It seems to be an emergency. I thought we'd run over—"

McGavock snarled. "No soap! If I take it on, I'll do it alone." He rubbed a knuckle thoughtfully behind his ear. "When can I catch a train?"

"Trains don't stop there, Luther," the old man said mildly. He produced an envelope. "Here's a bus ticket. Good luck."

When the door swung shut behind McGavock, the chief turned to his secretary. A pleased cat-and-canary look came

McGavock, in close, connected three times—and the chubby man went backwards heels over breakfast

into the old man's watery eyes. He ripped off the new collar, tossed it in the wastebasket. "Ah!" He breathed happily. "That's better... You know, Miss Ollinger, I was afraid for a minute that he was going to call my bluff. Luther McGavock is the best man that ever drew my pay. But he's dangerous, touchy. You have to handle him like a black panther—with an electric prod."

BARTONVILLE WAS A little splash of houses and ramshackle business buildings in a nest of wooded, red clay hills. McGavock typed it the instant he stepped from the bus. It was lazy, quiet, intelligent—the sort of Deep South town he liked.

The Main Street sidewalks, raised two feet or so above the street, were hot in the sunlight. Hound dogs lay curled in the piercing heat and grizzled mules with riding saddles waited patiently at hitching posts for their masters. The few stragglers in view were mostly lean mountain men who returned his casual scrutiny with polite curiosity.

The town was evidently a county seat. Across the street was a barren court square with its customary park benches and old stone courthouse. The whole set-up, the rutted road, the mules, the court square, was typical, familiar. McGavock picked up his Gladstone and started down the sidewalk.

The one hotel, the Bradley House—a moldy, clapboard building with fly-specked windows—appeared deserted. McGavock walked into the musty lobby, waited a moment for his eyes to adjust themselves to the half-gloom.

A spiderish man in a Roman stripe silk shirt with pink rosetted sleeve garters put down a tin cup at the watercooler and sauntered behind a battered desk. He threw out a card with the practiced fingers of a tinhorn gambler. McGavock signed it.

"Luther McGavock," the clerk read. "Memphis. I'm Cal Bradley—Cal for Calhoun, suh, not Calvin. I own this hotel." He waited for enthusiastic congratulations, none were forthcoming. "What, may I ask, brings you to this garden spot?"

McGavock said: "I'm representing Boggs."

The man in the striped shirt blinked. "Boggs? You've got me there. What are boggs?"

"Boggs," McGavock announced scathingly, "are not things. Boggs is a man, a millionaire. Porthos R. Boggs—the Memphis celery king. He has more dough than he can spend. That's why he hires me—I help him burn it. They told him that Bartonville is good bird country. I'm here to look things over and buy a few hundred acres of land if I can find something that suits us."

Bradley asked slyly: "Are you a hunting man, suh?"

"Heck, no!" McGavock jeered. "I don't know a snowshoe rabbit from a horned owl. But neither does Boggs. Ha." He pointed to his bag, ordered curtly: "Take this up to the room. I'm going out to catch a little air."

FOR SOME REASON or other, McGavock had expected to find his client living in a so-called Georgian showplace, one of those pillared mansions that always reminded him of a movie set. He was pleasantly surprised.

The squat, brick cottage was intimate, homelike. Its double-span cedar shingles were butted with bright green moss and the wind and rain of decades had buffed the old brick to a soft rose. The small, neat lawn was hedged with a spindrift of lilacs. Through a trellis of wisteria, he caught a glimpse of a cool flag-stoned backporch.

An almost obliterated nameplate on the gate said: *Malcom Jarrell, M.D.* McGavock took the turfed path to the door, clanged the lever bell-pull.

The door was opened by one of the queerest human specimens that McGavock had ever seen. A little pigeon-chested man in a seedy herringbone suit. He had a massive, shaggy head. From the bridge of his spectacles projected a short V of wire holding a second, squarish set of lenses: a Bebe binocular of the sort used by dentists and naturalists. He unhooked the contraption from his goatlike ears, frowned.

"I'm Lute McGavock." The detective introduced himself. "I'm charwoman for the Atherton Browne Detective Agency. I hear you've got your lines fouled. I'm here to help you untangle them. You're Dr. Jarrell?"

The seedy man shook his elephantine head. "There isn't any Dr. Jarrell. That was my great-grandfather. But I'm the man you seek." He studied McGavock gravely. "So you're the person Atherton selected. Come in, sir."

Then, astoundingly, in direct contradiction to his words, he closed the door behind him and ushered McGavock—not into the house, but around it.

In a vine-hung nook, on the flagstoned backporch, two wire-legged chairs were set by a kitchen table. On the table was a box of cubeb cigarettes, a partially eaten chocolate bar, and a wire cage containing a rat. The rodent was as big as a young pig, scaly-tailed, malevolent. *"Sigmodon hispidus,* the cotton rat," Jarrell remarked. "He doesn't like us, does he? I'm a naturalist, in a small way. I sit by the hour and study him."

McGavock said nastily: "You've got a stronger stomach than I have."

"I have a strong stomach," Malcom Jarrel answered quietly. "Or I couldn't tolerate you. You have an unfortunate personality, sir. There's something about you that makes me seethe. Something insolent. However, this is no time for character analysis. If Atherton foists you on me, I have to take what he sends. I'm just a poor country cousin and can't expect his most expensive talent. What about the garden mulch?"

"Says what?"

The big-headed man pointed out to the lawn. The setting sun, long sunk behind the crest of hills, dappled the yard in amber afterglow. Great sphinx moths, dusk feeders, were already shuttling among the delphiniums. McGavock had a feeling of unreality—as though he were a visitor in some eerie, goblin world. Unconsciously his gaze followed the line of Jarrell's heavy-jointed finger. In the rear of the grassy plot was a grape arbor; beside the grape arbor was a small pile of clean, fresh straw. "The garden mulch," Jarrell repeated. "It can't stay where it is. It's bleaching my lawn."

McGavock said tartly: "I'm no horticulturist. All the way down from Memphis and you—"

Jarrell smiled sadly. "There's a dead man under it."

THE STORY WAS quickly told. The man was Lester Hodges—a recluse. He lived in a shack at the other end of town. Jarrell had been awakened the night before by a dragging sound outside his window; he'd slipped into a robe, gone out to investigate and had found the body of his old friend.

The naturalist had then covered the corpse with mulch straw and had ensconced himself on the back porch to wait for aid from Memphis. Sixteen hours on the deathwatch—no meals, no visitors. No break except when he'd phoned his cousin.

McGavock got to his feet, wandered out into the yard.

The detective laid aside the straw in fastidious handfuls, uncovered the body bit by bit—like a geologist exposing a rare fossil.

"His head," Jarrell said. "Look at the back of his head."

It wasn't pretty. Hodges was a birdlike man in his seventies, hard-bitten, wiry. A large roofing nail had been driven through his skull—into his brain. The metallic nail head, as large as a nickel, lay flat and firm against the old man's silvery hair.

"I can't understand it," Malcom Jarrell complained. "It's practically impossible! I can't drive a nail into a box and do it satisfactorily. Say the slayer crept up on him in his sleep, even then how could he do it? Imagine! Holding the nail in position with one hand and swinging the hammer with the other. Those roofing nails are like big tacks. It isn't feasible!"

"You're on the wrong track," McGavock contradicted him. "I think I know how it was done. A novel and a brutal weapon—but a simple and efficient one, too."

They hesitated by the gate. "I've a batch of important questions to ask you," McGavock said. "But they're personal and I've got you placed. You'd bat me around with evasions until I wouldn't know where I was. So—I'll circulate around town and collect a little lowdown on you—and you'll have to come in with me. Then maybe we can get someplace. I've handled clients like you before. In the meantime, I'm giving you advice and I want you to heed it. Go to the sheriff and tell him the whole yarn. Leave me out, of course, but tell him everything else. It'll be embarrassing but we'll have to do it if we want to flush our quarry."

Jarrell made a pretense at pondering. "Wouldn't it be a better idea," he said carefully, "to wait until nightfall and then to take Lester out into the hills and leave him by the road?"

McGavock was withering. "Who do you think it'll fool? Not the guy that unloaded him in your yard. Just try to dispose of that body and they'll have hemp around your neck so quick you'll think your ascot slipped!"

TWILIGHT WAS BLENDING into night—it was that period that the natives called dusk-dark—when McGavock returned to the main drag. The air was sweltering. Somewhere, beyond the bridge, a revival meeting was getting under way. High-pitched voices lifted their rhythms to the summer sky. Storefronts blazed soft golden light. McGavock ambled through the jocular bustle of dallying citizens—family folk out for an evening stroll before bedtime, high school girls in their sweet-starched ginghams, village boys with pomaded hair and roving eyes. The detective located a hardware store, entered.

A clerk got up from the sidewalk bench in front of the store and followed him inside.

McGavock purchased a ten-cent compass.

The clerk was curious. "Buyin' a compass! I don't recollect seeing you in these parts. Are you aimin' to tramp the hills?"

"Skip it," McGavock said boorishly. "I'm not a revenuer. I see you have quart whiskey bottles as well as oak casks that can be converted to thump kegs. There's no copper on display but doubtless you've plenty hidden in the back room. Don't alarm yourself, I'm not in town to bloodhound any of your rural customers."

The clerk was abashed, befuddled. "You'll have to excuse me, Mr.—er—"

"Hodges." McGavock was expansive. "The name is Lester Hodges. At your service."

The clerk went bug-eyed. "Lester Hodges! Think of that. Listen, friend, we got a feller right here in this town by that very name."

McGavock reeled dramatically, grimaced with incredulity.

"Them's true words," the clerk insisted defensively. "Lester Hodges. Many a hour he's sat by that pot-bellied stove and whittled."

It came out like an appendix under a local anesthetic: where Hodges lived, his annual income—nil—and his likes and dislikes. "Why don't you look him up?" the clerk urged. "He might be kin."

"It's hardly likely," McGavock said dolefully. "All my kin were killed off in the battle between the *Monitor* and the *Merrimac*."

THE SHANTY WAS in a hollow at the edge of town. It was built flush into a red clay bank. Above it, as a background, the ridge road passed it over a wobbly wooden trestle. A full moon was rising down the valley and the trestle with its crazy-angled supports looked like a gigantic tarantula against the sky. McGavock stood across the path and sized things up.

His calculations told him he had a good ten minutes on the sheriff. Yet a lighted lamp burned in the window of Lester Hodges' shack.

The detective climbed the rickety stairs to the narrow porch and knocked. There was no answer. He twisted the knob and stepped in. The room was empty.

The furnishings were scant—a dilapidated iron range, a pallet on the floor, a fire-blistered bureau. And that lonesome lamp flickering in the window.

The bureau drawers held the recluse's food stock: a sack of dried beans, a little cornmeal, a rancid ham hock. McGavock glanced about him angrily—it was a difficult layout to frisk. There was no place to conceal anything.

He found them in the cold ashes of the iron range, and when he found them he didn't know what to do with them. A few tiny firecrackers and a shank of fishing line, in a tobacco can.

He stared blankly at the tin, thrust it in the pocket of his sack coat.

The lamp bowl was almost full, it had just been lit.

The detective had got himself into a spot and knew it. The little one-room shanty had no back door. He'd realized the lamp was a trap but he'd planned on a back door. Someone out in the night was waiting for him. Someone who had a sense of engineering: the light was placed so that when he left he'd show up like a treed possum.

McGavock made a quick decision. He blew out the lamp, swung open the sagging door and stepped out onto the narrow porch. "O.K., Sheriff," he shouted. "Come on in. You want to take a look at this!"

A shadowed figure materialized in the blackness of the trestle timbers. There was the liquid glint of moonlight on a blue steel shotgun barrel. McGavock realized he was facing a desperate killer.

The phantom wavered. McGavock thought, he's trying to grapple with the new break, trying to play it so that he gets the most out of it—he wonders what I've discovered.

A husky, heavily disguised voice called back: "Take a look at what?"

McGavock dropped like a plummet, rolled tumbler-fashion down the red clay bank. The shotgun let loose with both barrels. There was a deafening, coughing blast and the shrieking of splintered glass as the shanty window went into shard and dust.

A clump of sumac caught McGavock's fall. He got to his feet, listened a moment, heard nothing.

The detective made no attempt at quartering his attacker. He walked along a dry, brushy gulch, came out on a hillside and returned to the village through a weedy alley.

He drew up beneath the first streetlight, wiped his knees and elbows with his handkerchief, balled it up and lobbed it behind a picket fence. He was, he decided, fairly presentable.

The gent with the shotgun could wait.

One thing was certainly evident. Lester Hodges, the old recluse, hadn't met his death and been rolled in Jarrell's yard through some sort of grotesque accident. There was design behind this, cold-blooded merciless design. From now on anything might happen. The slayer was smart, cunning—and he knew he was being hunted.

THE BACK STREET brought McGavock to the rear of the courthouse. He circled the building, selected a bench in the deserted court square, sat down and redigested a few conclusions. An inspection of his ten-cent compass showed that it had not been damaged. Main Street was nearly empty. This was a town that really closed like a mouse-trap at the stroke of nine.

One window alone remained lighted. A little office with an eight-foot front beside the undertaker's. A desk was pulled up close to the window, a man sat behind it in a swivel chair. He appeared to be looking through the pane, across the street, into the court square—directly at McGavock. The gold lettering on the door said: *Hal Maldron, Attorney.*

McGavock got up, crossed the street. Hardly had his instep touched the curb than the man leaned over his desk and rapped on the window.

It was a shrill commanding rap—a piercing, arrogant vibrato. McGavock opened the door and strode in.

"If you want to speak to me," he exploded, "heist your pants off that sponge rubber cushion and address me like a gentleman. I don't go for window banging—"

Hal Maldron was a blubbery, grayish man with bad teeth and a pair of the smallest, cruelest eyes that McGavock ever looked into. He smirked at McGavock's rage. "Calm yourself, brother."

Maldron held up a hand, waved a huge horseshoe-nail ring. "It's this ring that does it, brother," he boasted. "It makes me the most hellacious lawyer in these hills. I'm sure-fire. I never lose a case. But why the ring, you ask? I'll tell you. Why chase around looking for clients, interviewing witnesses, suborning jurymen? No need for it. I just sit here in my swivel chair and let the world come to me. Across the street's the courthouse, yonder's the post office, next door's the undertaker's. What more could a lawyer ask? I'm plump in the middle of the county's bloodstream. Anyone with any kind of business has to pass my window sometime or other. Comes a prospect or a hostile witness, I just reach over and rap on the pane." A malignant look settled itself in his rubbery jowls. "And, believe me, they come when I call them!"

McGavock was speechless with fury.

"You got off the bus at seven fifty-eight," Maldron declared. "You registered at the Bradley House and then proceeded to Malcom Jarrell's, where he informed you that he was secreting a corpse. What you've been doing for the last half hour, I do not as yet know—but I'll find out. I summoned you in here to advise you that you are now working for me. There have been developments. Jarrell has given himself up to the police; he is at liberty, on bond. I'm representing him—"

McGavock managed to speak. "He's retained you?"

"That's beside the point. I said I was representing him. I'm being retained by another party, one who has his welfare at heart."

"Just who is this other party?"

Maldron showed his spotted canines. "That, too, is beside the point. I just wanted you to understand that there's been a shifting of conditions, a change of ownership, so to speak. You've been demoted. I'm head man. If you play with me, I'll keep you on the payroll. No cooperation and I'll send you scooting back to the city."

McGavock gave a low, strained laugh—a strangled sound, almost a whine. "I ought to kick your teeth in. Which wouldn't take much of a push." He held his breath, tried to control himself. "I'm not employed by Jarrell. I'm laboring for a guy named Atherton Browne. Try a tank-town frame on me and the boys will be in your hair like seventeen-year locusts. You'll learn a little about metropolitan detective agencies."

HE WAS STILL boiling when he reached the hotel.

Cal Bradley, fussing behind the desk, was acting as his own night-clerk. The spidery little man seemed self-conscious, over-polite. "Mr. McGavock!" he greeted. "About to retire? A good night to sleep, suh. There's a breeze from the north." He laid the key on the blotter. "Number eleven, at the end of the hall. The best room in the house." Abruptly, as an afterthought, he reached inside his shirt, dragged out a rumpled, soiled envelope. "This was left on the desk—addressed to you. I didn't see who placed it there."

McGavock ripped open the flap. The note was written on hotel stationery: *Hodges can't use your help now. Let the dead alone. Get out of town.*

"It's written on your letterhead—and unsigned," McGavock snapped. "I suppose the entire town has access to your paper."

Bradley sighed. "That's true. Everyone filches from a hotel." He brightened. "Just think. You've only been in town a few hours and already admirers are sending you unsigned letters. You make friends quickly, suh."

When McGavock was halfway down the corridor, Bradley's strident voice rattled after him. "Another thing. It almost slipped my mind. You've had a charming visitor—Laurel Bennett. She's dropped in three times within the last hour. Perhaps she wants to sell your employer, Mr. Boggs, the old Fern Springs resort?"

McGavock answered crossly: "I wouldn't know. I've never heard of her. If she comes again, I'm not seeing callers. I'm footsore and weary. I'm hibernating for the night."

2

The Heavy Loser

LUTHER McGAVOCK GAZED at his room and flinched. It was about ten feet square. The wallpaper was water-stained in coffeelike splotches; the worn rug was as thin as a bait seine. There was an oval crayon enlargement above a washstand, a crockery bowl and pitcher—and a lumpy iron bed.

The single, grimy window looked directly onto the tin roof of an adjoining shed. Bradley's finest room was no bridal suite.

McGavock stuck the tobacco tin behind the crayon enlargement. He opened his Gladstone and took out a belly gun, a stubby thirty-eight cut back almost to the cylinder—and a pair of wire clippers. He shoved the pistol under his coat, turned back the mattress and with the wire clippers snipped off a foot of stiff wire from the bedsprings.

The detective took the wire to the door, threw a tight turn around the doorknob, pulled the ends down and threaded them through the eye of the key. He tested the apparatus; it was steady, strong. No outside manipulation could jiggle the bit in the lock; it was tamper-proof.

Cheap hotels with shaky door locks were no new experience to Luther McGavock.

He raised the window, laid the towel from the washstand over the sill. A landmark to help him identify the correct room on his return.

McGavock crawled through the window, groped down the

tin roof, lowered himself catlike into the alley. The silence was oppressive, appalling. It was as though the village were quarantined. The detective glanced at the luminous dial of his wristwatch.

It seemed like two in the morning—yet it was scarcely nine-thirty.

EVERY SMALL SOUTHERN town has its leading family. The Bennetts assumed this position in Bartonville. McGavock had been aware of their prominence from the moment of his arrival. Everywhere he'd looked he'd seen the name: on the town's drugstore, the garage, the cotton gin. He could visualize the sort of home Laurel Bennett would be living in—a sleek white mansion with fluted columns and a veranda as big as a parade ground. She would, in other words, be occupying the house he had mistakenly allotted to Malcom Jarrell.

This time he was right. He found the place without much difficulty.

Pretentious, austere, it stood at the mouth of a short avenue of old magnolias. The porch light was on—McGavock was evidently expected.

Malcom Jarrell opened the door to his ring.

McGavock said dreamily: "I imagine a house, prowl around and locate it. I ring the bell and see you standing in the door-way. This case is dopier than a tael of opium. Who is this Laurel Bennett, what's your tie-in, and what does she want with me?"

The seedy naturalist tilted his monstrous head, stepped back, gestured the detective in. "We need your counsel. Mrs. Bennett is my godchild. She has a problem for you."

"A problem?" McGavock mocked him. "Now that's intriguing! A detective is like a doctor, anyone that comes along tries to panhandle a little free medicine. I'm up to my ears right now in a problem. Or haven't you heard? I'm trying to shoo the executioner away from you. It seems to me—"

Jarrell was crotchety. "Come now, you're not all that busy! This shouldn't take twenty minutes. Hear what Laurel has to say. I'm sure that Atherton won't object."

The lady of the mansion was just about seventeen years old.

A delicate figurine in black lace with a cameo at her throat, she leaned against the creamy marble mantelpiece and watched McGavock approach. Oil portraits hung high above her head. Antebellum ancestors: eagle-nosed gentlemen—firebrands— and haughty, whale-boned grande dames.

Laurel Bennett was slim, fragilely molded. Her glossy black hair was caught by a pearl bandeau. Her eyes were somber, brooding.

Seventeen years old, McGavock thought. He judged her age shrewdly by her lips. He tried to picture her in a middy blouse and Mary Jane pumps. It simply wouldn't work. The gal might be a child, McGavock decided, but she's not that kind of a child. She's wise, hard.

Her manner was impersonal, gracious. "I heard you talking to Mr. Jarrell in the hall," the girl began. "You seem reluctant to help me. You appear to believe that there will be no remuneration. Let me say that you are going to be paid and paid liberally. Present a reasonable statement to my attorney, Mr. Hal Maldron—"

"The window rapper? The guy with the eroded teeth?" McGavock was venomous. "So you're the party that had him bail my client. How do you people expect me to get anything done with all this meddling? Jarrell has popped off until—"

Malcom Jarrell said patiently: "You're balked. Completely confounded. So you're trying to put the blame for your incompetence on me."

McGavock barked at the girl: "What is this job you want me to do?"

"You're a man of experience," Laurel Bennett said throatily. "I think you'll be quick to sympathize. Gil, my husband, is middle-aged. Suddenly—for no reason that we can see—he has gone into an orgy of sowing wild oats. Not women, I mean, but drinking and gambling. It's mortifying, of course—most middle-aged husbands are proud to pay more attention to their young brides. If they're lucky enough to have a young bride, I mean. But it's not only embarrassing—it's critical. He's jeopardizing our security. He loses enormous sums. We have a joint account—he makes secret withdrawals. It has me half-mad. It can't go on!"

McGavock asked warily: "How do I come in?"

"He's out right now. At a place called Chunky's, a hell-hole down by the riverbank. I've been cruising around, I've seen his car there. I'll drive you up and leave you. I want you to get him out and bring him home."

"Is that supposed to cure him?"

"You could scare him on the way back," the girl suggested. "Tell him some terrible cases where men drank themselves into disgrace and their pitiful wives starved in the gutter and things like that."

"O.K.," McGavock agreed. "Let's go." He threw a parting remark at Malcom Jarrell. "Spend the night here. I'll see you in the morning. I want to ask you about your cotton rat."

Jarrell answered him amiably. "I'm an early riser. Any time after sun-up."

CHUNKY'S PLACE WAS in the river bottom about five miles out on the old swamp trail. A desolate, poisonous five miles. Snake-infested sloughs, milky with muddy water, thrust fingerlike from the dense second growth along the roadside. The headlights of Laurel Bennett's car played on a ceaseless tangle of wild grape and willow and water oak. The air was brackish, dank—stagnant.

The girl was silent, intent on holding her swaying car to the boggy trail. McGavock sat beside her and whistled. It was a habit of concentration that he was unable to break. And he always whistled the same thing, the same way. The tune was *The Letter Edged in Black*.

"Cal Bradley," he remarked, "thinks I'm a sap on the purchase for shooting land. He suggested that you might be anxious to sell me a pleasure resort, a place known as Fern Springs. Fern Springs is a new one on me and I thought I knew them all, from Florida Bay to Puget."

Laurel smiled stiffly. "It hasn't functioned since nineteen-ten. Maybe you don't know it, but the south is studded with old, abandoned resorts—tucked away in wild, unreachable places. Back at the turn of the century, in the red-spoked carriage days, it was fashionable to summer at some health springs. The fad passed but the old buildings remain. Almost any county south of the Mason-Dixon has a couple. Fern Springs belongs to me, it's back in the pine country. It's always belonged to my family and is not for sale. I'd sell my mother's wedding ring first."

McGavock said: "I'm not in the market for a wedding ring, but I'll keep your offer in mind."

She cursed him. He lay back on the cushions, closed his eyes and listened with real enjoyment.

Laurel Bennett braked her sports car at a bend in the road. "It's just around the corner. You'd better go the rest of the way on foot."

"How will I spot him?" McGavock asked.

"They'll all be drinking," she said bitterly. "But he'll be drunk. They'll all be gambling—but he'll be losing his shirt."

Abruptly, without warning, he reached forward and turned on the dash. Deftly, before she could prevent him, he laid the ten-cent compass on her knee. The needle was as steady as a rock.

The girl flushed angrily, knocked his hand aside. "If you want to take bearings," she spat, "take them from yourself!"

He gave a raucous, unpleasant laugh. "I'm not taking bearings. This is my electric eye. I'm just making sure that you're not preparing to put a two-inch roofing nail into the back of my skull when I step out." He restored the gadget to his pocket.

She caught him by the lapel as he slid through the door. "Watch yourself. They don't like strangers."

He bared his teeth. "Neither do I."

The building, the size of a domestic garage and covered with tar-paper, was a black ulcerous sore in the moonglow. Its windows were caulked to the frame with soggy, mildewed quilts. Not so much as a wavering cobweb of light showed. A moody scene, depraved and threatening. McGavock was familiar with these backwoods gambling dives. They were dynamite.

There were a few clay-caked jalopies in the clearing, and a powerful, gleaming coupé—Gil Bennett's.

McGavock knew better than to advance and knock. He slowed up at the fringe of the timber, called: "Hello. Hello, in there!" A ritual for strangers and one that had better be observed. The door opened.

A chubby, muscle-bound man with a receding chin stepped out. He was wearing a lemon yellow polo shirt stuck into new overalls and carried an army automatic casually at his side—as though it were a monkey wrench.

McGavock said: "I'm a friend of Cal Bradley's." He walked into the patch of light. "I'm a traveling man."

The chubby man chewed it over in his slow mind. "I guess you're all right," he decided. He led McGavock into the hut, closed the tar-paper door.

IT WAS A low, vicious crowd. There were seven men in the room—three sprawled sullenly at a rough-sawed makeshift bar at the back; the remaining four were deadlocked in a game of stud under a hissing gasoline lamp.

Gil Bennett was in the poker game. He was easy to spot. Dressed in a quiet business suit, he was the only man present wearing neither leather boots nor denim. He was a decent-looking guy in his middle fifties. McGavock wondered what devious pressure had cast him into marriage with so young a wife and then perversely, had driven him to such a deadfall as this.

The detective rested his shoulders against a wall joist and watched the game. There were two bottles of red whiskey on the table and the liquor was kept in constant rotation. Bennett's playmates lolled and simpered and put on a silly show of being skin-tight. The businessman appeared to be cold sober.

When Gil Bennett took the bottle to drink, he grasped the neck with his fist close to the bottle's mouth. The foxy pup, McGavock thought, he's *tonguing it*, cutting off his intake.

"I hate to break this up," the detective said cheerfully. "But Mr. Bennett's roast is burning. He has to hustle home."

There was an ominous silence in the little shack.

Gil Bennett asked: "Did my wife send you?"

McGavock nodded. "That she did."

The chubby houseman strolled over. "Out!" he ordered hoarsely. He tossed his knobby, dwarfed chin towards the door. "You're not welcome here." He grabbed McGavock's wrist.

McGavock relaxed. He twisted his trapped wrist, caught the stocky man's forearm in a grip of steel—a double-lock. His opponent stiffened. McGavock stepped straight into him, thrusting his thigh behind the chubby man's knee. The chubby man went backwards heels over breakfast and McGavock, in close position, hit him three times at the hinge of his jaw. He was out before he struck the floor.

It was touch and go for a split second. Anything could have happened. Then everybody laughed. The show of brutality exhilarated them. A gambler with a Mexican leather-work holster peeping from his shiny blue serge suit got up from the table and shook McGavock's hand. A downy-faced youth at the bar hauled a mouth harp from his hat and began running off minors. There was an air of general festivity.

IN BENNETT'S COUPÉ, on the way back to town, McGavock made an astounding discovery. His companion, in spite of all his bottle tonguing, was drunker than a shoat in a silo.

"How long have you been haunting that dump?" the detective asked genially.

Gil Bennett hiccoughed. "About two weeks. And, boy, have I had bad luck! All the time I lose! At first it wasn't so bad, seven-eight dollars. Now the jinx has really got me. I run as much as twenty bucks in the hole as regular as clockwork." He shook his head fuzzily. "I try to outslick them but I can't seem to make any headway—"

"How much have you lost to date?"

"One hundred and eighty-three frog skins. Down the old sewer. That's plenty bucks. Wow!"

McGavock grinned to himself. The case was finally cracking; at last he was getting his teeth into it. "It's a heap of small change," he agreed. "But it's not what breaks up wealthy family life. Mrs. Bennett said your losses were enormous—that was the word she used. I thought it sounded fishy. I couldn't see how the town big shot, you, owner of the cotton gin, garage, et al., could find any real financial competition among the local bedrock sportsmen. Why then the secret withdrawals?"

Bennett chuckled. "You catch. This gambling business is a ruse. The Bennett Cotton Gin, the Bennett Drugstore—phooey! Everything I own is in partnership with my wife. And I don't mean matrimonial partnership—I mean business partnership. Hal Maldron looks after her end and the way they whipsaw me is nobody's business. Every time we get a little money ahead they put it into reserve pools and running expenses and stuff like that. I couldn't tell you within ten thousand dollars what my present capital is."

McGavock prodded him. "And?"

"I've got plans. They probably seem wacky to you but they're the best I can do. My wife and I have a joint bank account. That's my only access to cash. I make big withdrawals, as much as the traffic will stand. I send the money out of town to a city bank. I've got it deposited under a different name. I can make a fresh start any time they give me the bum's rush. All I'm waiting for now is for Laurel and that leechy lawyer of hers to sock me with their divorce—"

"Divorce?" McGavock perked up.

"Sure. I bet they've got the papers all filled out." He went cagy. "What are you pumping me for? Where did you come from, anyway? By golly, you're a detective working for Hal and Laurel!"

"I'm a detective, all right," McGavock confirmed. "I might as well admit it. You're the only one who doesn't seem to know it. But I'm not working for Hal Maldron. I'm employed by a slave driver in Memphis. I'm here to find out who knocked off Lester Hodges—and, more important, how come?"

That sobered him. "Old Les Hodges has been murdered?" The idea seemed to give him some inner fear. "That's going to be a blow to Malcom."

"If so, he's standing up under it extremely well," McGavock remarked. "Why should it affect him?"

"They were bosom pals. The town's two nuts. Hodges illiterate, Jarrell overeducated." He said in a strained voice: "Laurel and Hal aren't mixed up in this, are they?"

"Not so far as I know," McGavock lied. "Why do you ask?"

Bennett pulled up in front of the court square, idled his engine. "Alcohol's treacherous. It makes me think I'm smarter than I am. Forget the whole thing. Thanks for your interest—and good-night."

McGavock produced his compass, handed it to his companion. "Listen to me and listen carefully. Are you sober enough to understand me? Good." He glared at the drunken man with a fond fierceness. "The slayer of Lester Hodges used a mean weapon. A magnetized hammer, like bill-posters use, only I imagine this was a big baby, like carpenters use. He carried the tack on the hammerhead, followed Hodges down a dark street. At the right moment he reared back and swung. That's the way it was done." The detective paused. "I bought this gadget for myself but I've decided to hand it over to you. If anyone approaches you with a bulky package, a bundle, something that might conceal a hammer, stall 'em while you make a few careless passes with this compass. If there's a magnet in the vicinity, the compass needle will whip around and point it out."

Gil Bennett scoffed. "Why give it to me? I'm in no danger." He slammed the car door.

McGavock watched him from the street, saw him place the gadget tenderly in his breast pocket. The black coupé whammed off in a screeching of gears.

"He's afraid," McGavock said. "He thinks something is after him—and he doesn't know just what it is!"

McGAVOCK HAD ORDERED Malcom Jarrell to spend the night with the Bennetts for a very definite reason. The detective wanted to give the little vine-covered brick cottage a thorough searching—and he wanted a free hand while doing it. One thing had bothered him all evening, the incident that had occurred when he had first visited his client. Jarrell had met him from the inside of the house, at the front door—yet he had closed the door behind him and led the detective not into the house, but around it.

McGavock had the impression at the time that he was being decoyed away from something, that the naturalist had been interrupted in something he wished to conceal.

It was pretty obvious that his client had been lying to him like a trooper ever since they had joined forces. According to Jarrell's story he hadn't left the back porch for sixteen hours, except to phone Memphis. The cubeb cigarettes and the half-eaten chocolate bar were evidence to the contrary. One doesn't keep a reserve of such tedium-breaking luxuries on one's back porch to be conveniently handy for just such an emergency. There had been other funny stuff, too. The naturalist's report had been as full of holes as a second-hand snood. He'd said he'd been awakened by a dragging sound outside his window—yet the corpse by the arbor was a good thirty yards from the house.

McGavock reconstructed it this way: *Jarrell had probably seen the killer drag the body into his yard.* Maybe he had recognized him, maybe not. In any event, the naturalist was reluctant to discuss it. It didn't look good.

The detective scowled. It wasn't the first time he'd had to plow through a client to get at the criminal.

LUTHER McGAVOCK SWUNG open the squeaky gate, made a quick, cautious survey of the shrubbery. The white moon high overhead, now harsh and bright, struck the frothy lilac hedge to shimmering silver, laid ragged shadows of black velvet on the close-clipped lawn. It was indescribably beautiful—unearthly. McGavock thought, It's no wonder the big-headed naturalist is half cuckoo. I've never seen a place like this. It's actually narcotic. A human couldn't live in this dream world and retain his sense of values. It's a place for vampires and ghouls, creatures who flourish from the grave.

Lester Hodges had been taken to the funeral home, the mulch had been restacked in the stable lot. Only a few wisps of scattered straw by the arbor testified to the gruesome tragedy.

He inspected the rat in its cage on the porch. Its ruby eyes glared at the hooded flashlight in the detective's hand. "If you could talk," McGavock said thoughtfully, "we'd get this thing over in three minutes. You're the kingpin in this bloody mess." He fumbled about, discovered the key behind a flowerpot and entered Malcom Jarrell's kitchen.

He worked through the kitchen, the dining-room, the bedrooms. It took him twenty minutes to discover it: the hiding place in Malcom Jarrell's study. The detective lifted a Spanish tile in the hearth. Beneath it, in a narrow, boxlike space, lay a bulky brown envelope.

McGavock picked up a small hooked throw-rug from the floor, draped it over a student lamp on the desk, flicked on the light and examined his find.

The envelope contained a thick bundle of clippings, letters and papers held together by a rubber band. It contained something else, too—a little fuzzy, gray ball of hair about as big as a small marble. The detective's first unpleasant reaction was that he was looking at a wad of human hair, the hair of Lester Hodges.

But this hair was too fine, too dry.

Rat hair? Hardly likely. The fibers were much too long.

McGavock grinned. He realized what he held in his fingers, knew that this was evidence to hang a killer.

He wondered if Jarrell fully realized its significance. Probably yes. It all fitted in now. His call that evening on his client. Jarrell here in this cozy study, interrupted in his analysis of the furry object. It explained the Bebe binoculars and Jarrell's sidetracking him around the house.

McGavock slipped off the rubber band, fanned out the papers on the desktop and started through them systematically.

The first item was a yellowed newspaper clipping with a block headline. From the *Bartonville Clarion,* dated August 7, 1909:

NORTHERN GUEST VANISHES AT FERN SPRINGS
Devil's Elbow Claims Wealthy Manufacturer

A prosperously dressed individual giving his name as T. James Cortwright had, according to the article, registered at the Fern Springs resort on the night of the sixth. In a brief talk with Calhoun Bradley, the clerk, he had declared that he was from Cleveland, Ohio, and had inquired courteously if any of his fellow townsmen were, by chance, among the resort's guests. With regret Mr. Bradley informed him that the resort was patronized in the main by local gentry and expressed mild astonishment that even Mr. Cortwright had himself heard of its existence in such an out-of-the-way corner of the country. This remark had somehow angered the Clevelander. He had opened a wallet, paid for a month in advance, and had retired to his room.

Mr. Bradley had attempted to mollify him by informing him that the resort's season was at its height and that later in the evening there was to be a lawn party. Mr. Cortwright had made some unsociable remark and had left the desk.

The next morning a mountain man, snaking logs, had discovered the gentleman's hat and wallet a quarter of a mile from the hotel buildings. They lay at the edge of a patch of treacherous quicksand known as Devil's Elbow.

An examination of Mr. Cortwright's room showed that his bed had not been slept in. The management was attempting to inform Mr. Cortwright's family.

McGavock said to himself: "So Bradley was clerk. And the season was in full swing. Ten to one, Jarrell was there—and Maldron, and Bennett."

The next clipping, dated a week later, said:

CORTWRIGHT DEATH SUICIDE
Absconder Succumbs to Remorse

Here, the tale took a fantastic twist. Communication with the Cleveland police disclosed the stunning fact that T. James Cortwright was none other than Thompson J. Wainwright, a badly wanted absconding broker who had looted his firm of seventy thousand dollars in cold cash.

It seemed obvious to the Cleveland police and to the *Bartonville Clarion* that Wainwright had selected Fern Springs as a hideout and suddenly, for some unfathomable reason, had an uprising of conscience which induced him to take his life. What had become of the booty, no one could find out. The conclusion was that he must have spent it.

McGavock shook his head. Such goings-on!

How could a stranger, in the night, locate a patch of quicksand he couldn't possibly have known to exist? Why hadn't he taken his hat in with him? And just what kind of a conscience was it that Mr. Cortwright-Wainwright possessed? One that drove him to suicide yet refused to return his plunder to his victims. Horsefeathers!

There were three letters, each bearing a recent postmark and mailed a week apart. Each was addressed to Lester Hodges and each contained a blank sheet of paper clipped with a wire paper clip.

Bennett had said that Lester Hodges was unable to read. *Someone had used the envelopes to send him money.* Bills. And small bills probably—Lester Hodges changing a large banknote in Bartonville would have caused a sensation.

McGavock bundled the stuff back up, snapped on the rubber band and replaced things as he had found them—under the Spanish tile.

THE LIGHT IN the window of Hal Maldron's law office had been extinguished. The window-rapping attorney, like his fellow citizens, was home in bed—fighting mosquitoes in his old-fashioned nightgown, trying to get some sleep. McGavock palmed the brass knob and got out his key ring with its assortment of keys. The third one did it. He slipped in, left the door ajar behind him.

He knew just what he was going to do and how he was going to do it.

A wire basket on the lawyer's desk containing signed but unmailed correspondence gave the detective a specimen of Maldron's signature. It was bold, fancy, with loops and flourishes. The sort of signature a pompous man assumes cannot be forged.

The detective placed his hat over his flashlight, rummaged

for a piece of scrap paper. He dipped the attorney's steel pen in the inkwell, got a generous nibful of gummy ink and wrote:

The bones of Thompson J. Wainright are at Fern Springs. Seek and ye shall find!

Hal Maldron

McGavock wrote in large letters, lines wide-spaced. He filled his pen twice during the short inscription. The signature was a marvelous replica.

Quickly, McGavock slid the worn desk blotter out of its corner brackets. The underside, as he suspected, was new, unused. He blotted the message on the blotter's reverse—with the care of a master engraver.

The detective crumpled the paper, stuffed it in his hip pocket, refitted the blotter in the brackets in its original position—so that his handiwork was concealed.

Again on the street, the office door locked behind him, he gave a short, mirthless laugh. The entire operation had taken less than two minutes. He couldn't help thinking of Atherton Browne, wondering what the old man would say. It had been a busy evening with a rather heavy routine: three breaking and enterings, one assault and battery, one forgery.

It had been a busy evening and a profitable one, too.

McGavock had found out why Hodges had been murdered, had a good idea who the killer was. He understood now the double irony in the anonymous warning he had received: *Let the dead alone.* There was more than one corpse involved in this case. He was confronting a veteran, a two-time killer.

From the tunnel-black alley behind the Bradley House, he

could see the white towel hanging from his open window. He caught the shed's low eave, drew himself up onto the tin roof.

His room was just as he had left it. The tobacco tin behind the crayon enlargement, the wire key lock on the doorknob. McGavock undressed, donned a violent purple suit of cossack-style pajamas, and was asleep by the time he hit the sheet.

3

―――

The Hammer

THE DETECTIVE WAS just finishing a pungent, savory breakfast of chicken pie and eggs in the bare matting-floored hotel dining-room when Calhoun-not-Calvin Bradley materialized at his table. The puffy proprietor dragged out a chair and sat down. "You may be the owner of this flea-trap," McGavock said darkly into his coffee. "But the law books will tell you that I have a tenant's lease on this table. Scram!"

Bradley said artificially: "Did you have a sound night's sleep?"

"I did. In spite of that broken-down bed—"

"It's that bed," Bradley said smugly, "that I wanted to speak to you about. When you check out of here, you will notice an added debit of $6.80 on your bill. That is for mutilating my best bed—clipping the spring, suh, and twisting it through the key! I'm shocked—"

McGavock asked bleakly: "How do you know?"

"I saw it, suh. With my own eyes." The hotel man rolled his eyeballs reprovingly. "Shortly after you left the desk last night—to hibernate—I was under the impression that I heard you call me. I knocked on your door. No response. I rattled the panel. All was quiet. I became frantic. I've had guests with heart seizures. I raced around to the alley. With the aid of a ladder I reached your room from the outside. You were gone. I must say I was grieved to observe that you had—"

"Go 'way!" McGavock ordered. "You're constricting my digestive juices."

Bradley settled himself comfortably. "You're a deep one, full of dodges. It seemed a bit eccentric at the moment but this morning I think I understand. *Toujours l'amour.*" He squeezed a lewd wink from the corner of his eyelid. "Someone was telling me that they happened to notice you on the old swamp road with Laurel Bennett last night." He left the sentence up in the air, on a note of inquiry.

"You'd better take a reef in that limber tongue of yours," McGavock said quietly. "Or it will bring on an Act of God. You don't kid me a bit—I've been pumped by experts. You, and the whole population, know all about me by now. Who I am and what I'm here for. When the cat gets out of the bag in a village like this one—it divides and scatters. I met Mrs. Bennett by appointment—that was business. I went out along the swamp road and manhandled your friend Chunky—that was pleasure. I'm a detective and I'm here to find out who killed Lester Hodges."

Bradley tittered. "Who do you favor?"

"I favor you."

The hotel proprietor asked mockingly: "How do you make that out?"

McGavock folded his napkin in a neat cornucopia, got up. "The man that killed Wainwright killed Hodges. Lester Hodges' murder was bred in the homicide of that absconder back at Fern Springs thirty years ago."

Bradley said innocently: "Wainwright? I never heard of him." He went through a grotesque facial contortion, pretended to remember. "Oh. You mean the man that fell into the quicksand? I recall what you're speaking of now. A tragic incident. I was clerk at the time. I'd almost forgotten. Wainwright wasn't murdered." He lowered his voice confidentially. "The affair was very strange. I've thought about it a great deal. What became of the money? No one has ever answered that. Would you like to hear my personal hypothesis?"

"I would, indeed."

"It's this," Bradley announced brightly. "Wainwright didn't commit suicide. He just used Fern Springs as a blind to throw pursuers off his tracks. He signed up at the resort, paid weeks in advance, learned about Devil's Elbow—probably from the servants. That gave him an idea. He sneaked out of the back of the building, placed his hat and wallet on the edge of quicksands and left the neighborhood that very night. You see, he had a small cowhide satchel with him. It disappeared when he did. That proves my point. He hightailed and took his seventy thousand with him. Right today he's doubtless a pillar of society in some place like Johannesburg or Rio."

There was logic in the hotel man's statement—and McGavock had to admit it. "If that's your story," he rasped, "stick with it. It strikes me you're mighty clear on the details—considering it happened three decades ago."

Bradley simpered. "That's my story. And will remain my story—until a better one comes along."

LAUREL BENNETT, HERSELF, was standing in the sunny foyer of the lobby waiting for McGavock. She was wearing jodhpurs and a baggy pearl-colored brushed wool sweater. A short, braided quirt was tucked into her armpit. The bright morning light was harsh, unkind to her. There were tiny crow's-feet at her temples, her lips were drawn, fagged. "I thought you'd never get up," she said. "I've been watching for you from across the street. Let's go somewhere and talk, someplace where we'll be alone. I'll meet you at the cemetery in ten minutes."

McGavock was ugly. "We'll do nothing of the kind. No clandestine conferences for me! If you have anything to unload, let's have it here and now."

"But this is too public—"

He prepared to brush past her. "O.K."

She clutched him desperately by the sleeve. "It's about the hammer! You have to listen. I've found the hammer!"

"I've lost no hammer."

"Don't taunt me. You know what I'm talking about. Gil came home with your compass last night and told us why you had given it to him. This morning, before anyone was up, I took it out in the toolhouse and found the hammer. It was in a big wooden chest with the rest of the tools. Its head was magnetized. It pulled the compass needle. I tried it out; it picked up nails."

McGavock said gravely: "Don't tell me you disposed of it!"

She raised her eyebrows innocently. "How did you know? That's exactly what I did. I took it out in the country and threw it in the river. I'll never tell anyone where. Wild horses couldn't drag it from me."

"It couldn't have been Gil's hammer?"

"Oh, no. It was a new one—I'd never seen it before." She smiled deprecatingly. "It was in Gil's tool chest but that doesn't prove anything, does it?"

McGavock guffawed. "Sister, you're a thing of beauty and a joy forever. You're more fun than a stampede at the circus. I wish I wasn't so busy; I'd like to give you more of my time. Cal

Bradley tells me the town is pairing us off together, gossiping about our little trip to Chunky's last night. Answer me this: wasn't it you, yourself, that put out the story?"

Rage swept into her eyes.

"I think I'll leave," McGavock said hastily. "You're getting set to touch off a string of oaths." He left her standing there— frustrated and furious.

MALCOM JARRELL WAS seated on the side steps of the Bennett mansion in smoking jacket and carpet slippers. He had his four-lensed spectacles hooked on the bridge of his nose. He was feeding brown sugar to a procession of big, black ants. He'd bend down, watch for a second, and then scribble a note on a jumbled sheaf of papers. Hunched with his stubbled chin between his scrawny kneecaps, he reminded McGavock of some shabby sea monster.

"You'd better turn around," he said placidly as McGavock came into his vision. "And go straight back to town. The sheriff just phoned. He's mad enough to top the high cotton. He's waiting for you at Lawyer Maldron's." The naturalist smiled. "If I wasn't so occupied here, I'd trot along. It'd be amusing to hear you bluster. You're going to have to do a bit of explaining—"

"It's you, my erudite friend of fur and feathers, it's you, suh, who have a bit of explaining to do." The detective bore down on him. "I want to know about that rat of yours. I want to know all about it."

"His name is Bertram," the naturalist said owlishly. "He's deficient in vitamins A, C and D—"

McGavock spat, "And don't take me for a sleigh ride. I'm talking about his hind leg. Just above the ankle, there's a raw place in the fur—a band of flesh where the skin's been rubbed off. What caused that?"

Jarrell nodded sagely. "I'm treating him for it. Bertram was caught in a trap. The mark of the trap's jaws—"

McGavock said happily: "Boy, you really think on your feet! That's a snappy answer. Now let's see what you have to say to this. As a matter of fact, there's no raw place on his leg at all! I know. I checked."

Malcom Jarrell's composure cracked. His florid cheeks went gravel-gray, sucked in, his eyes darted wildly—past McGavock's shoulder, past his hip, evading the detective's steady gaze.

The naturalist licked his lips. "I owe you an apology," he croaked. "I certainly misjudged you. I should have known that Atherton wouldn't send me a fool, that you must be smarter than you acted. Grant me this request: don't question me. Let sleeping dogs lie."

"No can do," McGavock said coldly. "I'm after a killer. Let's hear about Bertram, the whole story."

"You leave me no choice." Jarrell gritted his huge jaw. "I'm afraid you've guessed the worst of it. A few weeks ago a citizen of our town, someone Lester Hodges had known all his life, came to him with an extraordinary business proposition. Who this person was, Lester refused to tell me. The rat was involved in that business deal."

"Of course," McGavock declared. "That's been perfectly obvious from the start. You were keeping Hodges' rat for him. No naturalist would confine such a large animal in such a small cage. It's cruel. That was so Hodges could tie a string to its leg without the beast whipping around and fanging him."

"Exactly."

"What was this business deal?"

"This person employed Lester to search between the floors of an old, tumbledown health resort out in the pine country, Fern Springs. Hodges was half-mad—"Jarrell's voice was patronizing, amiable. McGavock remembered Bennett's statement: The two town nuts—Jarrell and Hodges. "Lester was half-mad," the naturalist repeated. "He tackled the problem with a system of his own. He tied fishing line onto the rodent's leg and used him some way in the search. I don't know how on earth he induced the animal to act."

"He was searching for obstructions under the floor," McGavock explained. "He placed the rat in an opening by the baseboard. Floor joists run parallel—under every floor there's a series of small tunnels. It was pretty clever. It saved him ripping up goodness knows how much floor space. It was the most plausible way to do it.

Malcom Jarrell frowned. "But how did he make the animal obey?"

"He scared him through with tiny firecrackers, a commodity obtainable at any Deep South country store. Hodges slipped his pet into the floor, popped off a firecracker—and judged by the length of slack in the line the progress his animal was making under the floor. Did the old man find what he was supposed to?"

"I don't know. I should say he was slain before he was successful. He'd come over in the evening and talk to me in a vague sort of way. I got the impression that he and his employer were satisfied with the way the business was going. His employer was paying him a steady salary of four dollars a week—sending him banknotes wrapped in blank paper. Lester was quite excited over his good fortune."

McGavock said: "You're being candid with me? You're telling me everything?"

Jarrell had his old poise back. "Oh, quite. You'll have to excuse me now. You have work to do." He resumed his scrutiny of the black ants. "And so have I."

AS SOON AS McGavock laid eyes on the local law he knew that he was in for a catch-as-catch-can tussle.

The sheriff of Linden County was the direct antithesis of the old-style rural sharpshooter that pinned his rusty badge to his gallus elastic and toted a .38-in-a-.44 frame at a holster on his hip as big as an English riding saddle. The young man that lolled on the corner of Hal Maldron's desk was modest, friendly, self-effacing. He was dressed in well-cut blue-gray tweed. And his fingernails were a little over-manicured.

It was the fingernails that scared McGavock. This lad must have plenty on the ball. The hard-bitten mountain folk of Linden County wouldn't have elected him if he was as sappy as he seemed. The coon-hunting hillmen selected their sheriff like they selected their hound dogs—for brains and guts and stamina. McGavock had the strange feeling that he was in the presence of a hotshot, deliver-the-goods career man.

The young man smiled. "Howdy. I'm Steve Robley—the current and temporary head of our local crime and punishment bureau. It's mighty swell of you to look me up. I hope I'm not imposing?"

McGavock was stunned. "No," he said carefully. "It's a pleasure. Is Maldron, here, a deputy of yours?"

Hal Maldron lifted his fat lip, exposed his decayed teeth. "Yes," he announced, "I am."

"No," the sheriff said, "you're not. I'm sorry, Hal, but I'm going to have to revoke your authority for the duration of this brief but pleasant interview. We mustn't intimidate our new friend with a belligerent show of force." He got out a stubby briar pipe, loaded it, got it going. "I've gone over the hammer, Mr. McGavock. I can't find any prints."

McGavock remarked: "I left the hammer under the body. As a proof to you that I wasn't down here to tamper with evidence." It was a bluff, a case of life or death. He surged with relief when the sheriff nodded.

"The very conclusion that I myself came to. I must say it gave me a bit of surprise—I'd always been under the impression that private detectives were not so cooperative."

"I've tried it that way," McGavock said. "It's the hard way. Now I cooperate." This boy really had a deadpan. He wondered if he was being maneuvered out on a limb. "Can I be of any service to you?"

"Yes," the sheriff said slowly. "You certainly can be. I'm stumped. What's it all about? Who'd want to murder harmless old Hodges?"

McGavock was impressed. "This is a long story. And a muddled one. I work for an agency in Memphis. For twenty years now we've been investigating a case for a brokerage firm in Cleveland. Back in nineteen-nine they had a guy abscond with seventy grand. He came down here to Fern Springs and vanished."

He had them entranced. They were swallowing it, every word. There could be no doubt of it.

Maldron said helplessly: "Why didn't you say so last night! I didn't apprehend that you had such powerful backing. You people have been working on a case in this vicinity for twenty years? I can hardly believe it!"

"We've been working on the case—but not in this community. It was the slaying of Lester Hodges that gave us the break we've been looking for."

Sheriff Robley was flustered. "I'll be perfectly honest with you, Mr. McGavock. A certain party—"Maldron looked miserable. "A certain party summoned me last night by an imperative phone call. He said that you were retained by a cousin of Mr. Jarrell's and that you came down here from Memphis for the sole purpose of obstructing justice. He said that he'd go into court and swear that you had consulted him last night about his client and had attempted to entice him into illegal conspiracy."

"These sure-fire lawyers," McGavock said pleasantly. "No wonder they win cases. They butter their bread on both sides. Who's he representing—Jarrell or you? I may say at this time, that we in Memphis have had occasion to speculate a little about this Maldron. In fact, it wouldn't surprise us to learn that somehow he's directly involved. He knows something. He was at Fern Springs in that fatal August when Wainwright disappeared. He—"

Maldron glared. "And so were Bennett and Malcom and Bradley and half the town."

McGavock shook a finger dramatically. "Then, sir," he declaimed *basso profundo*, "then why, sir, did you write us that unusual note—the one about Wainwright's bones, seek at Fern Springs and ye shall find?"

The lawyer fidgeted. "Nonsense. You're out of your head."

Steve Robley looked suddenly intent. "Go on, Mr. McGavock."

"That's all," McGavock said. "Comes in this crank letter signed 'Hal Maldron' talking about a dead man's bones—"

The sheriff said softly: "The letter was typewritten, of course?"

"Not as I remember it. Written in big letters, in ink, as I recall it."

The young sheriff stepped to Maldron's desk, inspected the surface of the much-used blotter. He rubbed his chin, looked at the ceiling for a moment, turned the blotter over. The inked imprints stood out in heavy black scrawls. The sheriff took a pocket mirror from his comb-case, held it above the inscription.

"'The bones of Thompson J. Wainwright are at Fern Springs,'" he read. "'Seek and ye shall find!' Thank you, Mr. McGavock. You've been of great assistance. I'll not keep you any longer."

Alone, on the sun-splashed sidewalk, McGavock wiped a trembling hand across his forehead and said, "Whoo!" So the hammer was under the corpse all the time. He'd started his investigation by muffing the murder weapon. It had been a nerve-racking ten minutes. They had been waiting for him, all set to drive him out of town. He'd sidestepped it. For how long, he didn't know—but for the time being, anyhow. And time was what he needed.

"Six hours," McGavock decided. "Give me six hours more and I'll blow this thing seven ways to Christmas!"

GIL BENNETT WAS in his office at the cotton gin. A little room not much larger than a chicken coop, its walls were plastered with commercial calendars—wild ducks in topsy-turvy flight, prize bulls, and turgid maidens in air-brushed bathing suits. Bennett sat on a rocker with a spliced leg by a cluttered roll-top desk. Laid out before him were a wine glass, an egg, a bottle of pepper sauce and a salt cellar. "Glad to see you," he said. "Hitch up and dismount."

The only other article of furniture in the room was a battered church pew along the wall. McGavock stretched himself out full-length, propped himself up on the arm, and grinned. "Do you think you'll live?" he asked.

Bennett's voice was hollow. "I doubt it." He broke the raw egg in the wine glass, dusted it with a sprinkle of salt and doused it liberally with pepper sauce. "A prairie oyster. Will you go along with me, sir?" McGavock shook his head. The businessman took it at a gulp. "You must break the yolk with your tongue as it goes down," he said. "Ugh!"

McGavock remarked sententiously: "The wages of sin." He laughed. "Get that wilted expression off your face. You're afraid I'm going to continue our conversation of last evening. I'm not. You were a guest at the Fern Springs resort back in nineteen-nine when a guy named Wainwright drifted in with a satchel of hot money—and evaporated. Do you happen to remember the attendant circumstances?"

"Very well, indeed." Bennett was grim.

"Swell. The place, I understand, is now owned by Mrs. Bennett, who inherited it. The episode occurred some years before Mrs. Bennett was born. Who did it belong to at the time?"

"To an invalid relative of hers down in Louisiana. She inherited it at his death. Mrs. Bennett, by the way, comes from New Orleans. She's not actually a native of our country."

"I see," McGavock said. "If the resort had an absentee landlord, who ran the joint? Bradley?"

"Scarcely! Bradley was just a general utility man. Malcom Jarrell was the titled manager."

"I see. One thing more. Have you any personal theory as to what happened? I mean, were you satisfied at the time by the way the thing was explained?"

Bennett's answer was calm, detached. "There's always been bad friendship between Malcom Jarrell and myself. Everybody in town knows it—you should understand it before I express an opinion on so grave a point. My answer is no. I wasn't satisfied at the time and I'm less satisfied today. I think Wainwright was killed and his money was stolen."

McGavock was silent.

"It's this way," Bennett amplified. "We live in a small community here. We know each other—and our families have known each other—for a good many years. We can guess the income of our neighbors to a plugged nickel. Malcom Jarrell has a most scanty income—yet he has prospered."

McGavock retorted: "Isn't the same true of Cal Bradley?"

"In a way, yes. But Cal's case is a little different. He's a low, cunning trickster. Men like Cal Bradley are destined to prosper despite all laws of order and decency."

McGavock got to his feet, slapped his hat against his thigh. "I'd hate to go into court with that kind of a brief." His eyes narrowed. "You're holding back something, aren't you?" He dropped his hat on the floor, picked it up and cocked it on the crown of his head. "Don't let me shove you into anything."

Bennett answered wryly: "I won't. There's more to this mess than shows on the surface. Whenever you—"

He was interrupted mid-sentence by a timid knock on the door and the entry of a stalwart young hillman. The caller was dressed in a plaid cotton shirt; a three-inch brass-studded belt held up his faded denim trousers. He confronted them with wooden composure. "Which one of y'all might happen to be Mr. Bennett, the man that owned that ol' Fern Springs bat den?"

"Me," Bennett said. "And I still own it. Or rather Mrs. Bennett does. Why?"

"I'm Asie Tenniman. I'm yore south neighbor back there in the pine country. I shore hate to tell you, suh, but ain't nobuddy owns that building no more. It was farred down to ashes at daybreak this mornin'. I'm sorry I couldn't bring the word no sooner. Hit's eighteen miles by muleback an'—"

"Are you telling me," Bennett asked, "that our resort has been burned?"

"And I don't mean maybe. Some mighty mean folks live out there in the timber." The hillman added carelessly: "My woman claims she heard a boiler let loose jest about the time we seen the red."

"Shiners?"

The boy wouldn't commit himself. "I couldn't hardly say, suh. I'm jest a-telling y'all what I know. Good mornin', gentlemen."

And he was gone.

McGavock cut out: "Eighteen miles in and eighteen miles back—on a mule. And not a penny, not even a word of thanks."

"You don't understand these people," Gil Bennett observed quietly. "If I'd offered him money he'd have thrown it in my face. It's a favor and I'll remember it. Maybe sometime I'll have a chance to pay a doctor's bill or something for him… What do you make of it?"

The detective fanned the air. "It's too much for me!"

4

Seek and Ye Shall Find

THERE WAS A telegram waiting for him on his return to the hotel. A pimple-faced kid with a muff of uncut hair skipped it across the register with an insolent flourish. He was wearing an oversize alpaca coat and black-ribboned nose glasses. "And who are you, my scrofulous adolescent?" McGavock inquired.

"I'm swing man to this joint. Mr. Bradley, he's takened him a day off. He's got a misery."

"Mr. Bradley's ill? You don't seem overcome with grief."

"Not me. It ain't no shingles off my smokehouse." He paused. "That's shore a nutty telegram in that there envelope. I chanct to hold 'er up to the light. I can't make no sense out'n—"

"You got a fine start, son." McGavock was warm in his encouragement. "Just keep on candling private correspondence and you've got a big future before you."

Behind the locked door of his room, McGavock slit the envelope, extracted the yellow flimsy. The message was signed Atherton Browne. It read:

EIGHT FOUR ONE COMMA TWO TWELVE FIVE
COMMA ONE THREE ONE COMMA TWENTY ONE
FOUR COMMA SIX ONE SEVEN COMMA ELEVEN NINE
THREE YOU'RE NOT ON A VACATION.

McGavock glowered. He went to his Gladstone and got out

his copy of *Dr. Trimble's Hygiene for Babies*, the Browne Agency keybook. Page eight, line four, word one gave him *what*. Page two, line twelve, word five was *if*. Laboriously, the detective leafed back and forth, broke down the code.

The deciphered message read: *What if anything are you accomplishing—you're not on a vacation.*

McGavock purpled. He grabbed the book till the veins stood out on his wrist. He drew back his arm to dash the volume against the wall, froze, grinned. He uncapped his fountain pen, settled down and filled out an answer.

It took him twenty minutes to get it the way he wanted it. The final draft said: *Page one seventeen, paragraph three, in toto.*

Paragraph three on page one hundred seventeen of *Dr. Trimble's Hygiene for Babies* said: *Keep your nasal passages clean!*

He left the wire with the kid at the desk with the injunction that he get it off immediately—and headed for the Bartonville garage. He wanted to rent a car and take a look at what was left of Fern Springs.

Sheriff Steve Robley was lounging beneath the shady marquee of the Magnolia Drugstore. He uncrossed his ankles, picked a short cigarette stub out of an ivory holder, put the holder in a little velvet-lined case. "Luther McGavock!" He saluted the detective. "The Man of Forty Faces."

McGavock came to a halt, squinted. "What's the rib, Sheriff?"

Robley gave him a quick, friendly grin. "You've really got this town on its ear. They've been comparing notes on you. I've had a dozen warnings about you. To Cal Bradley you're representing a mythical celery king named Boggs. Malcom Jarrell thinks he's your client. You tell Maldron and myself that you're representing some brokers in Cleveland. The clerk at Jones' hardware store tells me that you bought a compass from him and that you are not McGavock at all but a man named, singularly, Lester Hodges." The sheriff's lips quirked in a boyish smile but the skin about his eyes was tight. "Furthermore and furthermore. That 'seek the bones' message on Hal Maldron's desk blotter is just a little too good to be true. It makes me uneasy. I've put a call through to your agency in Memphis to check it but can't seem to get any satisfactory response. They must have the letter on file—if such a letter exists."

"Of course they have," McGavock declared. "That letter's going to clear up this case."

"That's my car yonder by the watering trough." The sheriff pointed lazily to a low, tan job bright with metalwork. "I was just pondering a trip out to the old resort. I'd like a little company. Think I could shanghai you into going along?"

McGavock frowned. "Don't pressure me. I got a schedule that's swamping me." He considered. "O.K.," he agreed. "If we can get back before suppertime."

THE DRIVE DEEP into the hills was rough and tiresome. Just out of town they struck the sloping red clay road and started their winding climb. Through a gap in the foliage, they could glimpse the village. It lay in the dank liquid-green of the bottoms, its buildings like tiny matchboxes. Main Street seemed one long, rambling shed. McGavock made out the red-painted cotton compress, court square and—in the distance—the rickety wooden trestle curving above the cut with its long, spindly supports. The trestle by Hodges' shanty where his attacker had opened on him with shotgun slugs… Great oaks closed about them and the picture was gone.

The high ridge caught the hot sun's rays, illuminating the tree shafts with preternatural clearness. The earth was brassy, scorched.

They turned from the pike, followed an indistinct trace of wagon ruts—and then, abruptly, it was cool, gray shadow. They were in the pine country.

Sheriff Robley stopped his car at a fork in the trail. "That's Devil's Elbow. Where Wainwright's hat and wallet were found. Shall we get out?"

McGavock glanced at the sink hole. It was a vile, grassy bog, saucer-shaped, bordered by dense hazel bushes and speckled with the sickly pastel blooms of wild orchids. "There's nothing here for us," he remarked. "Wainwright never saw this place."

"Perhaps you're right," Steve Robley agreed grudgingly. "It's the old hotel that holds the clues I'm after."

"Then you'll have to sift the ashes," McGavock gibed. "It's been torched."

The sheriff listened attentively while McGavock told him about Asie Tenniman's report. "So we drove out here for the trip! This is another of your tricks! What's behind it?"

McGavock said: "I've got a hunch. Play along with me—I think we can turn up something interesting."

THE OLD RESORT, deep in a bowl of giant pines, was a shambles of flaming timbers. It was as if some giant hand had caught up the burning building, crushed it to splintered wreckage, and had dropped it, jackstraw fashion, to a blazing inferno. They could hear the vicious crackle and snap of the tinder-dry joists long before they turned into the little hollow.

The heat was searing, terrific.

"What are you thinking?" McGavock asked.

"I'm thinking the same thing you are," the young man answered calmly. "If this fire's been going on since daybreak I'll eat a box of .38s. The building's been exploded—and I should say within the last twenty minutes."

McGavock pointed to a blurred tire tread in the soft ground. "That's not a bear track. Our killer's been here, done his little chore—and gone."

The dapper sheriff was nettled. "We'll jusk ask a few questions of that hillman's wife, Mrs. Tenniman, who saw the building burn at daybreak. It looks like connivance."

"Mrs. Tenniman can wait." McGavock scowled, surveyed the surroundings with moody concentration. "Wainwright was killed in the hotel. There was a lawn party going on, a big fiesta out front. He signed up with Bradley and retired to his room. He'd been there a few minutes when somebody, another guest, knocked on his door, lured him into this guest's room and knocked him off. It's an old pattern, it's been done dozens of times before."

"It's very possible."

"I'm telling you that's what happened. The killer then went to Wainwright's room, got his cowhide satchel with the seventy grand and took it back with him to his room. Now listen to this, because the time's going to come when I want you to remember it: the murderer pilfered the satchel, pried up a couple of planks in the floor and hid it there."

"I don't see—"

"You will. It worked so well that time that he tried it later. And that's how we're going to catch him."

Steve Robley said suavely: "Well, we've got the body in our room, what are we going to do with it?"

"We're going to wait until about eleven thirty, when the lawn party's in full swing, and then we're going to lug it out a side door and dispose of it." McGavock added casually: "You don't happen to have a shovel on you?"

Steve Robley smiled. "Yes, I have. There's one in the car. I came prepared for almost any contingency. Don't look surprised." He walked away, returned with the two short-handled spades. "This is going to be pretty hopeless, isn't it? Where do we start?"

"We don't dig until we reason it out," McGavock declared. His words sounded silly to him. "Let's get the lay of the land, let's prowl."

The ferny springs, from which the resort had gotten its name, were halfway up the hillside. They lay in a grotto of fetid fronds—back beneath an overhang of black wet rock. There were seven of them and they drained into a silty pool where a rusty iron pipe carried their curative waters down the slope to an ornate pagoda-like bath-house.

McGavock leaned over the pool, peered into its scummy, yellowish depths. "And this stuff was supposed to be healthy! Yow!"

"He didn't toss the body in there," the sheriff said dryly. "That water was in constant use at the time. I don't see any bones. Do you?"

"No," McGavock answered. "But we will. Hold your horses."

At one side of the pool, far under the shelving overhang, a V trough had been cut in the limestone at the rim to check the overflow. A steady stream of water poured from this trough, struck a slab of shale and flattened out to a tiny brook which meandered down the bank in a little pebbled channel. McGavock began to whistle. He whistled *The Letter Edged in Black*. He raised an impudent eyebrow at the young sheriff. "Just like Attila! I'll give you odds."

Robley showed wavering signs of temper. "Don't be cryptic. This thing is getting me down."

McGavock declared: "It has to be so. Our man's an engineer. Everything he does shows balanced planning."

He lifted the slab of shale from the brook, jammed it up against the drain trough in such a way that it diverted the overflow from the pool. A new runlet angled off down the hillside. Except for a few shallow puddles, the brookbed went dry.

"Get to work," McGavock ordered. "We dig in this dry channel." He cleaned a handful of tangled watercress from the ravine, thrust his spade blade into the gravelly earth.

"I'll start part-way down," the sheriff said, "and work up towards you." He disappeared down the slope in the brushy shrubbery.

Ten minutes later the sheriff's loud, clear voice called out excitedly: "By golly! Luther, I've found it!"

McGavock grinned at the young man's unconscious intimacy. "You've found what, Steven?"

"I've found the skull!" He sounded perplexed. "Wainwright must have been a midget. This looks like a child's skull."

"If you're not satisfied with your skull," McGavock yelled back, "come up and pick one from me. I've found three."

In a grisly hour they excavated the bones and skulls of six bodies. Two children and four adults. They laid the macabre relics on the marsh grass. Sheriff Robley was thunderstruck, nauseated. "A graveyard," he whispered hollowly. "A ghastly funeral trench! What sort of charnel work went on here? I'll have half the town in my cells as soon as I return! It makes me dizzy. I can't seem to make heads or tails—"

"Charnel work is right," McGavock agreed gravely. "I was afraid of something like this." He looked old, cruel. "But I've got our boy in the bag. Meet me at Malcom Jarrell's tonight about eight and we'll go to town." He scraped the sandy loam from his shovel, started for the car. "Let's chat a bit with that south neighbor—Mrs. Tenniman."

THE ANCIENT TWO-ROOM cabin, with its log door-step and its pack of yelping fox dogs, nestled at the turn of the trail. It was almost concealed by the waxy, swooping branches of aromatic pine. A wizened old woman, barefooted and smoking a juicy-looking pipe, sat in the runway. She pretended not to notice them as they approached.

The sheriff took off his hat. "Good evening, ma'am. Are you Mrs. Asie Tenniman?"

"I hain't her sister."

"I understand that at sun-up this morning you heard an explosion at the old hotel and that a few moments later you saw the sky redden as the building caught fire?"

The old woman chewed her pipe stem.

"I'm Steve Robley," the sheriff said placatingly. "Don't be afraid to talk to me. You probably knew my father. We mean you no harm. We understand—"

"You understand! You understand! Who-all's bin a-tellin' y'all these tales?"

The sheriff answered complacently: "Your husband, Asie."

The old woman said sweetly: "Now hain't that a marvel? If you was any sheriff at all you'd know your county. I'm a widow-woman. Asie's bin dead and gone three year now. The big-pox takened him."

There was a flustered silence.

McGavock put in his oar. "You tell us you're a widow. Those look to me like mighty fine fox hounds. Do you hunt foxes?"

The old dame went into a frenzy of rage. "Yes, by daddy! I hunt fox and I hunt deer and I hunt bear. And I got me a thirty-thirty inside that can roll you up like a cigarette paper. And if you fellers don't quit pesterin' me and git gone I'll shore haul 'er out!"

In the car, on the way back to town, the sheriff said: "The man that gave that false report to Bennett was an impostor. What did he look like?"

"He had a plaid cotton shirt and a flashy brass-studded belt. He was about eighteen years old. Do you make him?"

"I think I do. He's a character—and a bad one—from over in the Hostetter's Store neighborhood. How he got into the picture, I couldn't tell you. Maldron's defended him time and again—but that doesn't mean anything."

"Of course not."

There was an awkward interval.

The sheriff changed the subject. "Back there, before we started to dig, you said something about Attila. What did you mean?"

"Attila the Hun," McGavock explained. "That was the way his brother tribesmen buried him. They wanted to hide his body so they dammed a stream, buried him, and then turned the water back in its channel. I wonder how many anonymous killers have done it since!"

The sheriff parked behind the courthouse. "Promise me

this," McGavock said earnestly as they separated. "Promise me you'll do nothing stringent until you hear what I have to say at Malcom Jarrell's tonight. Be there on the dot—and bring your buddy Hal Maldron."

The sheriff was hesitant. "It's mighty irregular—"

McGavock soothed him. "If it's the credit you're worrying about—don't! I don't want any headlines. All I want is this slayer."

That did the trick. Robley smiled. "I wasn't thinking of headlines but if you put it that way, it's mighty fine of you. I'll be seeing you."

THE DETECTIVE HAD an early supper at the Bradley House. Its lord and master was nowhere to be seen. But the boy in the alpaca coat was in a talkative mood. "A fellow was a-saying you're a detective," he observed. "You and Steve Robley been out all evening, ain't you? Fellow was a-saying y'all are teamed up to ketch you'uns a badman."

McGavock grabbed the boy's wrist, punched his hand in the inkwell, slapped it on a piece of paper. He gave the brat a terrible leer. "Fingerprints," he explained. "I'm not passing up anybody. I'll just send these up to Nashville and—" He paused, studied the paralyzed clerk thoughtfully. "Maybe you'd like to turn state's evidence?"

"But I don't know nothing about nothing."

"The heck you don't. Where's Cal Bradley?"

The adolescent licked his lips. "He's out in the country somewhere training a bitch pointer."

"Why didn't you say so in the first place? Why all the secrecy?"

"I swear I couldn't tell you. He threatened me not to. That's all I rightly know."

"If you see him before I do," McGavock ground out, "you tell him the sheriff said he's to show up at Malcom Jarrell's at eight."

He was dog tired. He rubbed his unshaven chin, knew that a bath and shave would freshen him, but decided to wait a little. In a far corner of the lobby—back in a sort of alcove—he could make out the outlines of a couple of comfortable-looking chairs in the half gloom. He sauntered over, sank down into cool, deep-cushioned leather and closed his eyes. He was half-asleep—thinking about that little ball of gray fur beneath the tile in Malcom Jarrell's hearth—when he heard footsteps advancing toward him.

Laurel Bennett burst out: "I have to see you. Thank goodness I've found you—" She was dressed as she had been that morning: baggy sweater and worn riding breeches. There was a disheveled, dramatic rumple to her hair.

"You haunt me," McGavock grated. "It's not right. You're a married woman. What now?"

"I have to confess," she said demurely. "I storied to you this morning. I didn't find any hammer. I just wanted to study your psychological reactions. When I was at college I wrote my thesis on—"

"Sure, sure." McGavock yawned. "Some other time, please!"

She ground her heel on the floor. "Where I come from," she stormed, "people pay me the proper respect."

"If they don't they get horse-whipped, eh?"

She went suddenly docile. Her somber eyes fastened themselves on him, intent and warm. "What makes you so attractive?"

McGavock kicked out a chair. "Sit down. What's all the bedlam about this time?"

"This. I've just been consulting with my attorney, Mr. Maldron. We want to retain you. Not through your agency, you understand, but on sort of a freelance job. We're so impressed with your energy and capability that—"

"That what?"

"Well, it's this way. I'm just a young girl. Gil came down to Louisiana and married me before I realized what was happening. Swept me off my feet and brought me back here with him. Now I'm beginning to regret it."

"How so?"

"My husband doesn't love me. He makes big withdrawals from our account and sends them to Paducah. He's keeping another woman up there. On my money!"

"Think of that!" McGavock snorted. "You overrun yourself, my child. Last night it was that Gil was gambling his dough away—now it's a new twist."

"You must believe me," she pleaded. "I'm sure I'm right. Hal, Mr. Maldron, says it's quite possible."

"How do I come in?"

"We want you to go up to Paducah right away and browse around. We want you to trace this woman down and get information on her. You can name your own salary!"

"It sounds highly attractive," McGavock decided. "But I'd like a couple of weeks to think it over." He ogled her. "I'll have to write my congressman." He called to her as she strode away. "Be at Jarrell's tonight at eight. The sheriff's orders—and bring your husband."

HE SAT THERE for perhaps five minutes, in a glow of pleasure at her anger, and then, on impulse, got to his feet and walked diagonally across the lobby—towards the rear. There was a door just beyond the desk which aroused his curiosity.

He turned the knob, pushed open the panel and stepped out into a small, enclosed court.

The little space, paved with brick and fenced on three sides with rotting eight-foot planks, appeared to be the hotel dump. Rusty bath tubs, broken crockery lay scattered in trashy litter. A wooden gate with a shoestring latch, inset in the fence by the alley, led down a short flight of stone stairs to an arch of brick. The entrance to an old cellar which lay behind the building's foundations.

McGavock descended the stone stairs, walked warily into the musty blackness. Just inside the arch, he stopped, got out his pencil flash. It was a "plunder room," a storage place for broken furniture.

He flicked his light in a swinging survey, across the great hand-hewn beams above his head, about the loamy, crumbling walls. Then, with the mathematical precision of a hawk circling for a field mouse, he crossed the floor with his beam, began a painstaking, clockwise examination of the cellar's cluttered contents.

He felt, knew, that he was in the presence of death.

His light indexed the hodgepodge: chests and highboys, cobwebbed and battered; rolls of rugs and matting disintegrating in the yeasty dampness.

From a frayed, red silk settee—in the heart of the untidy jumble—the corpse of Cal Bradley watched him with popping, lifeless eyes.

McGavock clicked his tongue, took a quick step forward. The hotel man's hair was a bloody spongy mass. "Our man likes hammers," McGavock thought. "And he's learning to get along without nails. This is a ball-peen job." He inspected the victim without the slightest twinge of sympathy.

Bradley had been dead for at least six hours. In death, the man's real nature showed itself. His puffy, spiderish face was grooved in lines of greed and malice. McGavock turned away in disgust.

On the earthen floor beside the settee was a granite wash-bowl full of gasoline. In the center of the bowl was a paving brick. On the brick, its base just awash with the gasoline, was a china teacup of gun powder. A new plumber's candle was thrust into the cup of powder.

The nape of McGavock's neck crawled. "He was coming back tonight to give it the works! When everyone was asleep. He's willing to burn down half the town. A fire here and all of Main Street goes like excelsior. And, according to his plan, I'm upstairs sawing wood."

The detective pocketed the candle, dismantled the apparatus. He dissipated the powder about the ground, carried the gasoline out into the courtyard and poured it on the paving bricks. "It's hardly likely he'll be back before dark—and I'll have him by then." McGavock frowned. "I hope."

The pimpled clerk was squatting behind the desk, his ear glued to the radio. A program was just signing off. "... *How will Kent escape from the cannibals? Who is the mysterious little man with the blow-gun? Will Professor Lamphert discover the chemical which can unpetrify a human being? Listen tomorrow, same station, same hour.*"

"Exciting, eh?" McGavock made a comical arch of his eyebrows.

The kid nodded. McGavock said: "Give me my key and the house sponge. I'm going to my room and take a bath."

"We don't have no house sponge. You're supposed to use your wash cloth."

"Skip it."

McGavock's room had entertained a caller.

All the bedclothes had been torn from the bed, thrown on the floor. The mattress had been ripped in vicious slashes, its cotton batting pulled out in handfuls. His Gladstone had been dumped on the carpet, there was a muddy footprint on his purple sateen pajamas. The tobacco tin behind the crayon enlargement was gone.

The detective took in the chaos in cold, seething rage.

The final shock was waiting for him at the washstand.

Four black, lumpish objects lay on the flower-embroidered face towel. At first he thought they were potatoes. Like a kick in the stomach, it came to him what they were: rattlesnake heads. Meaty, evil-looking things, severed just back of the jaw.

"This cinches it," McGavock decided. "This is the lad that touched off Fern Springs. The footprint on the pajamas—that's where he got wet shoes. And that's where the rattlesnakes came from, too."

He slid a slip of paper from under the ugly things. A note, in the same script as that he had received the night before, and also on hotel stationery, said: *These vermin got in my way. You see what happened to them. God be with you.*

McGavock considered. "He's scared. He's blown his top. He's mouthing threats. From now on we'd better watch our step—he's hysterical."

Fatigue disappeared with the first splash of cold water. He

bathed to the waist, gave himself a brisk rubbing and selected the least crumpled of his shirts from the disorder on the floor. A shave, twice over, finished the job in short order.

He was all set to wrap this business up.

5

Murder Spa

BY THE TIME McGavock hit the sidewalk the air was breathless—sultry. There was the electric threat of a summer storm about to break loose. In the southwest sky, above the hillcrests, smoky thunderheads were gathering in a diaphanous haze. Even the hound dogs had vanished from the rutted road. The few mules left at hitching posts, their ears flat against their necks, stood stark and fearful in anticipation of the coming squall. McGavock didn't like it. Rain would bring an early nightfall and he was playing against darkness.

Lawyer Maldron lurked in the doorway of his office. The detective had the sensation that he'd been waiting there a long time for McGavock to pass.

He was a different lad from the one that McGavock had quarreled with last night. Somehow, in twenty-four hours, the attorney's cruel ego had withered almost to the vanishing point. "Good evening, sir." He was downright servile. "Could I speak with you a second?"

McGavock asked sarcastically: "What's the matter with the horseshoe-nail ring? Don't tell me you've given up window rapping?"

Maldron forced a cavernous laugh. "I don't rap for my friends, it's not polite." He threw a loop in his lower lip, screwed up his face. "That note on my blotter. You wrote it, didn't you? It was a joke?"

"I wrote it," McGavock said genially. "But it wasn't a joke."

Maldron was hugely pleased. "You admit it? Would you mind informing the sheriff? He's been after me—"

McGavock jeered. "Amnesia has come over me. I don't have the slightest idea what we're talking about." He asked sharply: "In the old days, back when Fern Springs was doing a rush business, how did the out-of-county guests get there? It's a long walk for gentlefolk."

Maldron was perplexed at the question. "They didn't walk, of course. Most of the guests were from right here in Bartonville. Those from out of the county came by train. There was a junction about eight miles from the resort. A surrey was sent out for them. Is that what you mean?"

"That's what I mean." McGavock turned up his coat collar. A sudden spray of raindrops, a premature warning of the storm on the way, whipped down the sidewalk in a swirl of tiny silver crowns.

The sheriff was not in his office at the courthouse. A turnkey greeted McGavock warmly. "Steve's done got Buck."

"Pardon?"

"I'm a-sayin' Stevie's done picked up Buck. He won't talk, though. Stevie says, should you drop in, for you to go back and make a try at him." He pointed a thumb over his shoulder. "He's at the end of the cell block."

McGavock said speculatively: "O.K. I'll see what I can do."

Buck was the phoney Asie Tenniman, the mountain boy with the plaid shirt and brass-studded belt. He was stretched full length on his bunk, reading a Sunday school paper. Every few minutes he'd take a glass jar of snuff from his pocket and rub a pinch of the powder into his gums. He looked at McGavock with glassy eyes, as though the detective were an unpleasant figment of his imagination. "You might's well leave me be. I hain't got nary a thing to say."

McGavock became chummy. "What you reading, Buck?"

"This-here paper was here when I come in. I'm a-whilin' away the time till Hal Maldron gits over to see me. You fellers'll be sorry then. I'm fixin' to sue y'all—"

The detective listened amiably. "But you haven't answered my question. What are you reading? It looks like a Sunday school paper."

The mountain boy said smugly: "That's what it is. It's a Bible paper. I'm reading a piece about how a lady preacher lived forty year amongst the Eskimos and spread the word of—"

McGavock took a little red leather book from his inside pocket. He leafed through it with great concentration, selected a page, tore it from the book and flipped it through the bars of the cell to the floor. "When you finish up the lady preacher you might start on that. It's a copy of the state arson laws."

"Arson laws?"

"That's right. You threw Bennett and me off the trail while somebody rushed out and torched the old hotel. You're as guilty as the man that held the match. I've just been in consultation with Mrs. Bennett and she says it's the pen for the lot of you."

The mountain boy was thoughtful. "I'll make you a swap. I'll tell you what I know—if you'll promise to have Maldron scorch over and git me out of this."

"I'm not in a position to make such a trade. This is worse than arson—it's murder!"

The corridor and the cell block were growing dark. The boy looked out the small window at the smudgy clouds heaping themselves around the hilltops. "I think I been foxed," he said woodenly. "This-here was supposed to be a prank. I'm shootin' me a game of nine ball down to the Shamrock when Gussie says I'm wanted on the phone. It's a funny voice. It sounds like a woman tryin' to talk like a man—or maybe a man tryin' to talk like a woman, it's hard to place. Anyways, this voice says for me to go to Bennett and tell him about the fire—like I did. I was to go to Bennett's tonight at ten o'clock and Mrs. Bennett herself was to pay me ten bucks. I don't know anythin' about any murder and till the sheriff picked me up I didn't know that Fern Springs had really been burned. I'm a good boy. I'm deacon back in the settlement where I come from. I tithe, I eschew the ways of evil, like it sayeth—"

McGavock tossed him a crumpled package of cigarettes. "You don't know it but you're a lucky kid. Stay right where you are. The streets aren't safe for you tonight."

THE FIRST DEEP growls of thunder were bumbling across the opaque heavens as McGavock strode down the magnolia avenue of the Bennett mansion. The lawn shrubs were swaying to the pressure of the wind, showing the undersides of their leaves in silvery glitters. The great white mansion was a sulphur yellow beneath the racing storm clouds. Gil Bennett, in his singlet, wearing whipcord slacks and buckled sandals, was on the side lawn. His sparse hair, licked by the oncoming gale, lay plastered to his shiny pate. He was batting a wooden ball over the bent-grass sward, immersed in a solo game of croquet. He swung the mallet with a limp left hand; in his right he carried a jumbo sixteen-ounce mint julep. He waved to McGavock, beckoned him in.

"At it again, eh?" the detective observed dryly. He eyed the pint-sized goblet. "Tomorrow it gives prairie oysters. Where's Mrs. Bennett?"

"She's at Malcom's." He looked unhappy. "I'm supposed to join her there." He belched. "Ole Malcom, the man of nature, with his six eyes. That man gives me the creeps. I'm getting fortified." He walked to a wicker lawn chair, picked up a blazer jacket, slipped into it. "I thought you told me you weren't working for Hal and Laurel?"

"I'm not. They've been tempting me but I haven't succumbed. While I've got you alone I'd like to learn a little more about that divorce your wife is preparing to hang on you."

"You mean what I said last night? Forget it. It was just an alcoholic hallucination."

"That's what I thought at the time, it sounded like a drunken sympathy gag. Now, I'm not so sure. Do you want to come in on this with me or not? There's more at stake than meets the eye. There are wheels within wheels—if you get what I mean."

Bennett gave his head a blunt, decisive shake. "No thanks. You're a pal, and I appreciate it, but I'm a family man and I handle my own affairs."

"Your wife says you are sending money to Paducah. Where did she get that idea?"

"I gave it to her. She's been prying around, pumping me in a delicate offhand way about that money I've been withdrawing. I told her that I was footing the bills for a kid in finishing school up in Paducah. It wasn't very nice of me but she had me wacky with her nagging. Boy, did she show her claws!"

McGavock said: "That I can believe. Where are you sending this money, by the way?"

Bennett grinned. "Wouldn't you like to know! I'm sending it to a big bank in a little town on the West Coast. More than that, I'm afraid I can't tell you. It's perfectly legal, you understand. It's my own money." He seemed uneasy. "Why the gathering at Malcom's? What's Old Spooky trying to pull?"

McGavock laughed. "Time will tell. It's not Jarrell's party— it's mine. The sheriff and I are going to saw this business off. It's the finale."

"Wheels within wheels is right!" Bennett studied his fingerails. "You've got your little scheme, Maldron's got his— and I've got mine. And ten to one, all our schemes, all our plans, are perfectly transparent to Malcom Jarrell. Well, as you say, time will tell. Let's go."

THE STORM HIT them a half-block from Jarrell's cottage. It opened up with a deafening clap and a raging sluice of water. Lightning flayed the black sky. They broke into a lope and, sheltered by the arching maples, managed to make Jarrell's front porch.

Laurel let them in. She was wearing her jet lace semi-formal with the cameo at her throat. She seemed unnaturally stiff, apprehensive. Bennett brushed past her, towards the study. The girl stayed McGavock with an arresting hand. "I've discovered the most horrible thing," she whispered.

"Another hammer?"

She flared. "You're impossible!"

McGavock said quietly: "I can make a good guess as to what's disturbing you. You found the headless bodies of four rattlesnakes, didn't you? Well, dismiss them from your mind.

They're a plant. I've got the heads, I knew the bodies would turn up somewhere."

"It's too repulsive! They're back in the kitchen—in Malcom's bread box."

"He's a naturalist, isn't he? Maybe he goes for gamy food. They're quite tasty if you pretend you're eating crab."

There was an atmosphere of subdued hostility in the study. The naturalist, his four-lensed spectacles hooked on his monstrous head, was busy sorting and mounting butterflies. He hardly seemed aware of the fact that he had company. Gil Bennett, his cheeks and ears flushed with open antagonism, lolled in the window bay. Behind him, the squall lashed the leaded panes in cracking gusts.

"Where's the sheriff?" McGavock asked.

"He'll be here later," Laurel said.

"That's just as good," McGavock commented. "Maybe we can thrash out a little domestic difficulty before he arrives. Are you planning to divorce your husband?"

Jarrell snapped an iridescent azure wing, fretted. "You have no idea how brittle these things are. I've ruined three since you people have been here. You distract me. Can't you go away and come back tomorrow?"

"No, you don't," Bennett said firmly. "Not in this downpour. Where's your southern hospitality, sir?" He addressed McGavock. "You've been here a day, now. What have you found out?"

"Plenty," McGavock answered. A bell in the hall clanged. Sheriff Robley, in a swanky gabardine raincoat, walked in on them. "Where's Bad-Tooth Maldron?" McGavock demanded.

"I don't know." The sheriff was annoyed. "I couldn't find him. I left messages for him all over town."

"There are a few things I'd like to run over," McGavock remarked. "Just to help us get organized. This case breaks itself into two installments: the old hotel murders, thirty years or so ago, and the present situation. You understand, this isn't what is generally known as a murder chain. It's just sort of a double outburst. The second, or contemporary, affair dovetails into the older business."

Sheriff Robley's calm eyes held him as he spoke. "I'm sure you're right, Luther. But it's the current mess that concerns me. Who killed Lester Hodges?"

McGavock ignored him. "Put it this way: why was Hodges killed? Hodges was working for a rascal. The old eccentric was employed to search Fern Springs for the cowhide satchel in which Wainwright carried his seventy grand. This rascal had long suspected that the absconder had been knocked off. He reasoned that the satchel lay hidden beneath the flooring of one of the rooms. He'd been clerk at the time—"

Jarrell said petulantly: "Why the mysterious circumlocution? If Cal Bradley is the rascal you're talking about, why don't you say so!"

"Check. Names it is." McGavock watched the naturalist's nimble fingers in the lamplight. "Cal Bradley, as room clerk of the old inn, knew who had which room. Find the satchel under a certain floor and he'd know for certain who had slain Wainwright. He hired Lester Hodges to locate this satchel. Hodges did his searching by means of a rat."

"Did he," Bennett asked, "find the satchel?"

"No. But he made the killer nervous. This prowling, this attempting to uncover an old crime, got our murderer jumpy. He got him a magnetized hammer and a two-inch roofing nail and knocked off Lester Hodges. Is that clear?"

"It's clear enough," the sheriff agreed. "But it's highly speculative. Why isn't Cal Bradley here with us tonight? It appears he holds the key."

"He's absent through no choice of his own," McGavock retorted. "He's shuffled off this mortal coil. He's in the cellar of the Bradley House—stiffer than a briar root—"

THERE WAS A gasping silence. Laurel Bennett murmured: "We're doomed—all of us! There's an unholy hand at work among us. What have we done to merit such a fate?" She flung out her arms, crossed her hands piously over her heart.

McGavock barked angrily: "Won't you shut up! This is no time to mug for a spotlight." The storm outside dropped with a cleaver-like slash, there was only the low whine of the wind.

The girl cried dramatically: "Why isn't Hal here? Have they slain him, too?"

An oily voice from the doorway said: "Not me, Mrs. Bennett. Hal Maldron can take care of himself." The attorney barged his gelatinous body into the center of the assembly. "Sorry, Malcom, to pop in this way. Guess you didn't hear me ring. Got your message, Sheriff. Hustled right over. I was home peeling a bunion off my— But you folks aren't interested in that."

"You're all bunion, if you ask me," McGavock observed. "Quiet, please. Where was I? Oh, yes. Now let me tell you about Fern Springs. In its heyday it was a fashionable resort, no doubt very popular. It was more than that—it was a murder nest. I don't mean that the management was involved. I mean that somebody saw certain possibilities and summer after summer turned them to his bloody advantage. Jarrell, I'd like to ask you this question: who carted the guests to and from the railroad junction?"

The naturalist considered. "As I remember it we had a station wagon but we rarely used it. Usually the incumbent guests would take the out-of-county people to the railroad in their personal carriages. We were all one big family."

"Among you regulars," McGavock said, "there was a man who plied a terrible trade. He struck up friendships with wealthy guests. In weeks of intimacy he learned about his victims' contacts, learned who could be disposed of safely. Lonely men and women came to Fern Springs. Many of them would have no one to miss them. When their stay was up, he wheeled his buggy from the stables, gallantly offered to drive them to the junction." He paused.

"That, of course, was their last ride. He murdered them around the first bend—for their travel money. Men, women and children."

"It doesn't seem practical," Maldron argued. "Murder for a pittance."

"Pittance, says you. Wealthy vacationists went well-heeled in those days. I'll wager he cleared two thousand in a season."

"But Wainwright—" the sheriff put in.

"He broke his routine for Wainwright. And well he might! It netted him a fortune. He slew Wainwright the night he registered. He was afraid to wait, afraid that the absconder might slip from his clutches. Wainwright was his blunder. That's how I found out who he was."

"I knew who he was all along," Malcom Jarrell chirped up. "I saw him drag Hodges' corpse into my yard."

"You keep out of this," McGavock said. "When we need your

comment, we'll ask for it. To continue the story. Hodges, working for Bradley, snooped around until he got himself eliminated. I appeared on the scene. Somehow, probably through Bradley's loose gossip, the killer learned a city detective was after him. He lay in wait for me at Hodges' shanty and threw a handful of number four shot at me, sent me a warning note at the Bradley house. I didn't scare. The next day he changed his tactics. He sent a hillboy named Buck around to Bennett's—when I was present—to say that Fern Springs had burned at dawn and then hightailed out to fire the building. Actually, there was no evidence in the old building, it had been long since removed, but he had heard about newfangled methods of detection and didn't know but what maybe a fluoroscope or something would turn up evidence."

"By the way," the sheriff remarked. "I've got Buck in the hoosegow. So far he won't talk—"

"He doesn't need to. He talked a little to me—and that is enough. Well, our killer by now is as busy as a squirrel in a hickory tree. He fires the old building, hunts out some rattlesnakes—those rocky ledges must teem with the vipers—zips back to town. He lures Bradley into the cellar, bashes in his head and sets a firetrap. He leaves the snake heads in my room with a final threatening note, scampers over here to Jarrell's and stashes the snake bodies in Malcom's bread box. He's really putting out steam—he's fighting for his life."

Maldron cleared his throat heavily. "It all comes back to me now… How well do I recall that summer in nineteen nine. Every insignificant detail stands out crystal clear. Gil Bennett flouncing around among the ladies, taking them hither and yon in his yellow-spoked trap and livery stable mare. Gil was shabby in those days—"

Jarrell said: "Hal, the time comes when I must speak the truth. You're my choice."

Bennett spoke quietly. "And you, Malcom, are mine."

THE SHERIFF NARROWED his eyes. McGavock looked cynical, happy.

"The thing that gives it away," Bennett explained, "is the rattlesnake theme. You'd know where to go to catch them and how to do it. You couldn't get Hal Maldron within ten yards of one. But there's much more to it than that. You were manager at the time of Wainwright's disappearance. You were no doubt right there at the desk when Cal Bradley signed him in. He looked prosperous, talked with a northern accent, and acted suspicious. You waited a bit, called him to your room and murdered him. Mr. McGavock says that Hodges used a rat in his prowling. Everyone in this town knows that you kept that rat for Hodges. I charge that Hodges was employed by you, that you murdered him on your own lawn and called in this city detective."

"Such a rigmarole!" Jarrell's massive head peered about the room. "I've no time to indulge in tomfoolery. Clear out, all of you, with your absurdities—"

McGavock said plaintively: "What about me? Doesn't anybody wish to hear my accusation?"

They stared at him.

"Maldron's correct. Gil Bennett's our man!"

"That's a serious charge," Steve Robley said gravely. "Is it official?"

"Of course I mean it to be official. He's a gory killer if you ever saw one."

Gil said whimsically: "Old pal, you've turned on me. And I bet you've built up a good case, too."

"Listen to it," McGavock whipped out. "And form your own opinion. It was you—old pal—and no one else, who planned and executed this entire massacre. You promoted your murder market at Fern Springs back in nineteen nine and buried your cadavers in the brookbed. You killed Wainwright, took his satchel to your room, looted it and hid it beneath the flooring. Cal Bradley suspected this. He employed the crackpot Hodges to ferret out the evidence. You killed Hodges—it would be simple for a man in the garage business to obtain a magnetized hammer—"

"But you gave me your compass to protect myself against this slayer—"

"You are a sly customer. I was fighting deceit with deceit. As I was saying, you killed Hodges and when I appeared on the scene attacked me. This morning when I visited you at the cotton gin, you saw me coming, grabbed a phone, called the Shamrock poolroom and asked for Buck. You disguised your voice to throw suspicion on your wife. Buck appeared, put across his little act and departed."

McGavock shook his head. "You made a mistake there, my friend. You may not pay a man for a thirty-mile trip on mule-back but you at least *thank* him. It was a slip—I smelled a rat."

"I'd like to hear the rest of this tale." Sheriff Robley was modest.

"The rest of it you know. Buck stages his act and Gil, as soon as I leave, drives out and torches the place. While you and I are out there digging around, he's back in town beating in Bradley's skull. He'd planned to lay in wait for Buck when

Buck showed up tonight at the Bennett mansion for his pay. With Buck gone, he figured he'd be safe." The detective smiled harshly at the businessman. "You know, Bennett, you plan well but you talk too much. You gave yourself away a dozen times. When you attempted to arouse my suspicions against Jarrell you said that he had prospered unnaturally. If anyone in this village has prospered unnaturally it's you, yourself—garage, drugstore, cotton gin. Last night in your car you invented a divorce that your wife was going to slap on you. This morning you realized that I could chase that down and expose it so you flew to Mrs. Bennett and got her excited about an imaginary dream girl you were supporting in Paducah."

BENNETT DRAWLED: "IT'S pleasant listening to you orate—but do you have any proof?"

"Scads," McGavock answered. "Scads. Your gambling at Chunky's. A ruse to cover your withdrawals: *you were paying blackmail to Cal Bradley!*"

Bennett was completely relaxed. "The wildest sort of slander, sir."

McGavock spoke to Laurel. "That baggy pearl-gray sweater you've been wearing all day, is it yours?"

She tried to follow him, gave it up. "No. It's Gil's—but I like it. It's so roomy."

"Gil Bennett!" McGavock's voice was tight. "You were wearing that sweater when you dragged the body of Les Hodges into Jarrell's yard. Wisps of brushed-wool came off on the old man's corduroy. Jarrell saw the whole thing through his bedroom window but was doubtful as to your identity. He came out with a light and combed the gray hairs off before he covered the body with straw. He has that evidence beneath the tile there in the hearth—a little ball of wool. His testimony will hang you—"

Gil Bennett arose and turned his back on them. He stepped into the little bay window and began kicking out the leaded panes.

Hal Maldron seized him by the elbow, pulled him back. Bennett gave his torso a half twist, shot the lawyer through the shoulder and continued his glass smashing.

Sheriff Robley said calmly: "Bennett, you're not giving me any choice. I'm going to have to kill you."

Bennett dropped his pistol, advanced dazedly to the sheriff, who snapped on a pair of handcuffs.

"The satchel?" the sheriff asked.

"Bennett has it," McGavock announced. "Beneath the floor of his office. When I was in Bennett's office at the cotton gin I gave the floor special attention, dropped my hat, as a matter of fact, to give it a little closer inspection. The boards had been taken up and renailed. You'll find your satchel there."

Laurel Bennett burst out: "I'll never feel comfy in that old gray sweater again. And I loved it so!"

McGavock said sardonically: "But think, babe. You're married to a homicidal beast, a notorious public character. That means headlines, and reporters and three-column photos. I'll bet none of your bridesmaids back in Louisiana have done as well as that!"

The girl threw herself into his arms. "You can always see the bright side to everything!"

Let's Count Corpses

The sheriff could only count two kill-corpses. "And one to carry," corrected Luther McGavock, adding up the tidy toll.

1

Apparatus for Suicide

McGAVOCK, TILTED BACK in his swivel chair, was reading the lovelorn column in the newspaper when Miss Ollinger, the chief's secretary, tapped him on the shoulder. McGavock said: "Dear Miss Ollinger. I am a sensitive boy fourteen years old and am in love with the wife of our butcher but her parents will not consent to our marriage. What shall I do? Signed, Perplexed."

The spinster drew herself up. "Mr. McGavock, please! Don't be lewd. I haven't the slightest idea what you're talking about and I certainly don't want you to explain it." She announced stiffly, "Mr. Browne desires a word with you."

McGavock had worked in every major agency in the country. He was small, wiry—and hateful. His coarse black hair was cut in a short pompadour and there was a jeering quality about his deep-lined face that aroused instant hostility in strangers. Until he'd found this Memphis outfit, he'd never felt at home. He operated under a roving license, a contract that the agency could repudiate if he dragged it into hot water.

Old Atherton Browne knew him for what he was: touchy and dangerous. He liked what McGavock brought in but didn't want to learn too much about his methods.

McGavock lounged through the frosted glass door into the chief's sanctum. The old man glared at him with baleful,

*He pointed it as McGavock
as though it were a gun*

mucous-rimmed eyes, beckoned him over to the curly-maple desk. "How do you like the deep South, son?"

McGavock said indifferently: "One place is as good as another. What is this?"

"You don't fool me one bit, Luther." The old man was malevolent. "You're happy, you're contented. You love the South. You think it's all magnolias and dueling pistols and belles in hoopskirts. I love the South too—but I'm a Southerner and it doesn't fool me. It has more facets than a double-cut brilliant—"

McGavock gave a nasty snort. "You sound like you're tight."

The old man produced a legal size envelope, slid out a sheet of paper. He opened it, laid it on the desk top. There was a scrawled message on the paper and an enclosure—a little three-inch triangle of what McGavock took to be fawn colored felt.

McGavock picked up the scrap of felt and examined it. The hairy nap on one side was very short; in faint, bluish letters were the initials *S. T.* "What in the world might this object be?" he asked.

"That's a dog's ear. It came to me in the mail this morning."

"A dog's ear!" McGavock dropped it on the desk. "What are those initials doing on it?"

"Good foxhounds are very valuable," the old man explained. "Sometimes during the chase they stray from the pack and get stolen. Many hunters tattoo their dogs on the inside of the ear to identify them." He stared at McGavock as though he were attempting to hypnotize him. "Read the note."

The communication, written in an elongated angular script, was brief.

Sirs:
They broke into my kennels last night, cropped my hound's ear and stole him. I'm sending you all that they left me. Return the rest of the animal to me—dead or alive—and I'm prepared to pay you five thousand dollars.

Sprague Tatum
Halford

"Halford is a community up near the Kentucky line," the chief informed him. "Hills and bobcats."

McGavock was chilly. "When a human tracks a dog—that's news. I'm not interested."

"I hardly thought you'd be," the old man said sadly. "So I put a call through to Jason in St. Louis. This business has some pretty risky angles and I'm just as glad to have some other outfit handle it—"

McGavock perked up. "Risky?"

"Why certainly, Luther. There's bad medicine cooking up there in Halford. Why does this Sprague Tatum write down here to me? Why doesn't he turn his case over to the local law? And ponder that dead or alive offer. Five grand strikes me as a little dear for a carcass."

McGavock wavered. The old man said crossly: "And if that's a hound's ear I'll put it between crackers and eat it. I was raised with dogs. That ear came from a bulldog—and a big one. A boxer, I should say."

McGavock flattened his lips. "I put in three months with that bunch at Jason's. They don't like me and I don't like them. Cancel your call. I'll take a try at it."

THE STATION AT Halford looked like it had been rolled up to the edge of town by a drunken cyclone and left beside the railroad tracks as a practical joke. Its warped clapboards were sprung from the sheathing and the swayback roof was composed entirely of tarpaper patches. McGavock strode down the platform and entered the little waiting-room.

The station-master was behind his wicket, fiddling with a little cardboard disc. He gaped as the detective approached, exhibited a mellow set of old ivory tusks. "Hidy, friend," he greeted. "This-here dinkus is a marvel. Hit's a perpetual calendar. Tells a body his birthday ten year from now. When was you borned?"

McGavock answered smoothly: "In the fourth Heavenly Stem, the tenth Earthly Branch, in the Hour of the Tiger."

The station-master puckered. "Yo're a-prankin' me—"

"It's a fact," McGavock insisted. "My people were missionaries in China. Listen, Colonel, I'm going to be in town for a few days. Suggest a good place for me to stop. I'm a nervous wreck—so the hotel's out."

The station-master considered. "The sexton, he takes in boarders. But you won't much care for it there—all he does is talk shop. And there's Melinda Dawson. She's at the Teacherage."

"I had some private family in mind."

"Melinda's private. You'll like her iff'n you can stand her." He chuckled. "She got a tongue like a Canada thistle. She taught her forty year and retired and, dadnab it, they cain't git her to move out'n the building."

McGavock nodded. "Thanks."

The station-master pawed the air. "Hold on! Well, I'll be glorified! A idee jest hit me. I can take you in myself. If you don't mind bunking double with me on a pallet—"

McGavock said gravely: "I'd be afraid to do it. I always sleep with a razor in my hand. To fight off nightmares." He gave a lunatic leer, picked up his luggage and departed.

The village, like a bolt of bright calico, stretched between the railroad track and the river. It was just after suppertime—the hottest part of the day. The business section was deserted.

The sun, arrested above the distant ridges, was poised for setting. The wooded hills were a harsh, metallic green in the dancing heat waves. A sharecropper jolted by in a mule-drawn wagon, his wife and family seated rigidly beside him in a row of kitchen chairs on the wagonbed. Soft, vaporous clouds of summer dust puffed from the mules' hooves, settled on McGavock's glossy, city-polished shoes. From a hackberry in the churchyard a mockingbird cut loose with a tranquil imitation of a melancholy whippoorwill. "Cropped ears and mocking-birds," McGavock mused. "I know these docile towns. They can pack a mean brand of violence."

When McGavock laid eyes on the Teacherage—he knew it was for him. Ancient, unpruned lilacs, bristling with dead-wood, arched around the tiny porch. Lush, sweet-scented violets bordered the walk. Here's where I stay, he decided.

The old lady that answered his knock was lank and with-ered—as tall as a tall man. McGavock followed her into a clut-tered living-room and introduced himself. She subjected him to a careful scrutiny, seemed satisfied, and proffered him a big brass key. "Your room has an outside entrance," Miss Melinda informed him severely. "But that doesn't mean you're to come in intoxicated. I presume you're going out again before you retire?"

"I am," the detective confirmed. "I want to look up a friend of a friend. Perhaps you can help me. Do you have a man in town named Tatum?"

"There are two Tatums," Miss Melinda answered primly. "And both are no-accounts. One is Sprague Tatum who lives with his dogs at the end of Court Street. You'll probably not catch him at home until later. Someone said he's been up in the timber all day breaking in a pair of stiff boots. Then there's his brother, Darnell."

"It's Darnell I want."

Miss Melinda registered distaste. "Anybody who wants him should have him. I'd hate to give you my church-going opinion of Darnell. He stays with that over-privileged nephew of his in a pretentious white brick house at the other end of town." She got down to business. "The rent for your room will be one dollar per night. May I ask your profession?"

"I'm down here studying the canebrakes."

Miss Melinda batted her eyes. "The canebrakes. I don't quite understand."

"I don't get it myself." McGavock shrugged his shoulders. "But orders are orders, eh?" He laid a twenty dollar bill on a starched doily. "They tell me it might take years!"

SPRAGUE TATUM'S HOME was easy to spot. A sprawling, green shingle bungalow in an eroded, grassless yard. A garish split-boulder wall flanked it on three sides and at the far rear, among the outbuildings, was a low gray shed. The yippings and yowls of hungry hounds told McGavock that this shed was his client's kennels. There was no sign of life about the place.

McGavock rang the doorbell, listened attentively. There was no response. He let himself down from the edge of the porch into a bed of iris, circled the building and made his way toward the group of sheds at the back.

There was a small red barn, a tool-house, and the dog-runs. He beamed his pencil flash through the meshed wire of the kennel. A nice pack of blooded dogs. Springers, coonhounds and beagles; every one of them warm-eyed and friendly. They burst into sonorous ululation at the glow of his light. He flicked off the torch and proceeded to the barn.

The barn had been remodeled to serve as a garage. A workbench ran along one wall, oil drums along another. There were eight of these huge oil drums—decked to a height of six or seven feet. The fact that they were decked suggested to McGavock that they were empty; loaded oil drums are tough to maneuver. There was something funny in the way they stood there—so neat and orderly in the center of the wall space. McGavock squinted at them.

He heaved one of the tall cans to the floor and discovered what he had suspected. They concealed a door.

It was a low, massive door of two-by-eights with a wrought iron hasp and a heavy combination padlock. The lock's steel shackle had been cut with a hacksaw. McGavock lifted it from the staple, swung open the cumbersome panel. It led into a stuffy boxlike room, entirely windowless but for an iron grating in the ceiling. There was the smell of dog here, too. But a different sort of smell—a wild, feral odor. The cell was empty; a trace-chain leash lay coiled on the cement, an upset water pan beside it.

"Here's where our client's animal lost its ear and vanished," McGavock decided. "They had trouble taking the beast. Look at that upset pan." He puzzled. "It was a big creature and fierce. Now explain this: why does a man with a mean watchdog keep him in such an out of the way place? It looks like Sprague Tatum was protecting his dog—instead of vice versa."

Suddenly, he laughed. "I get it! And old Atherton muffed it! Wow! This is going to be some case."

He replaced the oil drums and returned to the green bungalow.

He was standing by a scrubby, undernourished rosebush in the gathering twilight when he was startled to observe that the kitchen door was wide open. Cautiously, he ascended the back steps, meandered into the darkening building. A quick prowl of the downstairs uncovered nothing of interest.

The bungalow was a story and a half affair, with a single, dormered master-bedroom. It was in the master-bedroom that McGavock found the dead man and the suicide apparatus.

McGavock switched on the overhead light. The dead man sat in the middle of the room in a rush-bottom chair. He was a wizened little fellow in his early sixties. He wore a gates-ajar collar and a shoestring necktie. There was the scent of vaseline on his thin hair and his goatee had been carefully dyed to hide its gray. His chin was on his chest. He'd been shot in the back of the skull.

Behind him, lashed with adhesive tape to the standard of a bridge-lamp, an old Iver Johnson .32 was pointed in the general direction of the crown of his head. A string from the trigger of the gun looped back of the lamp standard and ended in the lap of the corpse—was, in fact, tied to the dead man's thumb.

The pistol was a .32 but the hole in the man's head was the work of a .45.

McGAVOCK FACED THE contraption, peeped into the gun's cylinder. The chamber on the left, which should have contained an empty shell, showed a shiny copper-nosed slug. The gun had never been fired.

Until McGavock saw the farewell note pinned on the dead man's lapel, his natural impression had been that he was confronting his client. The note, however, told him differently.

My Beloved Brother, it read, *Knowing that you are out of town for the day, and having no gun of my own, I have taken the liberty—despite our brotherly enmity—of dropping in and using one of your many firearms. I'm leaving thirty cents on the dresser to reimburse you for the cartridge. Farewell, Your un-brotherly brother, Darnell.*

McGavock said playfully, with a broad minstrel-show dialect: "That's sho' a heap of brothers for one little note!" The handwriting on the message was uncannily similar to the dog-letter the agency had received from client Sprague. It was a backwoods attempt at forgery and not a bad job.

He'd walked into a frame for his client—and a pretty slick one.

The detective gave his mouth a wry twist. He could just hear the local law diagnose the set-up. Sprague, they would be forced to decide, killed his brother with a .45, arranged the suicide contraption, dashed off the note in his, Sprague's, script.

McGavock got busy. The corpse was wearing narrow, foppish oxfords. He took off the dead man's shoes, switched them so that each was on the wrong foot. He dismantled the apparatus, put the adhesive tape and spurious note in his wallet. He was on the verge of dropping the .32 into a dresser drawer when an inspiration struck him and he changed his mind. He tucked the pistol into his belt. "You go along with me," he said. "I got plans for you."

He clicked off the light, stood for a moment grinning in the lavender dusk. "I think," he decided, "that will get us out from under. Now we'll visit that over-privileged nephew in the big white house."

The reflector name-plate on the gatepost gave McGavock a

good idea of what sort of man he was about to run into. There were two little gilt-and-black glass signs, one above the other. The top one said, *Joyce Roger Preston*—and the one under it, *Deliver All Goods in the Rear.* McGavock snarled. A snobbish and deliberately arrogant insult. In a village like Halford, where everyone was kith and kin, the injunction was completely unnecessary. It was like demanding that your neighbor wear clean underclothes.

The lad that opened the door to McGavock's ring fitted the picture perfectly. He was sandy-haired, fish-mouthed, and was garbed in a fancy pair of draped pants that reached up to his chest. He posed on the threshold, in the light from the hall, and stared at McGavock's turquoise shirt front as though the sight nauseated him. "All right, all right," he whipped out churlishly. "What's on your mind?"

McGavock said gently: "I have something to deliver and I'm not taking it around to the rear. It's this: in about a half an hour the sheriff's going to pay you a very embarrassing call. I hope you're fully prepared."

That knocked Preston back on his heels. "Come in," he ordered. He tried to put the old haughty man-in-the-saddle tone in his voice—but couldn't quite make it. "Come in and explain yourself, sir."

"That I will," McGavock agreed affably. He trailed his host down a short bright hall, ornate with much pier glass and marble, to a book-lined study.

PRESTON IGNORED HIS guest. He unlocked a cabinet, poured himself a glass of sherry from an etched decanter, replaced the decanter and locked the compartment. He got out a hammered-silver cigarette case, made a great fuss over selecting a cigarette, snapped the case shut and stowed it in a pocket. No courteous offer of wine, tobacco, or even a chair. McGavock watched the show with great interest. In the South, where the tradition of hospitality is so sacred, such a routine didn't happen accidentally. The detective realized he was being given the works.

"Now, sir," Preston announced boorishly, "I am ready to hear what you have to say. And it had better be good. I have a short temper, sir."

He's edgy, McGavock decided. I'll let him toast a bit.

The detective ogled the handsome furniture, the brocade window drapes. He picked up a flat book from the corner of the mantel, leafed casually through its pages. Abruptly, he V'd his eyebrows. A photograph album. Page after page of tombstones: big ones and little ones, all kinds, and nothing but tombstones. "What crackpot took those?" he asked curiously. "I've heard of all kinds of camera addicts but this graveyard stuff is a new slant to me."

Preston flushed angrily. "Mr. Darnell Tatum, my uncle, took those pictures. He's a genealogist. He needs them in his profession, establishing lineage." He shifted impatiently. "What was that about the sheriff?"

"Don't give me that sheepdip!" McGavock blustered. "How can you sit there and act so innocent? You know very well what I mean. I'm your victim. You people have been using the mails to defraud and I'm one of the many guys you hooked. Here I am, running my beanery down in Memphis when I see that ad in the paper: 'Are You Royalty? Send Twenty Dollars for Your Family Crest.' Well, I send this Darnell Tatum the twenty berries and what do I get? A dinky four-page pamphlet giving the history of the MacGuggen clan. My name's McGavock not MacGuggen. I've written a dozen letters asking for my refund and you people won't answer."

Preston was flustered. He made an attempt at clearing away the fog of words. "Stop referring to me as 'people.' Your story has me completely confused. It's my uncle, not myself, who is the genealogist. If Uncle Darnell ever inserted an ad in a paper, I never heard of it. You are dealing with gentility, sir!"

"Gentility!" McGavock guffawed contemptuously. "Me just a poor laboring man and you people gypping me out of twenty bucks. Is that the way you built this big house?"

Preston was devastated with horrified rage. His face blanched in fury, his hands trembled. "This house, sir," he shouted, and his voice was squeaky and wavering, "belongs to me. I am extremely wealthy in my own right. My uncle dwells here because he finds the menage of his brother Sprague uncouth and unfriendly."

McGavock chopped out abusively: "Where is this Uncle Darnell? Where can I find him?"

"I haven't seen him all day but I can tell you where he is. At this hour he is out at the furnaces."

"What furnaces? You're kidding me."

Preston was back in the old haughty groove. "The furnaces are the furnaces, sir. Those ruins just out of town. It's Uncle Darnell's favorite evening stroll."

The young man showed McGavock to the door. He became suddenly ingratiating, almost servile. "There won't be any publicity, will there?" he asked anxiously.

McGavock said: "That's entirely up to your uncle."

THE COURTHOUSE CLOCK was banging out nine when McGavock returned to the main drag. The shops were having their final flurry of business before closing. There was good-natured, almost merry feeling in the balmy summer air as sleepy citizens gathered in knots beneath the stanchioned awnings for a touch of pre-bedtime banter. McGavock, as he ambled through the jovial townsmen, caught tail-ends of their heavy handed, bucolic repartee… "Does yore wife know yo're out?"… "kin eat more chicken than a hongry preacher"… "Eddie, here, done cut his lip on a busted fruit jar!"

The tough little detective listened wooden-faced; these were the kind of folks he liked.

One turn around the stem and he found just what he'd expected: The Blue Bell Cafe. Its location, in an alley just off Main Street, its black painted windows, were familiar characteristics. He'd seen its counterpart in a score of other towns. Halford was bone dry—The Blue Bell was Halford's blind pig.

He pushed through the door. A hillman in moccasin boots and denim trousers was lolling at a high counter chatting with a teen-age boy in a soiled apron. Behind the boy, on a dusty shelf, were a half-dozen cans of pork and beans; the cans were corroded with rust.

The occupants cut off their dialogue as McGavock entered.

"I'm a stranger in town," McGavock said. "And I'm thirsty."

The boy said politely: "They's a mighty fine well of drinking-water in the hitching lot behind the co'thouse."

McGavock grimaced. "That's where it belongs, in a hitching lot. For horses and mules, yes; for me, no." He went bellicose. "No soap, eh? You take me for an alcohol tax man. Phooey!" He fanned the air with his hand.

They watched him with courteous amusement. He addressed the counter-boy. "I'm Lute McGavock. I'm a sportsman. I'm going to be around town for a few days but right now I'm a little short of funds." He fumbled in his belt, came out with Sprague Tatum's Iver Johnson and laid it on the bar. "This is an old style gun but it's still in good working order. How about advancing me a couple of bucks on it until tomorrow."

The kid's eyes glinted. He said with reluctance, "We don't pawn."

The hillman covered the side of his face with a horny hand and winked. The counter-boy picked up the cue. "Mr. McGavock, meet Mr. Abbott," he said. "Mr. Abbott, he's a sporting gent, too."

Mr. Abbott murmured, "Pleased to meetcha." The kid sauntered to the end of the aisle, disappeared into a back room.

McGavock's new acquaintance was not a pleasant specimen. He had puffy, slitted eyes and a loose, cunning mouth. He studied the detective speculatively, brutally, as though he were in a stockyard buying pork on the hoof.

"Keep your pistol, bud," he said.

Mr. Abbott dug into his shirt and produced a wad of bills the size of a potato. He peeled off two greasy singles. "I'm glad to accommodate you."

McGavock took the bill in silence.

Abbott said: "So you're a sporting man?"

"That's right. You know how it goes. One day you're in the dough and the next you may be a little short. I'll see you get this back tomorrow. I've a stake coming through in the morning mail."

Mr. Abbott said slowly: "If you're a real sporting man and like it rough and ready, I got something on the fire that'll mebbe interest you."

"Yeah?" McGavock acted cagy. "What is it?"

"Don't rush me," the man in denim answered. "I gotta know a little more about you." He thumbed his black felt hat up on his forehead and walked out into the night.

ALL IN ALL, it had been an extremely informative evening. Facts which at first had seemed so fluid, so muddy, now were clarifying themselves, crystallizing. It was time, McGavock decided, that he had a look at his client. Sprague Tatum must certainly have arrived home from his phenomenal boot-breaking jaunt in the uplands.

The backstreets of Halford were alternate patches of silver moonlight and black shadow. These householders of Halford loved their shrubbery; every tiny cottage had its shroud of syringa and crape myrtle, gnarled, low-sweeping trees lined the sidewalk.

The detective had just passed from the moonglow into a lip of shadow when a cheery voice hailed him: "Can you bake a cherry pie, Billy Boy?"

McGavock came to a stop, peered about him. "Howzzat?"

Thirty feet or so away, a man stepped out of a hedge.

The figure, blurred and indistinct, was carrying something that resembled a walking stick on a tray. McGavock opened his mouth to question him as the man raised the queer paraphernalia to his shoulder. He pointed it at McGavock, awkwardly and carefully, as though it were a gun of some sort.

Intuitively, McGavock dropped to his knees.

Almost simultaneously there was a dull, snapping sound,

a muted *thock!* The detective pawed at his belt buckle for his pistol. The phantom wheeled, struggled into the hedge and disappeared.

McGavock got to his feet and started a painstaking search. It wasn't long before he found it. A piece of steel about the size of a short lead pencil. Embedded, arrowlike, in the bole of a maple—about on the level with his chest. He balled his handkerchief around it and pried it out. It had penetrated to a depth of a good two inches.

He stopped at the first streetlight to examine his find. It was a triangular taper-file, ground and whetted until each of its three edges were surgically keen. "I knew they made butcher knives out of files," McGavock muttered. "But this is certainly something for the book. Yow!"

The green bungalow, from eaves to foundation and from end to end, blazed with lighted windows. The clay lawn was scarred with a maze of crisscrossed tire tracks. McGavock read the signs with laconic accuracy: the sheriff and the undertaker, with their cavalcade of friends and admirers, had swooped down on the place, staged their jamboree—and pulled out. The murder had been discovered, reported, investigated. The corpse of Darnell Tatum was pigeonholed on its cooling slab and the high sheriff of the county was embarked upon a homicide.

McGavock's client greeted him with extravagant eagerness. He literally dragged the detective into the house, shoved him into an armchair, pushed a footstool under his ankles. McGavock said coldly: "Don't fondle me! I've been trying to get in touch with you since—"

His client interrupted him. "Have you found the dog?"

SPRAGUE TATUM WAS a handsome devil. He was of the type frequently referred to by middle-aged women as distinguished-looking. Well over six feet, he had a chest like a bale of cotton and a vigorous, robust manner that contrasted attractively with his fleecy, snow-white hair. A de luxe outdoorsman, he was dressed in a black-and-red check shirt and tailored hunting breeches. "The dog will have to wait," McGavock declared. "What were all those tire marks out in the yard?"

"The law,"Tatum answered. "I've just been visited by the law. I got home a little while ago and found the body of my brother in my bedroom. He'd been murdered." He said it with great enthusiasm—as though he were recounting the flushing of a covey of quail.

"Goodness gracious! Who killed him? You?"

"Of course not. They suspect me but the idea is absurd. When I found him he was as stiff as an eight-zero fish hook. He'd been killed this morning and I've been away all day."

"Now that's very entertaining," McGavock said blithely. "A wonderful town, Halford. Things happening every minute." He took the whetted file from his pocket, handed it to his client. He told of the attack on him, described the strange gadget the man was carrying. "What was it the guy had?" McGavock demanded.

Tatum turned the silver of steel over in his blunt fingers. "He had a crossbow."

"A crossbow?" McGavock scoffed. "Fah! Medieval romance it gives, eh?"

Sprague Tatum smiled bearishly. "No, nothing so fancy as all that. Just an old Dixie-style crossbow. It's a strange thing but many a Southern kid back in the hills who never heard of

Henry the Eighth has his home-made crossbow whittled from the heart of a cedar fence post. Had one myself. Shot rats with it—used nails as ammunition. My dad had one, and before him, my grand-daddy. Every male from seven to seventy can make one. Tracing a crossbow in these parts would be impossible."

McGavock said fiercely: "That's what you think! I'll have that ginzo by the scruff of the neck by sundown tomorrow." He simmered. "What kind of hocus-pocus goes on? Your brother's murdered under your own roof and you don't turn an eyelash. Guys jumping out of hedges and shooting crossbows at me! And all you're hopped up about is that stolen dog. Where did you keep the hound, by the way?"

Sprague Tatum's answer was innocently casual. "I have kennels back of the house."

So it was going to be like that. Lies from the start. "I noticed them," McGavock said tartly. "What kind of a dog was this?"

"A large brindle bulldog."

"A watchdog?"

Tatum was vague. "Not exactly a watchdog. Just a brindle bulldog."

"Just an ordinary, run-of-the-mill five thousand dollar dog, eh?" McGavock gibed. "Well, he seems to have brought on a case of homicide. Now let me tell you something about murder, my friend: anyone can kill. That's just the first and easiest step. To kill and cover, is a different story. I'm going home now. I'm going to bed. But before I pull out, I'd like to leave this little sermon with you. When you hire a detective, don't doubletalk him. He may be just a bit smarter than you are. Clients, you see, are amateurs; maybe just once in a lifetime they'll employ a detective. The detective, on the other hand, is a professional; his life is just a series of clients. He gets to know their dodges pretty well. And no detective worth his salt will act as a blind for any crime. Just think that over. I mean every word of it."

He slammed out of the house, left the big man paralyzed with amazement.

2

The Houseboat

THE COURT HOUSE was locked up for the night. McGavock rattled the worn bronze thumb-latch and cursed. This was an eventuality that he'd overlooked. Up to now he had bypassed the local authorities. McGavock knew these country set-ups. If he didn't make some show of co-operation, and make it quick, come morning they'd be on his neck like berserk bumblebees.

He wandered out into court square and dropped onto an iron park bench. Giant magnolias caught a puff of breeze from the hills and clicked lazily in the stifling air; their stiff, dead, last year's leaves lay about the ground like crisp curls of half rotted leather. A velvety bat, attracted by the coal on his cigarette, slipped out of the overcast sky with a whisper of wings, looped back into the black night. The row of shabby store fronts along Main Street was deserted, desolate.

"A town that's made to order for a killer," he observed. "And believe me, it's got one. He who kills and runs away will live to kill another day—or words to that effect. I'd better not fumble."

He snuffed out his cigarette, took the antique Iver Johnson from his belt and laid it in the magnolia leaves by his feet. "I'm through with you now," he said. "You don't fit into this case. From now on it's finders keepers. You've done your work for me—and done it nicely."

Miss Melinda Dawson had retired. The Teacherage, swathed

in its lacery of fronds and blossoms, was dark. McGavock turned from the pavement and entered the yard. He took just three and a half steps on Miss Dawson's glazed brick path when the blinding beam from a powerful flashlight exploded in his eyes. A worried sandpaper baritone said: "Wal, I'll be x-squared! So you're the feller from the city. I'm Sheriff Sackett."

"Oh!" McGavock smiled. "Glad to meet you, Sheriff. I've been looking all over for you. Just came from the—"

A huge hamlike hand appeared in the pool of light, slapped McGavock four times about the torso—under each arm, at the small of the back, at his belt buckle. McGavock gagged with rancor. "Do that again," he blurted venomously, "and it brings disaster. I don't go for pawing. Now stand aside. I'm hitting the hay."

Sheriff Sackett's voice rasped petulantly. "I got trouble. Let's set yonder on the curb and pow-wow. I'm all balled up."

"Tomorrow. I'm tired. I've had a long trip."

"And a busy evening—according to talk that's going around. Sprague Tatum tells me that he's hired you up from Memphis. I cain't help wondering what for?" The sheriff sighed. "Hit's got me addled."

McGavock said coldly: "I came here to catch a dog thief. I get to town to find that my client's murdered his brother. That automatically releases me. Tomorrow, I catch the first train back to the city."

The sheriff's boots scraped nervously in the spongy darkness. "Don't be in no rush to leave. To tell the truth, I'd sure like a little help on this."

"Not me." McGavock was decisive. "Sprague Tatum killed his brother. I don't work for a murderer."

"Lissen," the sheriff whispered. "Should I prove you that Sprague never kilt Darnell, would you reconsider? Sprague's innocent. That's a gospel fack. We ain't putting it out to the public but it's so."

"The body was found in Sprague's bedroom, wasn't it?"

"Why, sure." The sheriff's rasping voice was loaded with secrecy. "But when we undressed Darnell down to the undertaker's we found he was wearing his shoes on the wrong feet! Now Darnell was a fancy dresser—he wouldn't never have done that. Do you catch on? It means Darnell was slew sommers else. He was maybe in house slippers when he was destroyed. They put on his shoes and toted him to Sprague's. It was a frame."

"Well, I declare." McGavock sounded impressed. "You've argued me into it, Sheriff. I stay. It's my duty to protect my client. From now on, you and I work in the same harness, eh?" He changed his manner, barked curtly, "Then turn that light on yourself. Let me see what kind of a man I'm talking to."

The sheriff gave the torch a backhand flip. McGavock boggled. Sheriff Sackett was a roly-poly fat man—scarcely five feet tall. He was wearing a wrinkled linen suit; his pongee shirt was unbuttoned to his breastbone and a prismatic necktie draped, lasso fashion, over his shelf-like bay window. A serviceable walnut handled .38 was visible beneath the skirt of his coat.

Sackett shut off the beam. "I ain't much to look at. I appreciate yore interest, suh. Thank you and now, goodnight."

THE GUEST ROOM at the Teacherage was an amazing experience for McGavock. He struck a match to the squat, hobnailed glass lamp on the dresser and invoiced his new quarters. It was like a visit to the museum. A cowhide trunk, a marble-topped washstand, two priceless Georgian chairs and a canopy bed. The bed fascinated him; he turned back the covers at the foot and counted six feather mattresses. He got into his pajamas, scratched the back of his head and realized that he wasn't sleepy.

Suddenly curious as to what old ladies kept in cowhide trunks, he lifted the lid and investigated. There was nothing in the trunk but a small, mounted deer's head. McGavock carried it to the light. All in all, it was an extremely repulsive object. It was old, so old that moth larvae had channelled the dead fur. He gazed thoughtfully into the bulbous amber eyes, read the metal plate on the wooden plaque.

Presented to a Good Friend
by
Darnell Tatum, 1932

McGavock yawned, turned the specimen over. A yellowed paper label, about the size of a cigarette paper, read, *Blakesly Jones, Taxidermist, Split Birch, Michigan.* He replaced the shabby trophy, climbed up into the billowy bed.

In two minutes he was asleep dreaming that he was back at the Blue Bell Cafe trying to swap foxhounds with a Michigan taxidermist who wouldn't deal because he, McGavock, wasn't oldtime Southern gentility.

The detective was awakened the next morning by a chattering of birds as a blacksnake raided a robin's nest outside his window. That was the way his day started. He stripped to the waist, splashed cold water on his scarred chest, and dressed.

Miss Melinda was setting a mole trap on her front lawn as he went out for breakfast. She greeted him as he advanced. "Off to the canebrakes so early?"

He shook his head. "It's edibles I have in mind." He paused and glowered. "Last night when I talked to you about Darnell Tatum you screwed up your face like his name was an emetic to you. I find a deer's head in the trunk in my room presented by him to you, A Good Friend. I don't get it."

She showed no resentment whatever at his prying around in her personal effects. "My redeemer! I'd forgotten all about that atrocity. That means absolutely nothing. Every autumn for the last twenty years Darnell has gone to Michigan on a hunting trip. On every return he brings back a carload of those hideous heads. Almost everyone in town has one. We take them politely and stow them away in attics or trunks. It's a vanity with him—Nimrod, the Great Hunter. I think he buys them. I don't think he could hit a steamboat with a handful of sand." McGavock listened sourly.

A meal of sugar-cured ham, and—believe it or not—scrambled duck eggs, put him in good fettle. The town's sole restaurant was the hotel dining-room. He tipped the waiter—and managed to milk a little information. Abbott, a notorious local badman, lived in a houseboat a mile up the river.

He walked out Main Street to the water tower, left the highway, cut through a patch of runty roadside cotton and struck the bottoms trail. Brilliant butterflies caracoled through the steamy, golden air. Quick darting lizards, sunning themselves on rotting logs, inflated their emerald throats at him and scurried into the leaves. All was dazzling, rainbow color. And then McGavock entered a nest of willows—and left the morning sun behind him.

The great trees, rising high from the bank, flexed out over the river, their branch tips dragging the sluggish water. The shanty houseboat, long since unfit for navigation, was moored on the hard mud beach. In a tent of leafy shade. It was about as squalid a habitation as McGavock ever saw. The weathered deckhouse was roofed with tin tobacco signs, a crate of scaly-eyed, choleric chickens was jammed in the boat's bow. Abbott was at the boat's stern lowering a live-box of fish into the muddy stream. He had an eighteen inch channel cat hooked through the gill on his dirty thumb.

THE GAMBLER SALUTED McGavock with a predatory grin. "Howdy, sport," he called. "I'm just stirring up a bite to eat. Come in and set."

"Don't mind if I do." The detective crossed a narrow catwalk to the houseboat's deck and followed his host into the shack. In the far corner there was a built-in packingbox bed and a rumpled, filthy blanket. A granite coffee pot was bubbling on a kerosene stove. Abbott cleaned and dressed the fish, stripped off its satiny skin and dropped it into a cast-iron frying pan. He set out cups and saucers, poured black coffee. Into each of the smoking cups he put a spoonful of buttery-looking paste. "This-here is yaller of egg and sugar. It's a old steamboat trick—you cain't tell it from cream."

McGavock sipped it. It was surprisingly good. He took two one-dollar bills out of his pocket and tossed them on the table. "Here's the return of your loan. Thanks."

Abbott devoured the catfish with a great sucking of his teeth. He dropped all pretense at conversation until he had finished. In the center of the table were four shotgun shells. The cardboard cylinders had been cut open just below the waddling and shot—into the powder chamber. They'd been emptied of their explosive. McGavock pointed at them with his chin. "Don't tell me you're making a bomb?"

The hillman laughed uneasily. "By doggies, that's a good un! Plenty times I could use me one. No, brother, I ain't making no bomb—I takened the powder out'n them shells to test it. A man has to know what he's buyin' these days. Ain't it the truth?"

"Quite so." McGavock observed tentatively: "Last night you said something about a sporting proposition—"

Mr. Abbott piled the fishbones in a neat stack in the middle of his plate, wiped his fingertips in his armpits. "I was higher than a hoot owl. I didn't know what I was sayin'. I ain't got nare a thing." He added affably, "You put me in mind of a feller I knowed years ago—when I was a young hellion robbin' banks. This feller made out he was a ax salesman and doggone iff'n he wasn't a detective! Well, he hounded me from county to county till it was downright bothersome. All of a suddent he disappeared."

"What happened to him?"

"Durned if I know. I always figgered he got lost in the woods. I'm a-talkin' to the law right this minute, ain't I?"

"You are."

"Well, I'll be jumped-up and Joe-Diddled!" Mr. Abbott grinned patronizingly. "It couldn't be you're looking for Sprague Tatum's dog, could it?"

"No," McGavock said quietly. "I've found the dog. Tonight he'll be returned to his chain in Mr. Tatum's garage—won't he?"

Abbott was stunned. His lips sagged from their gums, fear came into his furtive eyes. "Why, it ain't possible!"

"You heard me," McGavock declared bleakly. "Tonight that brindle goes back to its owner. Those are my orders." He paled at the nape of his neck. "The next time we talk together don't spill a lot of gibberish about what a bad man you are. I'll let it go this time—but the next time you threaten me I'm going to reach out and slap you silly."

Abbott made a faltering rally. "Are you a-sayin' that I stole that mongrel? You cain't prove—"

McGavock coughed out a sneering grunt. "The dog goes back," he repeated. "As soon as it's dark."

ALMOST EVERY OLD-FASHIONED country mansion in the deep south has its "office"—and Joyce Preston's estate was no exception. These offices are conventionally similar: little one-room frame buildings tucked away in some corner of the house-yard. They are relics of another day and their original purpose was to give the master of the house a secluded retreat to tot up his domestic accounts and while away the hot afternoons in an atmosphere of dignified ease. Today they have fallen into disuse.

It was mid-morning when McGavock strolled through Preston's armorial gates. He stopped dead still in the gravelstone drive and sized the place up by daylight. Everything was in the best *post bellum* manner: the impressive white mansion, the formal gardens with their iron-swan fountain and latticed pergola, and the modest "office" half-shielded in a clump of privet.

He was bearing down on the house when his eye caught a flutter of color behind the window of the tiny building. He swung abruptly from his course to investigate.

The office door stood wide open. McGavock stepped inside.

The room was spick and span and flecked with saffron sun motes. The detective's wary glance took in the background, a rusty heater-wood stove, a cumbersome pigeon-hole desk—and centered on the girl.

She lay in a wheelchair. She was dressed in a short flowered skirt and apple-green blouse and her molten copper hair spread over her shoulders like icy fire. She gave McGavock a lazy, invalid smile. "Hello, there," she exclaimed. "I've worked out a new one. How do you like this: man's laughter?" She lifted a jade cigarette holder to her lips, blew a double column of smoke from her delicate nostrils. "Put them together."

McGavock thought he'd barged in on a mental case. "Howzzat?"

"It's a game I've invented. You take two words and put them together and get a new meaning. *Man's laughter;* put them together and get *manslaughter!* It's easy after you get the knack. And it's a lot of fun if you live alone like I do. Here's one I worked out the other day: King Louis came to the throne in 1774 and ruled for nineteen years. Pretty good, isn't it? Get it? Came to the throne and ruled, *and drooled,* for nineteen years!"

"Excuse me." McGavock turned to leave. "Farewell. I'll be seeing you—" He gave her a pitying stare. "You're a sick girl. Company disturbs you."

"Sick in a pig's eye! I'm in better health than you are. Oh. You mean the wheelchair?" She laughed. "I've always wanted a wheelchair and now that I've married a rich man—"

"Don't tell me you're Mr. Preston's wife!" McGavock's voice reeked disgust. "So I'm addressing Mrs. Joyce Roger Preston."

She caught the sourness in his tone and picked him up on it.

"Roger doesn't make a very good impression at first meeting but you'll find he grows on you."

"Grows on you like a wart!" He studied her thoughtfully. "What's this business about living alone. You mean he neglects you?"

She said hazily: "I haven't any kick coming. I married for money—and that's precisely what I got." She closed her eyes. "I've been hearing about you around town. You're the man that's staying with Miss Melinda. You're a detective, aren't you?"

McGavock held silent. Mrs. Preston groped under the chair cushion and produced a pair of bright yellow pigskin gloves. "This office is my ivory tower," she declared. "I come here and sit when I want to be in a world of my own. The other day I was sitting here when I heard a baby chimney swallow squeaking in the stove pipe. I got to poking around to see if I could help it—and I found these gloves."

"So what?"

"I scarcely know. You're a detective, maybe you can explain it. It's a puzzle and I don't like puzzles." Mrs. Preston was elaborately casual. "They're not Roger's gloves—he'd be horrified at the sight of them. They weren't Uncle Darnell's—he couldn't possibly have got them on."

"Maybe they're Uncle Sprague's."

"No chance." She shook her coppery head. "You couldn't pay Sprague to set foot on these premises."

"I give up." McGavock changed the subject. "Where's your husband, Mrs. Preston?"

"At the undertaker's—arranging the funeral." She fastened a drowsy gaze on the second button of his coat. "My friends all call me Wynne."

McGavock bowed formally. "Thank you for the detail. I'll note it in my report when I return to the home office."

MISS MELINDA DAWSON was chopping weeds in her vegetable garden. Lisle hose, the feet snipped off, were pulled on her forearms to protect them from the sun; she was giving the dry clods merry hell with a dull hoe. McGavock came around the corner of the walk with a little paper bucket of ice cream and two bottles of cherry pop. He went into the kitchen, located a couple of tumblers, put a hunk of ice cream in each of them and filled them with the ruby colored pop. He reappeared on the back porch, called Miss Melinda up into the shade. "Try this," he said. He handed her a glass of the concoction and a tablespoon. "Alcohol, no per cent."

Miss Melinda sank cautiously into a bottomless rocker. McGavock faced her on an up-ended butter crock. He announced: "I'm an investigator. I'm telling you because it's only natural to surmise that by now you know it. I've just taken a poll of the county and it appears to be an open secret. Yesterday I come to town to find a stolen dog and run into a batch of murder. Furthermore, I'm beginning to believe that Darnell Tatum's homicide is a good deal more—and worse—than that. This is high-proof, double-run crime. Small towns are pretty clannish. I'm cracking my way inside—but the going is tough. I'm asking you to give me a sketchy idea as to just what this Preston-Tatum layout consists of."

Miss Melinda finished her cherry pop, coddled the glass between her knobby knees. "The Tatums," she remarked, "are a streaky family. I can't understand it. If there was a murderer in the lot, it was Darnell himself. Sprague and Darnell hated each other. The obvious conclusion is that Sprague killed his brother. That's the obvious conclusion—but I don't believe it. I've known Sprague since he was in Fauntleroys and I earnestly insist that he's too shiftless."

"Here, here!" McGavock exclaimed. "We're not passing verdicts, we're attempting to assemble a few facts. Where did Roger Preston get all this heavy dough?"

"It was Roger and his money that caused the break-up between the two brothers." The gaunt old dame assumed a classroom attitude. "There was a sister, Clarissa. She kited down to Mobile and married a sea foods cannery. Her groom, Preston, was aging at the time and a few years after Roger was born the father went the way of all flesh. Clarissa immediately sold out her holdings, returned here to Halford and built that big house. She left Roger in a boys' school in Georgia. As a matter of fact, we here in Halford didn't suspect there was a child until two months ago when Clarissa died and her will, leaving everything to Roger, was probated."

McGavock asked: "What brought on the feud between the brothers?"

"Precisely that. Both Darnell and Sprague were aware of the nephew's existence, having visited him both at his home in Mobile and at school—but a definite lack of affection, even antipathy, between the mother and child had led them to believe that he would be cut off with a few dollars and that the bulk of the estate would go to them. They got the surprise of their life when the testament was read!"

"Life can be bitter!" McGavock said with relish. "Now tell me just how did this—"

Miss Melinda's cheek cupped in a cadaverous grin. "Roger

came to town and established himself in the big house. The two uncles were furious—they snubbed him cold. Then Darnell double-crossed his brother and sycophanted himself into the nephew's good graces. He moved into the mansion and lived high, wide and handsome on Roger's bank account."

"I catch," McGavock murmured. "No wonder Sprague hated him. I guess that explains that. One thing more. While I'm in town I want to take in all the scenery. What's this I hear about some furnaces?"

Miss Dawson said scornfully: "The furnaces are not scenery. They're just a clump of tumble down buildings out on Possum Hill. Years ago, before the war between the states, ironmasters had workings there. The ore ran out and the buildings have been abandoned for a half a century. Br-r-r! It's a ghostly place. If you want to see some really beautiful scenery go to—"

"I want to see the furnaces," McGavock insisted. "I like ghosts. It's the Frankenstein in me."

Miss Melinda rattled the spoon in the glass, set it on the floor. "A tasty potion," she affirmed. "I'll remember the recipe." She picked up her hoe. "What brought on this inquisition? I take it you have just been visiting your client." McGavock looked blank. The old school teacher said: "If you haven't you'd better—and soon. He's been tearing the town open looking for you. About a half an hour ago he came galloping up on his bay, screaming your name. Could it be that he's found another body?"

SPRAGUE TATUM WAS tinkering around his kennels. He waved McGavock across the yard with a wild flailing of his arm. The big outdoorsman had undergone a tremendous change since their last meeting. His gusty jocularity had entirely vanished. He was bubbling in frenetic rage. It was a strange, excited anger—with a definite undertone of panic. His massive face was distraught. "You can't do this to me!" he stormed. "You don't get a penny!"

McGavock said insolently: "What's the gripe?"

Hysteria fringed Tatum's voice. "It's you. Never have I seen so obnoxious a person. I've detested you since the minute I met you. You're not only disagreeable, you're inefficient. Can't you do anything correctly?"

McGavock chuckled. "The dog's been returned, eh? And you don't seem to fancy it."

"Come inside."

The huge beast was chained to a leg of the workbench. McGavock blinked. An ugly looking monster, higher than a man's knee, it was not brindle but coal black. Its right ear was cropped to the skull, filaments of slaver drooped from its lax mouth. "A wicked looking hellhound," McGavock observed. "He's not well. He's been living on a diet of gunpowder. I thought you claimed the critter was brindle."

"His natural color is chocolate brindle," Tatum confirmed. "His hide has been rubbed with lamp black to disguise him. How did you locate him? Who had him?"

"Didn't you see him returned?"

That touched Tatum off again. "No. He was sneaked in the garage here while I was down at the post office getting my morning mail." He began to gesticulate frantically. "I demand to know who stole him."

"Case closed," McGavock said tightly. "Make out your check for five grand and forward it to Atherton Browne—"

"Not one cent! Our agreement was the arrest and conviction of the thief."

"Our agreement," McGavock ground out, "was the return of the hound. Five thousand dollars—dead or alive."

"I don't want the dog. I want the man that stole it." Tatum went sly. "How do I know that the beast didn't come back of his own free will—"

"And chain himself to that bench leg?"

"Stranger things have happened!"

McGavock said quietly: "Sonny boy, you're writing yourself a mighty rough ticket. I don't like to be pushed around. If that's the way you want to play it, it's up to you."

What at first had been a faint, disturbing suspicion in McGavock's mind was now growing into a definite hunch. This was no casual, rustic murder. He was confronted with a subtle, bloody program promoted by an A-1 operator. He'd smashed into a web of vicious, hidden crime.

The detective returned to court square, entered a grocery store and purchased a handful of fresh green peas.

"Don't bother to wrap them up," McGavock said. "I'll just drop them in my pocket."

The clerk elevated his eyebrows. "You're a light eater, suh. That would just about make a mess for a hungry skunk."

McGavock declared: "Brother, you're closer than you imagine. That's why I'm buying them. To mess up a skunk."

EMBALMING WAS ONLY a sporadic sideline with Halford's undertaker. His real bread-and-butter trade was in ladies' footwear and millinery. When he was called upon to perform funereal functions he converted the workroom of his shop into a temporary mortuary. McGavock wandered down a vile alley, past a livery stable and a feed-and-grain platform, and poked his head through the door of the makeshift morgue.

It was a ludicrous layout. The backroom was a shambles of hosiery placards, hatboxes and miscellaneous litter. A nimble, nervous fellow in a seersucker jacket was tucking a sheet around a body on an improvised trestle table. "The department of arts and crafts," McGavock announced. "You've finished with him, I suppose?"

The undertaker became nettled. "Finished? How could I have finished? I'm no magician. I haven't even started—"

"Well, you better be getting around to it." The room was stifling hot. McGavock wiped the perspiration from his neckband. "This isn't the Arctic." He said blandly, "I'm from the Lodge. I've been delegated to check on Brother Tatum's obsequies—"

"What lodge?"

"The Cosmic Order of Rapacious Genealogists, Nashville Chapter. We want to be sure that he gets something pretty fancy." McGavock demanded severely, "Where are they going to stash him?"

The undertaker was shocked. "Mr. Tatum is to be buried in full ceremony in the family plot out at Pine Chapel. It's to be a private affair with only a few close relatives present. You may send a wreath if you like but I hardly think your presence will be welcome at the services."

McGavock slurred: "The Order of Rapacious Genealogists is not going to want Brother Tatum buried at Pine Chapel. That's out in the sticks, isn't it? Don't you have a cemetery right here in Halford?"

"Of course we do!" The undertaker was exasperated. "But as I've already explained, the Tatum family graveyard is at—"

The detective strolled over to the trestle table.

"If Brother Tatum's funeral is to be strictly by invitation, and I'm not invited, maybe I'd better take a farewell look at the dear departed."

He pulled back the sheet quickly—and gawked.

The body beneath the cover was Abbott.

The badman's piggish, lifeless eyes were dilated in terror. His left temple was a mat of splintered bone and gummy hair.

McGavock, caught off balance, exclaimed foolishly: "But this isn't Uncle Darnell!"

"Certainly not." The undertaker was primly rebuking. "Mr. Tatum came in last night. He has been taken care of and lies yonder behind that Keepshape Hosiery sign—in one of my best grade caskets. Mr. Tatum is a gentleman. Mr. Abbott, I'm sorry to say, is riffraff. In this business you meet all sorts of people."

McGavock said stiffly, "How long has he been here?"

The undertaker took off his seersucker jacket and rolled up his sleeves. "Mr. Abbott was brought in just a few minutes before your arrival, sir." He reached for a galvanized scrub bucket. "And now I must ask you to excuse me. This will take a bit of doing."

3

The Sepulcher of Baby Alice

JOYCE ROGER PRESTON, in powder-blue slacks— with a cerise stock at his throat, was posing on the court house steps. Knee slightly bent, arms behind his back, he was permitting the rabble to behold his charm. Only a couple of scavenger pigeons and a mangy mongrel seemed interested in him. Preston said coldly: "Run along! I have no desire to consort with you."

McGavock strode up, teetered back on his heels. "I know just how you feel. Here comes that odious man again." He was silent a moment, gloating. "The law wouldn't go along with you, would it?"

Preston asked frigidly: "What are you insinuating?"

"You've just come from the sheriff's office," McGavock declared derisively. "You've been trying to slap a warrant on me. You've found out I'm an investigator and you're burned because I foxed my way into your home last night. You've been thumbing through the law books to find some charge to pin on me but the sheriff won't listen. Right?"

Preston's voice was spiteful, malevolent. "Sackett has gone too far. He'll learn that I'm not without influence. He informs me that he has deputized you. If I were you, I'd think twice before I accepted—"

McGavock interrupted good humoredly. "Tut-tut!" The detective dug into his pocket and came out with a handful of green peas. "What in the world are these things?" he asked curiously.

Preston, in spite of himself, leaned over and peered. "Peas," he said.

McGavock pressed his point. "I know they're peas. What kind?"

"Just ordinary green peas." Preston was getting suspicious. "What's behind all this?"

"Nothing." McGavock tossed the peas to the iridescent pigeons. "I hear that your old man made his kale by canning crawdads and oysters down in Mobile?"

"That is substantially correct," Preston agreed smugly. He enjoyed discussing his wealth. "It was oysters and shrimps, to be exact. Crawdads, as I understand it, are freshwater; shrimps are marine."

"Now that," McGavock announced solemnly, "is mighty educational!"

He sauntered away.

The office of sheriff of Blount County was in a cement block annex winging out from the court house proper. It was an immaculate little room with white calcimined walls and olive enameled metal furniture. Sheriff Sackett stood at a barred window looking out into the hitching lot below. The cumulative impact of the afternoon sun was terrific. Outside, in the glassy colorless heat, jar flies shrilled their piercing, monotonous hum. From the cell block in the rear a doleful tenor sang, *"I wish I was a mole in the ground... If I was a mole in the ground I'd root this mountain down...."*

Sheriff Sackett said: "He came in here trying to get me to send you back to Memphis. I ain't afraid of his bank account.

He's crazier than a last year's bird's nest if he thinks he can boss me around." The undersized fat man assumed a harried, cornered expression. "Preston, himself, ain't in the clear—as far as I'm concerned!"

McGavock prodded him tenderly. "Suspect everybody, say I."

"It's more than a suspicion. Them shoes worry me. Like I told you Darnell wouldn't have never got them switched. That means he was shot at a time when his shoes was off and that the killer in his hurry got them mixed. Now reduce it to absurdum. What do you get? You get this: If Darnell had his shoes off that means he was at home. He was kilt at Preston's!"

"It's a convincing case," McGavock agreed. "But that doesn't mean that Preston did it. Maybe a tramp or burglar broke in and—"

"A tramp wouldn't tote no corpse clear across town!"

"I can see your point." McGavock seemed undecided. He said abruptly: "Preston has a photo album that belonged to his uncle. Pictures of tombstones. It might help us. Can you finagle it?" Sackett nodded.

"Good. Now here's something, Sheriff, that's going to embarrass you. I'm sorry but I'm going to have to bring it up." McGavock splayed his fingers, examined the knuckles of his hand. "I want the lowdown on those dog fights."

Sheriff Sackett flustered. "Dog fights?"

"That's what I said."

THE LITTLE FAT man walked to the cooler, drew himself three drinks of tepid water. He produced a cigar, punched an air hole in the back end with a desk pen, changed his mind and dropped it in the letter basket. "Where you learned of them, I don't know," he said at last. It was a struggle for him to speak. "You really cover a town when you work. You're right; bad stuff has been going on around here. Believe it or not, I'm as honest a sheriff as the next man. I hain't got no use for gambling. A trotting race, maybe—or a hand of stud, yes. But one thing I won't tolerate: pit fights. They're cruel and vicious and bring out the evil elements in a man."

"But you've been tolerating them!"

"No, by doggies! I've been trying to stomp 'em out but I can't get to first base. Fellers in this county are holding dog fights sommers. Where, I don't know, and who's behind 'em, I cain't find out. And when I do, I pity 'em. It hain't an ordinary crime, it's a sin. I gotta answer to my preacher for it ever blamed prayer meetin'!"

McGavock said: "Well, one thing more. What happened to Mr. Abbott? I've just come from the undertaker's—"

Sackett's thoughts were on other things. "Don't bother none about Abbott. It's a good riddance—that man was lower than swamp skim. He fell off a cliff over by Possum Hill. Some ginseng diggers found him about a hour ago."

McGavock narrowed his eyes. "Fell off a cliff, eh? Think of that!" He proclaimed gustily, "You're my temporary boss, aren't you? Well, Chief, I've got a report to make to you. The case just alluded to is now closed. There'll be no more dog fights. Abbott was the promoter behind them."

Sheriff Sackett expostulated: "I shore hope you're right!"

"It's not guesswork, it's a fact. Sprague Tatum hired me to come here and locate a stolen dog. This hound was the fighting type beast, a mean boxer. I met Abbott at the Blue Bell Cafe and told him I was a sportsman. He intimated that he had something rough and ready for me. He wanted a little time to line me up. This morning I paid him a visit at his houseboat. I found plenty evidence that he was my man. There was a pile of cut shotgun shells on the table."

"That's enough for me," Sheriff Sackett declared. "They feed the fighters raw meat and gunpower to make them crazy-bad."

"I didn't see the hound but I knew he was around somewhere, maybe tied off in the brush. I threatened Abbott, demanded that he return the beast at sundown. I must have scared him. He sneaked the dog back to Tatum as soon as I left." McGavock surged passion. "I saw the dog in Tatum's garage. He was smeared with lampblack. Tatum admitted it was the right animal but welched on his promised fee. If you want the proof that clinches it, go around to the undertaker's and look at Abbott's fingernails. Ten to one you'll find lampblack."

"I will," Sackett said slowly. He frowned. "I ain't liking the way it adds up. A month ago Tatum brought that dog in from out of state. He went around telling everybody what a tough dog he was and that he was pit-trained. He said he was a champion fighter and that he'd bought him to bring him to Halford and give him a peaceful home because he was agin pit fighting. He tole that story so much that everybody in town was sick of listening to it. It appears to me that Sprague Tatum is mixed in this business. Now that I think of it, it shore sounds like he was advertising a favorite."

"No," McGavock corrected. "He wanted his dog stolen. He was tempting Abbott to come and get him. He imported him for one purpose—to get Abbott to steal him—which Abbott did!"

Sheriff Sackett was befuddled. "You're a good man, McGavock. I might say the best I ever teamed with. But I cain't swaller that. He lures a man to filch his pooch and then employs you to come and get him back! It ain't scarcely reasonable!"

McGavock sat at the sheriff's desk, dragged up a typewriter. He rolled in a sheet of paper and, with frequent x-ing outs, tapped out a lengthy message. He ripped the sheet from the cylinder, reread it, handed it to the officer. "Have this telegram sent to Blakesly Jones, Taxidermist, Split Birch, Michigan. Send it over your own signature and demand an immediate reply."

The sheriff said unhappily: "What's deer hunting got to do with us?"

McGavock pretended not to hear. "And get your hands on that photograph album! I think we'll find that Darnell Tatum got what was coming to him, that he was as crooked as a stake-and-rider fence. And that somewhere among the pictures in that album he was foolish enough to preserve a record of his criminal work."

IT WAS THREE o'clock before McGavock got back to the hotel for lunch. The dining-room was deserted. The detective's morning acquaintance, the garrulous waiter, was off shift. The desk clerk, himself, a shuffling oldster with a roseate sunburned nose, took his order.

He was just polishing off the gristle-end of a heavily gravied, tough-fibered hill-cow steak when the old clerk tottered up to his table and handed him a small peach-colored envelope. The oldster loitered. "Read it," he ordered. "It was give to me to give to you. I know where it come from but I promised not to tell nobody."

In brown ink on strongly perfumed paper was written: *I have to see you right now—before the funeral tomorrow! Please don't fail me. Come to the bridal suite. At once. Wynne Preston.*

"Now she comes at me with a bridal suite!" McGavock scowled. "You trying to get me compromised?"

"Don't lay it on me," the old man exclaimed defensively. "I just work here. The bridal suite is up on the second floor—beyond the gent's washroom. Number seven, it is."

McGavock ascended the narrow, built-in staircase to the upper hall. He located number seven, grasped the knob and pushed open the door. The room was airy, high ceilinged. A faded carpet of twining roses was on the floor and the tall, vaulted windows were fluted with gingerbread molding. It had been a good twenty-five years since the mildewed bed had been slept in. Wynne Preston, a little-girl ribbon about her copper hair, was curled on a horsehair sofa reading a newspaper. The five inch headlines on the front page shouted, PERSHING PURSUES VILLA.

"Nothing like keeping up with the times," McGavock commented.

Mrs. Preston gave him a sultry smile. "I wanted something to read while I waited for you. I found this paper lining a dresser drawer. The actual fact is that this is news to me—it happened before I was born. How did it come out, did they catch this Pancho Villa?"

She was taking him for a ride and he knew it. "I don't like this funny stuff," he blustered. "Meetings in hotel rooms are dangerous business. Why did you want to see me *before the funeral?*"

She looked at him blankly. "Before the funeral? Oh, I remember now. I put that in to be mysterious. So you wouldn't let me down. What I really want is this: I want you to explain a phrase to me. I was reading a book the other day and I came across the expression *chance-medley*. What on earth does it mean? I take it, it's something legal."

"It is," McGavock answered. "And I'm no lawyer but I'll try to clear it up for you. Chance-medley is homicide by misadventure. Say when one man kills another, maybe accidentally, without evil intent. Chance-medley is sometimes confused with *chaud-melle*. That's when a guy kills a guy in a mix-up— without premeditation."

"Thank you," she said demurely. She brightened. "Then that's how Uncle Darnell was slain! By chaud-melle! He must have gotten in a fight with someone."

"Uncle Darnell's demise was premeditated murder. He got the bullet in the back of his head—" He cut off roughly. "You didn't summon me here to talk about chance-medley. Any good dictionary could explain it to you."

Wynne Preston's voice was soft, husky. "It's those yellow pigskin gloves, Luther." She even knew his first name! "I can't understand them. How did they get in that stovepipe in the office? I'm oppressed with a nebulous sense of horror. Something's going on around me that I don't know about!"

"Now let me get this straight. You're scared—and you base it all on those gloves. Is that right?" McGavock was bland.

"Yes, Luther."

He began to speak, fast and maliciously. "Then set your fears to rest. I've solved the puzzle of the gloves. There's nothing to—"

"You mean you've traced them?"

"I mean I've solved their puzzle. They were the bait to a trap, a trap set by you for me. No man ever wore those gloves. They were mussed and grimy—on the outside. On the inside, they were new—the little sticker price tag was still under the cuff. You bought them yourself. The whole thing was an act for my benefit."

Her eyes smoldered. "I don't like your tone! Whatever makes you say such things?" She controlled herself, said seriously: "Why should I do such a senseless thing?"

"I'll know the answer to that," McGavock retorted, "when I hear from a Michigan taxidermist." He added abusively: "Finish your newspaper. I don't want any traffic with you."

ALMOST SINCE McGAVOCK'S very arrival in Halford the evening before he'd been annoyed by Sprague Tatum's feeble—but ingenious—alibi. He could visualize the handsome giant taking the witness stand and explaining to an entranced jury with aching feet that he, Sprague, on the day of his brother's murder, had been on a jaunt in the timber breaking in a stiff pair of boots. The tale was so absurdly human and so simple that McGavock had not the slightest doubt that he could go into any court in the country and make it stick.

The job of exposing this silly story would be tough. Up to now McGavock had shunted it about in his mind, deliberately evading it because of its difficulty. There were only two possible angles in breaking the story down. The first was to catch the wily client in a conversational stratagem and force him to give himself away. Endeavor along this line, McGavock decided, would be a waste of time. The only alternative was routine legwork and endless questioning of possible witnesses. This

trial and error method would take weeks with no final guarantee of success. When a man claims he spent the day in the
woods he's made a statement that's hard to disprove.

That's the way it had seemed at the start—absolutely ironclad.

Then he worked on it from an inside point of view and the
thing began to loosen up. If he hadn't been in the woods, where
had he been? A day's a long time to fiddle around. Barring the
possibility of a trip to some place or other, the only natural
conclusion was that Sprague Tatum had never left Halford.
McGavock, like the Irishman and the lost cow, put himself in
his client's place. Early in the morning Tatum spread the story
of his fictitious jaunt. His job from then on was to keep out of
sight of the villagers. The safest place to hide, in fact the only
place in a town the size of Halford, was in a man's own home!

It was fantastic, it didn't dovetail with known facts, but cold
logic told McGavock that Sprague Tatum spent the day of his
brother's murder on his own premises.

McGavock ascended the hillside, knee-deep in feathery
sage-grass. A lazy hawk above his head quartered the glazed
sky in listless, suspended spirals. The detective stood in the
chalky, shadowless sunlight so that the outline of his figure
blended with a holly tree at his back. The little town spread out
in the valley below him. Down the slope, scarcely two hundred
yards away, lay the cluster of buildings that made up Sprague
Tatum's residence: the green bungalow, the low gray kennels,
the mill-roofed stable. From his elevation, he could see them
in their proper proportion and perspective—as though he were
studying a plate laid out on a table.

For five long minutes he was anesthetized in concentrated

attention. Softly and unconsciously he began to whistle; the tune he whistled was *The Letter Edged in Black,* and his tone was as clear and true as a rosewood flute. The bungalow and the kennels, set conspicuously in the open, were far too exposed to public gaze.

The barn was a different story. A ragged gulch, rimmed with dense scrub, hazel and elderberry, looped over the hill's ridge and descended almost to the stable's rear door. This way the dog had been stolen—and returned in broad daylight. It was the way, too, unless McGavock was very wrong, that Sprague Tatum had circled back home—after he had worked Main Street with his alibi.

McGavock descended the precipitous gully and opened the stable door.

He found himself in a small harness-room directly behind the garage. He halted a moment, holding his breath, waiting for the dog to bark. Through the thin partition, he could hear the animal's heavy panting and knew the beast was too sick to be interested in worldly affairs. Just beyond the threshold, and to his right, a rough timber stairway rose to a trapdoor. McGavock climbed the creaking steps to the loft.

The stable loft was low; the raftered roof arched in an inverted U from the ridgepole to the broad planked floor. The sole light came from a grimy circular window in the forward gable. The window was about shoulder high and there was a shiny patch on its surface where the crust of smut had been polished for better vision. McGavock peered out; he could see a corner of the kennel, the sidewalk, the bungalow's front steps and a section of the side of the building. The detective quirked his lips wryly. Here, from this peephole, client Tatum had watched on McGavock's first visit of the evening before.

McGAVOCK SAID: "IF he loafed away the day here, and now I know he did, he must have had food. The way he'd do it is this. He'd stop uptown, buy a picnic lunch, hit for the fields—and backtrack to here."

He subjected the loft to a painstaking search. It was the faint stench of an empty sardine can that uncovered the cache.

Crumpled up in a brown paper sack, and thrust between the kingpost and the floor joists, were the remnants of Tatum's hideout meal: a sardine can, a couple of buns, the rind of a slice of cheese.

And there was something else, too. A tightly crumpled sheet of paper.

A letter. McGavock smoothed it out. It read:

> Be sure to be at home tomorrow. All day. I must see you about you-know-what, just when I8ll call, I can't say. This is critical."

"Now the background begins to fill in," McGavock murmured. "Two days ago he gets this note. The day of the appointment, yesterday, he puts out the fake alibi, comes home and lays up here in the loft—waiting for his visitor. I've got him with his axle dragging."

A clamorous yipping and yapping came from the direction of the kennels—Tatum was feeding his foxhounds. McGavock descended from the loft, stepped from the stable door and confronted his client at the corner of the building. The big sportsman was carrying two pails of milk.

He set the buckets carefully in the dust at his feet and watched McGavock's approach with popping eyes.

"Where did you come from?" he asked.

McGavock said sweetly, "Make a guess!" His face roiled. He spit out, "I'm just a no-good, obnoxious, disagreeable person— but, brother, I've got you in a crotch!" He flourished the type-written note in the other's face. "Who wrote this?"

Tatum caved in. It was a sickening thing to watch, his florid cheeks went sallow, his bloodshot eyes darted spasmodically from side to side. He made a pitiful attempt at turning on the old high voltage personality. "The letter is from Darnell. But we won't get excited over it, will we?" When he spoke his voice was the voice of a frightened schoolboy. He blurted, "When I received it, I was flabbergasted. Darnell hated me. It didn't make any sense. I was suspicious. I went to the barn and waited. I thought I'd better size things up from a distance."

"You saw your brother arrive?"

"No. He must have gone in the house from the back door. I couldn't see the back door."

McGavock said happily: "As an alibi, it's terrible. The jaunt-in-the-hills yarn was much better. You're getting worse, fast."

Tatum ran his fingers through his rumpled, snowy hair. A cunning, calculating look crept into his eyes. "You're doing this to me for personal reasons," he exclaimed. "You're deliberately bringing calamity upon me. You're persecuting me just because I lost my head and spoke rudely to you. I apologize. Let's let bygones be bygones." He fumbled in his whipcord breeches and produced a legal-sized envelope. "I was just about to mail this."

McGavock took it from his limp hand. The envelope had no stamp; it was addressed to The Atherton Browne Detective Agency, Memphis. McGavock ripped open the flap, extracted a check. "Five grand," he confirmed. "That's right." He placed the check carefully in his wallet, dropped the envelope to the ground. "I observe," he said, "that the check is dated yesterday. My farewell sermon to you last night touched you up a bit. You made the thing out after I left. You've been carrying it with you ever since, in reserve. In readiness for just such a moment as this, when you're cornered. You and I are quits. I'm glad to shake you. One minute you try to mousetrap me and the next you're crying in your beer."

Tatum came to life. "Quits? Then you're going back to the city?"

McGavock laughed spitefully. "If you'd played square and paid off, I'd have been Memphis-bound eight hours ago. Now, I'm sticking around, on my own time, to see this mess straightened out. If any hard luck develops, you brought it on yourself, my friend."

McGAVOCK RETURNED TO the Teacherage for his gun. He was funny about firearms; he always liked them where he could lay his hands on one if he was convinced he might need it but hated to load himself down unnecessarily. A gun to McGavock was like a pipe-threader to a plumber; some jobs called for it, some didn't. When the occasion required, he got it out of the toolbox and used it.

His revolver was a wicked looking instrument—designed for quick and final results. It had a short barrel, a big convenient grip, and a bore the size of a cranberry. He had just stowed it behind his belt buckle and was snapping shut his gladstone when he saw Sheriff Sackett puffing up Miss Melinda's brick walk. The sheriff was carrying a flat parcel. McGavock walked out to the edge of the porch and greeted him. "You got it, eh?"

Sheriff Sackett nodded glumly. "I got 'er all right. But when re-election rolls around they's going to be another feller sitting in my swivel chair." He sighed mournfully. "The things you ask me to do. We got the society element in this town madder'n hornets!"

McGavock said sententiously: "Truth will prevail. Let's see that album." He leaned against the porch banister. "Before we go into this, I want to ask you a couple of questions. Who is this Mrs. Preston and how long has she been married to the current unspeakable?"

"Her name was Wynne Hargrave and she married him shortly after he come to town. Count her out of this. There ain't nare a worldly thought ever went through her sweet head. I've knowed her all my life and I'll vouch for her."

"She's local, eh?" McGavock pondered. "That was my second question."

"Sure she's local. She comes from a little settlement just south of town. Her pappy candidated for me two year ago when I run for office. Wynne went to high school here in Halford. When Mister Preston inherited from his old lady and moved in, he met Wynne at a strawberry festival and married her."

"Strawberry festival?" McGavock sounded surprised. "I thought he was too good for the hoi-polloi!"

"For about ten days, when he first come, he socialized—dawgged it to all the parties and frolics. Then he gigged Wynne and settled down to be a aristocrat. What did you want with that album? I've been through 'er page by page and I cain't find nothing out of place."

McGavock said: "Darnell Tatum was a genealogist. A genealogist is a guy you pay a fee to and he looks up your family line.

He uses histories, family bibles, court and cemetery records to establish degrees of consanguinity. He'll rig you up a pedigree. Sometimes, when there's a gap in his documents, he'll refer to old tombstones. Maybe in five years' hard work a busy genealogist would refer to, say, six or seven tombstones. They're only used as a last resort and are difficult to locate. Now in that album there are at least a hundred photos of tombstones. It's fantastic."

Sheriff Sackett demurred. "Maybe—"

"Maybe nothing! That album is phonier than a dime store diamond. One of those photographs really means something, the others are blinds."

"How can we spot the right one?"

"I don't know," McGavock answered. "But we have to, that's all. It's a clue to murder."

McGavock almost failed to snag it. It was about halfway through the book. A small snapshot, pasted on the same page with two decoys. The detective touched it with his thumbnail. "Here we are," he said. Sheriff Sackett craned his neck.

It was a photograph of a midget grave. The weathered marble headstone was carved crudely in the shape of a sleeping lamb. The chipped, faint letters on the tombstone's face said:

BABY ALICE
Daught. Lucy & Obed Preston
BORN JAN. 3, 1821
DIED MAR. 9, 1822
Welcome the Little Children
To Come Unto Me

"The Prestons are buried out to Pine Chapel," the sheriff commented. "What's wrong with that-there?"

"There's a screaming mistake in it. *That grave is new dug!*" McGavock grinned.

The sheriff fought it out. "It cain't be new dug. That-there's a hundred year old stone! But, durn iff'n you ain't saying true words." The enormity of the thing began to dawn on him. "Why somebuddy's been vandalizing Baby Alice's sepulcher. The Prestons and the Tatums ain't going to keer for that!" He blanched. "Somebuddy's gone and buried something new in there!"

McGavock nodded.

The sheriff amplified. "They've went and buried another corpse in the same grave! How could they have did it in such a little grave? They must have dug a deep hole and stood the new body in on its feet. Ain't that horrible!"

McGavock said quietly: "They didn't bury a corpse, they buried a suitcase." He knotted the skin at the corners of his lips. "It was Darnell himself that planted that suitcase. He buried it at night, probably, and came back the next day to photograph it. He wanted a record in case anything should happen to him."

The sheriff said with determination: "I'm gonna take a chanct on you. You was right about Abbott, he had lampblack under his fingernails. I seen Tatum and he admitted his pooch was blacked up when it come back. Now this graveyard desecration has to be looked into. That means me, I'm the sheriff. I want you to come along."

"Fine! When do we start?"

"We're heading for Pine Chapel in a hour."

McGavock growled irritably: "An hour? Why not right this minute?"

"I cain't get the afternoon off," the sheriff answered wretchedly. "My old lady's making me delouse her henhouse."

4

Quick-Drying Cement

THE CASE WAS really building up pressure. It was as vicious a scheme of murder-for-profit as the detective had ever encountered and the business was about ready to pop its valve. It was McGavock's landlady, entirely unknowingly, who actually cinched it. Hardly had the sheriff slogged away down the dusty street than Miss Melinda leaned her skinny elbows out of the bedroom window and yoohooed. "I judge a man, Mr. McGavock, by the company he keeps," she accused.

McGavock asked: "You mean the sheriff?"

"No," she corrected severely, "I don't mean Sheriff Sackett. I mean Dabney Spurlock. He's been around to see you three times in the last hour."

McGavock closed his eyes and made weaving motions with his hands. "Comes now, out of the crystal ball, the name Dabney Spurlock." He opened his eyes. "Who is he and what does he want."

"I don't know what he wants but I can tell you who he is. He's trash. He owns the circus—"

"Are you telling me there's a circus in town and I didn't know it?"

She sniffed. "This particular circus has been in town three years! It was a cheap-john rodeo. Dabney did rope tricks and his wife rode a bloated mustang. The show was supposed to be itinerant but Dabney hit town and just couldn't seem to get moving again. First his wife died, and then his trailer burned, and then his mustang died. He and his tribe of urchins live by petty thievery—out in a shack in Frogtown."

Frogtown was a semicircle of shanties at the edge of a swamp. The rickety, one-room cabins were built on pilings of railroad ties three feet or so above the miry ground; it was a desolate community. McGavock's guess was that there wasn't a plank or nail or strip of roofing in the entire settlement that hadn't been filched.

The most forlorn of all the stilted, shedlike houses bore a gaudy curlycued sign in red and yellow and blue: THE GREAT SPURLOCKS. Four pretty little girls, ranging in age from seven to fourteen, were lined up, ladder-fashion, on a long keg bench on the narrow porch. A barefooted, stoop-shouldered man with a pitchpipe was hopping about in the mucky grass, scolding, haranguing them.

"Let's try 'er agin," he ordered. "And you, Julie Jane, whup that thing!" The little girls picked up an odd assortment of instruments from the floor at their feet: a jug, a mouth harp, a saw and fiddle bow, and a washboard. The stoop-shouldered man tooted his pitchpipe and the kids went into a whanging rendition of *Jesse James*. "That's better," Dabney Spurlock said to his offspring. "Now git out and grabble we'uns a fry of turkle fer supper!"

Mr. Spurlock turned to McGavock. "How do you like 'em?"

"They're mighty sweet." McGavock was impressed.

"No they hain't. They're meaner than ringworm. But they're natchel musicians. Some of these days we'll be ready fer the road agin. You the detective everbody's talking about?"

McGavock flinched. "I can't deny it."

Mr. Spurlock crinkled his eyes. "Don't pay no attention to me," he said kindly. "I'm jest a-teasin' you." He pranced over to a crude log pigpen, dropped to his hunkers and reached into the interior. "Now if this blame sow don't nip me!" When he withdrew his arm, he was holding a crossbow. "Here we are! The doohinkus the feller shot at you with!"

McGavock examined the primitive weapon; it was stubby, powerful. He remarked: "So you saw him? Have I actually got a witness in you, then?"

Spurlock said regretfully: "I'm powerful sorry but they cain't be no testifying in no courtroom. You see it's this way. My little gals is putting up cucumber pickles. Wal, by happen-chance we don't have no cucumber patch. Last night, in the dark of the moon, they was in town accumulatin'."

"Stealing from the villagers, eh?"

Spurlock was mildly reproachful. "The good book sayeth, the pore man shall share his brother's vineyard. Now vineyard means a yard whar there's vines. Cucumbers grows on vines. I gotcha there, friend. As I was sayin', the little gals is in the alley behind the preacher's garage when they see this feller jump out of the hedge and throw down on you with a crossbow. He comes tearing down the alley and pitches the weapon over the fence into the preacher's garden."

"Did the little girls recognize the man?"

"They shore did—but we'uns ain't namin' no names."

"Then why mention it in the first place?" McGavock blew up. "Why make repeated attempts to get in touch with me and then—"

"Because it's my way of doin' things," Mr. Spurlock answered. The pupils of his gray eyes contracted. He said, offhand: "My granpappy won him a medal at Chancellorsville. I'm a State's Rights Secessionist and a doggone good Confederate."

McGavock said: "More power to you. But what has that to do with—" Suddenly he got it. "So that's it," he remarked. "You don't like Yankees."

Spurlock grinned. "Yo're reely a smart man. It ain't that I don't like 'em—I just don't keer for 'em.'"

WITH NO PARTICULAR purpose in mind, McGavock detoured on his return so that he passed the showy mansion of Joyce Roger Preston. It was a good half hour until his appointment with the sheriff. He felt in fine fettle, in just the right mood to indulge in a bit of enjoyable insulting. The breaks were with him. Young Preston was taking his ease in the shade of the cool veranda. A frosty tankard sprigged with mint in his hand, his feet in rope-soled sandals, he was doing his best to put out a one-man tableau of The Landed Gentleman Relaxes. He called cheerily to McGavock—with a complete reversal of attitude. "I say there— Come up, sir, and sit down. I was just thinking about you."

McGavock dropped down beside him in a wicker lounge chair. His host urged: "Let me fix you a julep."

McGavock shook his head. "No, thanks."

"Cigarette?"

"Nope." The detective asked insolently: "What's got into you? You're finally grasping the rudiments of polite breeding."

Preston chuckled affably. "You're certainly privileged to that remark. I'm afraid I've been a little unpleasant. A teaspoonful of baking soda in a glass of water changed all that, sir. I have dyspepsia, I've been out of sorts. A spoonful of baking soda in a—"

McGavock said, "Nuts!" He paused a moment, inquired coarsely, "How's for tagging along at your uncle's funeral procession tomorrow?"

Preston sipped from his tankard. He wiped off the frosty moisture with the palm of his hand, admired himself in the silvery surface. "I'd be delighted to have you join me. But don't expect any bangup spectacle. There'll just be the two of us… and Uncle Darnell. There'll be just a couple of cars. You and I in one; the undertaker, the body, and the Halford sexton, in the other. The sexton is an elder and will administer the rites—"

"What about Mrs. Preston and Sprague?"

"Uncle Sprague refuses flatly to attend. It's just as well. He's impulsive and would be certain to cause a scene." He hiccoughed amiably. "With Wynne it's a different story. She says why do people go to funerals? You just take something out and leave it and come back without it. She says if you look at it that way you can see that funerals aren't actually any fun. She's staying home and listening to the radio."

"You charming people!" McGavock got up. "I'll be going. I've got to see a man who delouses henhouses." His ear caught the sound of his words. "Delouses henhouses! I'm getting as screwy as Mrs. Preston. I'm making poems!"

The drive to Pine Chapel was a wild one. Sheriff Sackett manhandled his battered, clay-smeared coupé like a bulldozer on a short contract. They clattered down Main Street in a nimbus of dust, rattled and jolted over the loose timbers of South Bridge, and slewed from the pike full blast—smack into a clump of second-growth. McGavock clutched his panama—he thought the sheriff had gone mad. They cleared the mesh of branches and came out on a backtrail. From then on, the going got really rough.

The trail consisted of two dry, deep ruts almost to the hubcaps. Sackett jounced into the ruts, lined up his wheels and stepped on the accelerator. It was like shooting rapids in a canoe. "In the rainy season," the sheriff gasped, "these roads aren't passable."

After three miles of this terrific churning, when McGavock thought he could stand it no more, the fat man cut his wheel at a fork and they were in a trackless tableland of lofty stag-head oaks. The coupé shuttled through the tree trunks, over the leafy mold. "I don't see any road," McGavock remarked. The sheriff gazed thoughtfully about him. "They ain't none. We go by bearings. It's easy to get lost." Twenty minutes later they hit a shaley creekbed.

Sheriff Sackett sighed with relief. "Now we cain't miss." He bounced into the winding channel. "We just foller this dry stream."

"Poor Uncle Darnell," McGavock observed. "He's going to remember his last trip."

"Come falling-weather, they could never get him through. They'd have to put him amongst strangers in the Halford cemetery." The sheriff threw off the ignition. "We're here!"

THEY WERE IN a miniature, saucer-shaped hollow. The back-woods church, long abandoned, had collapsed beneath the futility of decades. It was as though the external force of time, like the tremendous pressure of subterranean waters, had thrust in its sides and demolished its warped-shingle roof. The rotting wooden skeleton glowed with trumpet vine and wild geranium. McGavock and his companion plowed through the tough, seedy sward; great green-and-gold beetles, as big as a man's thumb, rose from the ground before their advance.

The chapel's tiny graveyard lay beyond the wrecked building—near the margin of the clearing. The unkempt graves were overrun with weeds and Bermuda grass. And the sepulcher of Baby Alice was exactly like its neighbors: a tangle of sedge and bracken. Sheriff Sackett objected. "We must have mis-read that-there photograph. This grave hain't been tampered with. She's all overgrowed with—"

"Dig," McGavock commanded the sheriff. "You're observing a very extraordinary piece of landscape gardening. Our party came out here, buried his suitcase—and photographed the new dug mound. He wanted a record of his work. Then, after he had taken his picture, he planted bentgrass and fern, dosed them with liberal applications of commercial fertilizer—some of the new compounds contain a root-producing hormone. My guess is that he's been back many times since, tending his little plot as carefully as a veteran horticulturist."

Sheriff Sackett shoved his spade into the loose earth. "We'll see." Instantly, there was a *clank!* He scooped off the shallow layer of topsoil. The object, only three inches or so below the surface of the ground, was not a suitcase. It was a small lard can, hermetically sealed around the rim of its lid with sealing wax. The sheriff pried it from its resting place. He gave McGavock a jubilant, triumphant smile.

"O.K," McGavock said curtly. "I'm wrong. It's not a suitcase. But it's just the same as a suitcase. Open it up!"

Sheriff Sackett laid the can on the grass, eased the weight of his boot on its side and buckled it—springing the lid. Wrapped in a tablecloth were a classring, a scholarship key, a pair of nose-glasses—and a book. The sheriff picked up the volume and inspected it; it was titled, *The Essence of Finite Epistemology.*

He turned to the end-paper, read aloud: "'To our good friend, chosen by us as the campus live-wire and all around good fellow—from his classmates of '42.'" The sheriff complained. "More stuff has happened to me in the last twenty-four hours! Stuff like this!"

"We've got him," McGavock declared. "This is all we need. This and a memorandum from that Michigan taxidermist."

"Got who?"

"Got the killer of Uncle Darnell," McGavock answered crossly. "Let's strike for town."

It was sundown by the time they reached the tableland of staghead oaks. About them was the breathless silence of sluggish, sleeping timber; a wan day-moon, like a translucent fish-scale, had already started its slow climb from the horizon. The sheriff launched the coupé into its wild, darting shuttle through the shaggy tree trunks.

It's sundown, McGavock realized. And I told myself I'd have this smoothed out by sundown.

He said: "It's all over now, Sheriff, but the slicing and serving. If, after I leave tonight, you like what I've dished up—remember the Atherton Browne Detective Agency, Memphis. We co-operate. Tell your friends." He paused impressively. "Now, here's what I want you to do. Go back to your office and see if Blakesly Jones has telegraphed you from Split Birch. Get in touch with the following people and have them assemble at nine—at Joyce Roger Preston's. Stall them with some kind of yarn about your having turned up a new will of Clarissa Tatum Preston's. I want to see these bright and beaming faces: Young Massa Preston and his drowsy, smoldering helpmeet, big, handsome Sprague and Miss Melinda Dawson—"

The sheriff barely dodged a stump. "Miss Melinda? Why her?"

McGavock said: "Put yourself in her place. An old lady living all alone. No friends, no recreation. I want to give her an exciting evening. It isn't everyone who can sit in on a murder showdown."

SHERIFF SACKETT EDGED the over-aged jalopy into the hitching lot behind the court house. McGavock crawled out. He walked over to a wooden, algae coated watering trough, bent down and took a drink from the rusty iron pipe. He wiped his lip delicately with a violent purple handkerchief and nodded goodbye. "I'll be seeing you, Chief," he said.

It was on that brutal, jouncing stretch of rutted road on the return to Halford that the hunch had occurred to him. It was fantastic but the more he thought about it, the more certain he became that he must be correct. All day, ever since his first interview with Wynne Preston there in the estate's office, the image of the girl with her apple-green blouse and her copper hair kept flashing into his brain. It wasn't the girl exactly—it was the atmosphere of that room that persisted in disturbing him. The meeting in the hotel, for instance, left him cold. He kept visualizing the inside of the office, with the girl sprawled in the wheelchair—and always he had the sensation of sunshine, *too much sunshine.* He could get that far with it and then it would stump him. The saffron sunlight and the girl's copper hair and—

It was on the jolting, rutted road that his mind's eye suddenly filled in the missing detail. *It was an old office, but there had been a new floor!* Cheap, harsh yellow pine. That was why the place had seemed so bright and sunny.

There were no two ways about it, Joyce Roger Preston's office merited a return call.

The building, McGavock had observed on his morning's visit, was nested in a fence-line of osage, and was flanked from the direct view of the house by clumps of untrimmed privet. Access should prove comparatively simple.

It was near-dark when he pushed through the thorny branches of the osage hedge. He stood for a moment, in the fused shadows of twilight, at the off-corner of the small structure. Satisfied that his entry onto the grounds had gone unnoticed, he groped his way forward. He maneuvered the privet between himself and the lighted windows of the mansion. He walked plantigrade, heel and sole flatly on the ground, like a lynx—no foolish tiptoeing—and his footsteps in the dry twigs were casually and completely soundless.

The office was empty. He closed the door behind him, got out his pencil torch and went to work. As earlier in the day, there were but three articles in the room: the wheelchair, the cumbersome old pigeon-hole desk and the stove. He'd been correct; the floor, of mill-planed pine, was brand new, as garish and harsh as a packing box. He went to the wall, hunched down, and propped his flash on a package of cigarettes so that its beam struck the door-trim about ten inches from the floor. He fumbled in his vest and produced a cylindrical gadget that looked like a tire-pressure gauge: a machine-tool jimmy with a telescopic handle.

One slow, twisting pull and he had the baseboard pried from the wall. Beneath the baseboard were three bent finishing nails—flattened to the plaster. He squatted in reverie, smugly satisfied, arose and scrutinized the old desk.

It was of the eighteen-ninety vintage, when every house-holder was his own businessman. McGavock tried the drawers; they were locked. The desk was a kneehole job, one side designed in a cabinet for ledgers. He pulled the desk from the wall, levered off the molding strips and lifted out the back.

There was a half-empty sack of cement in the ledger cabinet. Any cement was interesting but this was particularly interesting. It was quick-drying cement.

He replaced the desk, shoved back the baseboard and withdrew.

WYNNE PRESTON WAS by the doorstep, in the murk of the shrubbery—waiting for him. She was in a backless evening gown, her flowing hair caught about by a triple silver chain. "Were you searching for something?" she asked. The whole setup was tailor-made.

McGavock said glibly: "No. I wasn't searching for anything. I'm leaving tonight. I just came back to the ole homestead to sit a few minutes alone in the gloaming and recapture those happy, romantic visions of—"

She said angrily: "Your humor is labored. I've a good notion to whistle for my husband."

"So that's the way you call him? I'm not surprised." McGavock grinned. "I bet he lifts his ears and comes flying. Do you have one of those soundless vibration whistles? The best trainers use them." Before she could retort, he inquired quietly, "How did you know I was here?"

Wordlessly, she raised her arm and pointed to the pergola about thirty feet distant. McGavock said balefully: "You were sitting behind that rose trellis, spying on me?"

"Yes, I was. I knew you'd come back. You simply had to! What did you find?"

McGavock asked reluctantly, "Can you keep a secret?" She nodded tensely. He said, "I've found a new will. A testament made out by Clarissa Tatum Preston just before her death and voiding all others extant." He swung into it—what the hell, he decided, give the girl a little something to worry about. "I'm turning it over to Sheriff Sackett."

For a second, he thought she was going to pounce on him. She moistened her lips. "That's preposterous! What does it say?"

"I haven't had time to peruse it—I've just scanned it. It says something about Joyce Preston's money being held in trust until his wife has a set of twins. The old lady was nuts about twins. She thought they were cute." He dropped his voice, became intimately confidential, "You got any twins?"

"No," she responded weakly. "I don't have any children at all."

He clucked his tongue sympathetically. "Twins are sort of a raffle. I understand that statistics place the odds at something like five-hundred-to-one." He elevated a satanic eyebrow. "Maybe I read that paper wrong. Let's wait and hear what the high sheriff has to say."

McGavock had been fully aware of one thing all through the case—he was confronted with an armchair criminal. General opinion to the contrary, McGavock knew the armchair criminal for what he was: snaky, merciless and elusive. Crime is like anything else—when a man puts a little thought on it he gets safer and surer results than when he slambangs his way through, trusting to quick thinking and luck. The armchair criminal hatches his own schemes—and the machinery he puts in action is devious and fiendish and original. He takes a lot of catching. He has a natural nose for loopholes; you have to check and double-check before you spike him.

There was only one way to fight an armchair crime. Brains were out, leg-work was the answer. You had to take the field and out-work him. If you collected enough information you soon saw that little filaments of evidence that seemed wispy tangents at first soon began to cross at a focal point.

The focal point in the murder of Darnell Tatum was the clump of derelict buildings out on Possum Hill known as "the furnaces."

Up to now, McGavock had never set eyes on them, yet he was in the position to know more about them than ninety-nine per cent of Halford's genial, easygoing citizenry. He knew, among other things, that it was at "the furnaces" that a local badman, named Abbott, now deceased, had thrown his series of nocturnal dogfights almost under the sleeping ears of the good sheriff and his fellow townsmen. McGavock knew more than that; he knew that Abbott's brutal animal-baiting was but half the story that the abandoned smelteries had to tell. About now, McGavock decided, was the proper time to investigate the other half of that story.

Possum Hill rose, like a great ghostly mound, just south of the village line. Supine cattle, pallid phantoms in the moonlight, turned lustrous gelatine eyes at McGavock as he threaded his way among them. The shaley slope, infested with treacherous flat-jointed hill cactus, made punishing climbing. His whip-cord chest muscles were taut with exertion when he reached his objective. The very difficulty of the ascent disturbed him. "There's a bug in my logic somewhere. This hill's too steep.

Things couldn't have happened the way I figured." He clamped his jaw. "Despite the topography, I'm right. I have to be."

THE FURNACES WERE a scar of wreckage on the moonlit hillside. Gaunt, gutted walls, heaps of crumbled brick, smoky stumps of ancient chimneys. Only one structure bore any resemblance to its original form, a low, squat storeroom about fifty feet long and about twelve feet high. "You're my baby," McGavock said. He tested the weathered door and, as he expected, found the huge, handwrought hinges well oiled.

Lightning had torn a gaping hole in the roof directly over the door; he caught a patch of mackerel night sky and a dusting of low-swinging stars. He flicked on his torch and took invoice of his surroundings. The room was a long dusty tunnel. Immediately over the threshold, at his right, was an arched alcove containing a narrow boxlike brick oven. "The brick kiln," McGavock judged. "They made the bricks for their buildings here on the spot." He swept the oven with his flashlight, shook his head. Its sides were split with zigzag cracks.

His nostrils isolated a faint scent, the odor of backroom poker games, of stale tobacco, sweat and foul whiskey.

At the far end of the long vaulted chamber he came across Abbott's handiwork. He found the dogpit. A square hole in the earth floor—five feet deep and six feet square. Here Abbott's sadistic, half-human customers had paid a fee and laid a wager. And watched dope-crazed dogs maul each other to death. The ground about the pit was littered with snipes and cigar butts. McGavock toed them with contempt. "I'd like to trace some of these cigarbands," he said grimly. "I'd hang a little disgrace on some two-faced, respectable churchgoers. Abbott knew his clientele."

He flicked his beam along the wall—on the shards of shattered bottles—and returned to the kiln in the alcove. He gave the oven a frustrated scowl, grasped the lever on the metal door and attempted to swing it open. It wouldn't budge. McGavock brightened. "That's better," he decided. He examined the door and observed that it was cemented shut. He picked up a long straw from the ground, stepped to the side of the kiln and attempted to feed the straw into a crack. The straw penetrated to the depth of the brick sidewall and met an obstruction. McGavock smiled happily.

"So that's the way it was done," he thought. "He came out here first—long before the actual climax. He came out here with his quick-drying cement, crawled inside the oven and sealed it air-tight. Had it all nice, and ready and waiting! If that's not premeditation! Wow!"

He had flipped off his torch and was standing with his palm against the panel of the door, preparing to depart, when he heard the scraping sound. It was a faint, almost inaudible rustle and at first he thought it came from the darkness behind him. He laid his hand on his gun-butt and held his breath. *Scratch-scratch-scratch.* This time it was definitely louder and to his confusion seemed to come from the outside, from the other side of the door. He recalled Miss Melinda's jocular reference to ghosts.

It's not possible, he decided. One instant it's behind me and the next it has passed *through me* and is waiting for me out on the hillside!

Then with a chill, he got it. It wasn't behind him and it wasn't in front of him. *It was above him—someone was on the roof!*

The next four seconds were an eternity of action.

McGavock jerked his eyes heavenward. Mackerel sky and spangled stars were blotted from the ragged hole over his head. Blotted out by the giant toadlike silhouette of a crouching man. The figure flung itself down at him. McGavock backstepped, too late to clear himself but soon enough to deflect the hurtling impact. The detective staggered off balance. There was a bestial grunt as his attacker caromed into the spongy blackness. A split second later the phantom surged up from the earth and McGavock had his arms full of bobcat.

The detective was puzzled—the man came at him with his bare hands. But it was life and death and no mistake. A sinewy arm circled his throat and McGavock felt a chest of rock crush against his own. The attacker's free hand sought out McGavock's windpipe—with thumb and forefinger, as though he were plucking the viscera from a slaughtered bull. It was a sleight that was instantly effective. McGavock's brain blanked out with an anarchy of pain. Maddened, insensate, McGavock came down with a terrific overhand and caught his opponent in the groin. The fingers slipped at McGavock's throat and the detective really went to town. He slammed the man back against the door with a Sunday punch under his ear, tried a haymaker, missed, and caught his attacker with the backlash of his elbow under the heart.

The man covered, groped for the door latch, and disappeared into the scrub. McGavock got his gun out, held his fire. He grinned, said: "I wouldn't have missed it for a week's wages. He had it coming to him. An hour from now I'll have him in manacles." He shrugged. "The guy's a screwball—coming at me unarmed." Absently, he flipped on his flash and swept the light about the ground.

A nice new lathing hatchet lay almost at his feet. The torch beam glinted on its nickel polish, showed a strip of dull glow down the edge of the blade. It, like the taper-file, had been honed to a razor keenness.

McGavock said soberly, "He dropped it when he lit." He rubbed a thoughtful knuckle across his chin. "Maybe I popped off a little too soon."

5

Let's Count Corpses

McGAVOCK'S WRIST WATCH said a quarter to nine as he banged on the door of Sprague Tatum's green bungalow. He was firing before the count, deliberately violating his agreement with the sheriff—but fifteen precious minutes were going to be needed in advance for setting a proper stage. When an armchair crook begins swinging hatchets, things are at the point of eruption.

Tatum let him in. The big man had shed his rugged plaids and riding breeches for quiet, conventional business garb. Three alligator hide traveling bags were stacked in the center of the living-room carpet. McGavock said mockingly: "Don't tell me that you've suddenly had guests drop in!"

Tatum hemmed and hawed. You could see that he wished he'd thought of it first but was afraid to go along with it. "No," he answered cautiously, "no guests. I thought I'd run down to Biloxi for a few days and inhale a little of that invigorating gulf air. As the poet says, I've got the wanderlust."

"I've no doubt of that." McGavock was bleak. "Hasn't Sheriff Sackett contacted you within the last few hours?"

"I believe I did hear the doorbell a short time ago but I was upstairs in the bath—"

"In the bath, baloney. You were probably under the bed. Get your hat. They're waiting for us around at Nephew Preston's."

Tatum blustered. "You'll have to go alone. I swore a sacred

oath on my honor as a gentleman never to put foot on those premises—"

McGavock picked up an expensive fedora from the hall-tree. "So I've heard. Let's ramble."

They walked in silence along the village streets, in the heavy humidity of the summer's night, McGavock always a little to the rear and side of his companion. Tatum was the first to speak. After a while, he said: "It's not that I wish to turn state's evidence, or whatever you call it—perish the idea!" He harrumphed, paused. McGavock made a spiteful sucking sound. Tatum said uneasily: "Did you happen to notice anything strange about that typewritten note. The one you found in my barn loft?"

"Of course I did." McGavock was solemn. "Do you think I'm blind? One glance at it and I knew you were a liar. Telling me that it was written by Darnell! That note had been carefully picked out on a typewriter by a novice. It had all the natural mistakes that an untutored beginner makes. No double spacing between sentences, no spacing after commas. And the most flagrant error of all—one that even you must have caught— was the I-8-ll for 'I'll,' where they all get tangled on their shift key. Did Preston write it?"

"I'd like to believe so," Tatum declared. "But Roger is a college graduate. If there were two men in town who should have known how to manipulate a typewriter I would have thought them to be Roger, who is highly educated, and Darnell, who used a machine incessantly in his profession of genealogist."

"Who do you favor?"

"Well, by the process of elimination, that leaves Wynne, Mrs. Preston."

McGavock pretended to be shocked. "We cain't arrest her," he said, imitating Sackett's petulant, sandpaper baritone, "she's as guileless as the fallen dew and her pappy done candidated for the sheriff. That leaves you."

"No," Tatum pled. "Don't say those things! Please!"

Joyce Roger Preston's big white brick mansion was a house with the jitters. The porch light was on, the garage light was on, and three concealed floodlights cross-lit every square inch of the spacious lawn and garden. Through the open, copper screened windows, McGavock could hear the shrill, scolding voices of spouse and bride as they crescendoed in trivial, wordy argument.

"Listen to that," McGavock remarked. "I swear, it sounds like a tobacco auction. Mrs. Preston is carrying the melody and Roger is coming in with the bass." He sighed, raised his hand to the knocker. "Maybe a little company will cheer them up."

Tatum made a feeble, final attempt at a balk. "I'm not going to allow myself to go in there and be insulted. Just because that branch of the family happens to have money—"

McGavock admonished him. "Hush-hush!" Roger Preston opened the door, bowed them in. He was flushed and excited. "What's this about a new will?" he shouted. "It's a fake!" He noticed Sprague Tatum. "You're behind this, sir! It's another of your gyps!"

McGavock said placatingly, "Greetings, Squire." The title soothed their host. He answered waveringly, "Oh, hello there, McGavock. Won't you come in?"

WHEN MOTHER CLARISSA employed an architect to design her humble quarters she saw to it that, if the emergency should ever arise, her living-room was large enough to throw a Governor's ball. McGavock was angered and astonished at the bizarre flaunting of so much money. The family portraits on the wall of cavaliers in satin and ladies with powdered wigs had all been turned out by the same hand—doubtless in some Chicago studio—and the shellac was hardly dry on their surfaces. The rose and cobalt pendeloques of the cut-crystal chandeliers swinging on their gold links, from the baroque ceiling tossed dazzling, prismatic light on the taut group. McGavock pointed a blunt thumb at an over-size, Circassian walnut concert piano. "I'm thinking," he said pensively, "that that little piece of furniture alone must have cost ten thousand cases of canned oysters!"

Everyone ignored him. Wynne Preston, her dainty transparent pumps scuffing the rich, deep rug nap, came forward to meet him. She stretched out a shapely arm. "Thank goodness you're here. Now we can get this muddle cleared up."

McGavock put his hands in his coat pockets, refused her handshake. He announced: "It's not me, it's Sheriff Sackett who's the law in this county. I'm just a ringside spectator."

They applauded him like a claque. Tatum declared emphatically: "You're too modest by far. You're a great detective. You found my dog, didn't you?"

Preston gave him a cordial, brotherly smile. "My uncle is correct. You're a great detective, and, I might add—a gentleman! It's been pleasant knowing you."

Wynne said provocatively: "A spectator learns things!"

"What's come over you?" McGavock demanded. "You're acting as guilty as a tribe of amateur chicken thieves." He turned to the copper-haired girl. "Yes, a spectator does learn things. In about eight minutes Officer Sackett and a friend will drop in. A little chit-chat before his arrival might show profit." He gave it time to sink in. "It's this way," he went on. "There are crimes and crimes. Take a swindle, for instance. The victim generally feels a deeper sense of guilt than the hardened crook that gypped him. It doesn't seem reasonable, but it's true. This brings us to murder, to Darnell Tatum and Abbott. As strange as it may seem, all three of you are affected by these two deaths."

Tatum asked pompously: "Are you inferring that each and every one of us is involved in the tragic demise of my brother? That's preposterous."

McGavock said complacently: "I've made my speech. Juggle it around any way you wish." The doorbell chimes went *glong-glang-gling*. "Here's the high sheriff."

Preston left the room and returned with Sackett and the old schoolteacher. The fat man was poker-faced; he held a folded telegraph flimsy in his hand. Miss Dawson blinked bewilderedly about the room through her steel rimmed spectacles. "Welcome to the wake," McGavock said. "We're just about to count corpses."

"Count corpses?" The sheriff was perplexed. "Abbott and Darnell—that's two."

"Ah! And one to carry makes three." McGavock addressed Tatum pleasantly: "Tatum, I charge you with premeditated murder. I've found the third body. Do you want to make a statement?"

There was a frozen silence.

Wynne whispered: "Now that it's really coming, I don't think I can stand it!"

"This," Preston said lightly, "is my idea of a pleasant party. I've always suspected Uncle Tatum of being a rascal. Isn't he even going to deny it?"

Sprague Tatum was mute with horror.

"It's true," McGavock said to the sheriff. "There's been a killing in your bailiwick that you know nothing about and Sprague's the bully boy that did it. He and his brother Darnell. It was a gory bit of butchering. It explains the brindle dog."

Deadpan, the sheriff said woodenly: "Iff'n it hain't too much trouble, I'd shore like to hear the evidence."

"We're wading in evidence. I place the crime some time ago. Say between the time when Clarissa Tatum Preston died and Preston came to take over. Here's what happened: Sprague and Darnell Tatum laid intricate plans. They lured their victim to the old office out in the yard. The mansion was, in that brief interval, temporarily vacant. They had the premises to themselves. As I was saying, they lured their victim to the old office and knocked him off. My guess is that they beat in his cranium, that's the way Abbott was slain. However they did it, they caused a mess. Stained the floor. Later, just after that as a matter of fact, when Preston and Wynne moved in, Mrs. Preston selected the little office as her pet playhouse. You say your piece now, Mrs. Preston, tell them about the gloves."

She blushed. "You seem to know everything. I used to loaf in the office. There was a funny brown spot on the old floor. One morning there was a new floor. Someone had laid planking during the night. I kept thinking about that ugly brown spot and decided that it was blood—"

"Which it was," McGavock broke in. "You suspected your husband. When you heard I was in town you bought a new pair of gloves and pretended you had found them in the chimney. You wanted me to investigate that angle."

"I was terrified. I was afraid I was married to a murderer—"

"The cadaver?" the sheriff inquired. "What became of—"

"That's the one I mentioned. The third corpse. The one to carry. They had already cemented the inside of the brick kiln up at the furnaces so that it was airtight. They took the corpse up to the ruins and entombed it.

"They had a mighty nice vault up there until Abbott pulled into the scene and began promoting his dogfights. He selected the furnaces as his arena. They had the same attraction for him as they had for the Tatum boys—they were secluded, clandestine. Now, the Tatum boys, after they had entombed their victim, worried about him. Preston, here, informed me that Darnell strolled to the furnaces every evening. Probably to check. They learned that dog fights were being held uncomfortably close to their brick kiln. What to do? The problem was to stop the fights without tipping off their crime."

THE SHERIFF NODDED. "Sprague picked up a mean dog and brought him to town. He knew Abbott would steal him. Then he wrote down to Memphis to get you to come up here and break up the fights."

Tatum pushed his wet lips into a desperate denial. "No. There's nothing to it. You can't prove it."

McGavock summarized. "You didn't have time to rip out the old floor in the office. You laid a new one over the old. I removed the baseboard; the original finishing nails are in the plaster where you raised it. There's the evidence: the bloodspot on the under-planking. Then there's the corpse up in the brick kiln."

Wynne Preston said speculatively: "But is that really proof? I mean there is a corpse and all that but I don't see how you can go before a jury and fasten it on to Uncle Sprague."

Sheriff Sackett said proudly: "Mr. McGavock wouldn't go and say such a thing iff'n he couldn't prove 'er in a court o' law. He must be holding back on us."

"No," McGavock declared. "That's the works, the entire slate. Take Tatum down to jail and drub a confession out of him."

They were all horrified.

"I'm sorry," Preston murmured regretfully. "It looks like stalemate."

McGavock bared his teeth. "Appearances are deceiving. We're just getting started. Sheriff, read us that telegram."

Sheriff Sackett unfolded the yellow paper. "She don't make much sense. Here goes—" He cleared his throat. "It's from that taxidermist, Blakesly Jones, Split Birch, Michigan. She reads thisaway: 'Name Scott Carson. Rarely comes to town. Lives in cabin in hinterlands. Professional guide. Darnell Tatum's favorite in these parts.'"

McGavock nodded. "Thank you, Sheriff. Now one thing more. Miss Melinda, here's the second and last question for you. This morning I observed you hoeing in your garden. What was that vegetable in the end row?"

"English peas."

McGavock said argumentatively: "They looked like just ordinary green peas to me."

Miss Melinda laughed. "That's because you're a Yankee. Yankees call them peas. We Southerners refer to them as English peas. You see we eat a great many kinds of peas here in the South, cow peas, whippoorwill peas, black-eye peas—"

McGavock turned to his host. "O.K., Carson," he said. "The old lady bagged you."

The foppish young man stared at him with cold albuminous eyes. McGavock knew he was facing a hard customer. Carson-Preston said indifferently, "And now it's me, eh?"

"It's been you all along. You're the goldfish in this bowl."

The sheriff groaned. "No second guessing, please, Mr. McGavock! You cain't solve no crime by just standing up and loose-mouthing people! These folks, is fine stock."

"Fine stock? Mebbe so, cattle are out of my line." The detective started to talk; he talked rapidly, lucidly. "Darnell and Sprague Tatum were well acquainted with Roger, their sister's son. They had visited him frequently at his prep schools and college down in Georgia. They recognized him for what he was—doubtless a selfish brat. When Clarissa died here in Halford the brothers hatched up a simple little murder scheme to piece into her estate. The plot was to substitute a conniving impostor for the heir. Darnell as a deer hunter had made many journeys to Michigan. It was only natural they should look there for their phoney facsimile—Darnell's favorite guide, Scott Carson.

"The real Joyce Roger Preston, fresh out of college, was brought to town secretly by the uncles with a great show of friendliness. He was taken to the office and slain. His body was interred in the brick kiln at the furnaces. Carson, here, came to town, was properly identified by the uncles as their nephew, married a local gal to make things look right—and established himself in this big mansion.

"Then the bleeding of the estate started. I imagine it was split three ways—Darnell, Sprague and Carson. The brothers shrewdly pretended a feud."

SHERIFF SACKETT ASKED: "Who kilt Darnell?"

"Carson did. He killed Abbott, too. The brothers were putting too much pressure on him. He figured out a little murder scheme of his own, one to eliminate them both at one whack. Taking advantage of their reputation for mutual bad-friendship, he wrote Sprague a typewritten note, purportedly from Darnell. The idea was to get them together in Sprague's bungalow and make it look like a good old time shooting fray with two bodies. Sprague was wary and hid out in the barn. Carson came prepared. He knocked off Darnell and left a frame—but you wouldn't understand that."

He glared at the circle of hypnotized expressions. "You, Carson," he barked. "You attacked me with a hatchet within the last hour—in the ruins on the hillside. You thumb-gouged me, Indian fashion—you learned that in the north-woods. Last night you took a potshot at me with a crossbow!"

Carson said: "You're singing into your hat. I'm Joyce Roger Preston and Uncle Sprague will swear to it."

"He can swear himself purple in the face. I've got you." McGavock barked: "Uncle Darnell left a little data for me in the grave of Baby Alice. Stuff he figured he might need himself sometime if you got out of control. Among other things, a pair of nose-glasses. A bit of back-tracking will reveal that the genuine Roger Preston had afflicted eyes. What's your answer to that?"

Tatum passed him some sign. Carson whipped out a long barreled, blue steel .38—and Sheriff Sackett shot him through the shoulder. Sprague Tatum threw his hands before his quivering jowls as if he were guarding off an invisible whip. "Be neighborly, Sheriff," he screamed. "Be neighborly!"

McGavock said pleasantly: "That was a quick draw, Brother Sackett."

The sheriff colored modestly. "Hit's a gift. I cain't seem to he'p it."

Wynne Preston eyed the stiff taffeta of her evening gown, twisted an ankle and studied her exotic slippers. "It's been a nice life while it lasted. Now it's back to the cotton patch for me."

McGavock said pointedly: "You're an injured woman. Think it over. They took away your good name, imposed a cruel fraud on you. I don't know how much there's left to the Preston-Tatum estate but I'd say you had a good chance of bending their ears in a lawsuit. If Brother Sackett, here, will testify as a character witness for you."

The sheriff nodded vigorously. "I shore will. She's a sweet, innocent child and her pappy—"

"Candidated for you!"

Why Meddle With Murder?

"Slashers aren't in my line!" protested McGavock—till he heard that a local hotshot was offering four grand for the answer to Larchwell's violent plague of murder. Then the wiry little dick was off like a bloodhound, hot on the trail of the coldest killer who ever plied his grisly trade south of the Mason-Dixon line.

1

Razor Mystery

McGAVOCK WALKED STIFF-LEGGEDLY into the office. There was a note on his desk, waiting for him. It said: *See me immediately. Atherton.* The detective lashed the paper from the desktop, crumpled it into a ball and glared about the room in insensate rage. Mid lunch-hour, the place was deserted but for the janitor's eleven year old son wrestling with a wastebasket. McGavock strode over to the lad, thrust out his chin. "You people can't do this to me! My vacation, started two days ago." He loaded his voice with blistering contempt. "First I get wheedling telephone calls coaxing me to stick around town. Now it gives pressure notes on the desk." He began to storm. "It's peonage. I won't stand for it!"

The kid said: "Hi, Luther. How's for butts on that cork-tip?"

The detective whispered from the corner of his mouth, to nobody: "Catch what I mean. They don't even listen to me. I'm just dross and dregs!" He laid his cigarette casually on a window sill and pushed through the door into the chief's sanctum.

Old Atherton Browne was sprawled in his swivel chair, a silly, maudlin grin on his face. He was almost drooling in bliss.

McGavock smiled sympathetically. "So it's finally happened, senility has actually reached out and grabbed you." He exhibited deep concern. "How does it feel? They tell me you live in a happy dream-world—"

The old man exclaimed: "Congratulate me, Luther. I'm a

McGavock swung his heavy-calibered gun at the trapdoor in the ceiling

great-uncle! Little Maybelle is to be christened this afternoon. My sister's son's daughter. Six weeks old and the living image of me!"

McGavock looked horrified, started to wisecrack, changed

his mind. "Little Maybelle," he echoed savagely. "You phone me out of bed and leave hurry messages on my blotter to gush about—"

The oldster beamed on him fondly. Most people found McGavock a hard man to take. Small, sinewy, tough, he'd worked in every major agency in the country. His coarse black hair was cut in a short pompadour and there was a salting of gray about his temples. He was a genius at getting results but there was a jeering, selfish quality about him that aroused instant animal hostility in strangers. Until he'd hit this Memphis outfit, he'd never had a real berth.

The old man shook his head. "No, son. I didn't summon you in here to gossip about my sweet little grand-niece. Bless her. A job of work has broken for us at Larchwell—a small town over by the Alabama line. I'd like you to handle it. It's a grisly sort of set-up and I can't make heads or tails of it. The village barber can't keep himself in razors. Someone breaks into his shop and steals them. This has happened twice."

"So now I'm a truant officer chasing schoolboys!"

"This isn't schoolboy stuff, Luther. I haven't given you the whole picture yet. Larchwell has had two murders. One night somebody swipes the barber's razors and that very night some Larchwell citizen meets a violent death. Both times it's happened!"

"A *sabreur,* a slasher!" McGavock was curt. "It's not in my line—"

"Not a slasher, son." The chief coughed politely. "You won't let me tell my story. There have been two killings but neither of them have been cuttings. The murders have been shootings, I believe. There's a man out there, a Mr. Dasher Phelps, who is curious about the possible connection between the robberies and the deaths and who informs me on crested stationery that the answer is worth four thousand dollars to him."

McGavock looked bored, almost halfwitted.

"That's the sketchy background," the old man continued. "I received this letter from Phelps with a five hundred dollar retainer and a news clipping. I've given you the gist of the letter. Here's the clipping."

A couple of inches of smudged, smalltown newsprint, it read:

Editor, *Larchwell Clarion*

Dear Sir:

I have written you five times about the inept and disappointing manner in which the local law enforcement is stalled on Larchwell's recent tragic killings. Why are you afraid to publish my letters? When Burt Gleeson, a countryman from the hills, was slain on our fair streets I demanded action. Nothing came of it. What's the matter with the Sheriff's Office, gentlemen? Some weeks later Jobe Allison was done away with in the same violent manner. Again I wrote you denouncing the abominable conditions.

Who is doing this killing?

What connection have these slayings with those barbershop robberies?

Why do you fear to publish my letters?

(signed)

Humanitarian

Editor's Note: Hogwash, Humanitarian! We're not afraid to publish you or anybody else: We've withheld your epistles from print because they have been scurrilous, vicious, non-constructive attacks on our sheriff—who is doing the best he can. If you're so smart, solve these murders yourself!

Across the margin was scribbled: *I intend to. I am Humanitarian. Send me a good manhunter! Dasher Phelps.*

McGavock hitched his shoulders. "I don't want any part of it. You're trying to tempt me. Get Pete Coyle to take it. Pete's the pet around this dump. I don't even have a decent contract with you."

The oldster listened blandly—their contract was a sore-spot between them. McGavock was dynamite—his employers liked what he brought in but didn't want to know too much about his methods. He worked on a special roving commission that the agency could void instantly if things got too hot. "Pete Coyle has his place in the organization," the chief reproved him mildly. "Pete's conservative. As a matter of fact, I can't spare him this afternoon. I'm sending him on a personal mission—"

McGavock gave a nasty laugh. "The cat's out of the bag. Let Pete go to Larchwell. I'll take over this personal mission."

"Fine!" That silly, maudlin look came back over the old man's face. He opened a drawer and laid out a small china platter. In the center of the platter was a picture of a cat on its hind legs with a fiddle tucked under its chin and, off to one side, an anemic cow was leaping over a moon. McGavock flinched. "What is it?"

"It's my baby plate," the old man announced proudly. "I'm presenting it to Maybelle. Pete Coyle is going to deliver it for me. He's to attend the christening, present this plate, and give the child a great big juicy kiss—"

McGavock said coldly: "I'm Larchwell-bound." He left me room with a painful display of dignity, closed the door softly behind him.

When Miss Ollinger, the chief's secretary, returned from lunch she found her employer in a tranquil mood. He picked up the nursery plate, handed it to her. "You can take this home with you tonight," he announced. "I've enjoyed looking at it. Thanks for bringing it down."

The spinster blushed, made a modest gesture with a limp wrist. "I was overcome, I mean I really was, when you asked to see it. My baby plate!" Tears brimmed her eyes. "You're a wonderful boss, Mr. Browne. So considerate of your employees!"

LARCHWELL PROVED TO be a larger town than McGavock had expected to find. It lay in the fertile belly of a succulent valley, low between two spiny mountain ridges. Four nights gone, the first heavy frost of autumn had spread through the uplands and now the cumbersome, circling hills were hanging in a crystallized wildfire of scarlet oak and maple and gum. McGavock stood on the curb and sized things up. Hardly a business building had been added or altered in the last eighty years, all were the same chunky model, their brick faces mellow sienna and umber in the sunlight, their upper stories balconied in ancient, delicate Spanish ironwork. It was four o'clock, the sacred interval of siesta. The pavements were abandoned. McGavock pulled down the corners of his lips. He knew just what sort of place he'd hit. One of those little secluded kingdoms of the deep south, lethargic, amiable—and explosive. "Like a sleepy bobcat," McGavock thought. "It looks so cozy you want to tickle it under the chin. Hah!"

He jaywalked the broad cobbled street, built of up-ended fieldstone in the dim past by slave labor, rounded the court-square, and kneed his traveling bag through a doorway marked simply—and sufficiently—*HOTEL*.

The lobby had the rotted, stale smell of an old trunk, a decrepit electric fan, its blades badly out of alignment, whanged and stuttered from a shelf on the wall, churning the musty air in a futile effort at reinvigorating the atmosphere. A man in neat pongee came out from the murk behind the desk to greet him, there was a cherubic look on the man's face, an expression of having just pulled off something pretty clever. With a start, McGavock suddenly observed that his companion was carrying a big blue steel automatic, a second later the detective realized his error, it wasn't a gun at all, it was a child's toy—a tin water pistol.

The clerk registered his guest, picked up the over-sized gladstone and barrelled it down a murky hall. He bowed McGavock into his room, adjusted the window shades. McGavock flipped him a quarter. The clerk caught it deftly, smiled, said: "Many thanks. I'll see that some needy person gets this." He didn't say it as a reprimand, he said it in a way to intimate that his guest had done a noble thing. McGavock sighed; he knew he was in Dixie.

The clerk made a little curtain speech before he departed. "Welcome to Larchwell. I hope your stay with us is a joyous one. It's only natural that I wonder at your presence in our lovely town, an answer presents itself. I suggest that you're here to investigate the shootings?"

McGavock said: "What on earth are you doing with that squirt-gun?"

"Centipedes—you know, thousand-legged worms. I fill my pistol with insecticide, you can knock them over before they reach a crack and vanish. The building's literally infested with them. In one more year I'll have them under control—I hope."

McGavock eased the panel shut. "Just a touch," he murmured to himself, "to make my stay a joyous one." He clicked the latch, turned to survey his quarters. Something dropped from the ceiling above his head and scampered into a crevice in the floor. A mammoth centipede, as long as his finger, furry and vile. McGavock cursed.

A sly, dogged look settled itself in his jaw muscles. "My vacation, started yesterday—and Atherton well knows it! O.K. I get ten days. Then, according to logic, I must be still on it.

Well, think of that. I will now fit the music to the words." He stripped to shorts and singlet, stretched luxuriously on the bed and closed his eyes. "May the devil take this Dasher Phelps, his razors and his four thousand dollars." He exhaled drowsily. "Boy! This is living!"

Rigid and tense, he stood the ordeal just three minutes. Eight minutes later he was out on the streets in search of his client.

The Dasher Phelps' layout was almost too good to trust. Genuine old southern mansions—general belief to the contrary—are very rare indeed. By far and large, the great majority of Georgian-pillared, formal-hedged super-homes have been built by non-plantation money and are about as *antebellum* as wrist-watches and boxed aspirin. Dasher Phelps' residence had all the earmarks of being the real McCoy. It was big and awkward and rambling. Its owner certainly dwelt in it but for one of only two possible reasons: either he was tied to it by chains of sentimental attachment—or he was too destitute to shift to more comfortable surroundings.

Client Phelps wasn't destitute, a poor man doesn't offer a detective agency a four grand fee to settle an academic point. This customer, McGavock decided, was an old-style, line-of-battle southerner.

McGavock crossed the expansive lawn—once arched with huge shade trees, now desolate with stumps and blighted deadwood—and ascended the steps to the sagging porch. He paused a moment, rattled the screendoor. A harsh, strained voice behind his back whispered: "Git thar fustest with the mostest! Thank you, suh, I don't believe I will. Hurrah for the Bonny Blue Flag!"

McGavock whirled. A gaudy Brazilian parrot was hanging in a cage in the honeysuckle vines. The parrot gave him an arrogant ogle and cut loose with the rebel yell. McGavock said severely: "Don't try to pick an argument with me. I'm on business. Some evening, maybe, when we're both free—"

SUDDENLY THE GREAT oak door swung open and a gentleman was bowing at McGavock. A quick decisive bow— as though someone had touched off a steel-trap. The detective invoiced his patron. Phelps was a small-boned, slender man with frayed coat sleeves, skin-tight trousers and expensive, custom made shoes. One of these lads with a kind of double cranium, he seemed all bulbous forehead, between his hairline and his nose were a couple of scholarly bumps about the size and color of a pair of grapefruit halves. He asked: "Are you the whatchumacallit from Memphis?"

McGavock bared his teeth. "I'm not a whatchumacallit. I'm a detective and, 'tis rumored down the corridors of fame, quite a good one. Don't treat me like your second-best plow mule, I don't like it. This town's been a gripe ever since I hit it. Centipedes, nutty roomclerks with water-pistols—and now you!"

Mr. Phelps got out a gadget, fussed around with it, connected it with his ear. "Please repeat," he ordered austerely. "I'm stone deaf."

McGavock sighed. "Skip it. Yep, I'm your man. McGavock's the name."

Again that quick, jumpy bow. McGavock followed his host into a sunny, sweet-scented parlor.

It was a surprisingly pleasant room. The ceilings were a good twelve feet, a battery of windows along one wall, opened from the top, let in the clean, fresh evening wind from the hills. There was the fragrance of autumn sumac and crushed pine needles. The detective seated himself warily on a fragile antique chair and waited for the curtain to go up.

It went up with a bang. Mr. Phelps posed himself before the sitting detective, reared back on his heels, arranged a blue-veined hand, fan-fashion, at the V of his vest and asked ponderously: "Are you armed, sir?"

"I am," McGavock lied. "Why?"

"Then, sir, prepare to serve your piece!"

"Howzzat?"

"I say be on the alert. Our lives are in jeopardy." He gave out with a fancy devil-may-care laugh. *There's been a murder!*"

McGavock said crossly: "So I've been led to believe. As I understand it, there have been *two*—"

Mr. Phelps looked astounded. "Is that so? I hadn't heard." Comprehension spread over his pinched features. "Oh, you mean those other deaths, those that you came down to investigate. I suppose, after all, they are actually murders. I somehow simply think of them as just killings. Just people, you know." He seemed distraught. "But this is different. This is serious. Finch Wyatt has been murdered!"

McGavock said dramatically: "Don't tell me it's come to that? Who is this Wyatt?"

"Why Finch Wyatt is Finch Wyatt. The person who manages my interests for me. A gentleman of great weight in the community. The sheriff is going to be on a spot this time for sure." He frowned. "I wouldn't want to be around him when he learns of it."

"Do tell!" McGavock's smile was honeyed. "When the sheriff learns of it, eh? Maybe we'd better have a few details on that."

Mr. Phelps nodded vigorously. "That would be in order." He carefully disconnected his ear-phone. "I do this," he explained bluntly, "so you won't interrupt me. I've an antipathy to being cross-examined. Finch's demise is not common knowledge as yet. How then, you ask me impatiently, do I happen to be aware of it? I answer thus: I have only now returned from a visit to his home. Once a week, at this time, I visit him to run over the past week's business. Well, I rapped on his door and got no movement within the house. This puzzled me, he usually greets me on the porch with the offer of a julep. There's a bay window that flanges out onto the porch, I peered in. Finch was lying on the daybed with a paper over his head to keep off flies. I thought at first he was napping. And then I saw the blood. His hand was hanging over the edge of the couch and his index finger was bloody red, as though it had been dipped in vermilion. He'd been murdered!"

"What did you do then?"

"I imagine your next question will be: what did I do then? Well then, sir, I became frightened and, to be perfectly honest about it—I sold out." He reconnected his ear gadget. "It's fortunate you're on hand. Drop the other matter at once and concentrate on Finch Wyatt. Things have taken on a personal, dangerous aspect—"

"Where does this Wyatt live?"

"In the futuristic house." He nicked McGavock out of his chair with a gesture of dismissal. "I'll not keep you any longer. I know you want to be out in town—earning my money."

McGavock burned. "You're right. I'll be wandering along." He got to his feet, added pleasantly, "A word of warning: treat me courteously. A guy that surrounds himself with talking parrots gets an exaggerated idea of his importance. "

Phelps took it with complacent good humor. "We'll get along. To keep the record straight, however, I'll have to pick you up on that parrot statement. Juniper has a malformed syrinx—I've had him examined by ornithologists. He's never uttered a sound since he's been in my possession—and that's been a good many years."

"Well, he's suddenly caught the gift of speech." McGavock put on his hat.

"Impossible. As I already told you, his *pessulus* is entirely inadequate—what makes you insist—"

"Suit yourself." McGavock spread his palms. "But let me tell you this, my friend: you've either got a talking parrot around or your joint is spooked!"

THE COURTHOUSE WAS solid, squat and sedate. It looked out on the cobblestone market-square with the air of a distinguished aristocrat mulling over the halcyon days of a prosperous youth. It had been built a century ago of good English brick, brick which had crossed the Western Ocean to New Orleans to be transhipped, time and again, by steamboat and mule and oxcart, to terminate its wandering journey deep in this fertile hill-locked valley. Chickasaw and Frenchman and Spaniard had lounged on its spacious steps. McGavock sauntered into the cool building, went the full length of a vaulted hallway and entered a door marked *Office of Sheriff*.

A bleary-eyed deputy was lolling with his feet on a battered desk, he had a barlow knife in his hand and was peeling a wart from the ball of his thumb. McGavock exclaimed: "Surgery, eh? Perhaps I'm in the wrong ward. Where's the sheriff?"

The deputy caught a rivulet of snuff, knuckled it back into

the corner of his mouth. "Sheriff's yonder." He pointed over his shoulder. "In cell four."

"In cell four!" McGavock recoiled. "It's mutiny. Wait until the Governor hears of this!"

"Pshaw!" The deputy snickered. "Sheriff's jest a-doctorin'. Go back and see for yorese'f."

The trip back into the cellblock was an interesting one. As far as mankind, the prison was empty, as for dogkind, that was a different matter. Cell one had two hounds, cell two had a setter bitch and a litter of puppies, cell three contained a brace of sleepy beagles. McGavock located Sheriff Jerl Dalton in cell four. He was, as his deputy had stated, doctoring.

The sheriff was seated on the bunk-edge, a redbone foxhound belly-up between his knees. He was running a pair of hand clippers around a wound in the animal's breast. "Durn!" he complained. "Here's gray fox season coming right at me and Sarah had to go and get herself fence-cut!"

McGavock remarked: "Funny-looking prisoners you got in this jailhouse."

"Them ain't prisoners," the sheriff answered seriously. "Them's jest dogs. Hit's cool and clean and comfortable, I keep them here for my friends. Cell one's Parson's coonhounds. Cell two's Lawyer Havely's bitch and her pups. Cell three's—" He broke off and gave McGavock a penetrating stare. "I don't seem to recall seeing you before. Are we acquainted?"

"I'm from Memphis." McGavock was deliberately offensive. "If you haven't heard of me, you will. I've been reading the papers, you boys are kind of falling down on your job. I'm on my vacation. I've decided to clean this town up for you."

Sheriff Dalton went white around his temples.

McGavock continued: "I got a system all my own. It's pure brainwork. I just take a stack of newspaper clippings and a telephone directory and work out a crime by trigonometry. Just like you'd cross-breed cattle. Catch the idea? Well, my statistics tell me that Larchwell is in a bad shape and that some guy named Finch Wyatt is likely to be the next casualty. That's my first tip. Five dollars, please."

A blank look came over the sheriff's leathery face. He said slowly: "I'm fixing to get mad." There was wonderment in his voice. "I ain't been mad for six year!" He laid the foxhound tenderly on the floor. "By gollies, *I am mad.*" His words poured out as cool and clear as spring water. "They've been killings hereabouts and we've been working on 'em but we don't have nothing to go on. Be that as it may, we ain't crying for no help from nare piddler from no city. Get out of my courthouse, you—you," he fumbled for a withering appellation, "you outlander!"

McGavock leered. "You may change your mind. If you need me, I'm at the hotel."

McGAVOCK WAS SYSTEMATICALLY combing the backstreets for the futuristic home of Finch Wyatt—when he ran into the sign. A little oblong of weathered tin staked into a wild, overgrown lawn. It said: *Jobe Allison, Optician.* Jobe Allison, he remembered, had been the killer's second victim. The little frame building, not much bigger than a shack, had an almost magnetic charm about it, an ancient wisteria had pried the gutters from the eaves, bricks were askew at the chimneytop, but something indefinite about it said it housed good-living. He felt an irresistible impulse, said: "I've got to talk to these people. Now. The corpse of Brother Wyatt will have to bear with me."

The brunette that answered his ring was about five-two, was built for appreciation—and had a glint in her eye like the business end of a bolt of lightning. McGavock asked pleasantly: "Am I addressing the master of the house?"

She beckoned him in, directed him wordlessly to a small living-room—and left him. McGavock had just about put together a plausible excuse for his intrusion when a man stalked up to him and said: "Well?"

The man was muscular, in his middle fifties, and had a meaty, phlegmatic face; he was dressed in a voluminous gray serge suit and wore enormous, elastic-sided comfort slippers. McGavock began glibly: "I'm the salesman from the optical supply house. I hate to corner you in your home but I'm pressed for time. Can you give me an order this trip?"

The man surprised him. He said thoughtfully: "Yes, I guess I can. I'm completely out of trocars and canulas. Send me the customary replacements—"

McGavock pretended to make a note. "O.K., Doc! Now, Dr. Allison—I am talking to Dr. Jobe Allison, am I not?"

"You are."

McGavock took it without blinking. "I just wanted to make sure. Someone was saying something about Dr. Allison being murdered. How these tales get started—"

The muscular man gave a great bull-like toss to his head. "You've been correctly informed, sir. There are, or rather *were,* two Dr. Jobe Allisons. I am one, my eighty year old father was the other. My father was brutally slain a few weeks back." He unbuttoned his loose fitting gray serge coat, slipped out of it and held it beneath the light. McGavock thought he'd gone wacky. "Here!" He pointed to a small patch between the shoulder blades. "Here's where the bullet went in—here, in the front, by the heart, is where the bullet came out. He was shot from the rear."

"You're wearing the victim's clothes?"

"Of course. They're my father's. One must be frugal in these times." He indicated the patching between the shoulders. "Nice needlework, don't you think? I learned to sew in the penitentiary. Just got out, by the way, a short time ago. Three years at Nashville for embezzling! I learned to re-bottom a chair, too."

McGavock said queerly: "You embezzle, you serve time and then you come back and take over your father's work in your old home town?"

Dr. Allison nodded. "I seem to catch a faint rasp of sawtooth *r's* in your speech—which suggests that you come from the northland, up beyond the Ohio River. Here in the deep south, we're a bit more tolerant about penal servitude than are our northern neighbors. We feel when we've served our time, we've served it and that's that. Why shouldn't I set up shop in Larchwell? My crime, which I paid for, was embezzlement. I'm a crack optician and my patients realize it!" A sixth sense told McGavock that he was being laughed at, a feeling grew on him that the chubby optician, back of his ponderous wooden face, was howling at him in silent, secret derision.

Dr. Allison escorted the detective to the front door. At the edge of the porch he fired his parting shot. "Maybe we'd better cancel that order for trocars and canulas—if it's all the same to you. Though I must admit it's interesting to hear of an optical supply house that stocks them. They're surgical instruments, you know, used by veterinarians—to relieve the bloat in cattle!"

Why Meddle With Murder? / 185

2

Scene of Crime

THE SUN HAD slipped beyond the distant, muffled hills and almost instantly dusk fell, the intense, smoky dusk of autumn, softening the village in a lavender veil. McGavock stood on the curb before the house of Finch Wyatt and scowled.

When Phelps called the place "futuristic" he used the right word. It was a screwball projection into a nightmarish hallucination. New, shiny, garish, it seemed to say: Larchwell is obsolete but I, Finch Wyatt, am a twentieth century hotshot. The building was sea-green cement, low and bulky, its corners were rounded to semi-cylinders and its roof was as flat as a dance floor. McGavock had seen plenty of *moderne* dwellings that he liked—but he didn't like this one. He stepped up on the narrow concrete ledge that did duty as a porch and peered in at the bay window.

The study was shadowy, impenetrable. The detective touched the door with cautious fingers, it gave inward beneath his touch.

He hesitated a split second, entered the dark hall. He didn't much enjoy the situation.

A quick prowl of the premises revealed six rooms, almost exactly alike: metal door-sills, harsh rough-plaster walls, rubber tiled floors. Convinced that he was alone, McGavock retraced his way to the study.

The way he figured, he had plenty of time. He carried a table lamp leisurely to a corner of the room, set it on the floor, placed his hat over it; the light was diffused, faint, but good enough to work in. The body lay on the daybed—just as Client Phelps had described.

It was a prosperous-looking corpse, glossy riding boots, neatly pressed pants and a nice globular pot-belly. It lay relaxed, the picture of a man who, with a luxurious meal under his belt, stumbles to the nearest couch, pulls a paper over his head and dozes off before the soporific taste of fat fowl and liqueur fades from his mouth.

That was the picture—but for one thing. But for the limp hanging hand and the gory, pendulous finger.

McGavock lifted the newspaper, bit his lip.

Finch Wyatt's throat had been cut from ear to ear. It was a thorough, conscientious job, the body was almost decapitated. The murdered man presented a queer, double-vision effect. The sprawled body seemed to be incidental property, it was the ghastly head with its popping china-blue eyes and flabby, blowzy lips that stole the show. McGavock murmured: "So this is the sort of sportsman I'm up against. Jugulation! At last he's begun to use his cutlery." He ran his palm meditatively against the grain of his chin bristles, bent over and subjected the corpse to a methodical search.

As he went through pocket after pocket, McGavock whistled. The tune he whistled was *The Letter Edged in Black* and his tones were as soft and warm and true as a rosewood flute. He cut off the melody with a snap, said, "I thought so!" triumphantly, and strolled to the lamp in the corner.

He had in his hand an open-end spectacle case which he had

found in Wyatt's breast pocket. Six razors had been jammed into the case. One, a graceful tortoise-handled instrument with a silken, hollow ground edge, was sticky with fresh blood.

A grim smile crawled up McGavock's cheeks, up to the crow's-feet which edged his wise, tired eyes. He took a square of kraft towelling from his wallet, wrapped the bloody razor in it, tucked it away. The remaining razors he restored in their spectacle-case container to Wyatt's pocket. He replaced the newspaper over the dead man's head.

He'd just finished arranging the paper over Finch Wyatt's half-severed head when the smell struck his nostrils.

It was an odor that he recognized as soon as he caught it, recognized but simply couldn't believe. It was the common, ordinary, indisputable smell of *burning toast*. McGavock had lived in too many walk-ups and one-room flats not to spot it for what it was: the pungent, carbonlike aroma of scorching bread.

The image that it conjured up was macabre, fantastic. Someone had slipped in, was sitting alone in the dark kitchen of this slaughterhouse calmly preparing himself a couple of slices of buttered toast!

McGavock shouted "Hey!" and listened intently. There was no responsive sound. He stepped into the hall, clicked on the overhead light. The kitchen was at the rear of the corridor, he could see the filaments of smoke drifting through the archway into the house. McGavock set his jaw, walked hard-heeled into the dark kitchen, snapped on the overhead fluorescent light. The kitchen was empty. He stood frozen in the doorway, tense, taking in the scene.

At first he didn't make it. The toaster, smoking merrily, was on the seat of a chair—pulled over against the wall. Just this toaster with its burning toast and the chair and nothing else.

Then his mind began to function—and things happened fast.

The toaster cord ran up the side of the wall, the transformer for the doorbell had been removed and the toaster was hitched directly on the current circuit of the doorbell! Someone had stood out on the front porch and by the childish device of pushing the doorbell button had set the toast to burning in the kitchen. But why? McGavock asked himself. Just then the hall light went out behind him, three shots cut loose down the tunnel-like corridor—and he knew.

He was being spotted—like a gigged frog.

He slapped off the kitchen light switch, dropped to his hands and knees and crawled down the darkened hallway *toward his attacker*. After the first volley there was silence, the killer was listening, figuring his percentage of success. McGavock transversed a third of the back hall, felt an open door, crawled into a bedroom. Three seconds later he was scrambling noiselessly out the bedroom window.

He dropped onto the spongy earth of a flowerbed—and all hell broke loose in the dark kitchen.

Blast after reverberating blast. The killer was using two guns, systematically cross-sweeping every square inch of the place. McGavock crossed the lawn to the sidewalk, started back to town. He grinned in unabashed self-congratulation. He'd had a close call but quick thinking had saved him.

It was a good trap, well-planned, but it had not snared him. Here's the way it had been laid out: the killer had set his toaster and *jammed the lock on the backdoor*, he'd then hidden in wait for the detective. When the time was propitious, he'd thumbed the doorbell, set off the toaster to lure McGavock back towards the kitchen. The first three blasts in the hallway were potshots to flush McGavock into the locked kitchen—where he could be disposed of at will.

McGavock said carelessly: "Doggone me, anyhow! Why can't I learn to tote a gun like other operatives? I could have had me a red-handed murderer." He didn't seem too bothered over it.

A spicy crispness swept down the valley. A stray wind, with a blustering threat of cold weather to come, rolled dry leaves in the gutter like twists of butcher's paper. McGavock thrust his chin into his cupped shoulder, held his hat to his forehead with the flat of his hand and headed for the hotel and supper. The ripe autumnal tang to the whipping air and the eager excitement of a manhunt gave him a sudden, ungovernable appetite.

He'd been in town only three hours and already he'd been jiggled like a pea in a traffic cop's whistle. Everybody and everything had taken either a verbal or physical poke at him. His client had offered him the old aristocratic rub-down, Dr. Jobe Allison had hoaxed him thumb-to-nose, the clerk at the hotel had placed him as a detective as soon as he laid eyes on him. Even a Brazilian parrot had given him the horse-laugh! This burg, Larchwell, had slapped him around, kept him off balance ever since he'd hit it.

From now on it was going to be a different story. A happy look brightened McGavock's lined face. From now on, he decided, he was grabbing hold of the reins and doing the driving himself. He was going to get the breaks—because he was going to make them.

McGAVOCK BARGED INTO the hotel under a full

head of steam, called, "I'm hungry!" as he passed the desk—
and plumped himself down at the first table he came to in the
dining-room. He was the sole customer, the barnlike chamber
was deserted. His acquaintance of the afternoon, the clerk in
the immaculate pongee, appeared in the doorway behind him
and began to shout. Then started a turbulent drama that struck
McGavock dumb. The clerk yelled: "Eddie! Willie! Jay! Serve
the gentleman!"

A cook and two waiters, dressed in ragged white aprons,
cleanly starched, began a seemingly interminable shuttling
from the swinging door to his table. Food, food, and more
food. All the time the clerk with the cherubic smile stood
by, his heels together, his chest arched—snapping his fingers
impatiently, goading his kitchen staff to a frenzied crescendo.

Abruptly, it was finished. A great vacuum came over the
dining-room.

McGavock gazed in awe at the table before him. There was
a glass of buttermilk and a glass of sweetmilk and a cup of
steaming coffee, there was green-tomato pie and yellow-to-
mato jam and pear butter, there was fried beef heart, hog jowl
and mustard, saddle of rabbit and marble cake. There were five
vegetables and a family-size crockery bowl of golden spoon-
bread. The roomclerk bent over and inspected it. "It's pretty
sorry, isn't it. My apologies. You caught us off guard."

McGavock said gravely: "It'll do until the main meal comes
along. Where have you people been all my life? Sit down, good
friend, and make small talk with me. I don't believe I caught
your name?"

"I'm L.C. Chisholm. That's an initial name; what it means,
I haven't the slightest idea. I've gone through life with folks

calling me Elsie—like a girl. Ah, me." He sat himself fastidiously across the cloth from his guest.

McGavock said offhand: "When I checked in, you asked me if I was in town because of these murders. How'd you guess?"

Mr. L.C. Chisholm pondered the matter. Finally he announced: "This isn't going to please you very much. I hate to tell you, but just this minute you've given yourself away. I take it now that you're a detective come to Larchwell to solve our recent murder epidemic. When I said you'd come to town for the shooting, I wasn't referring to the slayings—I was speaking about the good hunting hereabouts. We rarely see strangers but when they come this time of the year it's usually with game in mind. The dove season is on now, the quail season starts in a few days, as does the deer season. So you're after human quarry?"

McGavock held his answer until he'd polished off the last platter. Mr. Chisholm sat stoically by, watched him reach a state of repletion. McGavock chased a few derelict crumbs of marble cake into a pinch, swallowed them, got out his pipe. "My big mouth gave me away, eh? My boss would love to hear about that!" He got the pipe going. "Maybe it was a lucky break for me at that. If I get anywhere, I'll have to have some inside lowdown. How about it, Chisholm, will you play along with me? I'm warning you it's a risky and ungrateful business, befriending a detective on a homicide case. This town's got a crazy killer and, believe me, he's just beginning to roll. Yowsuh! He's a long way from closing shop!"

Chisholm said carefully: "I don't know as that I'm particularly frightened. I'd like to help you. What's weighing you down?"

"Many things." McGavock got organized. "Let's run right down the list. Where did Dasher Phelps get that parrot? And why?"

Chisholm smiled. "I don't know where he got it but I can pretty well guess why. Parrots are exotic birds. They're rare in the North—but many a southern home, especially the old-timers, has a pet parrot. It's the same way with peacocks. Did you know that there are hundreds and hundreds of pet peacocks roaming the lawns of southern homes?"

"No I didn't." McGavock was perfunctory. "And, I might add, little do I care. Let's not digress. Now, according to my information, the first of Larchwell's slayings was a man named Burt Gleeson. Just who was this Gleeson?"

"Nobody." Mr. Chisholm gave a deprecatory twist to his lip, McGavock read into it all the scorn of the townsman for his rural neighbor. "Gleeson was nobody at all. Just a sharecropping hillman from a settlement back in the timber. From a settlement called Indian Jump. Indian Jump, by the way, gets its name from the old days when an Indian captive jumped over a gulch and made his escape. A good story, eh?"

"Very good. I've heard it all over the country with different characters." McGavock rolled his eyes around the walls. "We're not getting anywhere. Let's try to peel this answer down and leave out all the local history. Here's what I want to know: Who did Jobe Allison, that's the son—the one that's alive now—embezzle from?"

Chisholm was fascinated. "Has Jobe been embezzling?"

"He said that's what they sent him to prison for."

"Prison?"

"Yes, prison. I stopped in at his home. A little brunette opened the door—"

"Miss Nancy, Jobe's sister."

"She asked me in. Up comes Dr. Allison. He tells me he's wearing his old man's suit, that he patched it himself and that he learned to sew when he was in prison for embezzling."

Mr. Chisholm choked. "That's Jobe for you. He's the town's first and foremost funster! Life is just one continuous series of laughs for him. That man would kid a bishop! He's a card! Jobe Allison's never been to prison, he's elder at the church. He is wearing his father's clothes, though that's because he's naturally stingy. He'd skin a flea for its tallow, as the saying goes. Yessir! Good old Jobe."

"Good old Jobe, the funnyman," McGavock repeated icily. He pointed to the far wall of the room. The plaster about a third of the way up the wall was dark, queer looking, this band of discoloration ran around the entire room. "What makes those walls look like that?" McGavock demanded. "I've noticed those marks in about every house I have seen since I arrived."

"Those are watermarks," Chisholm answered absently. "We had a bad flood here two years ago. Now that I've been putty in your hands and let you probe the recesses of my innermost being, I'm going to ask you to do me a very small favor in return."

Now it comes, McGavock thought. He said, "Anything. Anything at all!"

"Stop at the desk on your way out, if you will. I want you to return a book for me to the library. It's overdue. Tomorrow, I'll have to pay three cents on it!" McGavock flared, pursed his lips to curse. Chisholm said pointedly: "The trip will only take a few minutes and should prove definitely instructive."

THE BOOK THAT Mr. Chisholm gave him to return was titled *A Guide to the St. Louis World's Fair,* the volume was moldy, musty, had no paper pocket pasted on the back fly-leaf for a card, had, in fact, never seen the inside of a public library.

The Larchwell Library, McGavock had noticed earlier in the day, was situated on a side street beyond the courthouse. He started for it, got halfway across the cobbles of market-square—and veered from his course. He knew he was being gulled by the roomclerk—and didn't attach any too much importance to the episode. It was vitally important, however, that he pay a spot call to the barbershop and he wasn't sure just when these small town tonsorial parlors shut up for the night.

There was a portentous feel to the air. "Tomorrow," McGavock decided, "it gives a cold snap." The wind had died. McGavock smiled dryly, it was that season of the year, the time of first chill, so eagerly awaited for by farmers—the time known to them as "killing weather." Tomorrow would be cold and clear and fat sows would be dying left and right in secluded barnlots with little twenty-two bullets in their brains. McGavock said bleakly: "Killing weather is right. I've walked into a butcher's carnival."

The barbershop was at the end of a short row of stores and offices. The detective pulled up on the pavement before it, funneled his hands and attempted to peer through the crusted window. No soap. The pane was filmed with the grime of decades. He jerked open the patched screen door, twisted the doorknob and stepped inside. He said: "And the rabbit dwelleth in his warren and the mole in his dark den. Exclamations, second verse, third chapter."

The cubbyhole was filthy, rundown. Slabs of plaster had

fallen from the ceiling leaving exposed a skeleton of lath, the walls here too were watermarked, the floor canted at an angle like a listing deck. A sallow youth in a rumpled barber's smock was washing the back of his neck with the shop towel, he paid McGavock no attention. The only other occupant of the room was a hillman, sitting, elbows on knees, in one of a row of kitchen chairs. He was dressed in faded overalls, carefully ironed, and white shirt and tie. His rough-leather brogans were silvery with stove polish. When this lad comes to town, McGavock observed, he really dogs it. The hillman spoke in friendly argument. "They ain't no book in the bible named Exclamations, Mister. Yo're all sprangled up."

Before McGavock could retort, the boy with the towel put in his oar. "The Mayor's correck, Mister."

McGavock could hardly believe his ears. "The Mayor. *Is this man the Mayor?*"

They had a gentle smile at his expense. The hillman explained. "I come from out in the hills apiece. From a little settlement of scarcely more than five cabins. Fellers in town prank me about it, they call me the Mayor of Indian Jump."

The boy went back to sponging his neck. McGavock said eagerly: "I'm in luck. It so happens I'm writing a history of the county. Indian Jump's historical. I'd like to talk to you a little later in the evening. How about meeting me in the court square in, say, a half hour? There's five bucks in it for you." The hillman grinned, nodded.

The youthful barber said boastfully: "Mister, you see these lumps on my neck that I'm washing? You know what they are? Doc says I got me a genuwine touch of beri-beri."

McGavock agreed. "That, I can readily comprehend. I've

begun to realize I'm deep in the heart of the bury-bury country." He looked horrified. "What am I saying!"

THE LARCHWELL PUBLIC LIBRARY was in a
dwelling; it occupied the parlor of a little ivy-vined cottage.
McGavock strolled up the flag-stone path, entered the open
door. There was the odor of cabbage and bacon. A door at the
left of the hall was open, showing a neatly made bed, a slop
jar, and a vase of gilded cat-tails. There was the sound of wild,
discordant violin strains, and through yet another door, at the
back of the house, McGavock could see a white haired old
man, a little boy with a bright yellow violin, and a music-stand.
The old man was giving the little boy music lessons.

McGavock turned to the right and found himself in the
"library." There were three small bookcases with probably
five hundred volumes on their shelves. McGavock advanced
toward a kidney desk and vacant chair and cleared his throat.
The white haired music teacher appeared from behind a curtain
at the rear and raised his eyebrows. McGavock laid *A Guide
to the St. Louis World's Fair* on the kidney desk and said: "Elsie
Chisholm wants me to return this book for him."

A pair of steel rimmed clip-glasses dangled from the old
man's lapel on one of those buttonlike reels. He whipped out
the chain, like he was casting for a big-mouth bass, levered
the glasses on the bridge of his leonine nose and examined the
book. He nodded, said: "Be good enough to follow me, please."

The librarian-maestro led him behind mildewed portières,
down a flight of steps, into a white-washed, stone-walled cellar.
A girl sat on a three legged stool at a small table. On the
table was a lighted candle in a wine bottle—and a pair of the

biggest, rustiest manacles McGavock ever beheld. The old man mumbled an apologetic phrase and left him.

"I'm Nancy Allison," the girl declared. "Remember me?"

"That I do," McGavock announced vigorously. "How could I ever forget. You're the sister of that fun-loving comic, Dr. Jobe. What's this all about? Do practical jokes run in the family?"

The brunette said simply: "I wanted to consult you."

McGavock stood for a moment, panting. "You wanted to consult me!" Such fury tore through him that it was an effort to articulate. "All this rigmarole because you want to consult me. Secret stuff. Whisperings and plans with Chisholm, more whisperings and plans with the old librarian upstairs, conspiracy in a cellar, you've even got the old melodramatic scenery—a candle in a bottle!" He pointed to the cumbersome handcuffs. "Where did you get the bracelets, and what are they for?"

She remarked calmly: "I borrowed them from the case of relics at city-hall, they're good and strong, they were used on Yankees during the war between the states. I want you to take them and fasten them on Dasher Phelps so all these deaths will stop." She added archly: "You're a detective. Jobe told me how he tricked you into exposing it."

McGavock demanded boorishly: "What about Dasher Phelps? And don't give me any of the clowning your brother puts out."

She began to talk—and McGavock knew she was telling the earnest truth. "Dasher Phelps is my uncle. To understand what I'm going to say, you will have to let me break him down in a character analysis. You have to know precisely what kind of a man he is—"

McGavock put her back in the groove. "We can skip that. I know what kind of a man he is."

"Take the way he got all that wealth," she persisted. She amended hastily: "It was perfectly legal, of course, but Jobe and I, and all the rest of the county, can't help being puzzled. His sister left it to him. She was an invalid, she lived in an upstairs room of that old mansion of his. She never left her bedroom, she could barely leave her bed. Well, last year she died."

"Died and left him a pile of dough, eh?"

"I don't mean that. He didn't kill her. There was nothing suspicious about her death. If he'd wished to eliminate her, he could have done it years ago."

"Then what are you getting at?"

"Her last will and testament. In the entire history of our local courts, we've never seen such a will probated. She left everything to him, as was natural, all her property and cash, every single thing she owned—with the exception of a doorstop."

McGavock asked quietly: "And who did she leave that to?"

The girl's face was taut in the feeble light, terror crept into her eyes. "She didn't leave it to anyone. She kept it. The will said: *I'm leaving all my worldly goods to my brother, Dasher, with the exception of the red carpet-covered brick which I use as a doorstop. This doorstop I'm taking with me into the other world.*"

McGavock scoffed. "An old dame leaves a screwy will so that means the heir should fly around knocking off his fellow townsmen!"

"It's just logic," she said demurely. "It's just common sense—"

A tawny, quick-darting insect scrabbled across the table top, dropped to the floor. McGavock winced, said with loathing: "Another one of those worms! Gah! They turn my stomach!"

"Then you'd better leave town," she warned. "This is a city of centipedes! They came with the flood we had a couple of years ago. They've bred and multiplied in our damp walls and basements until most of us have gotten used to them. They came with the flood like the looter—only he left us, the centipedes stayed."

"The looter?" McGavock was elaborately casual. "What's this about a looter? I don't believe—"

"The looter," she explained with hard distaste, "was a vandal that terrorized us when we were in a state of disorganization. He took advantage of the flood and the chaos it brought to plunder and rob. Goodness knows how many homes and shops he burglarized. He specialized in jewelry and cash. The citizenry tallied up after it was all over. He must have profited by a good many thousands of dollars."

"Who was he?"

She gave a cold laugh. "Wouldn't Larchwell like to know! I think Judge Lynch would try his case." She paused. "He was seen several times, from a distance. He always wore a kind of kimono or woman's wrap-around house dress—but he was a man all right. He climbed and ran like a man."

"Well," McGavock said slowly. "This little interview has been one for the book. I'll doubtless be seeing you again. In the meantime, may I give you some advice?"

She nodded, breathless.

He pointed to the big iron handcuffs. "Never, *never* take a bath with those babies on. They'll pull you down the drain."

Her nostrils dilated in seething anger. "You idiot!" she hissed. "Why do I bother with you!"

LARCHWELL WAS PREPARING for slumber. The rectangle of shops and offices around the court square was fast becoming tomblike under a frosty autumn moon, blue shadows fell along the street, and high above McGavock's head the old slate roofs were glazed in luminous green moonglow. One by one, the show-windows darkened, night-lights, faint and weblike, flickered in the somber depths of the buildings. Merchants were bolting and locking their doors. Bolting and locking and barring, as townsmen had always done, against the thing that walks by night.

The wooden park-benches on the court house lawn were empty. McGavock made the circuit, checked them off. He thought his hillman friend had been overcome with timidity and had shied off. Three times, as he strolled about the grassless lawn, he heard the throaty, sonorous croak of a bullfrog. Then he got it, he turned to the court house, located the mountaineer hunched against a pillar on the broad steps. Your true hillman, he remembered, will sit on anything—a wagon hub, a curbstone, steps—anything in preference to a chair or bench. He feels less formal.

The Mayor of Indian Jump greeted him reprovingly. "You shoulda ketched on the first time I croaked at you. Bullfrogs done buried theyselves in mud for the winter by now." He added bluntly: "Jest what you want of me?"

McGavock knew his man, you'd get nowhere by going fast. He fenced politely, "I'm no weather prophet but I'd say it's going to turn mighty cold. Look at that moon."

The hillman said sententiously: "Warm winters make green graves, my pappy used to say." He pawed around in his mouth, took out his upper plate, produced a scrap of sandpaper and began buffing the denture. "I got new teeth. They hurt fireaceous bad. 'Scuse me while I cut 'em down a little."

"They say you come from back at Indian Jump." McGavock cued him in gently. "Did you know Burt Gleeson?"

"Waal, yes—" The hillman pumiced away at his false teeth. "Certainly-shore. I knowed Burt. You aimin' to put him in that history book of the county you was tellin' me about?"

"No. I'll be honest with you. I'm no author. I'm just a hard-working man like yourself, trying to earn a living." McGavock was grave. "Burt was shot down in cold blood. The same man that killed him, killed old Dr. Jobe Allison. I'm trying to dam this flow of blood. Will you—"

The hillman got to his feet. "I'll just be moseying along. I got eight-ten miles to cover—"

"Maybe I misjudged you," McGavock bit out. "Maybe you hold with murder."

The hillman showed no resentment at the insult. He sat down again. "No, I don't hold with murder," he explained calmly. "And I don't meddle with it, neither." He fought a moment with himself, declared: "Some of us folks out in the timber are mighty pore. We live on little bitsey rock farms. I ain't seen five dollars like you promised me since I don't know when. Right this minute I'm a-wearing a pair of under-drawers of tobacco sacking. A city man like you don't know what five dollars means to a feller like me. All right, brother, you pose the questions and I'll answer them. I only hope I'm doing the righteous thing."

McGavock said, "Burt Gleeson was a neighbor of yours. There are no secrets in the hills. I'll bet my arm you know exactly why he was slain."

The hillman observed soberly: "Let's be orderly about this-yere. Back in the hills we get lawed to death—so I know how to speak an affidavit. My name is Sibley Truelove. I hereby affirm and declare this-yere to be God's truth. I don't know who kilt Burt but I know why it was did. Burt was destroyed because he was messing around in something wrongful." He let that sink in, continued.

"One night I was walking home from town. I took a short cut through Three Ridges Hollow. They's a little log-road that leads into Hawkfork School. It was about eleven o'clock at night, and all of a suddent a big black automobile comes pushing through the scrub at me, down that log-road. I step back in the bushes and let her pass, I cain't make out who's driving but it's someone from Larchwell, shore. Now that gets my curiosity up. Three Ridges Hollow ain't nothing, it's just a hole in the hills with a tumbledown schoolhouse. I go down the trail to see what's what."

McGavock took out five ones, laid them on Truelove's bony knee.

The hillman said: "The schoolhouse was lighted up. Burt Gleeson was standing by the teacher's desk beside a barn lantern. He was holding something to the light, examining it. He must have heered me in the brush, he blowed out the lantern. I made tracks. Burt Gleeson was a mean old man, he'd ate more prison food than you could stow in a silo. He was no man to ketch in no guilty act."

"Guilty? Guilty of what?"

"The way I look at it, he and this feller from town had been robbing graves!"

"Whatever gave you that idea?" McGavock was skeptical.

"The thing he had in his hand when he put out the light. It was a little ladies' watch. One of them old-timey doodads that they used to pin to their shirtwaists. About as big as a two-bit piece with a pin on it. They ain't wore watches like that for thirty-year. It had come off'n some old-timey corpse. They ain't no other answer."

McGavock smiled. "Brother, you've really got the horror-viewpoint. Keep this interview close to your vest." He stood up, stretched the kinks out of his knees. "If we work this right, I'm going to be able to use you. Goodnight."

3

Hot Trail

AFTERWARDS, WHEN McGAVOCK could look back on the case in proper perspective, he saw that it was the new lock on the barbershop that actually tipped the whole business. He fooled with it just two minutes, saw that he couldn't pick it, and realized that if he wished to get into the joint he'd have to make it some other way. In his frustration, he stepped back to the curb to get an over-all picture of the set-up. The short business block was actually one narrow two-story building, at the uptown end was the bank, respectable and in good repair. From the bank to where McGavock stood in the blue shadows, the shops and offices fell progressively into neglect and dilapidation until they climaxed in the pestilent barbershop at their tail-end.

McGavock gave the lock a final examination and grunted. The youth with the beri-beri neck had lost too many razors to suit him, he'd finally taken the lesson to heart and had put out good cash for a good lock. The place was going to be hard to crack.

McGavock's quick eyes flicked attentively back and forth over the brick facing. And he noticed the grill.

It was an antique grill of cast-iron with small, diamond-shaped interspaces. About fifteen inches high by maybe a yard long. It was set around the corner of the building in the end wall—off Main Street. McGavock said pleasantly, "Just what the druggist prescribed! Think of that!"

The grill was low, a foot or so above ground level. McGavock dropped to his hunkers and inspected it. It was held in place by iron pegs set in the sandstone sill. The pegs were loose in their sockets, McGavock lifted them out. "So this is the way he did it." McGavock was astonished at the simplicity of it. "He came here at night with a muffled hammer and tapped the braces until the mortar crumbled. He could take them out and replace them at will. He had his own private entry!" The detective beamed his flash through the aperture, sidled through, and pulled the grill back to position behind him.

The building had no basement. He found himself in that sub-space between the floor-sleepers and the earth, the compartment was about four feet high and appeared to stretch the entire length of the block. He remembered the bank on the corner and wondered if his hunch was all wrong, if, after all, it was just a job of local-boy bank burglary. "It can't be!" he expostulated. "Forget the bank. It won't fit in!"

He swept the ground with his torch, the loose, dry loam was scuffled with footprints. They ran in a little trail about eight feet away from it *and stopped*. The earth about them was unmarked, there were footsteps going and coming—it looked as though the prowler had crawled into the sub-chamber, had gone eight feet, turned around, and returned. McGavock, hunched under the low rafters, gnawed the corner of his lip.

Suddenly it clicked, he turned his head, saw the trapdoor above him.

He shoved on the panel, heaved himself up and through.

He'd landed in the barbershop. In a little lavatory alcove.

It gave him a big grin. "So this is the way we go round the mulberry bush, eh? He didn't use the door at all! Lock the joint with a thousand locks and it won't keep him out." He bunched his handkerchief over his flashlight and checked the furnishings, detail by detail. One thing he was certain of: *his man hadn't come here for razors*—there'd been more important, less obvious reasons for his visits. The razors were necessary to him, perhaps, but were not the essential motive behind his prowling.

It was a brokendown shop, if McGavock had ever seen one. The one-lung barber chair was of a vintage long obsolete, on a packing box along the wall was a miscellany which served as a workshelf and held a cracked coffee mug—with an overworked brush in it, a soiled towel and a gallon of pink hair tonic. The floor was scarred linoleum. The detective glanced at the ceiling.

It was the old traditional small-town barbershop ceiling with the ads and slogans of local tradesmen painted on it, the theory being that tilted back in the chair the customer has no choice but to stare at his competitors' signs. *THE DAWN CAFE, SEE RAWLINGS-REASONABLE UNDERTAKER, THE FAMILY BOOTERIE—WHY PAY MORE?* and so on. One sign completely befuddled him. It seemed to read: *J.B. BLACK—I REAL ESTATE AND I LOANS.*

It took him a minute to work it out. And when he did, he knew he had something.

The sign actually read, *REAL ESTATE AND LOANS.* A crack ran lengthwise through the wide down-stroke of the *R* and *L,* divided them and gave the false effect of preceding each with an *I.* In other words, he was observing another trapdoor, he'd stumbled onto the ancient building's archaic firefighting layout.

McGavock said "Ha!" and strode to a broom closet and found exactly what he'd expected to see: a stepladder, new, spotless.

He dragged the ladder to the center of the linoleum, set it up, and a moment later was through the ceiling into the little room above the shop. It was more of a shaft than a room, it had no door or windows and was boarded the height of the second story. A dozen old buckets were arrayed beneath his torch beam, coils of musty rope hung from iron hooks of the wall. Cross-pieces were nailed on the exposed wall-joists forming a crude but serviceable stairway to the garret. "It's a natural," McGavock decided. "It's safer than a secret passage!" He fingered his upper lip in fierce, concentrated speculation, tried to twist his discovery around so that it made sense. It left him with a skull full of question marks. "Well," he decided, "we shall see what we shall see." He went up the cross-pieces hand-over-hand and climbed into the attic.

AND WHAT AN attic! Long and tent-shaped, it rose from the eaves to the ridgepole and stretched, block-long, from king-post to kingpost, the entire length of the building. A catwalk of loose planks had been laid across the rafters of its unfinished flooring. McGavock began a cautious tour of the stuffy, vaultlike eyrie. Regularly, every fifteen or so feet, an oak panel the size of a card-table top appeared—set flush to the floor. McGavock knew that he was passing over the offices and shops of the building's second story and that, in the old plan of things, these ceiling-vents had been installed as an aid to fire prevention. A bucket-brigade here had access to every second-story room.

He gave the first of the ceiling-vents a careful inspection. It was of thick seasoned hardwood, its hardware, hinges and lock, were on the under side. It seemed perfectly tamper-proof, to a casual eye, nothing short of a sledge hammer could force it.

The fifth ceiling-vent was marked with a scrawled chalk X.

McGavock dropped to his heels, pooled his flash on it—and smiled. That little chalk-marked square of oak explained a dozen things. It was a master key that unlocked a tangle of apparently irrelevant puzzles. It explained, among other things, the razors.

A panel, as McGavock suddenly realized, is simply a sheet of wood set into a groove in a surrounding, heavier frame. This inset board is held in place by a double lip on the frame—much as putty holds a window pane in place. Someone had neatly, and in a craftsmanlike manner, whittled back the upper, or exposed lip of the frame until the panel was cleared. McGavock's man had crawled into the cellar up into the barbershop, had borrowed the barber's razors, had proceeded to the garret and had used the razors to gimmick the ceiling-vent.

In the center of the panel was a lightly driven tack. A knob to lift it. McGavock raised the sheet of wood from its inset, flashed his torch down into the room beneath him. He was looking into an office-workshop. There was a desk and a chair and a waist-high wire mesh railing. McGavock deciphered the reversed letters on the door. They said, *JOBE ALLISON, EYES EXAMINED—WATCHES REPAIRED.*

McGavock nodded approvingly. "It had to be. Our killer is slowly materializing."

On his return journey he paused an instant in the barbershop, unwrapped the bloody razor from the kraft towelling and laid it on the workshelf by the shaving mug and hair tonic. "A grim and gory implement of murder," he decided in beatific appraisement. "The lost sheep returns to its fold." He hesitated a moment in happy conjecture, visualizing the sallow proprietor tomorrow morning when his eyes landed on it. "Say he opens shop at eight. By eight-one it'll be in the hands of the law—which is fitting and proper!" He considered. "I guess I've taken care of everything here. Now a quick swing back to Brother Finch Wyatt's—and then to bed!"

Wyatt's cement house was as dark as a cistern. Pressure on the doorknob revealed that the place had been locked up. It wasn't difficult to reconstruct the sequence of past events. The killer had sprung his trap on McGavock, the shots and the hullabaloo had frightened the neighbors. The sheriff had been informed, had ascended in his glory, carted off the corpse and padlocked the place. The murderer must have had a good ten minutes to make his escape.

McGavock selected a pass-key from his ring, threw the bolt and entered the house *moderne* for the second time in a few hours. He had a vague idea as to what he might find—but he hadn't the slightest notion where it might be hidden.

Starting with the study, and proceeding room by room, he subjected the house to a painstaking, tedious task. It was in the mattress of the living-room couch that he found it. A personal-account ledger. "Wouldn't you know it!" the detective observed. "Here's the guy with a futuristic house and a soggy old-style brain. Hiding stuff in a mattress is about as original and safe as hiding a key under a door mat!"

He examined his find. It was a long, canvas-bound journal. The posting on the front page read:

Oct. 5—Rec'd of The Archangel Gabriel $500
Oct. 29—do $900
Nov. 7—do $1200

Nov. 15—do. $1200

Nov. 27—do. $2500

McGavock said pointedly: "Brother, you tapped the archangel just once too often." He was in the act of closing the ledger when he noticed a folded paper between its leaves. He drew it out. The paper was heavy bond, legal length. The letterhead said: *Office of Sheriff, Larchwell.* The text of the communication ran:

Dear Finch,

It's surely nice of you to go out of your way and offer to help me on that terrible wave of looting we had here a time back when the flood got us, but to tell the truth I've just about give up hope of ever catching the lowdown cur. He didn't leave no clues of no kind. However, if as you say, you think in your sundry business activities round and about town you might run into something sometime, I'll enclose the list of plunder that you asked for. It follows below; in flood-times and such emergencies folks have a lot of cash on hand.

Mrs. R.P. Liggett $120

and cameo brooch val. $75

Bee Grocery. $1832.44

Joe Fisher $40

and diamond ring val. $475

William Collum. $270

And so on. There were many names on the list. The losses in cash alone ran to almost twelve thousand dollars. About halfway down the page, McGavock noticed this item: *Hannah and Dasher Phelps… $93 and small lady's chatelaine watch engraved* *with birds and butterflies.* He refolded the letter, shut the ledger, slid it back into the mattress.

He walked down the hall, clicked on the kitchen lights. It was physically impossible for him to shove off without taking a look at the scene of the recent gun-attack. This driving curiosity gave him the final big surprise of the evening. He was standing stock-legged in the center of the room, gazing at the plaster walls torn by the killer's bullets, when a voice addressed him.

The voice came from a recessed breakfast nook. It whispered: "Git thar fustest with the mostest. Thank you, suh, just about two fingers please. Hurray for the Bonny Blue Flag!"

The gaudy Brazilian parrot ogled him from its perch.

McGavock ambled over, said coaxingly: "Hello, friend. You see murder, eh? You catchum good look-see, eh? Who has been carrying you back and forth from house to house?"

The parrot answered promptly. It said: "I give you Gen'l Andrew Jackson, gentlemen—The Scourge of the Everglades!"

"Very funny, very funny indeed!" McGavock sneered. "You're obstructing justice and you'll live to regret it." He dumped a handful of sunflower seeds into the cage from a box by the sink, gave the bird a pan of fresh water, and stalked from the room.

A FIFTEEN WATT bulb was burning in the hotel lobby. A dollar alarm clock by the register said six minutes after ten and a little much-thumbed card leaning against Mr. Chisholm's inkwell indicated a small tap-bell and advised: *Please Ring if Services are Needed.* A doorkey was lying on the desk with a brief note in the roomclerk's script. The note said: *Mr. McGavock, here's your key. I have retired. Put on plenty of covers. Chisholm.*

McGavock picked up the key as though it were an obnoxious, repulsive thing, remarked aloud: "He just leaves it out here for anyone that might be interested in it. What a hotel, what a town! I wonder if I got any clothes left."

Sheriff Jerl Dalton arose from a lounge chair in the corner. He declared stiffly: "I bin through your belongings, sir. But I can assure you I ain't stole nothing."

McGavock said insolently: "I'm sure you had a warrant?"

"No." The sheriff was slow in speech, cautious, picking each word with care. "No, I didn't have no warrant. But the way it turns out, I did you a favor. There was a big shooting out to Finch Wyatt's a little earlier in the evenin'. Somehow or other I figgered you into it. I come here and went through your valise and found your gun. So that lets you out."

McGavock gave a cutting, I-told-you-so grunt. "We've been over this before—but I'll repeat: you better put a bodyguard around that man Wyatt. I've got a hunch he's in danger."

"He's dead." The sheriff was mildly reproving. "He's deader than a quarter's worth of dogmeat. Neighbors heard guns going off and called me. When I got there I found him with his throat cut. Natcherly comes back to mind my pow-wow with you on the very subject of this late lamented—"

McGavock said: "I confess everything. I stop into the jail and warn you Wyatt's in danger. You laugh me off. So I rush out and knock him off to make my story stick! Pretty smart of me, eh?"

Sheriff Dalton tried to calm him. "Ain't no need to fly off the handle! I ain't accusing you of nothing. Coroner says Wyatt was killed hours before you hit town. Now I know you ain't no lunatic like you claim to be, using arithmetic and telephone books to solve crimes. Dasher Phelps has been around to see me. He's told me all about you. He's been throwing you in my face. He says you're going to solve this case right over my head."

"Well?"

"By doggies, I got a feeling you might do it. You're the most nauseatin', irritatin' feller I ever talked to but you don't fool me one bit. You're wiser than a vixen-fox before a field of hounds. How you figgered Finch Wyatt into this mess beats me. You wouldn't want to inform me on this point, would you?" McGavock suddenly observed the sheriff's eyes, they were red rimmed.

"No," McGavock answered pleasantly. "I don't believe I would." The sheriff's eyes were really troubling him now, he was rubbing them with the heel of his thumb. McGavock had the queasy feeling that he was watching an adult male weep. The little detective said quickly: "How's for you and me working on this business together?"

"That's mighty kind of you. Hit was what I was hopin' for— but I was afeared to." He started to leave, added: "I'll see you in the mornin'."

McGavock asked diffidently: "This Wyatt, it's a blow to you, huh? He was a pal of yours, eh?"

Sheriff Dalton shook his head. "Nope. I despised him, he was a hateful man—along the lines of you."

"Then why the red eyelids?"

"I'm sleepy," the sheriff exclaimed indignantly. "Look at that clock! Hit's durn nigh a quarter after ten!"

4

Interview By Surprise

IN THE MORNING it was brisk and golden and sweet. McGavock, waking, had the faint memory of an interval of icy chill at dawn. The two hooked throw-rugs on the bed told him that sometime during the night he'd groped around the room for more cover. Now, with morning, the cold had mellowed to a gentle, invigorating burr. Autumn sunlight hammered through the wavy window panes in a whirligig of prismatic rose and violet. McGavock reached for a cigarette, said brightly: "This is the day that tells the tale." He lay back on the mammoth bolster, took three lung-filling longshoreman drags, swung to the edge of the bed and laid the soles of his feet on the frosty board floor. "Let us now be up and doing."

The detective caught Mr. Phelps in the act of just finishing his breakfast. The little man with the bulging cranium, garbed in a grotesque magenta dressing-robe, sat at a card table on his vine-hung front porch. He made elaborate pretense at being unaware of McGavock's approach. The detective stood at his client's shoulder, watched him spear a toast crust with sterling silver fork tines and swab an egg-cup, watched him pour coffee from an exquisite, engraved coffee service. Then, theatrically, he swung about, shoved the steaming cup at his guest and gestured toward a chair. "You startled me, sir." Dasher Phelps frizzled his eyebrows. "I'm a deaf old man. I didn't hear you come up the walk. Won't you join me—"

McGavock scoffed. "It's high time you and I got into the same harness. Always when I talk to you, it's horse-feathers." He pointed to the gleaming belly of the silver coffee-pot. The front yard, and the walk and the arching trees were reflected in it in perfect miniature. "You knew I was here. You sat there and saw me come up the walk. In my book, on page thirteen, you're a barefaced liar."

Mr. Phelps struggled in his dressing-robe pocket, he got out his ear gadget, connected it. "Please repeat. I had the strange impression you called me a liar."

McGavock said: "How fantastic!" He brooded for a moment in dark, roiling anger, asked at last: "Who's this Hannah Phelps?"

"Hannah was my invalided sister, sir, who lived with me here. She died recently."

"What's this about a chatelaine watch with birds and butter-flies on it?"

"I'm sure I couldn't tell you. How's our work progressing? I didn't bring you down from Memphis to quiz me about my deceased sister." His blue-veined hand, suspended in mid-reach for the sugar tongs, twitched. "Did you say birds and butterflies? My Redeemer! Where did you ever hear of it? That was stolen from the house by the looter at the time of the flood. Hannah was upstairs in her room—I was out with the rescue squads. The man broke in and took it, he took some money, too—"

McGavock declared pointedly: "Maybe, if things go right, we'll get it back." He flashed the subject into a new channel. "Sheriff Dalton keeps harping to me about some nutty will your sister left. It seems as though she cut you off with noth-ing but a brick doorstop."

"No, no!" Phelps waggled his chin. "You've got it all mixed up. She left me everything she had—except the doorstop. She wanted to take the doorstop with her."

"It's a slick trick," McGavock retorted, "if you can do it. Did she?"

"Don't be indecent. Of course she didn't. It's just where she left it. Upstairs. I stopped the clock, pulled down the blinds and left the room just as it was the second she died."

"Elevate yourself out of that chair," McGavock ordered, "and take me to the old lady's bedroom. And I mean now!"

The key to Hannah Phelps' sitting-bedroom was in the lock. McGavock loitered in the hall while his host entered and prepared the way for him. There was the rattle and snap of blinds being raised on their rollers—and turbulent sunlight tumbled into the somber apartment.

This business of locking up deadrooms always gave McGavock the shivers, and the brilliant sunlight didn't much help. There was a small ash bed with the headboard carved in clusters of fruit, the fruit was dusty. In the corner was a fireplace faced with glazed maroon tile, the tile was dusty. There were three or four red plush chairs and a turkey-red carpet was laid to the baseboards. McGavock walked to the window, observed that he was looking out on a second-story veranda. He pointed at the wall. "What's that room there?"

"That's my study." Phelps was prim. "It was my study, by the way, that was looted."

McGavock said insinuatingly: "Maybe the old lady robbed you. Maybe she got out of bed, walked along the veranda and filched your cash. Easy money, eh? Maybe she swiped her own watch as a blind!"

Phelps was speechless. "That, without doubt, is the lowest, most impudent calumny I've ever heard perpetrated!" He began to quiver.

McGavock guffawed. "I got you with your gadget on that time, didn't I? Forget it. It was just a speculation, there's nothing to it, you can take my word on that."

Phelps said: "Let's tend to business. Look under the bed."

Under the bed a square of carpet had been cut right out of the rug—exposing a square of bare floorboarding. The square was two and a half feet each way. "That's where she got the carpet to cover her brick," Dasher Phelps said. He sounded bewildered. "Why she ever took it right off the floor like that I haven't the slightest idea."

"Neither have I." McGavock was candid. "Where's this much publicized doorstop?"

Phelps bent to the floor, handed it to him. It was covered with carpet all right, and the carpet covering was an exact match for the rug on the floor. McGavock hefted it, turned it over. He became suddenly attentive, carried it to the light. The covering had been sewn with stocking thread, with fine silken thread such as was used to repair sheer feminine hosiery. "Did the old lady wear fancy stockings?" McGavock asked.

"Not fancy, no. But therapeutic. They were thick heavy affairs made of elastic; you see she had varicose veins." He recoiled. "What are you doing? Stop that, sir!"

"I'm ripping these seams." He laid back the stiff fabric. The doorstop contained just a brick. No papers, nothing else. Just an ordinary building brick. "I expected nothing," he explained. "And that's just what we find—nothing." He tossed the brick on the bed. "Finish your interrupted breakfast. I've got to see a man about some scratches on the back of a chair."

IT WAS SATURDAY and by the time McGavock returned to the business section Larchwell was beginning to hum with its weekly fair-day atmosphere. Every Saturday in Larchwell, summer and winter, was a day of fiesta, a day of gun-swapping, merchandising, street-corner debating and general all around goodfellowship seasoned with a dash of good, hard bartering. Hillmen chewing althea twig toothbrushes wandered the streets in slow dignity, searching for friends and acquaintances, apple cheek hill-mothers, frozen-faced and hostile to the eye of the townsman, towed diminutive replicas of their elders—little boys in overalls, little girls in sunbonnets—along the crowded pavements. Here, a farmer had taken a circle-saw out to the sidewalk to examine its steel, there, an old beldame struggled with a crate of chickens to pay her church tithe. On the cobblestones before the courthouse, an itinerant performer had rolled out a wagon wheel and was doing handstands and trick spins for the entertainment of a knot of idlers.

The laughs and catcalls and merriment were wine to McGavock's blood. "If I was half-bright," he decided, "I'd buy me a cottage here and settle down. These people have plenty that I'm short on."

The barber with the beri-beri was standing in his doorway telling and retelling to a constantly shifting audience the amazing story of how he found a bloody razor on his workshelf when he opened shop.

McGavock located an entranceway just beyond the bank and ascended creaking stairs. He sauntered along the second-story hallway until he came to a glass which said: *JOBE ALLISON, EYES EXAMINED — WATCHES REPAIRED.* A little bell tingled as he opened the door.

Dr. Jobe Allison, dressed in his baggy corpse-suit, was tilted back with his feet on his desk, playing with a piece of string, making a cat's-cradle. He got up hurriedly, swung open a gate in the wire-mesh railing and welcomed the detective with a hearty handshake. McGavock was non-plussed.

Dr. Allison blustered. "I'm sitting here boiling in shame for the little prank I played on you last evening and here you walk in—just in time for me to apologize! Of course, if you take the episode in its wider sense, you came into my home misrepresenting yourself, you asked for a drubbing and I administered it. But I don't like to look at it that way. When you simmer the thing right down to the bottom, it adds up to this: you're a detective and you have to make a living. Right?"

"I try to," McGavock said modestly. "But economists claim my standard of existence is pretty low."

"Ha-ha! An excellent sense of humor! Nancy tells me you are here in Larchwell to apprehend the person who murdered my revered father. Right?"

"Yes and no." McGavock nicked his eye overhead. The oak ceiling-vent looked innocently secure, it had big iron hinges and a padlock as large as a calf's heart. "What does that sign on the door mean?"

"This was my father's office. He had that sign put on. He used to repair watches as a sideline. I don't. I wish I could, but I can't—"

McGavock said casually: "When your father died, he must have had jobs on hand. What became of the watches he was working on when he was killed?"

"I returned them to their owners. There were four watches and a clock."

"What did you do with the lady's chatelaine, the little pin-watch with the birds on it?"

"I gave it to Nancy."

"It wasn't yours—how could you give it away?"

Dr. Allison's pudgy face broke into a meaty, unpleasant smile. "You've a sharp, malicious tongue, sir. I didn't steal it—if that's your implication. It was brought in by a hillman named Burt Gleeson a few days before his death. After my father died, when I was straightening up his business, I contacted Mrs. Gleeson. The widow said she had never seen it, her opinion was that her husband must have found it on the highway. I bought it from her—"

McGavock sighed. "It could only have happened in Larch-well." He glowered at the optician. "That watch belongs to the estate of Hannah Phelps. You've been negotiating in stolen property. Report the incident to Sheriff Dalton." Allison was stupefied. McGavock saw he was off balance and pushed his advantage. "Get up out of that chair." Dr. Jobe got up like it was hot. McGavock ran his palm delicately across the top rung of the chair's back. "O.K.," he said. "Sit down." Allison sat. McGavock began sniffing things. He picked up the doctor's steel pen, sniffed it. He sniffed, in order, the pen wiper, the blotter, an old apple core in the ashtray.

The doctor was bug-eyed. "Is that the way a detective works? Is that the way you trailed Gleeson's watch? Do you locate things by sense of smell?"

"I do not," McGavock answered curtly. "I'm just having myself a bit of wholesome fun. I'm a comic."

STANDING ON A street corner, McGavock was listening to two sharecroppers debating as to the proper way of blasting stumps—and proving their points by the prophet Ezekiel—when Sheriff Jerl Dalton came flying out of the mouth of an alley and laid excited hands on him. "Lissen!" The sheriff grabbed him by the elbow and dragged him to the privacy of an empty doorway. "Hit's done blowed up in our face! I've never seed such a case. The more a feller learns, the less he knows!"

"Watch it, Sheriff," McGavock warned. "You're making with the cardiac!"

"We found the razor. The killer left it in the barbershop last night."

"So now he's bringing them back?"

"That ain't the point. The point is: how'd he get in. Lucas, that's the barber, went and had a brand new lock put on his door. I took me a strong reading-glass and gave her the once-over, she hadn't been touched. For a while, it had me confounded. I got to meandering around and durn if I didn't stumble on the way he's been doing it. They's a iron grill at the back of the building that leads to a space under the foundations. Lucas has a trapdoor in his floor, the old-timers cut it there years ago. Well, this razor thief crawls in the grill-hole, comes up in Lucas shop, takes whatever pleases him—and crawls right out again!"

"Congratulations! You've solved the case!"

"I hain't solved nothing and you mighty well know it." Sheriff Dalton was flushed with frustration. "Why should a killer steal six razors when one is more than enough to destroy any man I ever laid eyes on?"

"Maybe he used the other five to practice with." Before Mr.

Dalton could retort, McGavock snapped: "No fooling, Sheriff—you're correct. Things are breaking left and right. I'm in a rush just now—but save an hour or so for me after lunch. I want you to drive me out to Hawkfork School."

Sheriff Dalton asked curiously: "What's a cave got to do with this-here?"

McGavock went suddenly wary. "Who's talking about any cave?"

"You are. Ev'body knows they hain't nothing out to Hawkfork 'cept an ole trivulous cave!"

NANCY ALLISON WAS in the orchard behind the house—feeding her chickens. She was poised in the whipping fall air and to McGavock, coming up the hillside through the sagebloom, it seemed almost that her loose gay-print frock, molded to her body, was a volatile rainbow vapor in the press of the wind. She called to him as he approached. "I'll be through with this in a minute!" Chalky yellow kernels of corn rippled from the red cob beneath the heel of her hand. McGavock took off his hat, to keep it from being blown from him, yelled: "No hurry! Take your time!" A sudden, powerful gust came down out of the distant mountains, caught an old hen from behind, carried her half across the chicken yard—and batted her tail-feathers into an Indian war bonnet.

Miss Allison came up to him laughing. They lounged in the clean grass beneath a gnarled peartree. McGavock announced off-hand: "If you love Chisholm, why don't you marry him?"

Her eyes widened. She tried to answer, gave it up, tried again. "Don't tell me L.C. has been crying on your shoulder!"

"Of course not."

"Then how'd you find out? Nobody knows about it but he and I."

"It's a long story," McGavock declared, "and you wouldn't be interested in the details. I just mentioned it to impress you with my prowess as a detective. Anything and everything is grist for my mill, nothing too large or too small. Now, let's get down to brass tacks. What did you find hidden in that brick doorstop of Dasher Phelps?"

She bent her neck forward, dropped her gleaming black hair over her eyes—flipped it back with a jerk of her head. McGavock grinned, she was stalling. She asked: "What doorstop?" McGavock said: "What doorstop?" He said it simultaneously and sarcastically, so that his words overlay hers.

He went on harshly: "You know what doorstop. The doorstop you were telling me about last night, the one Hannah wanted to take with her to the happy hunting-ground. You're wading out in deep water and heading for a step-off. As a friend of mine was saying the other evening—don't meddle in murder."

She expostulated. "Whatever—"

"You remember what curiosity did to that other cat!" He declared bleakly: "You went to Uncle Dasher's when he was away from home. You slipped up to Hannah's bedroom, cut the stitches on the doorstop and unwrapped it. What did you find?"

"I never heard anything so preposterous!"

"You took something out of it and sewed it up again. You had your pocket-book with you and in your pocketbook you had one of those little sewing kits with tiny spools of stocking thread in it that women carry with them for emergency repairs on their hosiery. For the last time, what did you find?"

She was appalled. "How do you discover these things? You've got to believe me. *There was nothing there. Nothing.* That's why I mentioned it to you last night. It has me completely baffled."

McGavock was convinced. "That leaves us one alternative. Someone pulled the same stunt you did, got there first."

"No," she retorted. "I'd take my oath on it. The doorstop had never been touched. It had the same old half-rotten thread on it that Hannah Phelps sewed it with. The carpet concealed absolutely nothing and that's the way Hannah left it,"

THE LITTLE DETECTIVE swung into the hotel with a wiry, jubilant stride, there were deep grooves at the corners of his lips, signs to anyone who knew him that he was flying the hurricane pennant. He'd been eating his guts out to ask Brer Chisholm just one question, and now he was in position to do it. He was loaded for bear.

The hotel clerk was sucking the oil from a new pen-nib. His cherubic face lit up at the sight of his guest. He saluted McGavock with a cordial wave of his hand. "The top o' the marhin' to yuz!" His Irish dialect was a torture to the eardrums. "I trust, sir, that you rested well?"

"I want to ask you a red-hot question," McGavock said happily. "Where were you about ten o'clock last night?"

Mr. Chisholm smiled. "In bed. In dreamland."

"O.K.," McGavock decided. "We'll shelve it for a second. Last evening at supper I asked you to come in with me and you agreed. All right. Tell me this: What's the business arrangement between the late Wyatt and Dasher Phelps?"

"Mr. Phelps, as I understand it, has various investments. Mr. Wyatt acted as sort of intimate adviser and manager to him.

I wouldn't place too much importance on this relationship. Finch Wyatt was an active and, in my opinion, sinister man. He was quite capable of independent ventures on his own—if you get what I mean."

"I get what you mean," McGavock declared. "Where did you say you were last night?"

"I said I was in bed."

McGavock gave him a predatory, sultry grin. "You and Nancy Allison look upon life and find it beautiful. I know about the small town romance. You want to get hitched but there's a horsefly in the ointment. This is all conjecture on my part but I'd say that Brother Jobe realizes his sister is an A-1 house-keeper and wants to keep a picket fence around her. I'll make a trade with you. If you tell me where you were last night I'll put the squeeze on Allison to release the gal."

Chisholm drew himself up. "I'd rather not discuss Miss Allison, in a public place with a stranger. Permit me to assure you that I—impelled by a logical urge to be helpful—"

"Biological urge, is right!" McGavock jeered. "So you won't deal? I'm sorry to hear it. It looks like I'm going to have to throw the sheriff on you. It won't get me very much but it's my only out."

"The sheriff? Just why—"

"Here's why. You've been double-dealing with me ever since I registered with you. You know a heap more about this dirty mess than an innocent man has on tap. I'm not saying you're guilty of anything catastrophic—I'm just saying that you've got something vital stored back in that noggin of yours—and that you won't loosen up."

Chisholm listened patiently. "To resort to an expression of yours, this sounds suspiciously like *conjecture*."

"Conjecture, my foot! It's fact. When I registered with you and you took me to my room, you asked me if I was here for the shootings. *Shootings* was what you said, in the plural, with an s! Later, at supper you tried to drag out the old red herring and cover up. Shootings means human beings, not wildlife. You wouldn't ask me if I was in Larchwell for the huntings, would you? You knew I was a detective as soon as you lamped me. You had guilty information."

Chisholm's lips moved soundlessly. McGavock spurred him on: "If you're getting that biological urge to tell the truth, I'd advise you to obey the impulse."

"I will," the hotel clerk said quietly. "I believe I will. Actually, I'm no more guilty of anything—than you are. You've got a way of twisting things that makes them seem quite different than what they really are. I knew you were coming to town because Finch Wyatt told me. He dropped in to see me on a bit of confidential business and mentioned it. He said Dasher Phelps was bragging to him how he'd sent to Memphis for you and how you'd clear up these killings. Wyatt thought it was funny. He said that in his judgment you, an outsider, wouldn't even get away from the post."

McGavock eyed him speculatively. "Confidential business with a neo-corpse. Sounds bad, mighty bad."

Chisholm remarked hastily: "Again you're getting the wrong impression. It was a perfectly harmless visit. He wanted me to keep an envelope for him in the hotel safe. A small correspondence envelope that felt like it had three or four new playing cards in it."

"Did he call for this envelope later?"

"He didn't have a chance. He was slain."

"Let's take a look at it."

Chisholm was flustered. "How you get me into these holes, I don't know. One minute it's banter and the next minute you've got me where I have to admit something. How did you know I wasn't here last night? Did you ring the desk bell for service?"

"I pounded heck out of it," McGavock lied. "I was cold, I wanted covers."

"I don't have the envelope," the clerk admitted. "I got to thinking about it there in the safe and got to wondering if it was going to involve me in something unpleasant. So, for Nancy's sake, I decided to get rid of it. I took it out to Wyatt's house—by the way, I saw you from the hedge as you left—and placed it in the mailbox. I knew someone would find it. They did. I went by this morning and it was gone."

"For sweet Nancy's sake, eh?" The veins stood out on McGavock's throat. "Do you realize just what you've done? Wyatt had reason to believe he might be knocked off. He had definite proof of who this party would be, he brought evidence down here and left it with you so that if anything should happen to him you would go scampering to the sheriff with his envelope. He could have put it in the bank but he wanted it back in circulation quickly. You took the thing around and stuck it in his mailbox. Who do you think has it now? I'll give you one guess. Answer: the killer has it!"

Chisholm said mildly: "That's too bad. I did it for Nancy."

McGavock took a couple of cigars from his coat, tossed one on the desk. "No thank you," Chisholm murmured. "They seem to give me a kind of vertigo of late. I used to enjoy them so much but now I hardly know I'm smoking."

McGavock stared sympathetically at the lovesick man. "I

know just how you feel, brother. Everything is lined with mother-of pearl. I've been there myself—for short visits. Well, as the poet sayeth, when a woman is really a woman, a good cigar is a joke. Yowsuh!"

5

Hillmen Are Tough

THE GUN McGAVOCK owned had been built to order
for him, it was designed for heavy duty. It was a .45 belly-
gun with a short, wicked bulldog barrel. It had seen plenty of
service but the detective was funny about it, he didn't want it
around him unless he was really going to use it. He left the
room clerk at the desk, went to his room, fumbled around in his
gladstone until he located it. He thumbed open the cylinder,
inspected the brass shell-butts, snapped it shut—and stowed
it behind his belt buckle. He had a bland hunch that it was
going to see action before the day was done.

He caught a quick lunch—a tepid salmon salad and a limeade—at an old fashioned apothecary's on court square, and met
the sheriff, goosequill toothpick in the corner of his mouth,
coming through the market wagons in the plaza. Wordlessly,
they paraded through the listless noonday crowd to a back-
street hitching lot. "This-yere's my conveyance," the sheriff said
proudly. "I'd like yore jedgment of her."

Sheriff Dalton spoke as though he were discussing a blooded
racehorse. There was nothing in the hitching lot except a
mud-caked Shetland pony and rusty, battered T-Model road-
ster. McGavock said: "It seems a cruel thing for two grown men
to climb on one little under-sized beast. But you're the skipper."

Sheriff Dalton spluttered. "I hain't talkin' about the pony—
I'm referrin' to the car, yonder. How do you like her?"

"This I will say." McGavock was over-polite. "Don't press me for an answer. What's one man's opinion anyway? Have you tried it out since the depression? Will it run?"

It ran, all right—like it had four engines under its hood. It was one of those special remade jobs used in the old days to out-run speed violators. Its dilapidated body was just decoy. It took off like a catapult, somewhere around the thirty mile notch, slammed in and out of a network of alleys and hit the highway clocking about sixty knots. "She's knowed four ways to the county line," the sheriff confided. "Her papers are made out to me personally. She's my platform and if I ever git froze out of office, 'y doggies, I take her with me!"

McGavock started to answer, churning clouds of deep sulphur-colored road dust gagged him. Two miles out of town the sheriff spun the wheel, slewed to a thumping stop before a unpainted country store. He leaned out of the car, called: "Save Miss Lucy a gallon of sorghum!" to an old man sunning himself on the porch, and cut the car off of the pike onto a side trail.

The next three miles were steady ascent, the powerful engine purred up the steep grade, higher and higher into the glory of the autumn hills. Redberry holly and hazel, great clumps of mistletoe matting the gaunt trees with birdnests—and always, above their heads, the canopy of frosted oak leaves, red-gold and waxen, like crisp, chilled flakes of molten metal.

They reached the ridge, struck the old logroad and started the dip. Three more miles of mighty bad going, and they pulled into an eroded clay barnyard. "We'll leave the car here at Mrs. Gleeson's," the sheriff explained. "And take it from here on down by foot."

"Mrs. Burt Gleeson's?"

"That's right. This little settlement is Indian Jump. Hawkfork is down in the holler."

McGavock absorbed the grandeur of the setting. They were on the rim of a precipitous depression; down below him, as though he were looking into a giant cauldron, was the froth and foam of brilliant foliage. The sheriff strolled about twenty paces up the hillside towards a small log cabin, halted a courteous distance from the doorstep. He cleared his throat carefully and yelled: "Hello! Is they anybody home? Hello?"

A woman in calico came out in the dog-run, squinted. "Who is it?"

"Hit's me, Miz' Gleeson," the sheriff said artificially. McGavock noticed that the sheriff was on his best behavior; it's him that's the outlander now, McGavock thought. The sheriff bowed. "If it ain't too much trouble, Miz' Gleeson, may I speak a moment with Shepardson-Beaumont? This is a friendly visit."

Mrs. Gleeson said woodenly: "I'll put it up to Shepardson-Beaumont." She disappeared into the house, returned almost instantly. "Shepardson-Beaumont says to make yorese'ves to home, gentlemen. He'll be right with you. He's stringing a banjo and cain't lay it down jest now." She left them.

McGavock said: "What are we waiting on? Who's holding us up?"

The sheriff was embarrassed. "A feller cain't just start out and poke around, not in this settlement. They take it unfriendly. Here comes our party!"

A little boy came out of the cabin and started down the path toward them. He had his head shaved and wore a cast-off little girl's dress stuffed into the top of his pants—like a shirt. He and McGavock sized each other up, there was an icy veil over his slate-gray suspicious eyes. Hard, McGavock decided, as hard and sharp and mean as a keg of nails—bent nails! McGavock said: "So this is Shepardson-Beaumont. Hi, Shep!"

The sheriff sensed the hostility, tried to act as peacemaker. "This is Mr. McGavock. He's from the city. I'll vouch for him. We want you to take us to the cave, son."

"Talk was going round that you folks was coming up the ridgeroad," the boy said belligerently. "Some of us wondered why."

Without any further word, he started down the hillside through the dense scrub. McGavock and the sheriff followed him.

THEY FOUGHT THEIR way down the sliding shale of a dry creekbed and came out into a small level clearing. In the center of the open space was a shantylike building of rough-sawed planking, a well-bucket on a rotting windlass, and a grapevine swing. "This-yere," the sheriff announced, "is Hawk-fork School." Their mountain-boy guide piloted them around the corner of the shanty, scrambled about twenty feet up the opposite hillside and said hostilely: "There you are."

The mouth of the cave was perfectly concealed from view by two natural dolmens of lapping limestone. McGavock was inside almost before he realized it. The detective had visualized the necessity of crawling through narrow openings, down long dank passageways, on his hands and knees and the layout was a pleasant surprise. Strictly speaking, it wasn't a cave at all, it was actually an eroded cleft in the limestone bluff—shuttered by those great, lapping rocks. The chamber was about twenty feet square and possibly ten feet high, it was well lighted. A small stream as big as a man's finger trickled from a ledge at the back and fell into a deep, black pool. McGavock said enthusiastically: "Now if we just had us a copper worm and a couple of barrels of beer!"

Master Shepardson-Beaumont gave McGavock a quick, intent look, new appraisal crept into his eyes. To the townsman, beer means simply beer—to the hillman moonshiner who has his own terminology, calling a chaser a tracer and charred kegs chartered kegs, the word beer has a peculiar significance: he says "beer" and means whiskey mash. The kid gave a wicked little twisted smile and said brazenly: "You ain't foolin'. I wish I owned me half of the double-back that's been run in this place!"

Sheriff Dalton was flustered at such outlawry being flaunted in his face. He cleared his throat, said, "Harrumph!" and turned austerely to McGavock. "Now, suh, here's yore cave. What's next?"

It was at the bottom of a narrow crevice back of the pool that they found the cache of jewelry.

McGavock was probing the blackness of a crack in the floor when his beam picked out the pillow case. It was lace-fringed, tied about the middle with a piece of cord and appeared to contain small, lumpy objects. McGavock said: "It's yours from here on in, Sheriff."

Sheriff Dalton peered down into the depths. "What is it?" The sack was ten feet or so below ground level, wedged by the tapering sides of the crevice.

"It's the non-negotiable plunder, jewelry and the like, stolen by the looter when you people had the big flood."

"Well, I'll be corrugated!" Sheriff Dalton bent over, peered again. He straightened up, thumbed the little red ball of flesh on the end of his nose. "If them's valuables, I want two witnesses afore I take that-there out." He considered. "Yo're one but little Shepardson-Beaumont here's a minor. Son, would you fan out and pick up some good neighbor?"

McGavock could tell that deep under the kid's deadpan he was plenty excited. The little boy said stolidly: "Why not?"

The kid strolled casually to the cave's entrance, stepped out of sight—and reappeared instantly with a man in tow. Just like that: out and in!

The man was Sibley Truelove, the Mayor of Indian Jump. Gone was his city finery, his stovepolished brogans and white shirt, he was dressed in husky denim work jacket, moccasin boots, and carried a double-bitted axe on his shoulder. He ignored McGavock completely, said: "Hidy, Shurf! I was just cuttin' a little tie-timber when the boy comes up and says—"

McGavock spoke to the mountain-boy. "That's his story, here's mine: you had him waiting in the vicinity. How many other good neighbors are hanging around in the brush?"

The kid grinned impudently. "Jest Mr. Truelove—and he's enough. He's head man in these parts. They ain't nothing he don't know or cain't do."

The sheriff spoke respectfully to the hillman, explained the situation in detail. The Mayor leaned his ax against the side of the cave and waited. McGavock said: "So your name's Truelove. And the boy says there isn't anything you cain't do." He pointed to the crevice. "The stuff's down that crack. Maybe you can conjure it up for us."

There was a twinkle in Truelove's eye. "Mayhap I can!" He

thrust his horny hand into his jacket pocket and produced what looked to McGavock like a small, three inch grapplinghook, three large fish-hooks set back-to-back, with a common shaft—fastened to a shank of strong fishline. "Now, Shurf," Mr. Truelove remark genially "this-here's a treblehook. You're fixin' to inform me hit's illegal to have one so I'll jest beat you to the draw: I know it. I tuck this away from a feller I caught using hit. This feller was trying to feed a starving family but the law's the law."

He turned abruptly away, lowered the hook into the crevice. He swung the line back and forth, the hook caught. The hill-man pulled up the bag.

Sheriff Dalton opened the pillow-case, looked into it. He said: "Great Day!" He passed the open bag about the circle: to McGavock, to Truelove, to little Shepardson-Beaumont. The bag contained a good double handful of jewelry: brooches, cameos, bracelets, watches. Mr. Truelove gazed upon the assortment with polite interest, as though he were running down the table of contents of a new church hymnal, the little mountain-boy looked bored, almost disgusted—but his ears were fiery red with suppressed excitement and expectancy.

"Now looky here," the sheriff declaimed. "You-all witness this." He exhibited a small wire with a split lead button at its end, he twisted the wire about the sack, clamped the button shut. "That's all, gentlemen," he orated. "You kin disperse."

McGavock said: "One thing more. Are there any bullfrogs in this part of the country?"

The little mountain-boy nodded. "Plenty. But they've went and buried themselves for the winter."

McGavock rasped angrily. "Wouldn't you know it! Just my luck. I'd give twenty bucks to hear a bullfrog croak."

Sheriff Dalton, in a burst of comradeship, slapped McGavock on the back and laughed. "Makin' jokes! I never seen the like, I swear!"

The Mayor of Indian Jump picked up his axe, passed through the dappled light of the cave's mouth, disappeared into the brush.

THE DRIVE HOME began in silence. The great sun, slipping down its western arc, hovered a brief instant over the plumed hill crests and vanished. The long, crisscross shadows of tree boles dissolved in gray twilight, by a trick of radiance, the golden leaves above their heads were struck to a final incandescent flash, went suddenly dull and lusterless. At last McGavock spoke. "Tell me about the late Hannah Phelps, Jerl. What kind of a human was she?"

Sheriff Dalton, one hand resting in fond proprietorship on the reclaimed plunder in his lap, was feeling his oats. "Jest a woman, Luther. Jest a pore, sick, crazy woman."

"Just a tattered page from Life's scrapbook, eh?"

"Yo're a strange feller, Luther. One minnit yo're talking as pretty as a preacher and the next yo're actin' like that other thing, like the adversary. Yo're correck. Hannah was a tattered page."

"Well, quit counting votes, take your hand off that pillowcase—and describe her to me."

The sheriff bridled, controlled himself. "First thing comes to mind about her is, of course, them funny photographs she was always takin'. She liked to take roof-top pictures. You see Dasher's house is up on a hill, Hannah could lay there on her bed and see down on half the town. She used to prop herself up with pillows and take pictures with a little ole camera she had. Pictures looked crackbrained to me, flopsided and all, but I heered fellers up North called 'em art and printed 'em in magazines."

McGavock mulled it over. "She amused herself that way. I call that good sense."

"Do you call them valentines good sense?" The sheriff was sardonic. "Jest after the flood she began sending out valentines. I bet she sent out two dozen of 'em—I got five myself. They were handmade valentines and she sent 'em out all times of the year, didn't make no difference what month it was!"

"She sent valentines?"

"That's what I said." Sheriff Dalton paused, continued ponderously: "Some folks think that because I hain't got a hair-trigger mind, I hain't got no mind at all. Now that ain't exactly true. Say they's a bobcat takin' my shoats. I don't grab me a two-barreled gun and rush around in the woods lookin' for him. I sit down in a corner with a chaw of tobacco and figger him out, I think about what kind of a partickilar feller he is and kind of study him out. Then one night he shows up and I'm waiting for him. It costs me a lot of young pigs. *But I get him.*"

A chill went down McGavock's back. He knew suddenly that he'd misjudged his man. He asked: "You mean you know who's doing these murders?"

"I hain't got that far yet. I'm workin' on another problem. For about a year, now, I've been meditatin' on Hannah's will. Take it this way: Hannah is a invalid. She cain't leave her room. She wants to make a doorstop. She has to have rug to cover it so she goes and cuts up the carpet. Ev'body knows about that. Here's what bothers me: *Where did she get the brick?*"

McGavock saw it all now. How strikingly simple *when you remembered the brick!* The envelope that Wyatt left with Chisholm, Wyatt's payments from the Archangel Gabriel, the valentines, the three murders. He said casually: "She must have asked her brother to bring her one."

"I asked Dasher just that," the sheriff retorted. "He says he cain't recall ever supplyin' her with no brick."

"Consider the case solved," McGavock declared quietly. "We've snagged our man." He battled with a few tag-ends, added: "I'll show you the answer tonight—in Hannah Phelps' deathroom. At nine sharp. You bring along Chisholm and Jobe, I'll pick up Nancy Allison. Don't ask me why. We want every-body present." He paused, warned grimly: "And keep a good eye peeled in the meantime. Things are heading up a little too smoothly—I'm not sure I like it."

McGAVOCK HAD SUPPER at the quaint, old-fash-ioned apothecary shop. It was a tough decision to make—the taste of salmon salad had loitered in his back teeth ever since lunch—but the way he saw it, it was the wisest thing to do. Stay out of sight, he decided, off the streets and away from the hotel and give the works a little time to get set. He selected a booth at the rear, behind a big cardboard sign of a man with athlete's foot, and dallied over tepid limeade and salmon croquettes. It was completely dark by the time he paid the suspicious drug-gist and stepped out onto the pavement.

The way he doped it, it would be a good hour and a half before things began to crack. For the first time since he hit town, he had a little leisure on his hands. He started like a homing pigeon for Jobe Allison's cottage, the memory of the optician's colossal rib about the trocars and canulas had seared him for twenty-four hours. "There's something about that lug that gravels me," McGavock observed. "Maybe I'd better have a bit of raillery with him. For business and/or pleasure."

Nancy Allison met him at the door. She seized him by the wrist and almost jujitsued him into the living-room. She was so glad to see him, she was almost off her trolley. She was dressed in coral crepe, with a touch of fluffy gray fur at the throat, and McGavock wondered—as he had wondered so many times before—at the ability of southern girls, even those so far removed from the world of style shops, to garb themselves so electrically. Miss Allison exclaimed: "Whatever did you do to Mr. Chisholm? He proposed!"

McGavock snorted. "Phooey! I'm not here to hold hands. Where's brother Jobe?"

"This is Saturday night. Jobe doesn't come home. He gets a sandwich at the hotel and goes back to the office. I fix him a big supper when he comes home at ten o'clock."

McGavock asked keenly: "How long has this been going on?"

She answered carelessly: "Ever since father died. Why?"

McGavock gave a malicious laugh. "You've had a wonderful time since your father died, haven't you? In a town like Larchwell, Saturday night is the social high-point of the week. What do you do? You stay home and cook meals." He gave her a quick brutal glance. "You say Chisholm proposed. Did you accept?"

She bit her lip. "No, of course not. Jobe needs me. But it was a pleasant experience."

"Well, sister," McGavock said coarsely, "one thing I'm going to do before I leave this town, I'm going to cut your tether and let you run." He exhaled noisily. "Where's that little chatelaine watch, the turnip with the birds and butterflies, your brother told me about?"

"Jobe dropped in for it about an hour ago. He was rather excited."

"Now he's acting sensibly. He took it to the sheriff, eh?"

"No, he didn't. He told me he was taking it back to the office to go over it with a loupe. You've got him all agitated. He thinks the two of you have stumbled onto something important."

McGavock said: "The louse!" He shook his head. "He doesn't know what it's all about but he's trying to chisel in at the climax." He snapped: "Do you wear a coat with that outfit?"

"No."

"Well, let's get going. I want you to hear what I have to say to him."

The rectangle of shops about the court square was caught in that doldrum between suppertime and the first flurry of Saturday night trade. Sidewalk stragglers had vanished. Townsmen were at home at table; here and there, back in alleys and hitching lots, hill-folk in wagons and buggies and surreys ate packed lunches and discussed their day's adventures in non-committal monosyllables.

McGavock ambled across the deserted market place, the girl chop-chopping beside him in her tiny, high-heeled pumps. They turned from the sidewalk into the old office building. McGavock, systematically cautious, halted her in the entranceway, said: "You stay down here. When I'm ready for you to come up, I'll whistle."

He was halfway up the rickety stairway when the shots banged out.

They came from inside Dr. Allison's office. There were five of them and they sounded like one long, rolling roar of muffled thunder.

The next thirty seconds was a scramble of violent action. He heard the girl below him stifle a scream. He started up the steps at a lope, there was the sudden smell of musky perfume and press of warm flesh as she threw him to the wall and passed him. She was in the room ahead of him before he could stop her.

Jobe Allison's head and shoulders lay slumped on his desk-top. His tawny hair was matted with blood. The girl rushed toward her brother, McGavock tripped her, sent her sprawl-ing. He swung his heavy-calibered belly-gun at the trapdoor in the ceiling. The panel was in the act of being eased into place. McGavock could see the tips of four white fingers as the vent closed.

Nancy Allison shrieked: "Don't! Don't shoot!"

McGavock emptied his gun. He went at it methodically laying one slug through the panel and five in a patterned circle about it. He heard the scuffle of feet on the ceiling joist above his head and knew he'd missed. McGavock said calmly: "It's just as good. I want you but I want you alive."

The girl exclaimed frantically: "Let's get up there! Let's get up there and catch him!"

"So now you want to catch him." McGavock replaced his gun. "It would be a waste of time. He's gone with the wind. You can be mighty sure he had a good safe exit all waiting for him. You don't seem too broken-hearted over your brother's death?"

She was plenty brief. "I'm not. Tell me what happened, so I can get the sheriff."

"He wanted that watch—and, by the way, he got it. When

Jobe went to the hotel for his sandwich, our man came in through the office door and secreted himself up there behind the panel. Jobe returned, the slayer shot him, dropped down, got the watch and fled back to his nest."

The girl seemed dazed. "But I think that attic's boarded up. How did he get away?"

"I don't know—but, believe me, I'm going to find out." He hesitated. "Do me a favor? Pop in at Uncle Dasher's about nine, will you, chick?" He turned, left her, walked hard-heeled down the stairs.

He found the answer to the quick escape in the alley back of the building. A long rope dangled down the brick wall. McGavock flashed his torch up the wall-face, a slatted louver-window under the eaves had been removed. He bared his teeth. "I've got him nuts. He's like a white mouse on a treadmill—he's putting out steam—but he's not getting anywhere. He's had his show. Now I'll have mine."

6

Killer Walks In

SIBLEY TRUE LOVE, the Mayor of Indian Jump, was
ensconced in his favorite nook—in a shadowed recess between
the fluted columns on the court-house steps. There was a
harried, faintly hostile air about him as McGavock approached.
McGavock said warmly: "Brother, you've got a smart noodle.
I see you kept our appointment. I wasn't sure, back in the cave,
if you caught my double-talk."

The hillman retorted nervously: "Yep. I caught it."

"What's wrong with you? Are you scared of something?"
McGavock inquired solicitously.

The Mayor laughed hollowly. "I'm scared of ever'thing.
I never see a man like you for stirrin' up things. You got
me sleepin' with kicking-boards on my bed—I'm just that
jumpy."

McGavock grinned. "You haven't seen anything yet. Life is
just beginning for you. I've got you all booked for a big time
tonight." He took out a fold of bills. "Here's fifty dollars. It's
more than I promised you but I'm going to ask you to put on
a little act for me. At nine o'clock sharp I want you to come to
the home of Dasher Phelps and ask to see me. There will be a
crowd of people in the room. I want you to ignore them all and
walk straight over to me. I want you to make out that you're all
hot and bothered. Can do?"

"Guess so."

"One thing more," McGavock amended. "I want you to say something. Just one sentence."

"What's that?"

McGavock told him.

"That's slander," the hillman objected. "If I go sayin' things like that about people, I'll get into trouble."

"I'll back you up." McGavock was curt. "Fifty dollars. All or nothing."

"I'll take hit. And by golly when snow comes and the nights are long I'm gonna get out my old guitar and set in front of the fire and make me up a song about you. They hain't had nothing like you in Larchwell since the big revival meetin' seven year ago."

Dasher Phelps' ramshackle mansion was completely dark. It stood on its desolate, moundlike knob, ominous and sepulchral against an autumn sky of milky clouds. "Luther McG," McGavock muttered angrily. "The Great Detective! He thinks of everything—almost. He plans a big *dénouement* but forgets to tip his client. There's no one home. I'm locked out."

He tried the screendoor, it was unhooked. He gave the broken down frame a series of vicious kicks, called: "Hey!"

A scornful voice behind his back said: "There's a lady present, sir! Watch your language." Came a withering laugh. "Hurrah for the Bonny Blue Flag."

McGavock snarled. "It's you, huh? Old get-thar-fustest-with-the-mostest!"

Dasher Phelps spoke from the tangled vines. "Control your temper, please. I'm preparing to retire and your tone agitates me." He came forward. He was wearing straw slippers, over his skintight trousers he had a much befrogged pajama coat. "Now that I've got the three of us together," McGavock ground out, "I'm going to get this cleared up."

"Tomorrow, please. I'm retiring."

"Hah! That's what you think. But more of that later. First this batty parrot: On my visit here yesterday afternoon, I find him on your front porch; later, he jumps up at Finch Wyatt's. Now he's back again. I thought you claimed he can't talk."

"I said my parrot, Juniper, can't talk. Juniper's upstairs in my study. This is, or was, Mr. Wyatt's bird."

"O.K. Go on from there," encouraged McGavock.

Dasher Phelps was amiable. "Yesterday, after you left, I sauntered out on the porch. I found General Grant hanging in the vines—"

"General Grant? How come—"

"He's a fine bird. When Wyatt bought him he was already named. Well, as I was saying, when I returned from finding Finch's body there was no parrot on the porch, that was why I got you all tangled up in talking about Juniper. When, after you had departed, I discovered General Grant I knew he had come from Wyatt's and that Wyatt had not brought him. Reasoning suggested that the murderer had placed him here to inform the world that I had paid a visit to Wyatt's around the fatal time-period. Someone, it was evident, was attempting to involve me. I waited until night and returned it. I realized this morning that Wyatt's bird would have no one to feed and water it, I made application to the sheriff and he allowed me to offer it temporary shelter."

McGavock listened intently. "So that's it. You've acted a bit outside the law but I can't see there's been any harm done. You don't customarily receive guests in your pajamas, do you?"

"I'm not having any guests tonight. I'm going to bed." He gave the detective the dignified dust-off. "Good evening, sir."

"Good evenin' to you-all."

"Good evening, gentlemen."

Sheriff Jerl Dalton and Mr. Chisholm materialized on the porch steps. Phelps pawed at his neck-line, blurted: "Who is it? Oh. I see." Relief sounded in his voice. "You've caught me a little *deshabillé*. No women-folks, eh? Good evening."

From the path, Nancy Allison called: "Good evening, everyone."

McGavock said dreamily: "Now if we just had some ice cream and cake!"

HANNAH PHELPS' DEATHROOM wasn't any cheerier at night than it had been in the morning. Dasher Phelps, his thin hands clutched about the red china bowl of an ornate kerosene lamp, led the procession through the door. He placed the light on the dresser, the garish pink plush furniture and turkey-red carpet blossomed into being. Phelps exclaimed modestly: "Now if you'll excuse me a moment while I slip on a robe—"

McGavock said petulantly: "You look O.K. the way you are—I'll strip to the waist, myself, if it'll make you shut up." He announced: "Well, good people, Larchwell's splurge of killing is ended. And High Sheriff Dalton solved them."

Dasher Phelps went goggle-eyed. "Not Dalton. He couldn't solve a grade-B chicken theft!"

"That's the impression he gives but it's deceiving." McGavock glared about the circle of fascinated faces. "He solved the puzzle of Miss Hannah's doorstop and when you break that down you've practically solved the works. He asked me this question and I'll put it on to you. Where did the old invalid get her brick? She had to get it somewhere in this room. Where?"

Chisholm volunteered the answer. "There's only one possible place. The fireplace."

It didn't take them long to locate it. The loose tile just under the mantelshelf. Behind the tile was the small oblong hole from which the brick had been taken. Nancy Allison asked curiously: "What does it mean?"

"It means a great deal." McGavock began to lecture. "This is one of the simplest crimes I've ever been up against. It had all the earmarks of being grotesque, fantastic, but actually it's nothing but robbery and murder. The thing that held me up was the doorstop. I kept thinking that the doorstop itself meant something. Actually, it had no significance whatever, it's the hole from which the brick was removed that's the key."

Nancy said brightly: "Do you mind if I sit down? I see this is going to take time."

"To the contrary," McGavock retorted. "We're going to get it over before you could take a headache tablet. Here's the outline of events as they occurred—and please observe how elementary they are. Larchwell has a flood and the state of civic disruption brings a vandal out of his den—a looter. He pillages day and night. One day when, according to Mr. Phelps, my client is out with a rescue squad the thief comes here. He loots the study next door but deliberately stays away from this room—which he knows to quarter an invalid. As I say, he loots the study, comes out on the veranda and climbs down the vines to the ground. He thinks he hasn't been observed. He's wrong. He's not only been observed—he's been photographed! Little

Old Hannah, propped up on her pillows has caught him full view as he slid over the veranda rail."

The sheriff was galvanized. "Iff'n Hannah knowed, why didn't she speak out?"

"She did, in a way." McGavock scowled. "But nobody understood. The old lady, bedridden like she was, was afraid to make a public accusation. She gave the negative to Dasher and he posted it to the city to be developed. He was always doing this job for her and thought nothing of it. When the prints came back, she was scared to have them around. She made a hiding place behind the tile. That left her with an extra brick, she cut up the carpet and covered it into a doorstop. The psychology of her cutting up a good carpet diverted attention from the brick. She wanted her secret to come out when she was dead and out of the threat of harm—so she put that goofy clause in her will to attract attention to it. She thought anyone could figure it out."

Mr. Chisholm gaped. "And no one did!"

"Ah, yes, my friend. Someone did figure out Hannah's dodge. Finch Wyatt, like everyone else in the county, was intrigued. He doped it out. He came here and found the photos. With good proof against the looter he then asked Sheriff Dalton for a list of goods stolen. With this list he knew just how much pressure he could put on. He put on a little too much pressure—and the vandal killed him. Mr. Phelps, I want to ask you this—"

Chisholm asked: "Then those were the photos of the criminal Wyatt brought to me to put in my safe. And I turned them right back to the thief?"

"Correct." McGavock looked at his watch. The Mayor of

Indian Jump was ten minutes late. McGavock began to sweat. "Now—"

Sheriff Dalton cut in. "How about the slayings, how do they tie in?"

"Very directly. The criminal has his plunder—which divides itself into cash and jewelry. Jewelry, in this small town is impossible to negotiate, it's useless to him. Now there's a small watch in the batch, Hannah's chatelaine, which falls into the hands of a innocent party—Burt Gleeson of Indian Jump. The killer maybe gives it to Gleeson in payment for some trivial obligation. He thinks: There's Gleeson way back there in the hills—no one will ever hear of it. The watch gets out of order." McGavock paused. "It's this watch getting out of order that sets off the fireworks.

"Gleeson brings it into town to get old Dr. Allison to repair it. The looter, learning of it, slays Gleeson to stop his mouth, breaks into the barbershop, steals the razors and tries to cut his way through Dr. Allison's ceiling vent to recover the timepiece. He fails."

Nancy said quietly: "So father had to go next."

"That's right. Your father was the second victim. The killer repeated his attempt to break into the shop. He failed this time too. By the time he finally got in, your brother had taken the watch home with him."

Phelps said pathetically: "To think that Finch Wyatt was engaged in such dishonorable—"

Downstairs the doorbell tinkled. McGavock grinned. "Hold on to your hats. Here comes my runner."

MR. TRUELOVE, McGAVOCK decided, was a mighty poor actor. McGavock had instructed him to act excited, he came in shaking and quivering and rolling his eyes like a high school kid in the dagger scene from Macbeth. It was so badly overdone that it was ludicrous—but it certainly got the audience. Phelps said: "Man! Man! *What's wrong?*" Chisholm was hypnotized, Nancy Allison looked as though she were about to faint. Sheriff Dalton said severely: "Stop that twitchin', suh. What do you want here?"

Truelove crossed the turkey-red carpet, confronted McGavock and exclaimed: "I know who's been doing these-here killings!"

McGavock said cheerfully: "That you do, pal. You speak from the heart."

The hillman was confused. He tried it again. "I know who's been doing these-here killings."

"We heard you the first time."

The Mayor faltered, looked helpless. "Ain't that what you tole me to say?"

"Exactly. I wanted the sheriff to have the pleasure of hearing it from your own lips."

Mr. Truelove looked uneasy. "But hit's just a joke, ain't it?"

"What do you think?" McGavock waved him to the sheriff. "Jerl, here's your man. The looter that terrorized Larchwell during the flood. Three-times killer in this city of centipedes—"

Sheriff Dalton wavered. "Now, Luther, we got to have more than yore say-so on this. You got any proof?"

McGavock spat. "Plenty. This is the boy that's been up to all those tricks. He's a little batty, maybe—he thinks he's the smartest man in the world. He figured he was riding high and out-thinking us, that's why he showed up tonight. He was giving me a big laugh up his sleeve ever since I met him. He's the boy that's been breaking into the barbershop—and here's the way he did it: He went in through the grill under the foundation, up into the shop. From the barbershop he climbed up into the old fire-room. From the fire-room to the attic and from the attic down into Dr. Allison's office. He went back over the course to get out."

The Mayor said woodenly: "Yo're makin' up lies agin me just because I'm a pore feller from the woods."

"You're smart enough to wire an electric toaster to a doorbell," McGavock observed. "But that's your limit." He addressed the sheriff: "How'd you ever muff Hannah's valentines! They were all full of stuff about *true love*, weren't they?"

Sheriff Dalton nodded. "Yessir! They was. Ever' doggone one of 'em!"

The Mayor of Indian Jump began to argue. "If they ain't nobody goin' to stick up fer me, I'll stick up fer myself. You say I climbed down in Dr. Allison's office and *clumb back up!* How could I have did this?"

"You dropped down. You got back up by putting a chair on the desktop."

"Then why didn't nobody see the chair when they come in next morning?"

"He's got you there!" the sheriff opined.

"We're not judging blue ribbon cattle, Jerl," McGavock said darkly. "We're trying to corner a blood-thirsty murderer. I'll tell you how you did it, Mayor, you lowered a cord with a treblehook from the attic—you remember that treblehook you flashed out at the cave this afternoon? You caught the chairback with the hook, swung it out and set it on the floor. There are scratches on the chair to bear me out."

The sheriff demurred. "I cain't do hit, Luther. Not on that. Anybody coulda made them scratches—"

"Laugh this one off," McGavock laced out. "I've got a living witness for you."

Truelove was derisive. "Now hain't that sompin'! Who is this party?"

"The barber," McGavock answered; "I haven't talked to him yet but *he has to be a witness.* He doesn't know it, but he is. It can't be any way else. The barbershop is the pivot to that whole circuit you make to Allison's office. To get through the barbershop ceiling you had to have a ladder. Barbers have no need for ladders. Yet there's a nice new ladder in the barbershop closet. How does this sound: I say that you bought the ladder, took it around to the shop and asked your friend to let you store it there until you got a chance to haul it out to Indian Jump. You probably told him you bought it at a bargain. Just ask the barber, Sheriff, and he'll—"

The hillman whipped out his pistol. The long barrel was just clearing his hip-bone when Mr. Chisholm let loose with a right hook, the gun went spinning, and Truelove, catching the full impact of the blow in his throat, went to his knee. Sheriff Dalton snapped on the handcuffs. Chisholm explained proudly to the room at large: "Carrot juice four times a day and punching bag ten minutes before each meal."

Dasher Phelps spoke ponderously. "Mr. McGavock, I shall, of course, see that your agency gets its stipulated fee. *But*—" He marched up to the sheriff, grasped the officer by the fingers and gave him a windmill handshake. "But first I must apologize to Jerl Dalton. Sheriff, permit me to be the first to congratulate you in solving a sordid and difficult case. Larchwell is indeed honored in having such a man as—"

Nancy Allison was looking at Mr. Chisholm, she was glowing with adulation. She burst out: "L.C., you've saved us all. You've saved us from being murdered. Larchwell can never repay you for this night's work!"

McGavock asked abjectly: "Can anyone tell a stranger when the Memphis train leaves?"

The Turkey Buzzard Blues

Expense was no object to those who wanted law and order brought to the crime-reeking village of Rockton. "I am willing to pay anything up to and including ten dollars if I am completely satisfied with results," was the first indication of the golden harvest waiting to be reaped by McGavock. And when Layton told him expansively, "I'm prepared to pay you twenty-five dollars cold cash if you can prove to me my father was murdered," the private detective knew for certain he was onto something good.

1

Murder Valley

A SOFT SPRING river-wind blew in through the open windows, riffled the papers gently on McGavock's desk. McGavock yawned. The janitor, puttering about the waste basket, straightened, leaned on his broom. "And then," the janitor explained, "after I'd done burnt this here corpse with pine knots, I'd sift the ashes fer little stuff—buttons and teeth and sich. I'd take this little stuff and cram 'er down my ole muzzle-loading shotgun and fire the charge straight up in the air. By golly, whur's your *corpus delicti* now? It's a perfeck crime!"

"The shotgun," McGavock warned. "We've got to dispose of the shotgun. Let's see. You could cut off the barrel with a hacksaw, thread the ends and screw it into your plumbing system somewhere. The gunstock you could whittle into a—"He rolled his eyes. "Sh-h-h! We're being eavesdropped!"

Miss Ollinger, the chief's secretary, drew herself up in affronted dignity. "I'm not interested in your diabolic small-talk." She made a prim, Pekingese mouth at him. "Something very important has broken. Mr. Browne wishes to consult you in his office immediately."

McGavock looked stupid. "Wishes to consult who? Him?" He pointed at the janitor. "Or me?"

"And I'd advise you to hurry."

McGavock got lazily to his feet, sauntered across the room and entered the chief's sanctum.

*The garrote was a slender
thong of green rawhide*

Old man Atherton Browne greeted his ace detective with an expression of abject misery. "They're going to make me retire, Luther," he said in a low whisper. "The doctor tells me I have a mighty bad heart." His ancient cheeks wrinkled in rivulets of self pity. "I'm a gonner!"

McGavock was taken aback. "You retire? In a pig's eye! When is this coming off?"

"Who knows?" The old man was vague. "Now, Luther, you and I are just like father and son. Here's my problem—and it's confidential. If I leave, I'm going to have a look over the staff and select a sort of general manager to take my place." He coughed politely. "You've been much in my mind. I was wondering if—"

"So that's it!" McGavock hooted. "You're trying to sell me a load of goods! I don't catch what you're getting at but I don't want any part of it. Me, your new manager. Haw! Pete Coyle's

the pet around here—and you know it. He's respectable, he shaves three times a day and carries a pocket shoe-shine kit. I'm just riffraff, I don't even have a decent contract with you!"

The oldster studied him with tragic, mucous-rimmed eyes.

McGavock was a small man, wiry and tough. His coarse black hair was cut in a short pompadour and there was a tweedy sprinkling of gray about his temples. He had a taunting, selfish quality about him that aroused instant animal antagonism in total strangers. At some time or other he'd been with about every major agency in the country. A genius at getting results, he was a hard man to take. He'd never felt at home until he'd hit this Memphis outfit.

His employers liked what he brought in but didn't want to know too much about his methods. He worked under a roving license—an agreement that the agency could repudiate if things got too hot. This one-sided arrangement was a constant gripe to him.

He leaned his sinewy shoulders against the wall. "You sent for me," he announced coldly. "Why?"

Atherton Browne sighed. "Something has come our way, son, that has all the earmarks of being dynamite. Something big. And it's going to take real talent to crack it." The old man was benign. "There's a bonus in it for you if you'll handle it."

McGavock was silent, wary.

The oldster produced a cream-colored envelope, slipped out a sheet of folded paper and waved it in the air. McGavock took it wordlessly from his fingers. A note, written in the tiny shaded letters of another era. It read:

Atherton Browne, Detective Agency

Memphis, Tennessee.

Dear Mr. Browne:

As I understand it, you people have commercial policemen for hire. I would like to rent one as I have a situation here which the local law refuses to consider seriously. I've got tramps in my girls' dormitory. Please send me a man to put an end to this irregularity.

I am willing to pay anything up to, and including, ten dollars if I am completely satisfied with your results.

Yours respectfully,

Simon Tetcherall Layton, M.A. Litt.D.

Pres., Layton's Female Academy

Rockton.

McGAVOCK LAID THE paper on the desktop, grinned.

"So this is your dynamite? He pays anything up to ten bucks—and you're going to split me a bonus out of it! Furthermore, that letter's dated three weeks back. What is this? A rib?"

The chief was grave. "No, Luther, it's no rib. I've heard of the Laytons back in Rockton. They're a powerful and wealthy clan. There's big money in this—but we have to earn it. I want you to do down there and, ahem—insinuate yourself into a generous fee."

McGavock was savage. "Not me! You don't catch me fooling around with any girls' dormitory!"

The chief chuckled. "Layton's Academy has been out of existence for thirty years. The old buildings still stand, I believe, but the college passed its vogue and closed its doors at least three decades ago." He became persuasive. "Do what I advise, Luther. Give it a go. I'm a southerner and I know the pulse of these people. Something, a sixth sense, tells me there's something pretty devilish stewing back there in Rockton." He leaned forward. "We may be late already. To be perfectly frank, I smell murder!"

McGavock was impressed in spite of himself. He asked dubiously: "How do you get murder out of—"

"Instinct, Luther. An old man's instinct." The chief was firm.

McGavock faltered. "O.K." He bared his teeth. "But this time you'd better be playing it on the square." He wheeled, slammed out of the room.

Miss Ollinger, from her desk in the corner, cleared her throat self-righteously. "Mr. Browne, I don't wish to appear officious—but I'm afraid I've caught you in a lapse of memory."

The chief smiled evilly. "How so?"

"You showed Mr. McGavock the *old letter*—but you forgot to mention the *new* one, the one we received this morning."

The oldster put on a great display of exasperation. "By Gad, you're right! Oh, well, I guess there's no harm done." He slid a second letter from beneath his blotter pad, clipped on his glasses and reread it:

Atherton Browne, Detective Agency,

Memphis.

Gentlemen:

About three weeks ago my aged father sent you a note requesting the services of a detective. You quite sensibly ignored it. Today, in arranging my father's papers, I came across several drafts of this communication to you.

I am writing you to ask you to take my father's letter out of your files, to destroy it, and to consider the correspondence closed.

I regret to inform you that my father was mentally unwell at the time of the writing and, having taken a turn for the worse in the meantime, has since hanged himself.

Yours truly,

Doxie Layton

Rockton.

"No," the chief repeated. "There's no harm done. Mr. McGavock's an exceptional man, Miss Ollinger. He works much better when he's—er—unburdened with trivia."

THE TOWN OF Rockton, buried in the hill-country, was no cinch to reach by rail. Three times, in the scant hundred miles, McGavock was forced to change trains. He was tired and grimy and irritable when the one-lunged local finally churned its way up the spur track to the dingy depot. The station platform was deserted. McGavock picked up his oversized Gladstone and headed for Main Street and a hotel.

The burg was a lethargic, easy-going Southern community of the type so familiar to him. A little larger, maybe, than the average—he guessed its population around four thousand, a county-seat. The town's business section formed a scattered rectangle, two blocks deep, around court square. Where Main Street faced the courthouse the pavement was roofed by one long, continuous marquee supported by gas pipe stanchions set in the cement curb. It was suppertime and the sidewalks were abandoned. In the purple quiet of the spring evening, hounddogs, slumbering in shadowed entrance-ways, awoke to the sound of his footsteps and stretched—dipping their forelegs at him in formal canine bows. His nostrils caught the woodsmoke scent of kitchen ranges, the faint lemon fragrance of bursting magnolia blooms. This was the sort of town he understood, this was the sort of town he liked.

The hotel was a squat, boxlike building of discolored brick. An ancient sign above the door said: *Simmons House.* McGavock swung his travelling bag across the threshold. The quaint, old-style lobby was fresh and pleasant. The small room was a rotunda in the best classical design, circular and domed, two stories high, and galleried about the second floor was a mahogany railing. A portly, frowzy man in an uncreased black stetson and with cigar ashes on his rumpled vest was piddling with a newspaper behind the desk.

McGavock set down his Gladstone, said: "Am I addressing Mr. Simmons?"

The portly man laid aside his paper. He had a puffy sallow face and protruding, china-blue eyes. He proclaimed ponderously: "Mr. Simmons was killed in eighteen fifty-four hunting buffalo in the Nebraska Territory."

"I hadn't heard." McGavock rocked back on his heels. "Are you the clerk?"

The frowzy man smiled paternally. "I, suh, am Robertus M. Leach. Sometimes referred to as the Honorable. In my impetuous youth I did a short hitch in the Legislature at Nashville. At the present time, however, I am, more or less, a man of leisure. I—"

"Swell. Fine. I want a room. Can you register me?"

The puffy Mr. Leach was overcome with regret. "That I cain't do, suh. Harvey, the gentleman who officiates over this hostelry, is up to the Gipsy Tearoom having himself a coke-and-ammonia. He will no doubt return within the next few hours."

"So soon?" McGavock was sugary. "In that case I'll just sit here on the stair-step and wait for him. No—on second thought, I won't." He ambled toward the door. "I think I'll look over your town."

Mr. Leach, the Honorable, nodded. Suddenly he screwed up his face and called: "Loosahatchie!"

McGavock came to a dead stop. "What say?"

"I hear," Mr. Leach shouted, "that the spring rains have flooded the Loosahatchie River!"

"I'm not surprised." McGavock was polite. "Heavy rains have a way of doing that to rivers. Is it serious?"

"Oh, no. Not serious."

McGavock waggled farewell, stepped out on the sidewalk.

A telephone directory at the corner drugstore said: *Layton, S.T., r 721 Ashwood Ave.* That was his man. A bit of indirect conversation with the garrulous young pharmacist behind the counter gave him pointers on locating Ashwood Avenue.

Number 721 Ashwood was an angular, slate-roofed cottage. There was a scholarly, precise atmosphere about the place. The neat, velvety lawn was enclosed by a low box hedge, the shrubbery at the gate had been trimmed to square pillars surmounted by geometrical spheres. McGavock strolled up the turfed brick walk. The porchlight was on, there was a brass plate on the door: *Dr. Simon Tetcherall Layton, M.A., Litt. D.* There was something else on the door, too—a big, showy funeral wreath.

McGavock glared. "Our client's dead! Wait until old Atherton Browne learns of this!" He clanged the old-fashioned lever bell-pull.

The door was opened by a waspish little fellow with a cut-away chin and droll, squinty eyes. He wore a rose-colored dressing robe, a calabash pipe drooped from the corner of his mouth. He made a fork of his index and second fingers, lifted the pipe from his lips, exclaimed cordially: "A human! Why bless your heart! I'm in the mood for company."

"I want," McGavock announced loftily, "to enter my niece in your female academy."

This struck his host as vastly humorous. "That, friend, will take a bit of doing. Who do you think I am?"

McGavock spat. "You're Doc Layton." He gestured to the name plate. "I can read, can't I?"

The fellow in the dressing room robe grinned. "I'm afraid you're a little twisted. This is Dr. Layton." He touched the wreath with his pipestem. "The late Dr. Layton. I'm Charlie Lusk, his amanuensis and general handyman. Come in and sit down." He stepped back. "You can help me keep the cats away—those rascals."

McGAVOCK STEPPED INSIDE. It was a house of death, all right, and there was just one word for it: spooky. The soft-carpeted hallway with its dull, dark woodwork was illuminated by a single dim night bulb. A rubber plant, a hat rack and a crockery umbrella-stand were lined along the wall. Lusk jerked his thumb toward the parlor. Through partly open sliding doors, the detective could see a casket on sawhorse trestles, could glimpse a mound of musky, odorous lilies and tuberoses. "There he lies," Lusk declared jocularly. "Waiting for tomorrow's festivities. Burial at ten. Would you like to look at him?"

McGavock walked forward, gazed down at the tranquil face of his client. There was nothing extraordinary about the professor—winged collar, shoestring necktie and long silver hair. Nothing extraordinary except his bulbous forehead. "He had a big brain," McGavock observed. "What happened to him?"

"Two days ago he hanged himself in the attic." Lusk's friendly casual voice seemed ghoulish in the hollow, high-ceilinged room. "I myself found him. It gave me quite a start." He arched his eyebrows courteously. "May I pour you a snifter?"

On a card table in the corner of the room was a cut-glass decanter, a high-ball glass and a platter of sandwiches. Charlie Lusk had been having himself a one-man party. McGavock remarked: "You don't appear too cut up over it."

"I'm not." The secretary was amiable. "Why should I be? I'm standing this deathwatch tonight because I'm getting paid for it. The family simply isn't interested. I'm serving Dr. Layton in death just as I served him in life—for good old frogskins. You're obviously a man of the world, you get my point of view."

McGavock was bland. "Yes. I do. What's this about the family not being interested?"

"I was referring to the son, Doxie, and his wife. They're interested in the demise, I guess—they're the ones who inherit." Lusk picked up a hardboiled egg, sprinkled it with salt and pepper. "They just can't be bothered with the functional details of the obsequies and interment. They stay holed up in that big white house of theirs out at the end of Locust Street and let me handle the funeral duties. I swear, they'd have had me embalm the body if they could have gotten away with it. Those people really pinch pennies." He stowed a bite of bread in the side of his mouth, and said: "You can't enroll your niece at the female academy—it's been closed for thirty years."

McGavock looked disappointed. "That's what I get for putting it off!" He paused, asked: "What made the professor hang himself?"

"Just before his suicide he went stark, raving mad."

McGavock looked skeptical. Lusk said breezily: "It's the truth. And how! Living around with him like I did, I saw signs of it every day."

McGavock pursed his lips sententiously. "Old folks are funny."

"Professor Layton wasn't funny—he was downright potty. Stuff like this: a couple of weeks ago, on a warm day, I come into his study. He has a roaring fire going in the fireplace. He shoves a broomstick into the coals, drags it out and stares at it—like he was reading a thermometer! I ask, 'What goes on?' He says, 'Charlie, it's just right, just hot enough.' What do you think he did then?"

"'Tis an engaging tale, indeed," McGavock declared. "What did he do then?"

"He took out his dentures, upper and lower plates, and tossed them on the fire. They were old-timers, made of hard rubber, and they blazed away to a fare-you-well. I was bug-eyed. I said, 'Dr. Layton, why did you do that?' What do you think he answered?"

"I give up."

Charlie Lusk shook his head. "He said that he was tired of masticating with substitutes, that he was going to grow himself a set of the real McCoy—and him eighty years old. He said he was going to do it through sheer will-power! That was the first time I realized he was nuts. Two weeks later he went up in the attic with a piece of clothesline and hanged himself."

McGavock put on his hat. "Well, I'll be wandering along. If you'll see me to the door, I'll let you get back to your wake."

Lusk was reluctant to see him go. The secretary lingered on the front porch, said cheerily: "Thanks for the pleasant visit. It's been a long time since I've talked to a city-man. If you're going to be around town—look me up."

McGavock nodded vigorously: "That I certainly shall."

MAIN STREET WAS coming to life. Already the citizenry was straggling to town from its supper tables. Here and there, a few townsmen in their shirt sleeves and broad-brimmed hats gathered on sidewalk benches and collected in court square to enjoy the gentle spring evening in communion with each other. Little moppets in pigtails and starched calico, and chuckle-heads with shaved craniums galloped, knee-high, up and down the pavements trying out their lungs. Womenfolk were home over their dishpans, later they, too, would appear, in modest, protective groups of twos and threes.

McGavock foraged up and down the side streets, located

a general store that catered to rural trade, and entered. An adenoidal, fuzzy-faced youth was sitting on a nail keg, greasing his brogans with a scrap of bacon rind. He gaped at the detective's approach, showed a mouthful of mossy green teeth, said: "He's to home, doggone him, a-eatin' his way through a mess of hog jowl and hoe-cake."

"Who?"

"The party yo're a-wantin'." The buck went back to his greasing. "I'm jest the boy."

"Oh, come now." McGavock was stern. "That's the wrong psychology. You're breeding an inferiority complex. Hitch your wagon to a star, put your shoulder to the wheel, look at the world through rose-colored glasses—and get me a spool of white darning thread."

The youth got to his feet, lumbered behind the counter. "Thur you are, mister." He laid the item on the glass showcase. "Spools of thread, I kin git. Hit's beans and rice and stuff that has to be weighed out that throws me. Them durn scales shore gives me a wrassle. Oncet—"

"I know just how you feel." McGavock was sympathetic. He turned, waved his hand in the vague direction of court square. "I'm a stranger here. What's that big building I passed, the one with the clock? Is that Dr. Layton's female academy?"

The buck was horrified. "No, sirree! That's we'uns brand new co'thouse! The old academy hain't nothing but a bat-nest down on the river road. Hit's nothing at all! Anything else?"

McGavock walked to the front of the store. There was a display card on the counter and clipped to the card was an assortment of tawdry, imitation pearl necklaces. The printing read: *Genuine Imitation Simulated Pearls—25¢*. McGavock detached a strand from the card, paid the boy. "I'll take these, as well."

The youth considered this a good buy. He said: "Them's as purty as a red shoe, hain't they?"

McGavock nodded. He fastened the necklace around his throat, started for the door, stopped. "How do they look?" He suddenly unclasped them, dropped them into his coat pocket. "I don't believe I'll wear them after all."

The buck was slack-jawed with relief. "That's better, mister," he said earnestly. "Them ain't fer fellers—them's fer gals!"

The river road looped out past the cemetery, descended a shaley grade at the corporation line, and wound its serpentine way into the brush and scrub of the dank, lush bottomlands. It was here, in a fetid saucer-like depression, that McGavock found Dr. Simon Tetcherall Layton's academy for females.

There were three buildings in the clearing—one a squarish two-story affair, and its mate, a slightly larger edifice with a cupola. Gaunt and bulky in the night, they were dismal reflections of the buffeting of time and neglect. "Rot and decay," McGavock muttered. "But oh-so-lovely in the sight of Professor Layton, M.A." The wreck with the sagging cupola, the detective decided, would be the old recitation hall. The squarish building, then, must be the female dormitory. The two structures were set facing each other. Behind the dormitory, at the edge of the brush, was a ramshackle woodhouse. Just these three specter-like relics of another day.

2

The Ghost Strikes

McGAVOCK STARTED ACROSS the spongy swamp-grass, and a light sprang up within the dormitory building.

A soft, shifting light—the beam of a hooded flashlight. The yellow gleam began at the front downstairs and then, progressively, it began a tour of the floor, room after room—a window lighting, then darkening, and the next in succession lighting in its turn.

Someone, McGavock realized grimly, is searching for something. The torch came abruptly to a halt in the last window. And now, McGavock thought, he's found it.

Rapidly and silently, the detective crossed the clearing. He advanced on the old dormitory from the rear. He groped his way along the narrow passage between the woodhouse and the building, circled the corner. His eyes swept the brick facing.

The flashlight lay outside the window, on the window ledge. A big coon-hunter's torch. Its lens was muffled with a bandana. It lay so that its beam was through the grimy window, into the room. McGavock went suddenly taut. He'd been trapped and he knew it—but the realization came too late.

Things began to happen.

Out of the shadowed entrails of the woodshed behind him, an avalanche of flailing arms and sweaty clothes threw itself upon his back—a bestial tornado of frenzied fury. Bubbles of fiery pain burst beneath McGavock's eyelids. In the flash of a split second, he felt his consciousness slipping from him. He was being beaten and kicked in an effort to drag him from his stance, but the black pain in his body was so excruciating that the blows felt as though they were coming from far away—from another world.

Blindly, in a haze of torture, McGavock got his elbow under his chin, and pivoted. He slammed out, backhand, with everything he had. His knuckles sank into soft flesh, there was a jarred grunt. Battling now, entirely in animal reflex, he let loose with both barrels, fists and feet.

And then, suddenly, it was all over. Somehow he was alone, on his hands and knees in the swampgrass, fumbling at his throat. He slipped the noose from his neck.

The garrote was a slender thong of green rawhide. He got stiffly to his feet, tossed the contraption into the weeds. For a long moment, he stood in the silence of the night—regaining his strangled breath.

The deathtrap had been simple and effective. He'd been expected, possibly he'd even been followed. When he'd appeared at the edge of the clearing, his attacker had started laying his bait, had walked down the far side of the building, flashing his light into each window as he passed, creating the illusion that he was prowling around inside. At the last window, he had placed his torch on the sill and hidden himself in the woodshed with his rawhide thong. It was foolproof, it couldn't miss.

McGavock tucked in his shirt, straightened his collar. "And Doc Layton died of strangulation. My, my." He patted his pocket to make sure he hadn't lost his necklace and thread. As vitality crept back into him, he became bull-mad. He gave the old dormitory a venomous, farewell glance. "What's here will have to wait. I want to talk to people. I want to talk to this Doxie Layton. And I mean now!"

Anyway one turned it, McGavock decided, it came out murder. There was too much throttling going on to be anything else. A cruel, sneaking killer was on the loose in Rockton. "I don't know what it's all about," McGavock simmered. "But I'm going to find out. He made one big blunder—and that was when he put the tap on me. I'm going to have this baby's hide if I have to pay the freight myself!"

Charlie Lusk had said that the professor's son, Doxie Layton, lived with his wife in a big white house on Locust Street.

McGavock hit Locust, kept going until he reached the end of the pavement. The house, on a small wooded hillock, was white all right, and plenty big. A showy, many-columned Georgian affair, it was overloaded with verandas and wings and porte-co-chères, like a debutante's wedding cake. McGavock pulled down the corners of his lips in distaste. "Me, I'd rather live in a nice, dark cave." A brass carriage-light was bracketed to the gatepost and a procession of similar lights, winding along the gravelstone drive, lit up the broad lawn. McGavock struck out across the yard, dead center, in a beeline for the porch. He took the porch-steps in a lope, clanged the knocker on its escutcheon.

The Honorable Robertus M. Leach opened the door and bowed him in. McGavock pulled up in the foyer, arms akimbo. Inch by inch, his cold eyes flicked over the ex-politician, took in his bloated dewlaps, the rippled vest with its smudged cigar ashes. "Up at the hotel this evening you were an ex-Senator—" McGavock put a lunatic tremor in his voice. "Now you're

Doxie Layton! A quick change artist, bedad." He recoiled, said imploringly: "Don't tell me you were the corpse I saw in Professor Layton's casket."

The frowzy man waggled his hands and head in violent denial. "Wait a minute, let me get a word in. I was Robertus Leach uptown, I'm Robertus Leach here. Mr. Doxie's in the library."

McGavock followed him down a lavish hallway, glittering in baroque gilt and prismatic chandeliers. Leach paused at an ornate, iron-studded oak door, dipped his shoulder. "After you, suh."

The mansion's library reeked wealth. The luxurious, powder-blue rug had a two inch nap. The walls were pressed leather and the rare colonial furniture gave off a lustrous, shimmering patina. There were alabaster figurines and oriental vases and busts of famous poets—but, as far as McGavock could observe, there were no books in the Layton library. Two easy chairs sat face to face by a cribbage board, on an inlaid taboret. A man leaned forward out of one of these chairs, looked directly into—and through—McGavock. He screwed up his face, asked petulantly: "Who was it, Bobby?"

Mr. Leach shrugged. "Just a person, Doxie. I brought him in."

"Well, take him out."

McGavock flattened his lips, said roughly: "You're Doxie Layton. I'm Lute McGavock, from the Browne agency. About three weeks ago your old man wrote us a letter asking us for a detective. I, my friend, am he."

LAYTON PICKED UP the deck of cards, gave them a dexterous one-handed cut. He was a rugged, handsome man in his middle-fifties, broad-shouldered and lean-flanked. His cheeks and ears were bronzed and weathered. One of these thousand-acre plantation owners, McGavock decided—this man had ridden many a rough mile on horseback. He was one of those strange mixtures of the metropolitan and the rural that you find among the landed elite. His madras shirt and soft flannel coat were right off Park Avenue but there was a white patch of skin at the nape of his neck where his black hair had been hacked off in a country-boy haircut. He said coldly: "I wrote your agency two days ago cancelling my father's request."

"Well, your letter never arrived." Even as he said it, McGavock realized he'd been finagled. There sprang into his mind's eye the vision of old Atherton Browne saying: *It's my sixth sense, Luther. I smell murder.*

Layton smiled frostily. "I sent it and you received it. Please leave."

McGavock controlled himself. He declared woodenly: "Layton, as of this moment, your father lies in his casket, a murdered man. Murder is my trade. I'm ready to pick up from here and go to work for you. What do you say?"

Layton turned his stony face from McGavock, addressed Leach. "Laroux, down at New Orleans, predicts a whacking good year for cotton, Mr. Bobby."

Leach puckered his forehead. "Maybe so, Mr. Doxie, maybe so. If the grass doesn't take it."

McGavock was sugary. "This is a wonderful town, this Rockton, where an old gentleman like Professor Layton can get knocked off and no one bothers about it." He grinned maliciously, weighted his words carefully. "Tell me, Layton, is this ex-politician a personal friend of yours?"

The plantation owner smiled. "What is the man talking about, Mr. Bobby?"

Leach shrugged. "That, I couldn't say, Mr. Doxie. Perhaps, Mr. Doxie—"

McGavock blew up. "Stop giving me that Mister Gallagher-Mister Shean routine." He purpled. "Don't bat me around like I'm a frog in a churn. Say you did write my boss voiding your father's request for services—I didn't know anything about it. I came down here in good faith to help you people out of a jam." He began to shout. "If you don't want to do business with me, O.K., it's up to you. But don't get hoity-toity with me, I can't use it!"

McGavock's voice snipped off in midair. There was a dead silence. Wood-sounds of the spring night came, muted, through the open casements: the shrill purring of tree-frogs, the lonesome ululation of a mating bobcat. Layton rolled a wheat-straw cigarette in tanned, blue-veined hands. "Why," he asked meticulously, "why did you ask me if Mr. Leach, here, is a friend of mine? You see him in my home. You see him playing cards with me."

"You'd play cards with an acquaintance. He'd have to be an intimate friend before you'd let him read your mail."

Leach said: "If you're walking towards town, suh, I'd be delighted to join you."

"Wait until you hear what I have to say—maybe you'll have a change of heart." McGavock went into detail. "You, Layton, showed Leach the note you wrote to us cancelling your father's request for services. You thought your letter would keep us away. Leach is a little foxier. His guess was that it would bring us on the run. He figures out mailing time, decides if I show at all I'll show up today. For some reason, it's important to him to know if a detective is on the job. He checks train schedules from Memphis, knows I'll have to stay at the Simmons House. He's there to give me the onceover when I pull in. He made the error of treating me like a yokel—I'm not. I'm a damn good detective."

Layton studied the fire on his cigarette, his hand was as steady as a rock. He said: "I didn't let Bobby read the letter to you. He was in my office the other morning just as I was finishing it. He was headed for the postoffice and kindly offered to take it along with him. I gave it to him—flap sealed."

The Honorable Robertus M. Leach laughed awkwardly. "Watch yourse'ves, gentlemen, the play is getting a little rough."

"Why horse around?" McGavock was insolent. "You opened the man's letter—why not admit it? You were in the Simmons House, waiting for a stranger from Memphis. When I came in, you thought you had spotted me but you had to make sure. You uncorked your Loosa-hatchie gag. You asked me if the Loosa-hatchie River was flooded by the spring rains. The Loosa-hatchie throws an arc around the Memphis area about twelve miles out of town. To get here on the railroad, I had to cross it. If I'd answered definitely, yes or no, I'd have given myself away." He winked at Layton. "That's just a free-gratis sample of my wares."

Layton's neck corded. He said calmly: "I like the sample. I'll have to have more of same, Mr. McGavock. May I consult you tomorrow morning at your hotel? Thank you." McGavock started for the hall. The frowzy Mr. Leach retrieved his black-thorn walking-stick from the floor by his chair, said: "Good-night, Mr. Doxie, let's not jump to hasty conclusions. Let's sleep on this mare's nest, all of us. As my old grandmother used to say, the morning's wiser than the evening. Mr. McGavock, will you permit me to accompany you as far as—"

Layton's voice was icy. "Goodnight, McGavock. Leach, you stay. I'd like a chat with you."

McGAVOCK HAD A problem and, as he saw it, it was going to prove a tough one. He'd tackled many a case where there was suspicion of homicide, but no body. In this set-up, conditions were reversed, he had the corpse and no one seemed much interested. Sooner or later, he realized, he was going to find himself confronted with a scoffing version of the local law. He decided to take the bull by the horns and get it over with.

The big clock on the courthouse steeple said eight twenty-five, the sidewalk throngs were thinning out, townsfolk were herding their families, heading for home and bed. McGavock crossed the square, ascended the broad steps and entered the courthouse.

It was a new building, smelling of unseasoned plaster, and aromatic varnish. McGavock ambled down the unlevel cement corridor, located a frosted glass door pane marked: *LUDLOW CHILDRESS, Office of Sheriff.* The door was open and McGavock sauntered in.

The room was tidy, efficient-looking. The one window was heavily barred and the gray walls were bare except for a single cartridge calendar depicting a sunset scene of a voluptuous Indian maiden in a birchbark canoe. On the floor, along one wall, was a row of six two-gallon pottery jugs. Sheriff Childress sat behind a shiny, golden oak desk. He was a husky, big-boned man in a pony-skin vest—he had the dewlaps of a bloodhound and there was an expression of apathy on his stolid face. He sat like a man frozen. He watched McGavock breeze in, said tensely through motionless lips: "Take it slow and easy, good friend, for God's sakes. You're a-fixin' to bring back my misery."

McGavock introduced himself, presented his credentials. The sheriff waved the papers aside. "I cain't read no writin' now. I gotta keep a good firm holt on myself. Any minute now, my misery she's due to come back on me."

McGavock said persuasively: "This is water down the old sewer—but I'll make a go of it. Heist yourself up out of that swivel chair and strap on your gun. There's been a murder."

"My gun's already strapped on. I ain't never without it," Sheriff Childress rebuked him. "Now about yore murder, let's reason hit out. Whenever they's been a killing, I always hear about it. I'm sheriff, someone always tells me. Q.E.D. Logic *ad mandamus* tells us they hain't been no murder. If they had been a killing, son, I'd of heered about it." He looked smug.

"Yo're hearing about it now." McGavock was patient. "That's what I'm doing now. I'm trying to tell you—"

"Who, according to you, has been kilt?" The sheriff smiled paternally.

"Simon Tetcherall Layton. And don't laugh."

"I cain't he'p it!" Sheriff Childress grinned. "Old Doc Layton kilt hisself, that ain't no crime. Yo're a stranger, friend. Fellers in town has been pranking you. Hyuh-hyuh-hyuh!" The sheriff rolled back in his chair, closed his eyes and broke into a bellowing guffaw. "Yes, 'y doggies, some 'un's done sent you to me on a foolish errand. They wasn't nothing—" The sheriff stopped in mid-sentence. His features went rigid, contorted in pain. "For Heaven's sakes," he said hoarsely. "We've went and did it. We brought back my misery."

Sheriff Childress groped in a desk drawer, produced a cigar box and opened the lid. McGavock stared inside and flinched. The box was alive with about two dozen scurrying beetles, shiny black bugs with elongated, jointed bodies. McGavock had seen just such bugs in rotted logs. The sheriff studied the scampering insects, caught one deftly between the ball of his thumb and forefinger. He tilted his head, inserted the beetle in his ear and—to the horror of McGavock—*squeezed,* McGavock licked his dry lips. "What—?"

"Earache. I got me a spanking mean earache." The sheriff closed the box-lid, sighed. "They ain't nothing like the juice of a betsey-bug for a ear misery."

"It's a new one on me!"

"Mebbe so, son, mebbe so. But mountainfolks has used them for years. Now kindly evacuate and lemme alone. I'm a sick man."

McGavock was resigned. "I guess I'm going to have to use the pearls, after all." Sheriff Childress wiped his fingers fastidiously with a fluffy purple handkerchief. McGavock said pleasantly: "Well, brother, don't say I didn't warn you. When things begin to crack, don't come to me with a high pressure gripe. I've offered to co-operate, I've laid the dope on the line—and you've given me the brushoff. I'm going back to the hotel. I will say this before I leave: tomorrow at ten in the morning, they're burying the old professor. At precisely that moment, while the cottage is empty, I'm going to be in Doc Layton's house turning it off for whatever I can find in the way of clues. I leave you this option—you can either pick me up there for breaking and entering—or you can use your noodle and hop onto my wagon."

Sheriff Childress sat motionless, his eyes went glassy. "Praise Jehovah," he whispered. "She's a-easing up on me. Go away, friend, go away."

IT HAD BEEN a waste of time, just as McGavock had suspected it would be. He didn't much like the looks of it. It was going to be pick-and-shovel work from the very beginning. He was in a nettled mood as he walked the lonesome street toward his hotel. The shopfronts along Main Street were already burning their nightlights behind grimy, flyspecked windows. The wooden awning above his head made a half-tunnel of shadow across the pavement. He pushed through the door of the Simmons House, strode with angry clicking heels across the tiles to the desk.

McGavock registered. The clerk, an amiable, mild-mannered specimen with crescent eyeglasses, blotted his signature, said courteously, "Your room is 207." He handed the detective his key. "I've had your bag taken up. They tell me that tannic acid will do in an emergency."

McGavock started for the stairs, walked six steps and stopped dead still. "What was that crack about tannic acid?" He turned. The clerk was nowhere in sight. Halfway up the stairway, he heard the clerk's detached voice addressing him again.

"Tannic acid," the voice called genially, "is for bad burns. You're playing with fire, suh!"

The second floor gallery was horseshoe-shaped. A murky corridor, covered with straw matting, led off the mezzanine into the vitals of the old building. McGavock, his fingers splayed on the mahogany bannister, paused a moment at the head of the stairs, peered down into the well of the rotunda.

Potted plants, clean tiles, shabby furniture—it was a peaceful, lethargic scene. That little lobby was Rockton in a capsule: *too* peaceful. Nothing, come murder and mayhem, could cause a ripple in the even tenor of its ways. He cursed, shook his head, and started for room 207 and his gun.

It was then that he saw the girl.

She'd been standing in the shadows, behind him, before a closed door. Just a faint shimmer of filmy voile in the dark mezzanine. He pretended to ignore her, wandered casually past her, but she stepped directly into his path, blocking his way. He shoved roughly into her, threw her off balance with his shoulder, said: "Whoops. Excuse it please."

The girl's hand dropped to the doorknob. "Just step inside, if you will." Her voice was low, commanding. "I'm in trouble."

McGavock made gurgling, derisive noises. The girl's tone became steely. "And don't be lewd. I'm Hallie Layton. This is not a bedroom—this is the music room."

"Why didn't you say so!" McGavock arched his eyebrows. "I'm a sucker for a fugue." He followed her across the threshold. She shut the door and faced him.

They were in one of those special parlors that old-time hotels reserved to protect their female guests from the ribald inspection of a masculine world. The Victorian wallpaper was printed in great clusters of violent lavender grapes, there was a broken-down pink plush sofa, a battered piano with a dime-store table lamp on it, and a miscellany of tattered brocade chairs. "So you're Doxie's old lady?" McGavock teetered back, gave her a harsh, unfriendly inspection.

Mrs. Layton was well worth an ocular tour. Svelte, long-legged and graceful, she was a gal with poise. Her lipstick had been put on with a brush and her blue-black hair, falling back from her white forehead, lay about her shoulders in glossy, waxen symmetry that spelled time and care—but it was McGavock's shrewd guess that here was a kid that would rather knock down a quail or saddle a horse than open a vial of imported perfume. In the first place, she was pretty, in the second, she was expensive. Her dainty, white frock was childishly simple—but it had cost somebody plenty scratch. She showed her wealth in her manner, too. McGavock gauged her age at about nineteen-point-zero, yet she stood before him with the self-assurance born and bred in a heavy wallet. She arched herself haughtily, said: "I've told you I'm in trouble. You're a detective. Will you help me—or won't you?"

"So you know I'm a detective." McGavock ogled. "Could it be you were listening at the keyhole when I was in conference with your husband and Leach?"

She shrugged it off. "Who cares. Yes, I admit it. I'm scared. I heard you say that Father Layton had been slain. I know what that means, it means the extermination has begun."

McGavock waited, deadpan. The girl amplified. "It's Fiddler Joplin. He's always in trouble with the law—and he blames it on us Laytons. He comes up for trial next court-day for taking fish illegally—he probably blames that on us, too."

"Malarky!"

"It's true. I'm making it sound silly but it's really something deep and hateful. To get the right idea, I'll have to give you a few facts. Don't think I'm boasting. The Laytons—my husband, my late father-in-law, and myself—control about two thousand acres—"

"Yoicks!"

"It's large, but there are many larger plantations." She took a deep breath. "Half of this was owned by my late father-in-law, half by my husband and myself. We ran it like a commercial enterprise. My father-in-law managed his section, we managed ours. The whole was under the supervision of my husband. We had periodical auditings and so forth."

"How does this Joplin fit in?"

"Most of our land is fertile bottoms but part of it is hill country." She was embarrassed. "Joplin is a squatter. He has a small hill farm called Joplin's Mill. We own the title to the property but the Joplins have lived on the land for a hundred years. About a month ago, Daddy Layton—for some strange reason—suddenly took Fiddler to court and tried to eject him from the land. Fiddler claimed title by prescription and adverse possession, which means he'd been using it and had actually settled on it. The jury upheld Fiddler, as it should have, and my husband and myself were in sympathy, but you see it was Daddy Layton's land."

McGAVOCK WAS BLEAK. "That's bad. But it doesn't quite add up. Evictions give shootings in barbershops. They don't give tricky murders like the old professor's."

Her lip curled. "You don't know Fiddler Joplin. He's a schemer. He's cunning. The squatter affair wasn't all, either. About a week before the attempted eviction, Daddy Layton tried to get through a true bill accusing Joplin of 'shining.' The sheriff had him in jail three days questioning him. It was this seeming persecution, coupled by the fact that Joplin's Mill had been in the family so long, that made the jury uphold the defendant."

"There you are." McGavock grunted. "I've never seen anything like the deep south hill country for lawsuits." He rubbed his jaw. "I'll work for you, sister. Who is this Charlie Lusk?"

Distaste show on her fine features. "He's an outsider."

"So am I."

Pretty Mrs. Layton exhibited the first signs of snobbery. "I mean he hasn't any connections. Any family or anything. Sometime ago, Daddy Layton took it into his senile brain to get a personal secretary. He wanted a girl, but we put our foot down on that. What would Rockton say, a young city female living with the old professor? We put an ad in the Nashville paper and it brought us Charlie Lusk. Daddy only wanted to pay him six dollars a week, Charlie held out for fifteen, so we made up the balance in secret to him."

McGavock asked politely. "Are you and Mr. Layton going to the funeral tomorrow?"

"I suppose so. Certainly."

McGavock was urgent. "The old man was killed. There's some clue, some place in that cottage of his, which will clinch it. I tried to get in tonight but this menial Lusk wouldn't let me past the threshold. Can you get him away in, say an hour, and keep him away for twenty minutes?"

She considered. "Yes, I can. I'll call him up from the drugstore and tell him that effective from the moment of Daddy Layton's death his salary was cut automatically to the original six dollars." She smiled. "That'll bring him flying out to Doxie with his mouth full of argument."

"Swell. Now, two things more. How does this Robertus M. Leach tie up with you folks, and where can I get a drink of whiskey?"

"Since Anderson went back to Arkansas, Mr. Leach has taken over his place as sort of a stop-gap. Mr. Leach's position is only temporary." She noticed McGavock's knotted forehead, explained. "I keep forgetting that you're a stranger. Anderson was our business advisor. He worked with Doxie but had nominal charge over the entire Layton acreage. He planted, jockeyed for proper prices with the buyers and so forth. A month or so ago his mother died and he went back home to Arkansas. My husband's more of a farmer than a businessman. He picked up Mr. Leach to keep his ledgers until he could locate a—er—more competent person." She met his eyes squarely. "That's the whole story. We've got Scotch, rye and bourbon at the house. I'll have a bottle sent around to you when I return."

McGavock shook his head. "It won't do. I got a galvanized stomach. I favor popskull moonshine."

She stared at him in uneasy pity. "I've heard that private detectives were like that. Well, there's a place in the cellar back of the old abattoir, but I don't recommend it. It's a low and dangerous crowd. It's run by an ex-convict named Pokey."

"Fine!" McGavock was ecstatic. "Just the thing. I'm only dregs myself."

Room 207 was neat and antiseptic-smelling. There was a brass bed, a framed magazine print of Sam Davis, the boy martyr, on the wall, and a huge cupboard-like wardrobe. McGavock stepped through the door whistling. He stood for a moment in the center of the room, taking in the comfortable surroundings. He cocked his thumb and forefinger at the wardrobe, hissed: "Come out of there Jesse James, and you too, Frank, I got you'uns covered." He walked to the window, tested the latch.

The big Gladstone was by the foot of the bed. He laid out his pajamas and dressing slippers, fumbled around and located his revolver. McGavock was funny about his gun. He didn't like to carry it unless he thought he might actually need it. A gun, the way he saw it, was just a tool of the trade. He wouldn't have carted it around with him twenty-four hours a day any more than he would have carried a Stilson wrench or a pair of wire clippers—just on the off-chance they might come in handy.

McGavock's gun was designed for heavy duty. It had a short barrel and a heavy bore, the walnut grip was battered and worn. It'd seen plenty of action. It was a tight case, he reflected, he'd seldom gotten away to a tougher start. But things were breaking at last. The wiry little detective was an opportunist, an expert at pushing his luck. It's like a pebble on a hillside, he decided, you get just one small rock pried out and, *whambo!* down comes the landslide.

He killed five minutes by his wrist-watch to give the gal time to clear out of the hotel. At the end of this period, he stuck his gun behind his belt buckle, turned out the lights and locked the door behind him.

3

Moonshiner's Hide-out

POKEY'S PLACE WAS a bit hard to find. In the alley back of Main Street, a ramshackle loading-platform ran the full length of the block, each merchant having his own backdoor outlet to it. Built in the old days, this platform was wagon-high, about four feet from the ground. By careful use of his flash, McGavock discovered that beneath each shop, back under the platform, was a door leading to what had once been the merchant's storeroom. Rot and decay had changed that custom. The doors on many of the basements were completely missing, others were sagging from disuse.

The red-clay alley was rutted, foul with the dung of mule and horse, and as black as a cave. McGavock made his way down the line. At the end of the row, the final building perked up his interest. An almost obliterated sign said: *Thos. Barlow & Son, Fresh Meats.* The old abattoir. It was foul, dilapidated; its windows were gaping with broken panes.

McGavock beamed his torch under the platform. The basement door was new. It was a strong affair of two-by-eights, of white pine, fastened to the jamb with barn hinges. McGavock bent his back, stepped under the platform and swung it open.

The dive was low and mean. McGavock knew these small town deadfalls for what they were: dynamite. There were just three men in the cellar—two customers and the proprietor. The place was vile, musty, the brick walls sweated to patches of fungus mold, the bare earth floor was spongy from age. The proprietor lolled behind a short packing-box counter at the front of the room, chatting with one of his customers, the other customer was spread-eagled on his back in a tangle of filthy bedclothes on a cot in the corner. His jaw was canted at a rigid angle—he was drunker than seven hundred dollars. McGavock paused in the doorway and admired him. He was a big man, six feet three or four, and his greasy carrot hair was shaggy and matted. With McGavock's sudden appearance, the proprietor and his companion clammed up like they'd swallowed alum.

McGavock touched his hat brim. "Salutations, good brethren." He advanced casually into the room, leaned his elbow on the packing-box counter. There was a stony silence. McGavock said breezily: "Well, here I am, boys. The man you've been waiting for."

The proprietor was brutish, unshaven, with evil little eyes. Like his two customers, he was dressed in overalls. "We ain't wantin' nobody, mister," he drawled. "Jest turn yourse'f around and go right back out that door." McGavock glanced at the customer by his elbow. A small, wrinkled hillman with the pointed face of a field-mouse. The detective addressed him, "How about a dram of nice charred whiskey? Would you take a drink with me?"

There was a moment of confusion. The mouse-faced man was in a spot. It was an invitation that you don't refuse unless you wish to infer an insult. The hillman thought it over. He remarked carefully: "If you got her, stranger, I'll drink her." He passed the buck right back to McGavock.

"Fair enough." McGavock showed his teeth. He said to the proprietor: "You're Pokey. This is a blind pig. I want a pint of your best rye. I want something that's been charred in a heart keg to a natural red. I don't want any green stuff that's been colored with manure or iodine. I don't want anything that's been touched up with lye to give it a gag. I want something that's come from copper, not tin, and—"

Pokey's face broke into a beam. "You shore want a lot. And durn iff'n I hain't got it." He went to the cot, rolled back the drunk, produced a pint bottle from under the mattress. He set the container on the counter, drawled: "One dollar, please."

McGavock was astounded. "You never saw me before. You're taking a chance, aren't you?"

Pokey's eyes were cruel. "Hit's you that's taking the chance, poddner. If you're an alcohol-tax-man sombuddy's in fer some hell-raisin'."

McGavock uncorked the bottle, shoved it across the counter to the mouse-faced man. The hillman tilted it back, took a five-ounce drag and choked. "'Scuse me," he said politely. "That last swaller, she went down my Sunday pipe." McGavock offered the bottle to the proprietor who took the traditional, courteous sip, and returned it. McGavock completed the ceremony.

The ritual finished, McGavock remarked convivially: "I'm a hunter and a fisherman, gentlemen. Zooks, how I love wildlife! You've got some fine hills hereabouts. They must be loaded with game."

The mouse-faced mountainman hiccoughed, nodded. "They is at that. They reely is." He took an althea toothbrush from his pocket, sprinkled a pinch of snuff on his lower gum, and rubbed the powder into the flesh. "Yes, sir," he declaimed when he'd finished the operation. "They's fish and I kin take y'all to 'em. Was you wantin' a guide?"

"Maybe yes, maybe no." McGavock looked sly. "He'd have to be the right man. I'm after gray foxes and I use chemicals and smokers."

There was a silence. The mouse-faced hillman was shocked. "A feller cain't take fox this time a year, and chemicals and smokers'll get you a trip to Nashville. They're a violation of the Fish and Game Act. Fox is out, but if you want trout—"

"Swell." McGavock prepared to leave. "Meet me at the Simmons House tomorrow morning. I'll have the jugs."

Again that strained silence. Pokey said: "You'll have the what?"

"The jugs. We'll jug them," McGavock explained. "You know how it's done. You put a little lime in the jug, make a small hole in the cork, drop the jug in the trout pool and *powie!* up they come. Blast them out, that's my style."

"You got a hellacious style if you don't mind my sayin' so." The little hillman was suddenly distant. "Yo're cryin' for a ball and chain."

McGavock argued. "We won't get caught, we'll be slick about it. They tell me Fiddler Joplin's been getting away with it for years. If he can jug fish, so can we."

That did it. The faces of McGavock's companions were drawn in coarse, livid anger. Pokey spoke and his voice was dull and dead. "It all comes out now. You ain't no alcohol-tax-man, yo're a sneaky game warden. Well, yo're wasting yore time, yo're jipper-jawing around tryin' to get evidence on Fiddler Joplin." The proprietor's unshaven cheeks contorted in contempt. "The rich folks, the Laytons, have got a grudge agin Fiddler. They're tryin' to frame him into prison."

McGavock sneered. "But I saw the jugs just this evening in the sheriff's office. That's evidence, isn't it?"

"It ain't enough to convict him and Sheriff Lud Childress durn well knows it. Fiddler Joplin takes game and fish like anyone else, but he takes it in season and he takes it legal. He had him those jugs fer another purpose."

McGavock broke into a raucous laugh. "That's a good one. I could see the holes in the corks—they'd been limed."

Pokey looked puzzled. "They was all set to explode, I know that. But he won't tell nobody what he was going to use them fer. Game warden, take my word fer it, he's innocent."

"O.K.," McGavock agreed. "I will. Take my word for it—I'm no game warden."

McGAVOCK STOOD IN the shadow of a foamy crape-myrtle tree and subjected Professor Layton's slate-roofed cottage to a cautious scrutiny. By now, if Hallie Layton had carried through her agreement, Charlie Lusk had shed his luxurious dressing-robe and had left the house. It was an eerie picture: the porchlight burning like a death lamp, the curtained windows, the funeral wreath swaying gently against the door panel in the fitful spring breeze.

McGavock swung from the sidewalk, through the box-hedge gateposts, up the glazed brick walk. He clanged the lever bell-pull, waited. There was no response. He tested the knob, found the door unlocked, and entered.

Systematically, he made a quick, thorough prowl of the ground floor. Off the corridor, to the right, was the old head-master's study. To the left was the parlor. The parlor was just about as McGavock had last seen it. The decanter on the card table was about empty and the platter of sandwiches nearly consumed, but otherwise everything was the same—

the center of interest was still the trestled casket with its heap of sultry flowers. At the end of the hallway was the kitchen, which McGavock passed up. Flanking the kitchen, on its left and right, respectively, was the cubbyhole which served the secretary as living quarters, and the larger, more comfortable master's bedroom.

Lusk's tiny room was cramped, but somehow cozy. There was a Spanish daybed, a small bureau and a friendly-looking, broken-down Morris chair with a shelf of books beside it. Three threadbare suits hung from a broomstick bar in the corner. The detective picked up the books, examined them one by one. The first was a paperback affair titled: *1001 JOKES, Fun for Young and Old*. The four others were instructional volumes on how to become a self-taught cartoonist. The flyleaf of each volume bore the scrawled signature: *Leslie Anderson, Little Rock, Arkansas.*

"Leslie Anderson," McGavock muttered. "Layton's business manager, eh? The lad replaced by the incumbent Mr. Leach. You're going places, Luther."

He got his big surprise of the evening when he flipped down the toggle and turned on the overhead light in old man Layton's master bedroom. The walls and floor jumped at him in almost blinding illumination. McGavock boggled. The bulb in the professor's ceiling fixture was at least two hundred watts in strength. Abruptly, he grinned. "Oh ho! So that's the way the land lays."

Working swiftly and efficiently, he began a minute search of the old man's quarters. The collar compartment of the cumbersome dresser paid off with an interesting document. A curt, arrogant letter. He unfolded the paper, read:

Dear Dr. Layton:

In response to your repeated conversations with me on street corners, in court square, at church—in fact wherever you encounter me in public—in response to these persistent conversations, I have finally been driven to take the matter up with your son, and my employer, Mr. Doxie Layton.

You say that you are old and infirm and that you wish Mr. Doxie to assume your holdings and acreage and that you are fully prepared to relinquish all title in his favor. You indicate that account-keeping and business management of so extensive holdings are, at your age, difficult and onerous.

I have, as I have indicated above, conferred with Mr. Doxie on this point. He wishes me to state flatly and finally for him that the idea of your deeding your property and estate to him at this time is not acceptable to him. He says that you are sufficiently vigorous and fully competent to handle your own affairs and that he hopes you will disabuse your mind of any doubts on this subject.

Mr. Doxie Layton has asked me to put his position in writing to bring an end once and for all to the matter. To be blunt: Mr. Doxie will keep his property and you will keep yours.

Sincerely,

Leslie Anderson

Manager, Layton Farms

"He's finally done it," McGavock said softly. "He's found a way to relinquish deed and title." He thrust the letter into his breast pocket.

The signature on the paper was in careful, angular script. The same name—in the front of the cartoon books in Charlie Lusk's room—had been round and fancy, almost illiterate.

You didn't have to be a graphologist to note the dissimilarity. McGavock went back to his prowl.

It was then that he made his big discovery. It was so cleverly concealed that he nearly muffed it. Three old quilts were stowed in the bottom drawer of the dresser. McGavock lifted them out. The drawer was lined with old newspapers. McGavock removed the papers. Cut in the wooden panel of the drawer-bottom was a hole. A small, rectangular hole, about four by eight inches. Just a hole. McGavock could look through it to the carpet beneath the dresser. For a moment, he was nonplussed. A strained, attentive expression grooved his face, brought out the network of wrinkles about his tired, wise eyes. He clicked his tongue, said: "For Gosh sakes!"

He replaced the quilts, shut the drawer, and stood up.

Professor Layton's room was a primer in crime. The two-hundred-watt bulb in the ceiling fixture, the ridiculous, huffy letter in the collar compartment, the squarish hole in the dresser drawer—they all fitted together to produce ironclad evidence to convict a murderer. McGavock's lips thinned. He was reforming his opinion of the old absent-minded professor.

He groped in his pocket, located the spool of thread and the imitation pearl necklace. "Now," he said, "a little hocus-pocus in the attic and then tally-ho for bed."

The attic stairs were at the rear of the hall, by the kitchen. The detective ascended a steep, narrow flight of steps, and found himself in a hot, stuffy cubicle. He heard the scratching scurry of startled mice and flicked on his torch. Two frightened bats took off from the rafters above his head and slapped their way frantically through the open louvers.

The garret was floored and represented the space between

the main story and the roof. Overhead, the timbers arched and pyramided into hips and gables. The place was bare, but for one article of furniture: an old leather-covered, claw-and-ball piano stool. McGavock caught the stool in his light, threw the beam directly upward. Hanging down from a rafter, over the piano stool, was about ten inches of cotton clothesline. "So this," McGavock declared, "is where they cut him down." He was hardly interested.

The garret floor was a patchwork of odds and ends of planking. The detective selected a spot about three yards or so from the pedestal of the stool, dropped to his haunches. He took off his hat, dented the crease at a forty-five degree angle. He placed his pencil flash in the crease so that it struck the floor before him in a pool of light. He probed in his vest pocket with a hooked finger, came out with a small cylindrical object that resembled a tire-pressure gauge: a machine tool jimmey with a telescopic handle.

He picked a floorboard at random, a warped three inch plank about two feet in length, inserted his jimmey and pried. It came loose with a squeak. On the lath and plaster bottom of the cavity thus disclosed between the joists, he spread a one dollar bill. He produced his spool of thread, broke off a length about ten inches long, laid the piece across the aperture at right angles to the elongation. With the chisel-blade of his tool, he withdrew the nails from the plank and refitted it in its original position. He dropped the spool into his pocket, tossed the bent nails over his shoulder, and inspected his work.

Everything seemed normal. Except that section of white thread. It ran along the floor for a couple of inches, disappeared by the edge of the plank, reappeared at the opposite joint and once again advertised its presence.

McGavock got to his feet, put on his hat. "Don't fail me, baby," he said. "I'm depending on you." His eyelids were hot and stiff. It had been a long, hard day.

Outside, on the street, he headed for the hotel and fresh, clean sheets. The sweet wood-scents from the crested hills swept in soft, soporific gusts through the little town. McGavock was asleep on his feet by the time he reached his room.

THINGS STARTED OFF with a bang the next morning while McGavock was at breakfast.

The ground floor of the Simmon's House was T-shaped. The lobby, or crossbar of the T, fronted the sidewalk and jutting back at right angles to the rotunda, behind the staircase, was a succession of utility and service rooms culminating in the hostelry's old-fashioned kitchen. The dining-room was located at the left of the hallway, immediately in the rear of the manager's office.

The room was high-ceilinged, airy and pleasant: curtains arched and billowed by the open windows and the morning sunlight, lemon-colored, splashed on white linen cloths and glinting silverware. Floor and woodwork gave off a faint sanitary smell from frequent scrubbings with lye-and-ashes. McGavock selected a small table by the wall and placed his order.

There was an open window by his shoulder and, constantly and persistently, throughout the meal, the curtain flicked and furled across his line of vision. He'd just demolished a platter of meal-fried drum fish and was topping the job off with sweet yellow tomato jam and beaten biscuits when suddenly, on an impulse of exasperation, he leaned forward and anchored the curtain to the table with the sugar bowl. To do this, he was forced to rise partially out of his chair. For a split instant, he had a good, clear view of the outside. That was how he saw the trespasser.

Directly beyond the window, possibly eight feet below him, was a small enclosed courtyard. Two sides of the courtyard were formed by a tall board fence, the inside L of the hotel constituting the remaining walls. A man came through a gate in the fence, from the alley. He was carrying his shoes in his hand.

It was the shoes-in-the-hand stuff that aroused McGavock's interest. The detective canted his chair, settled back where he could watch without being seen.

The man was a giant—six feet three or four—with tangled carroty hair. He wore faded overalls. McGavock placed him instantly: the lad at Pokey's, the big drunk who had sprawled in alcoholic stupor, spreadeagled on the cot in the corner.

The man stood for a second in the center of the cobblestone court and studied the row of second-story windows, He had the appearance of a man who was confronted with an emergency and didn't like to make snap judgments. A low coalhouse nestled in the crotch between the hotel and the fence. The man hid his shoes carefully in a stack of oak stove wood, frowned apishly. Abruptly, he raised his arms, grasped the coalhouse eaves in enormous, knotty hands. His shoulder muscles bunched. With lithe, unbelievable grace, by sheer strength of his biceps, he drew his monstrous hulk up from the ground onto the shed's roof.

McGavock was fascinated. In an animal crouch, the man ascended the slanting tin roof, to the row of second-story windows. He reared back on his hunkers, began waving his finger at the sashes, working his lips. He's counting, McGavock decided.

Finally the big man made his choice. He produced an iron tire tool, forced the window catch, and crawled out of sight into the building. McGavock closed his eyes, visualized the layout of the second floor. He counted windows himself—and smiled bleakly.

The big man had entered room 207, McGavock's room.

McGavock was deep in reverie when a pompous, blustering voice cut loose about six inches from his eardrums. "Well, well! I thought I'd find you here, suh! Partaking of ye old inn's matutinal edibles, I perceive. I'd like to join you, suh, but I have already enjoyed gustatory fulfillment. I will, however, accept one of yall's toothpicks." A pudgy hand suddenly grasped the china toothpick holder, upset the spindles in a heap on the tablecloth, pawed through them, selected one. McGavock turned his head, stared into the puffy, unctuous face of the Honorable Robertus M. Leach.

"UP BRIGHT AN' early, I see." McGavock was deliberately insulting. "Whose letters have you been snooping into this morning?"

Leach pulled up a chair facing the detective, lowered himself ponderously, in jelly-like convolutions. "You cain't make me mad, Luther." He chuckled. "I like you and besides I'm too all-fired happy, everything's bluebirds with me this lovely spring morning."

McGavock sneered. "I catch. Layton was going to tie the can on you last night and you talked him out of it. Is that what you mean?"

The puffy man looked offended. "You got the hatefullest way of saying the most simple things." He smiled serenely. "Essentially, suh, you done named the facks. I threw myself on his mercy. I explained to him that when I broke into that communication to you people in Memphis I didn't have anything but his interests at heart. I said, 'Mr. Doxie—if I'm your business manager it behooves me to manage your business and I cain't do that lest I know everything about everything.'"

"And he fell for it?"

Leach looked foxy. "Doxie Layton has what you might call the rich landowner psychology. His big obsession is land and raisin' crops. He don't like to be bothered with any kind of details that he can't figure out in terms of land or crops. When I saw he was writing a detective agency, I was afraid he was in trouble. It was my obligation to take the burden off my employer. I explained it to him last night after you left and he understood. I was just doing my duty, Luther."

"Don't call me Luther." McGavock's voice was creaky. "You're snake-eggs in my book!" He controlled himself, asked: "Do you really have Boss Layton's interests at heart? O.K., then. Answer me a few questions. Who was this Lester Anderson, what did he look like, and what were the circumstances of his so-called resignation?"

Mr. Leach looked mildly astonished. "So Les is involved in this? I'm not surprised. I never liked the man." He pressed his finger deep into his fat cheek, went through the motions of deep thought. "Les didn't resign, he hightailed. One dark night he just up and skedaddled, left Mr. Doxie stranded—that's how I came into the picture. What did he look like? Let's see. If I were describing him in court, I'd say that he was middle-aged, handsome, a good dresser, and all-fired cold-blooded. What I call the northern-type business man, the kind that would put his grandmother out picking cranberries if it would show black on the family ledger."

"A northerner? I thought he came from Arkansas."

Leach disgorged his toothpick. "So he said, but who knows? That's my description of him, would you like my *impression?*"

"Very much."

Leach was solemn. "I can put it in a single word: skittery."

McGavock was silent.

"Here's what I mean," Mr. Leach explained. "You'd be in a room and all of a sudden Lester Anderson would step out of the closet. It gave me the chills. I never visited Doxie but he pulled it on us. We'd be talking, and suddenly he'd pop out on us."

McGavock threw his voice deep in his chest, said in a hollow baritone, "Robertus M. Leach, the Honorable, I'm going to ask you to make a statement. Last night there was a scuttleful of cigar ashes on your vest, a condition which had the appearance of being habitual with you. However, this morning I observe that they have vanished. I am a detective; such details intrigue me. What became of those ashes, suh?"

Leach batted his eyes. "I brushed them off." He drew himself up like a pouter-pigeon. "You're a mighty sorry detective, suh, if you think my vest has anything to do with this-here affair. I'm going to Dr. Layton's buryin'. I always make a particular point of brushing off my vest whenever I go to a buryin'."

"Spoken like a true gentlemen." McGavock pushed back his chair, got up. "Expect a large crowd at the funeral?"

"Just the four of us. Mr. Doxie and Miss Hallie, Lusk and yours truly."

McGavock cocked an eyebrow. "How's chances of crashing the convention?"

"It could be done, but I wouldn't advise it. Frankly, you wouldn't be welcome."

McGavock said viciously: "You folks wait until I throw a funeral, and you want to come! You'll be sorry then!" He slammed out of the room, left Mr. Leach in a befuddled stupor.

McGAVOCK WALKED HEAVY-HEELED down the matting-floored upstairs corridor. He came to a noisy halt by the door of 207, rattled his key against the escutcheon and listened. There was no sound. He inserted the bit in the lock, threw the bolt, and entered the room.

The barefooted giant was standing awkwardly in the center of the carpet. He was a hard-looking specimen. His shaggy, uncut hair fell in tangled tufts almost to his collar. His unshaven, slablike cheeks were stiff in sullen anger. McGavock asked crisply: "Who are you and what do you want?"

The man spoke in a wooden whisper. "I'm Fiddler Joplin, and I'm aimin' to find out yore weight. I'm fixin' to slap you back to whur you come from."

"You've been standing here, waiting for me, for twenty minutes? Why didn't you sit down? There's plenty chairs and a nice soft bed!"

Joplin flushed, indicated his mud-caked overalls. "I ain't wantin' to mess up nobuddy's furniture."

"Well!" McGavock was speechless. "Think of that!" He grinned. "Don't get too rough with me, that gives blood on the nice clean rug."

302 / Merle Constiner

The red-haired man dug in a hip pocket and came out with a claspknife, a wicked implement with a sheepsfoot blade. Joplin laid the knife on the wash-stand. "I'll put her here," he said reluctantly, "or elst I'll be cuttin' on you. When I start to fight, my elements gits up."

McGavock said gently: "What have you got against me, Fiddler?"

"Hit's been know-rated to me that yo're a durn, skunky spy." He spoke without particular malice. "Pokey says you was in his place last night, whilst I was asleep, that you was tryin' to work up some crooked evidence on me. Let me pose you this, are you taking money from them Laytons?"

"Not yet, but I hope to."

"Why don't you folks leave me alone?" Dark, turbulent anger, the dangerous, desperate rage born of long brooding, surged into his stolid face. He spoke in a low, monotonous mumble. "Why do high-class rich folks like the Laytons pick on a poor honest farmer? I'll tell you why: they got the black blood of Satan in 'em. For months now, they been persecutin' me. Here am I, out on my hungry-feedin' farm not harmin' no-buddy, mindin' my own business. Doctor Layton, which was that ole dragon, the Devil, and the pappy of the brood—as hit sayeth in the Gospel—Doc Layton, he gets the idee to persecute me. First he sets Lud Childress on me as a 'shiner.' The sheriff throws me in jail and questions me for three days. They ain't nothin' to hit, so he has to let me go."

McGavock listened to the cascade of hate. Joplin went on: "That was just the beginning. A week later the old professor tries to evict me, hails me into court. The Joplins have done live at the Mill since before Jefferson Davis, I reckon. The court upholds me. The old man gets a-plottin' and a-plannin'—and lays a new snare. They're tryin' to jail me for juggin' fish!"

"I saw six jugs in the sheriff's office," McGavock declared amiably. "They were yours, weren't they?"

"That's right. But—"

"And they were limed, they were all set to blast?"

"I reckon." The giant began to sweat, beads of moisture gathered on his low forehead. "It looks like they got me red-handed, but they ain't. I'm innocent." His eyes were furtive, cornered. "I cain't tell you no more. Don't crowd me." He took a deep breath. "I'm gonna whip yore britches," he said placidly. "Then pack up yore satchel and git yorese'f Memphis-bound. Yo're a trial and a tribbelashun!"

McGavock made the mistake of arguing. He said: "Now hold on, Fiddler. There's two sides to every question—"

The big man came at him. He came at him in a lunge. He took three nimble, running steps, like a bobcat on a tree branch, came to a sudden stop and unloaded his haymaker. The attack was so unorthodox that it caught McGavock flatfooted. When the red-haired man rushed, McGavock's reflexes falsely warned him that he was in for an eye-gouging wrestling match. The detective lowered his fighting guard, and Fiddler Joplin swung. It was a woodsman's swing, the swing of an axman. The giant's fist, launched in a great down-hand arc, caught McGavock in the cup of his shoulder. The mighty impact drove him backwards and down, threw him flatly against the wall.

Just that one terrific blow. Joplin made no attempt to follow it up. McGavock, his shoulder throbbing, crouched taut and tense—infuriated at himself for his blundering misjudgment, his posture was that of a man dazed and badly hurt.

A queer change came over Fiddler Joplin. The network of capillaries on his flat cheeks burned fiery red, his eyes went dull and slaty.

He said lifelessly, "I cain't help myself, amen," and reached for his clasp-knife.

McGavock clinched. He knocked the knife to the floor, kicked it under the bed. Joplin threw clumsy, bearish arms around him and McGavock hit him three times below the heart. The hillman staggered. McGavock disengaged, laid an eight-inch pile-driver at the hinge of the big man's jaw, measured him with a final heartpunch as he sagged. He was out before he struck the floor.

The wiry little detective went to the washstand, bathed his hands and face, dried them on the sleazy hotel towel. He paused a moment, gazed with moody, unseeing eyes at his handiwork—two hundred and forty pounds of it—on the gay, floral carpet. He said to himself, "Fisticuffs, good old-timey fisticuffs!" without realizing that he was speaking.

He left the room, locked the door from the outside, and tossed the key through the open transom. He heard it jingle as it hit the bed.

4

Gala Funeral

HIS EYE CAUGHT sight of two familiar figures as he descended the broad, sweeping stairs into the lobby. Doxie Layton and the secretary, Charlie Lusk, were perched side by side on a red leather sofa, beneath a dusty rubber-plant—waiting for him.

They were dressed, each according to his tastes, for the burying. The landowner was barbed in fine black cheviot, his vest was piped with silver braid and he wore high black shoes which had the suspicious appearance of being hunting boots beneath his trousers. He watched McGavock approach with thoughtful eyes, as though he were judging the staple of a very inferior bale of cotton. For Charlie Lusk, the funeral was obviously an outing. The secretary was rigged for a bullfight: his jacket was of goose-track tweed, his flannel slacks were vivid chocolate. His single contribution to the sobriety of the occasion was a mourner's armband. He leaned back, behind Layton's range of vision, and gave McGavock a wry wink.

They arose simultaneously as he advanced on them. He flagged them off. "Some other time, boys," he said. "I'm behind schedule."

Layton was nonplussed. "That's a rather brusque way to greet a client, isn't it? Last night you offered yourself to me for hire. I'm prepared, sir, to retain you." He pointed to the clock above the desk: it said a quarter to ten. "Do you wish to deal with me? Answer yes or no. I, too, am occupied this morning. The funeral procession leaves in fifteen minutes."

McGavock pretended amazement. "Not from here, not from the hotel! That explains a lot. First Leach and now yourself and Charlie, here. I wondered why the kith and kin were congregating at the Simmons House."

Layton was unperturbed. "You're a strange and irritating personality, Mr. McGavock. Large cities incubate queer hybrids, don't they? Nevertheless, I've come to a decision. I'm prepared to pay you twenty-five dollars, cold cash, if you prove to me that my father was murdered."

"O.K. Follow these instructions: take out the oldster's stomach, chop it up and make a solution from it. Analyze that solution. He was given sleeping powders—and then hanged." McGavock pushed his hat onto his forehead with the flat of his hand. "Twenty-five dollars, please. Just forward it to your favorite charity—if any. Now step aside."

Layton said coldly: "I'd amputate my living hand before I'd desecrate my father's mortal remains. I've talked enough with you, sir."

McGavock fumbled in his breast pocket, located the letter he'd discovered in the drawer of Dr. Layton's dresser. "Here's an exhibit," he remarked, "that I'd like to hear a little more about." He handed the paper to Lusk. "You were the old man's secretary. Did you ever see this thing before?"

Charlie Lusk scanned the page intently. "No," he answered. "No, I never have. The old man was trying to give away his property, eh? Well, well."

"Let's take a look at that." Doxie Layton whipped the paper from the secretary's fingers. He read:... *you wish Mr. Doxie to*

assume your holdings and acreage and are fully prepared to relin-
quish all title in his favor… Mr. Doxie wishes me to state flatly
and finally for him that the idea is not acceptable to him! Signed:
Leslie Anderson, Manager, Layton Farms. For a moment his
poise cracked. "What rigmarole is this?"

McGavock asked blandly: "Is the signature genuine?"

"Of course it's genuine. But that means nothing at all."
Layton got organized. "Why blast that Leslie Anderson! I was
lucky to get rid of him. He was obviously involved in matters
concerning me without my knowledge!" He wheeled on Lusk,
lashed out: "Did you know anything about all this, Charlie?"

Lusk said calmly: "No, I didn't. But I will say this. The old
man was crazy—though not about money. Maybe Anderson
suddenly jumped his trolley—"

"And talking about Anderson," McGavock put in, "what's
this I hear about him hiding in closets?"

"That's right." Layton was grave. "It got to be quite an embarrassing stunt in that period just before he left us. He was eaves-
dropping on me, there was no doubt about it. The butler's
pantry was his favorite. You can hear the conversation in the
parlor quite well from the butler's pantry. I caught him three
times while I was entertaining guests. I asked him what he
was doing. He said he was counting the jams and jellies, that
a good business manager checked up on everything. He was
guilty, flustered—"

"Shelf-conscious, eh?" McGavock grinned. "Am I a comic?
Wow!" He nodded. "I'll be seeing you."

Layton said angrily; "When Anderson comes back, I'll
penalize him. I'll cut his salary. Just to hold him in line. He
was a good manager, you know."

McGavock took three paces to the door, turned. "*Was* is the right word. Leslie Anderson will never pop out of another closet. He's deader than a dime's worth of chitterlings."

DR. SIMON TETCHERALL LAYTON'S tiny, slate-roofed cottage had undergone a change of aspect. In the bright crystal wash of a blue-and-silver sky, it seemed a different place altogether, it seemed cheerful, cozy. The specter of death had vanished. The curtains had been pulled back, the wreath was gone from the porch, and the casket of Daddy Layton was, at that very moment, rolling along over red clay back-streets to its final resting-place. McGavock strolled up the glazed brick walk, tried the knob. The house was locked.

An ordinary skeleton key did the trick. He stepped inside, kicked the door shut behind him.

A heavy hand reached out from behind portiers, laid itself on his shoulder. The booming, complaining voice of Sheriff Ludlow Childress broke the tomblike silence. "Mister McGavock, I, as an authenticated representative of law and order for Tilden County, do here and thereby arrest you for breaking and entering!" The dewlapped sheriff, pony-skin vest and all, materialized in the hallway, dangling a pair of rusty handcuffs. He was puffing. "You said you was gonna do it, but I jest couldn't believe it. Hain't you ashamed o' yorese'f—breaking into a corpse's domicile! Jest wait till the jury sits on you! Don't they respect the dead back in Memphis?"

McGavock grinned. "Hi, Ludlow. How's the ear-misery?"

"Hit's went away, thank you, but you cain't sweet talk yore way out'n this. This-here's a criminal act."

McGavock hardened. "So it's going to be that way, eh? You're siding with your constituents. Doctor Layton was murdered—and I'm prepared to prove it to you. But you don't want to listen. You're covering for someone. You don't want a homicide case—you'd rather have a breaking-and-entering charge against an outsider like me. O.K. You're the sheriff."

Sheriff Childress lowered his eyelids. "Yo're jest a-goadin' me into idle speech. Bob Leach warned me agin you. He said yo're slicker than a vixen, and dangerous. I ain't covering up no murder and you mighty well know it. You come here from Memphis, on your own, without no client, and are going around fomenting, trying to stir up a sitshiation, hoping the good Lord will drop a juicy fee in yore lap. Jest like Bob Leach was a-sayin'—we hain't needin' no troublemakers in Rockton."

"Sure, sure." McGavock appeared to be in deep meditation. He asked, apropos of nothing, "What kind of a knot was it?"

"What kind of a knot was what?"

"The knot in the rope up there—" McGavock pointed toward the attic. "How was the rope tied, the rope that hanged old man Layton?"

"Just tied to a rafter. Just an ordinary knot, I guess." The sheriff was tolerant. "Why?"

"I have a feeling you've passed up some very valuable evidence." McGavock was grave. "We do things differently in the city. We study the knot. If it's a bowline, a sailor tied it; if it's a carrick bend, a carpenter tied it; if it's a timber hitch, a lumberman did it. And so on." He closed his eyes, reminisced dreamily, "How well do I remember that time we found an old man all trussed up with lover's knots. A dead giveaway. We scouted around and arrested his housekeeper. Yes sir, they were having a secret romance—"

Sheriff Childress was uneasy. "A knot is just a knot to me. Mebbe we'd best step up and have a look."

"It'll pay you in the long run," McGavock promised. "That, I can guarantee."

The tiny garret was sepulchral, still. The golden morning sunshine, beating through the louvers, cut the shadows in a crisscross of moted, lucent rays. The halflight was weird, otherworldly. McGavock's searching gaze swept the floor in quest of his thread, found it, continued casually to the piano stool. Sheriff Childress clicked on his flash, beamed it at the length of clothesline dangling from the rafters. "There you are," he declaimed. "What do you make of 'er?"

McGavock went through the pretense of studying it. He looked flabbergasted. "I'm stumped! I never saw anything like it." He walked abruptly to the window, turned his back to the room, and stared morbidly through the slatted louver down into the little yard with its velvety lawn and frothy, lacey lilacs.

Sheriff Childress' plaintive voice said miserably: "Don't do me this-a-way! You get me higher than a kite—and then you go and let me down. Is this really murder, McGavock? If so— what are we gonna do?"

McGavock wheeled from the window, faced him. "We'll have to use the pearls, Sheriff. It's trickery, I admit, but we're in a hole. We simply have to use them. It's a ruse I've relied on over and over again—and I've always found it highly successful. Shall we give it a go?"

Sheriff Childress asked dubiously: "What pearls?"

"These." McGavock dug in his pocket and produced the imitation pearl necklace. He grasped the string loosely in his hand, so that his thumb held the strand between his first and second finger. Mr. Childress studied Ahem warily. He asked: "Is them genuwine?"

"No, they're fakes. This whole business is a fake. Now you take this necklace—" He wedged his thumb deftly through the strand, exclaimed: "Oo-o-ps! They broke!" The beads cascaded in the air, they rattled and bounced about the floor.

Sheriff Childress said: "Oh, my gracious!" He bent his portly frame, began picking them up. McGavock joined him, he went to the far side of the room, leaving the sheriff to work in the corner where he had planted the plank and thread. Results came quickly. Sheriff Childress grunted with astonishment, said excitedly: "You run on downstairs, Mr. McGavock. I gotta be alone."

McGavock, without looking up, asked: "Why?"

Sheriff Childress' voice trembled. "This ain't no time to ask questions. Git out'n here. I got a inspiration. And when I get a inspiration, I gotta be alone."

"About these pearls—" McGavock protested.

"Forgit them durn pearls," the sheriff ordered, "and leave this attic now! Wait for me down in the parlor."

"O.K." McGavock was amiable.

He stood up, strolled to the door.

He started down the stairs, heavily. He went down five steps and, without pausing or altering the rhythm, stamped back up again.

SHERIFF CHILDRESS WAS on his hands and knees, staring goggle-eyed at the floor. As McGavock watched, the good sheriff grasped the ends of McGavock's thread, lifted the plank, and his jaw dropped. He reached into the pseudo-hiding place and took out the one-dollar bill. McGavock said breezily: "Find something, Sheriff?"

Childress started. He blew out his cheeks, got awkwardly to his feet. "I tole you to leave me alone!" he quavered in rage. "I do swear, I hain't never, no time, seen nare a snooper like you!"

"What's that in your hand? It looks like a dollar bill."

"It is a dollar bill," the sheriff spluttered. "You done forced me into confiding in you, you done ketched me." He controlled himself. "Let bygones be bygones, Luther. I'm ready to co-operate with you. Facks is proving you're right; they's more to this than a mere suicide. It's murder, it's murder and robbery, it all comes to me like a visitation, I see the whole thing in my mind's eye. Charlie Lusk kilt ole man Layton."

"Take it slow." McGavock objected. "I don't quite see—"

"It's as plain as day. This dollar bill proves it." The sheriff spoke pontifically. "This here hole in the floor is a hiding place, ain't it? Why, sure. Old man Layton fixed it up. He took out this board and laid that thread under it so he could find 'er when he wanted 'er. Now, nobuddy would go to all that trouble just to hide a little ole one-dollar bill."

McGavock didn't like the way things were developing. He said: "Here's the way I see it—"

Sheriff Childress ignored him. "I say that Doc Layton had a treasure trove in that hidey-hole. He was a miser. Mebbe they was thousands and thousands of dollars there. Lusk, living here in the house with him, caught on to it. He gives the old professor some kind of a sleeping powder or something, takes him upstairs, and hangs him. In his greed, when he rifles the cache, he gets careless and leaves this one-dollar note—that would be easy to do." The sheriff gazed on his companion benevolently. "Thanks to you and yore meddlin', we finally got us a clue."

"That dollar bill," McGavock announced pleasantly, "is suspicious. It's an indication of some kind of guilt, perhaps. At this stage, it's a little perilous to go any farther. It is an opening, it does put you on some kind of a trail. It substantiates what I've been repeating: that there's dirty work in Doc Layton's demise." He beamed, reached out suddenly and shook the sheriff's hand. "Good-bye, old pal. It's been great knowing you."

Sheriff Childress looked troubled. "What do you mean, good-bye?"

"It's heigh-ho and off to Memphis for me, I guess." He smiled sadly. "This is turning out to be one of those cases I can't resist—I've solved dozens of them. But, as you and Bob Leach say, there's no place for me here in Rockton. I'm not needed. Good-bye—and good luck with your visitations."

"Now hold on there." Lud Childress cleared his throat. "Bob Leach ain't my boss. Stick around a few days. I claim Rockton needs you." He grinned suddenly, an honest, boyish grin. "And I know durn well I do."

"That's better," McGavock said quietly. "You've made a smart choice. I've got this case practically solved. It'll be over by eight tonight, and I'll see that you get full credit." He started for the door. "Look me up this afternoon. *Don't forget.*"

When McGavock came out onto the porch he circled the cottage, passed through the backyard, and left the premises by the rear. The little home was out at the end of Ashwood Avenue. Beyond the low hedge which marked the property's limit was sloping, rocky pastureland. McGavock's problem, as he saw it, was to reach Simon Tetcherall Layton's dilapidated female academy. And to reach it, if possible, without causing too much fuss or commotion. The path he took the night before had led him by the cemetery—so that was out.

He looked with distaste at the rough countryside, paused a moment to get his bearings—and started his hike. It started bad, and got worse. Using the town water-tower as a landmark, he skirted the corporation line. The first quarter-mile was tough going, Spanish needles and prickly-pears, and then, as he descended through a network of dry gulleys, it got increasingly meaner. Finally he reached the river level. Here the ground was vivid in bright green grass, treacherous swamp grass, alive with small metallic leopard frogs and cut by sluggish, muddy sloughs. McGavock kept a cautious watch for copperheads. He pushed his way through a tangle of hazel and sumach and found himself in the clearing.

The dismal buildings stood dank and dreary against their background of water-oak and looping muscadine. McGavock, with no attempt at concealment, made directly for the dormitory. The front door, sagging on its rotted sill, was ajar. The detective swung the panel on its squeaking hinges and entered amongst the cobwebs and mold. He found himself in what had originally been the reception parlor. The small, bare room had but two doors: the entry and a door leading back into the dormitory proper. The layout of the building was extremely interesting from a historian's point of view. McGavock had heard of such queer floor plans. The architecture was a relic of those days when females, under the guise of chaperoning, had been herded like sheep. Immediately beyond the parlor was the first bedroom. This, when the academy flourished, had been the bedroom of the house-mother. It, like the front room, had but two doors. Behind the housemother's room was the first student bedroom, with two doors. And so on—back the entire length of the edifice. The arrangement was such that when Simon Tetcherall Layton's gals went to bed at night—they stayed there. The rooms were linked chain-fashion. The only way a student could indulge in nocturnal courtship was to parade through a succession of chambers, climaxing in the house-mother's room.

McGavock shuddered. "How did the poor chicks ever get themselves husbands? They didn't. They graduated, went home, and settled down to a life of gilding cat-tails and painting pansies on china pintrays."

Each cubicle was like its neighbor—an east window, a west window, and a fireplace. It was the final, end bedroom that paid off.

This room was an exact facsimile of the others except for several extraordinary details. Something new had been added. On the mantelshelf, above the fireplace, was a granite wash-bowl half full of dirty water, a filthy scrap of towelling, a bar of yellow laundry soap—and a cheap mirror. McGavock smiled. This was spoor that had so excited Dr. Layton, the evidence which had driven him to write his 'tramps in the girls dormitory' letter to the Browne Agency.

McGavock worked, and worked fast. It took him just two minutes to find it. He could have pretty well described it before he found it. Up in the fireplace, back on the chimney ledge, he located the bundle. A newish, gray garment, tightly rolled. He laid it gingerly on the floor and spread it out. It was a one piece suit of jumper-type coveralls such as mechanics and farmers use—smeared with smudges of clay and stiff with great blotched stains that could only be dried blood. In the center of the roll was a small hammer and a little black leather kit. He realized that he'd found the murder weapon: a stubby, vicious brick-mason's hammer—the short hickory handle was streaked and red. McGavock was careful not to touch it.

He picked up the black leather kit, opened it. It was an expensive masculine toilet set. There was a pair of military brushes, an ivory-handled nail file, and an empty leather loop. "Swell!" McGavock exulted. "Everything here but the comb!" The name of the owner, gold-stamped within the kit's cover, said: *Leslie Leroy Anderson.*

McGavock rolled up the coveralls as he had found them, replaced them in the fireplace. He said: "You will try to strangle me, eh? I've got you now, friend. You're a gone goose."

IT WAS HIGH noon, the sacred hour of spareribs and okra, when McGavock returned to Main Street. Mankind had vanished from the pavements. The hot sun, directly overhead, burned down on court square in a dry, tremulous haze. There was a scattering of wagons and surries up and down the block. A mountain child in a tattered buggy, guarding his pappy's property from the world of outlanders, munched parched corn and watched McGavock with saucer-like eyes while the buggy's blue mule, following its young master's example, ripped off great sections of the hitching post and masticated them with moody delight. The eyes of mule and boy were on McGavock as he passed, and he saw in each the same tired wisdom of the ageless hills.

McGavock took off his coat, unbuttoned his collar. The thermometer in front of the Simmons House said ninety-one as he swung into the lobby. The mild-mannered clerk with the crescent eye-glasses greeted him pleasantly. McGavock said apologetically: "Brother, I owe you moola. I hate to admit it, but I've lost my room-key."

"You left it in your room," the clerk said genially. "The chambermaid found it there about a half an hour ago." He took a key from the rack behind him and laid it on McGavock's palm, his manner off-hand and casual.

"Whoa!" McGavock objected. "There's a mistake here. The key is number 209. I'm 207."

"You were 207." The clerk smiled placatingly. "You are 209 now. Sheriff's orders."

"Does the sheriff tell people where to sleep in Rockton?"

The clerk laughed good-naturedly. "If the exigency demands, yes. About thirty minutes ago the chambermaid tried your door. It was unlocked so—"

"But I left it locked!"

"That was your impression. However, as I have stated, your key was inside. As I was saying, the chambermaid entered and found your key on the bed. She found the body on the floor."

"She found the what on the floor?"

"The body." The clerk soothed him. "Don't get jumpy. All hotels have them at some time or other. This was a man known as Fiddler Joplin, he had a rather unsavory reputation. There's no need for alarm, you're not suspect. The killing must have happened at least an hour after you left. The sheriff, nevertheless, would like to talk to you if you can spare him the time."

McGavock's voice was bleak when he spoke. "What happened to this Fiddler Joplin?"

"He was strangled with a rawhide noose. By a confederate,

most likely. He was a big man, we don't understand how it was done. It's quite a mystery…" He paused, screwed up his face. "May I give you a tip?"

McGavock nodded.

The clerk said confidentially: "Cook tells me he has some mighty fine river-caught sturgeon. Just say that I recommended it and they'll do it up extra-special for you."

McGavock observed sweetly: "Just pack a little in a lunch pail and I'll take it with me." He started briskly for the door, stopped abruptly when he was half way across the lobby and turned to observe: "From now until eight tonight—I'm going to be long-gone."

5

The Noose Tightens

HALLIE LAYTON RECEIVED McGavock in the conservatory.

The detective was about halfway up the gravelstone drive, headed for the mansion's templelike veranda, when the girl appeared for an instant by a flowering crabtree at the corner of the building and beckoned to him. She did it with a great show of secrecy. It was pretty obvious that she had been waiting for him, that she was trying to divert him before he reached the porch.

He left the drive, cut across the lawn, and followed her wordlessly into a great glassed-in solarium.

It was a domed airy enclosure, mill-roofed with small paned windows—as large as a ballroom. There were rows and shelves of exotic plants and ferns, running certainly into the hundreds, and so much sunshine—refracted at a dozen angles by the slanting panes—so much hairy greenery and waxy foliage, numbed McGavock's senses. The heavy fragrance of the sullen blossoms layered the atmosphere in strata of musky perfumes. Hallie Layton stood before him, stared at him fixedly.

Long-legged and graceful, she was truly a beautiful woman. Her soft jet hair was caught at the nape of her neck with a little-girl ribbon. She was garbed in a loose-knee-length frock of oxblood and thread-of-gold and wore tiny spike-heeled velvet pumps. McGavock gave her an intense, personal scrutiny, said: "Well, well. So this is the way folks get themselves up for buryings in Rockton!"

She flared. "Don't be absurd. I wore black at the funeral. When it was over I came home and dug out the wildest clothes I owned. You know, like you'd rinse out your mouth when you'd swallowed a fly."

McGavock asked calmly: "You didn't like the old man?"

"I loved him. You don't understand. It was just the coffin and the big hole in the ground and everything." She bit her lip. "I'm funny. I can't stand the thought of a living creature losing its spark of life. I guess it's something psychological with me."

McGavock made his voice insolent, pointed. "Do you hunt?"

The door was open to the yard. Six white peacocks, in a snowy line, paraded through the archway into the room from the lawn, wandered aimlessly in and out among the potted ferns. "Of course I hunt." The girl flushed angrily. "I see what you mean—but hunting is entirely different." She tried to explain. "Death, like anything else, comes in degrees. Some deaths are tragic, some are logical and essential. Every time you drink a glass of fermenting wine or eat a slice of moldy cheese you're actually destroying life, but you think nothing of it, do you? What I'm saying is—"

McGavock watched the peacocks. "For your essay on death," he declared, "a great big phoey. Why did you flag me in here?"

She parted the fronds of a drooping bracken, took out a businesslike checkbook and a tiny gold pen. "How much do I owe you?"

"Why worry?" McGavock was vague. He said conversationally: "I've listened to some funny yarns about the old professor. Someone, I believe it was Sheriff Childress, was remarking that the oldster burnt up his teeth just before he died. They say that he was going to grow himself a real set—just by will power. Had you heard the story?"

She nodded. "Yes. It's a fact. Daddy Layton himself told me all about it. He was sitting before his fire one day and he suddenly got exasperated with his dentures. He decided he'd raise a set himself—mind over matter. He took out his plates and tossed them into the fireplace. It sounds strange but who are we to say that he didn't know what he was doing!" She shook the checkbook. "How much do I owe you?"

McGavock noticed that each of the peacocks had one big-jointed toe. It had been bothering him. He asked: "Why is it that those birds each have a swollen toe?" He pointed at the nearest snow-white fowl.

For a minute, she didn't understand. "Oh, that." She smiled. "Peacocks have a tendency to roam. When you buy them, you smash one of their toes and from then on they'll never so much as leave the grounds."

"Just up and smash it, eh?"

"That's what I said." She bridled. "Don't look so righteous. It sounds brutal, and maybe it is. But it's an old traditional preventive and I can't see that it's any of your business!" She went into a cold rage. "You're reared in a city and you come out here and try to tell us how to run our lives. Of course, we Laytons are just half-civilized, but we manage to subsist—"

"I guess you do. Two thousand acres!"

She said frostily: "Last night I lost my head. I went to the Simmons House and retained you. All right, that's a contract. This morning Daddy Layton was buried. That terminates our relationship." She put pen to paper. "How much do I owe you?"

"Five thousand dollars."

Mrs. Layton recoiled. "Are you joking? No, I see you're not. Why that's preposterous. You haven't done a thing."

"I've been pleasant company, haven't I?" McGavock grinned. "Five grand is the toll."

She recapped her pen, folded the checkbook, thrust it in her pocket. "That does it. You don't get one red penny. Maybe that'll teach you a little courtesy. We make a fetish of manners here in the wilds, you know." She gave him a thin, tigerish grin. "I'll buy your ticket back to Memphis—and leave it for you at the Station."

He lifted his hat from his knee, patted it onto his head, stood up. "The only trouble with owning two thousand acres, as I see it, is that you're subject to delusions of grandeur. Don't lay that bull-whip on me, sister, you don't see any ox yoke around my neck. You and I have a contract and you can't break it by just snapping your fingers. You're twisting facts a little, aren't you? Last night, at the Simmons House, you didn't hire me to solve the death of Professor Layton. You were afraid of bodily harm; you contracted with me to protect you. That agreement was certainly not unilateral, it takes two to break it. If you were in danger last night, you are in danger now. I refuse to release you."

She scoffed. "Try to collect a cent!"

"You no doubt know all about Irish setters and walking-horses, but I happen to be fairly well acquainted with the law of the land. By your own admission, Layton Farms is a partnership. If we can't collect from you, we'll put the pressure on your husband. If it's no soap there, we'll sue the estate of old Doc Layton. And when Atherton Browne sues, newspapers get out their red headlines."

She was saying something over and over, underneath her breath, and he couldn't make it out. He asked: "What are you mumbling about?"

She whispered sulphurously: "You dog, you mangy, mangy dog! You dog—"

He nodded in solemn agreement. "I'm afraid it's true. And now, if you'll excuse me, I'll depart from this charming bower of everblooming delight. And see a man about some jugs."

CHARLIE LUSK IN his chocolate slacks and goosetrack tweed jacket—minus mourner's armband—was coming down the broad stone steps of the courthouse as McGavock turned into the square. The secretary was a changed lad. His breezy, cocksure attitude had completely evaporated. His shoulders were slumped and he was dragging his feet like a man walking on skates. McGavock called, "Hello!" and Lusk, observing him, made a futile attempt at putting on his old happy-go-lucky routine. He fanned his fingers, waved, said, "Hi, sport." His voice bent, his eyes were confused, stunned.

McGavock chuckled. "I know just what's going through your mind. It's a dismal world, isn't it?"

Charlie Lusk licked his lips, choked up. "You're not kiddin'. The outlook is very black."

The impact of the sun was terrific. McGavock stopped in the chalky-blue shadow of a fluted pillar. "The high sheriff wants to pin a homicide on you, eh?"

"He's got the wrong person. It seems that while we were at the funeral, Childress was searching Dr. Layton's home. Up in the attic, he found some sort of a hiding place with a one dollar bill in it. He claims it was a big money cache. He says that I killed my employer and robbed him of his secret savings. All that Sheriff Childress wants me to do is, first, to admit premeditated murder; second, to confess that I stole thousands and thousands of dollars, and lastly, to restore the money. That's a brief sketch of my immediate future. It doesn't appeal to me." He tried to smile. Abruptly, he looked mildly astonished. "How did you know?"

"I was with him when he searched the house," McGavock answered. "I'm a detective, you know. Which brings to mind a detail that has us puzzled. We happened to turn off your bedroom along with the rest of the house. I noticed that you're something of a bookworm and that your tastes run to cartoon books and jokes. The subject matter is beside the point, what I can't get is the signatures on the flyleaves of these volumes. Everyone bears the signature: Leslie Anderson, Little Rock, Arkansas. Did you borrow them from—"

Layton looked scared. "The books are mine. I don't know who put that name in them—or why. I noticed it three days ago. It must have been done just after the old man hanged himself."

McGavock said thoughtfully: "The names are forgeries all right. No man would sign his address just Little Rock. He'd say 1066 Gashouse Terrace, or something like that, he'd give the street address. Are the books valuable?"

"The whole batch, secondhand, is worth maybe three dollars and a half."

McGavock frowned. "When do they read the will?"

"The what? Oh, the will. Tomorrow afternoon. It's just a formality. The relatives all have copies. The Layton family is kind of a business corporation. Everything goes back automatically into Layton Farms. Even the old man's reputation. Haw!"

McGavock frowned, wagged his head slowly. "It's a mess, Brother Lusk, it's a real mess." He turned on his heel, took the steps two at a time, and entered the courthouse.

Things were transpiring in the office of the sheriff. Mr. Childress was entertaining.

When McGavock first walked into the room, he didn't get it. He thought Mr. Childress had suddenly been struck loony. The big sheriff was tilted back in his swivel-chair. He had an unlit cigar clamped in his dewlapped jowls, he had taken off the paper cigarband, had placed it on his ring finger, and, at arm's length, was admiring it in melancholy gravity. He twisted his hand back and forth, studying his finger, clucking his tongue in outraged bewilderment. "Horrible," he said. "Positively horrible." He looked strained. "Would you mind saying that again?"

McGavock stopped, hard-heeled. "I didn't say anything."

Sheriff Childress was annoyed. "Oh, come in, McGavock. I wasn't speaking to you. Now that you're here, come in." He spoke past McGavock's shoulder. "I'd like to hear that story again—from beginning to end."

It was then that McGavock observed the sheriff's guest. He was sitting modestly back in the corner, behind the door. He was a little difficult to recognize at first—and then McGavock placed him. Pokey, the ex-convict that ran the bootleg dive under the old slaughter-house. He'd come out of his hole and he was dressed for society. He'd shaved and washed, he was wearing ministerial blue serge and was immaculate in white shirt and black tie. The lines in his brutish face were deep in sullen, anti-social anger. "I'll tell you again," he said. "But I don't expect you to do anything about it. Folks like Fiddler

Joplin and me don't throw much 'fluence. We don't do much candidating for sheriff, come election-time."

Childress exclaimed reproachfully: "Now, that ain't so, friend. I'm a pore man's sheriff!"

Pokey's eye lit up sardonically. "If you say it, I guess that makes it a fact." He addressed McGavock. "And you, accordin' to my notion, hain't any better. Fiddler was a friend of mine. He was found dead in your room up at the Simmons House. How do I know you didn't do it?"

"Answer him gentle," the sheriff advised McGavock. "He's a tolerable good boy, all-in-all, but he's got a bur under his saddle and a gun in his pocket. Fiddler's demise has upset him, he'd kill you at the wink of an eye. Tomorrow, he'll be all right."

McGavock said pleasantly: "Goodness! This is just like a cutback to old Arizona. What's bothering you, Pokey?"

"I'm scared and I'm mad."

The sheriff coaxed. "Tell him about it, Pokey."

"Something's going on around this town that's mighty, mighty bad. I don't know what it is, but Fiddler Joplin did. He got to broodin' over it. I tried to pump him but he wouldn't loosen up. I figured it was something to do with him and the Laytons, something to do with them persecutin' him. Maybe a lawsuit or something like that. Last night I learned different."

Sheriff Childress spoke from the corner of his mouth. "Listen to this, McGavock. It's horrible."

Pokey continued: "Last night Fiddler come into my—er—establishment loopin' drunk. He was talkin' wild about Doc Layton, calling him Satan, that old dragon. Well, he stumbled around for a little and fell down on the bed—passed out cold. He was in a stupor. Doggone, if after a time he didn't begin talking in his sleep. He kept sayin' one thing over and over agin. It chilled my blood to hear it. He said, *Splashed with blood from eye to bosom!* Just that one sentence. I bet he said it a hunnert times!"

Sheriff Childress walled his pupils at McGavock. "Get that? Splashed with blood from eye to bosom. Who was he referring to?"

McGavock declared soberly, "Now listen, Pokey, I'm after Fiddler's slayer—and I'm going to get that very party. But I want you to be honest with me. You claim that Joplin wasn't jugging fish. You, if anyone, should know." He indicated the jugs along the wall. "How do you explain those?"

Sheriff Childress cut in petulantly, "Of course he was a-juggin'. I got a phone tip and went out to his place when he wasn't to home. I found those jugs under his bed. The corks is pierced, they's lime in 'em, they're already to go to town." An idea struck him. "Are you intimatin' that they were planted there? That he was framed?"

"No," McGavock declared. "They were his jugs, all right. Weren't they, Pokey?"

Pokey nodded. "They was his jugs, he admitted it to me, but he wasn't set on takin' no fish with them." He got to his feet, stood a moment in the doorway. "If the law had any gumption, it'd know he was telling the truth. Where would he use them? They ain't nothing but shaller branches out in them hills. His place is fifteen miles from the river, it's too far. And if he had a notion to jug the river-pools, he would-a takened them down there at night and limed them when he got there. He wouldn't have toted all that evidence fifteen miles." He sauntered from the room, closed the door behind him.

Sheriff Childress was impressed. He said quietly: "The man is right. I never thought of it that way. Which makes things considerably balled up for heavens' sakes!"

"Get out your car," McGavock ordered. "We're heading for the hills. I want to take a look at Fiddler Joplin's cabin. And I mean quick!"

JOPLIN'S LITTLE FARM was eight miles, dead center, back in the very heart of the Blue Rock country. Blue Rock was a name loosely applied to a wild, almost impenetrable maze of wooded ridges directly east of town. The drive was just eight miles, but it took them an hour and a half to make it. The trip started out a slow, tedious crawl, and got progressively slower.

They left the city limits, hammered along the macadam pike at a creeping fifteen miles per hour. McGavock spat, said nervously: "What the matter with this buggy? Can't we do any better than this? We're investigating a murder, you know."

Sheriff Childress said complacently: "If I'd open her up, she'd bend the needle. Good cars are hard to get. I've had this baby ten years and I'm aimin' to keep her ten more." The ragweed and roadside sumac rolled by in a slow-motion panorama. McGavock closed his eyes, attempted to doze, when he was jolted forward in the seat. "We turn here," Sheriff Childress explained. McGavock could see no turn, only the long, straight highway.

Mr. Childress, suiting action to the words, whipped his steering wheel abruptly to the left. The car groaned, slowed off the pike, over the berm and shoulder ditch, into a corn-field. "They's more ways to get back into the Blue Rock country," Childress remarked, "than a razorback has ticks. But this-here is the shortest."

They drove along a fence-line of mock orange for a quarter of a mile and headed up a gentle hillside. Three times in fifteen minutes the sheriff dismounted and opened up gates, and they passed through herds of sheep and grazing cattle. The angle of the grade increased, the shale and prickly pears gave way to holly and scrub cedar. An unpainted frame, one-room church appeared on the hillside. Six wagon trails, like spokes of a wheel, led off from the church. The sheriff selected a particular trail, fitted the car wheels in the ruts and grinned. "We cain't miss hit now. We're on our way to the ridge."

"As I get it," McGavock said slowly, "Fiddler didn't live in a cabin. He lived in part of the old mill. Am I right?"

The sheriff nodded. "That's true. But how did you…" McGavock yawned, said: "Pokey just told us so, in your office, didn't you hear him?"

The sheriff objected. "Pokey didn't say nothing about… Well, here we are!"

Joplin's Mill was in a little tree-locked hollow. Looking down on it from the ridge, it was a mournful, shabby scene. At one time, it had been a tiny, mountain gristmill, thriving and busy, and now, its roof-line sagged, its shingles were warped and mossy. The woody, encroaching tendrils of the forest had reached into the clearing. McGavock asked smugly: "What's that big pool of water just behind the building?"

Sheriff Childress said absently: "That's the old millpond, Luther." He suddenly looked thunderstruck. "Oh, golly! Fiddler was going to jug fish in his own millpond!"

"Let's get down there," McGavock ordered grimly. "We're wasting time."

The building had long ago been partially dismantled by

the insistent plucking of the fingers of time. The old mill was little more than a heap of tinder, the back half had buckled completely and lay in a vine-covered mass of helter-skelter timbers and planks. There was evidence, however, that the fore-end of the building had been inhabited. A window had been cut into the siding, a new cut cedar log had been laid as a doorstep. Some of the old mill machinery had been salvaged from the wrecked structure and lay rusty and neglected under a crude lean-to behind the living quarters.

McGavock, like a homing pigeon, made straight for the lean-to. He asked: "Where's the millstone?"

Sheriff Childress pointed to a great circular rock that rested against the warped clapboards. There was an ugly blackish stain on its sandstone surface. The sheriff bent forward. "'y doggies! That's blood!"

"Of course, it's blood." McGavock was cross. "What did you expect? Sorghum? Let's go inside."

It was a pretty shiftless excuse for a home, McGavock realized. There was plenty of timber on the place, if Joplin had wanted to build himself something comfortable—but evidently Fiddler simply didn't crave comfort. The room was crudely furnished, the walls were papered against the wind with old newspapers, the floor was unevenly pieced of odds and ends of scrap lumber. In one corner, there was a primitive stove fashioned from an old oil drum, in another there was a clumsy homemade bunk. Two broken chairs and a rough-sawed table completed the picture.

It was the object on the table which drew their gaze, eclipsed everything else. Smack in the center of Fiddler Joplin's table sat a bird-cage. The cage was a beautiful example of mountain craft, ornately woven of white oak withes.

In the cage was a buzzard. It was the first buzzard that McGavock had ever seen so closely—and it wasn't pretty. Huge, gawky, and nauseating, it was hard to look at. Out of a blackish clump of tousled feathers, stuck its serpentine neck of reddish, wrinkled skin ending in an evil-eyed, big beaked head. Its odious, predatory feet were the exact color of pale human flesh. It studied them with stupid unconcern.

Sheriff Childress gagged. "My Redeemer! What did he want to go and keep a thing like that as a pet for?"

"How did he catch it?"

"They're easy to catch. Just bait a snare-noose. Kids in the hills catches 'em and puts paper collars on 'em. But this is different!" The sheriff purpled. "Cagin' 'em and keeping 'em is—"

"Sure, sure." McGavock walked to the corner of the room. There was a scuttle of ashes by the stove. He lifted the scuttle, set it out a couple of feet, and scuffed the floor with his shoe sole. Sheriff Childress frowned, asked: "What are you looking for? More blood stains?"

McGavock was curt. "Nope, no blood today." He picked up the bird-cage, stepped out into the open, and released the captive.

The vulture loped a few crazy yards, took off with great sweeping strokes of its wings. They watched it disappear into the sky. "And now," McGavock said, "we'll take a quick gander at the millpond—just to keep the record straight."

The pool back of the building was stagnant, foul. Brush and scrub grew down to the very edge of the scummy surface. A blue-black moccasin, as meaty and thick as the sheriff's wrist, sunned itself on a rotting log, water-spiders circled and zigzagged through the slimy algae. "How deep," McGavock asked curiously, "did they dig these ponds?"

Sheriff Childress was restive. "Now that," he declaimed ponderously, "I never did hear tell." He took out a big gold watch. "Shall we be gettin' back to civilization?"

6

Triple Killer

ON THE SLOW drive home, Sheriff Childress was morose. Once, on the ridge-road, with an expansive view of the valley below them, McGavock broke the silence. "So all this country is Layton Farms?"

"That's right, Luther." The sheriff was glum. "Everwhichway you look. As far as you can shoot a 30-30—and a heap sight farther. They're mighty fine people, the Laytons."

For nearly an hour, neither of them spoke. They reached the little church in their backtracking, passed it, began their itinerary through the endless pastures.

Finally, McGavock spoke. "What's wrong with you? I haven't heard a chirp out of you since we left the hills. Don't tell me your ear-misery has come back on you!"

"It's worse'n ear-misery, Luther, if you can imagine such a thing. I got me a bad case of the blues."

"The blues?"

"I'm subject to 'em. God pray you never get 'em, Luther. Hit's like yore heart is laden with worms and gallwood. I cain't get that buzzard off'n my worried mind. I got the turkey buzzard blues."

The car lunged out of the cornfield, onto the macadam. They passed the red painted cotton gin, entered the outskirts of town.

"The blues, eh?" McGavock remarked finally. "I know just

what you mean. And I've got the cure for them. Meet me tonight at Doxie Layton's. At eight o'clock. Bring Charlie Lusk along with you, and your friend, Bobby Leach, the Honorable. Bring your handcuffs, the ones that you've been trying to snap on me all day. I've got a murderer for you. And one thing more—be sure that you have a brand new percussion cap on your shooting iron. Quite frankly, I expect a fracas."

Sheriff Childress said in a hurt voice: "My pistol doesn't use percussion caps. It uses cartridges just like all these new-type revolvers!"

GRADUALLY, AS THE minutes ticked off, the light changed. Of the three of them in the lavish Layton library—McGavock, the master of the house and his wife—only McGavock seemed comfortably at ease. At seven-thirty the sun went down, splashing the honeysuckle on the window, laying a filagree of rose-and-gray on the shiny pressed-leather walls. Hallie Layton sat bolt upright, taut. Across from her, her husband, his lean weathered face half obscured by shadows, relaxed in his favorite overstuffed chair. The sun went down. And as the moments passed, the rose-and-coral of its rays faded from the luxurious carpet, faded to violet. There was a quivering instant of half-light, of afterglow, and the room was plunged into the diaphanous surge of spring twilight.

The plantation owner reached into the shadows, clicked on a table lamp.

McGavock said: "And from Las Vegas I went to a little place called Worthington, Indiana—my what wonderful adventures! From there I went to Miami and helped an old lady find her emerald necklace. Out in Colorado, some goof was cutting up people and putting them in beer barrels, so—tally-ho—out I go to Colorado—"

The clock on the mantel struck a quarter to eight. Doxie Layton remarked coldly: "We can see you've had an interesting life, Mr. McGavock. It's good of you to entertain us. But just what is the point of this call?"

"Just whiling away the tedium," McGavock explained. "Waiting for eight bells. At eight, we're going to nail your father's murderer. Didn't the sheriff mention it to you?"

He obviously hadn't. They didn't seem too jubilant at the prospect. Layton picked an imaginary speck of lint off the lapel of his Park Avenue coat, scrutinized it intently. The brunette twisted forward in her chair, her eyes were hot in anger but her voice was soft and reproachful. "Do you consider this the time and place for coarse dramatics, Mr. McGavock?" A note of personal hostility crept into her tone. "The earth is still fresh on Daddy Layton's grave. Why not postpone this until tomorrow—after the reading of the will?"

"That would be too late. We must do this now, or we'll never again get the chance."

Layton rolled a brown paper cigarette. "You've been talking out of the corner of your mouth ever since you arrived in Rockton. Whispering mysterious nothings." The plantation owner spoke peacefully, softly, but there was steel beneath his words. This is, McGavock realized, this is the showdown. Layton said lazily: "Explain yourself, and fully, before I throw you out."

"Some time ago," McGavock declared, "your father wrote us in Memphis. He'd found what to him appeared to be evidences of tramps in his old Academy dormitory. It was that letter, coupled with a bit of personal investigation on his own part, that caused his murder. Yes—don't screw up your face. Professor Layton was murdered. We'll never be able to prove it, of course, as long as you refuse permission for an exhumation and post mortem. However—"

"However, baloney!" Layton scoffed. "If you can't prove it why go further? Frankly, I must advise you that I consider you a charlatan. You're here simply as an opportunist. You realize that you've failed—"

"I can prove that Leslie Anderson was murdered. I can produce the body. I can prove that the party that killed Anderson had plenty good reason to kill Professor Layton. How does that sound?"

Layton laughed. "You're really fighting for a fee, aren't you?"

From the front door, the knocker clanged and banged on its plate. "That," McGavock observed, "sounds like some kind of a sheriff." The girl arose and left the room. She returned with her unwelcome guests.

Sheriff Childress came through the door like a man made new. The scent of action was in his nostrils, his face was flushed in excited anticipation. He looked upon McGavock with the trusting, happy gaze of a child at Christmas. Beside him walked Lusk, and a little behind him, to one side, tagged Robertus M. Leach. The frowzy man peered past the officer's shoulder, smiled, bowed and nodded at the assembly.

Grimly, McGavock watched them approach. "Now we can get this over." He pointed. "Sheriff arrest that man. Watch out!"

The big sheriff moved like a lynx. He pivoted, grabbed Leach by the forearm, wrenched it up behind his shoulders. The frowzy man spluttered and thrashed. Charlie Lusk jumped into the fray, he clutched Leach's flailing arm, anchored it.

McGavock said fiercely: "Not that one, not Leach! *Charlie Lusk's our man!*"

It took three of them, McGavock, Layton, and the sheriff, to put on the manacles. The little secretary ranted and raved. Sheriff Childress eyed his prisoner uneasily. He said: "It was did, jest like I knowed all along—by a doggone outlander! How'd he do it, Luther?"

Layton said amiably: "Now this, McGavock, is a different story. I somehow felt—er—that you were trying to frame me into it. Tell us about it."

RAISING AN EYEBROW, McGavock said: "It'll cost you five grand." Layton gave the go-ahead sign of a buyer at an auction, said: "Shoot!"

McGavock nodded. "And, I might add, it'll save you many thousands. O.K. Here's the set-up. It's pretty transparent—I'm surprised that you people didn't catch it yourselves. Lusk, here, as the old man's secretary, has been embezzling from his employer. That's the background. Anderson is the spark that touched off all this killing. Some weeks ago, when the time came for the annual auditing of the Layton Farms books, Anderson, as was the manager's duty, checked up on Professor Layton's. He found them deficient. He knew the old man wasn't stealing from himself, so he accused Lusk. Lusk admitted it, asked for time to make restitution. Anderson agreed. I'm guessing about this—but as you'll see, it can't be any other way."

Hallie Layton exclaimed: "Then it wasn't Fiddler Joplin after all?"

"Fiddler Joplin had his place, and it was an important one." McGavock laid it on the line. "Lusk's plan was devilishly simple.

His scheme was to lure Anderson to his place of death and murder him. The death-place, selected by Lusk for the scene of his crime, was secluded Joplin's Mill. He worked on old man Layton, told him that Fiddler was moonshining. The old man had Fiddler thrown into jail for questioning. That was to clear the premises for the killing. Anderson met Lusk at night at Joplin's Mill and was by him slain, yassuh!" He paused. "Lusk became worried. Fiddler suspected that something was wrong."

"I see." Layton's eyes were slaty. "The body is at the mill. Lusk then worked on my father, afraid that his crime would be discovered, prodded my father into attempting to evict Fiddler as a squatter!"

"Exactly. To no avail," McGavock continued. "Fiddler had good reasons to believe a murder had been committed at his place while he spent the weekend in the hoosegow. He—"

Sheriff Childress was skeptical. "How could he know?"

"He saw blood on the millstone. Remember what he said in his drunken sleep—'Splashed with blood from eye to bosom?' He was using old miller's terminology, handed down to him by his pappy. The hole in the center of the stone is the 'eye' and the depression is the 'bosom.' He suspected that Anderson had been slain on the place, he set out to locate the body and to thus vindicate himself in the estimation of his friends and neighbors. His methods were crude and primitive. He figured that any corpse on the place would logically be submerged in the old millpond. He caught himself a buzzard as sort of a feathered bloodhound to smell out the body—and set to work. He limed some jugs. In his handy-man way he was going to use these jugs exactly as folks use dynamite, he was going to blast in the pond to bring the body to the surface."

Lusk said hoarsely: "I'm no embezzler. I wouldn't know how to go about it!"

"Oh no?" McGavock scowled. "You're an A-1 forger, you know all the expert tricks. Your books on how to cartoon are a cover-up in case anyone catches you with trick pens and inks. You forged Anderson's true signature to that letter in the old man's collar drawer as an *exemplar* and then scribbled his name in those volumes in your room as a red herring. You use a high-powered shadow-box in your forgery. You've constructed a dandy. You've cut a hole in the bottom of the old man's dresser drawer; this is your box. You take that two hundred watt bulb out of the ceiling fixture—I bet you made the old man keep it—and put it under the drawer. A plate of glass goes on the hole, and you're all set to trace anything that comes along!"

Doxie Layton said slowly: "So he killed my father, too. Why?"

"As I said, he made a murder-appointment with Anderson out at Joplin's Mill. He expected mean, bloody work. He prepared a washbowl and towel in the old, abandoned girl's dormitory. After he'd despatched Anderson, he searched him, he took from his body, along, doubtless, with his wallet—Anderson's comb case. Lusk then returned to the dormitory, slipped out of his coveralls, washed, and combed his hair with the dead man's comb. The old academy, Mr. Layton, was your father's pride and joy. He was prowling around and found the wash bowl. That was why he wrote us. On a later trip he found more. He found definite evidence of murder. He found the weapon—and he found Leslie Anderson's comb."

Robertus Leach, the Honorable, puffed. "What has a comb got to do with this?"

"It caused the old man's death. I suspect that he recognized *two kinds of hair on it*, and placed one kind as that of his secretary. He brought it home with him and confirmed it. He quizzed Lusk in a roundabout way and Lusk got suspicious. The oldster got scared. He built a big fire in his fireplace and burned the comb. Just then Lusk, snooping, popped into the room. The old man was a quick thinker. He tossed his teeth into the flame so that the hard rubber of his plate would cover the odor of the burning comb. It didn't save his life though."

Layton was convinced. "That was why Les Anderson kept popping in and out of closets. He suspected his life was in jeopardy."

"Precisely. And—"

"If I've been embezzling," Lusk said slyly, "why didn't I pull out while I was in the clear?"

"No hurry," McGavock explained. "The books won't be balanced again until after the will is read. You've still got a couple of days. I bet your suitcase is packed right now."

Sheriff Childress was getting an idea. His face jerked and contorted. At last he spoke. "Now, Luther, you done a right good job. And we're shore thankful to you. I'm gonna dredge that mill-pond tomorrow and seine up Les Anderson. As I see our case, it depends on our finding Les Anderson's corpse. I hope to heaven hit's thur!"

Lusk gloated. "It won't be. Anderson's in Little Rock."

"It won't be," McGavock repeated. "But Anderson's not in Little Rock. There are new nailheads in the ashes of Joplin's bedroom. Anderson's buried under the floor—and you can bet he's down deep."

There was in instant of horror. Silence held the room momentarily.

Sheriff Childress protested. "That cain't be, Luther. When you and me was out there this afternoon, the buzzard in the cage was half asleep. If they'd been a cadaver around, he'da been all hysterical and excited. He'd certainly a-smelled it."

"Lusk buried his victim under Fiddler Joplin's floor. Didn't you?" The secretary crumpled. McGavock ignored him, said: "And now to finish off with a brief lecture on natural history. Most folks think buzzards smell carrion. They don't. Believe it or not, they're guided entirely by sight. They have eyesight many times more powerful than man, they're kin to hawks. They can be so high in the sky that a human can't see them, yet they've picked out maybe a tiny fieldmouse on the ground. Their eyesight is truly marvelous. Their sense of smell, ladies and gentlemen, is greatly overrated. Any questions from the audience?"

About the Author

I WAS BORN in this little Ohio village where I now live (although I left when I was four). My grandfather was a Methodist minister here in the '80s. Am married, no children; but our 150-pound Newfoundland, Lancelot du Lac, keeps our home and our village fairly active. I've lived a good half of my life in Tennessee and am very fond indeed of the Southern hill country. Have been dragged through four colleges, and assaulted with a M.A. from Vanderbilt. When I was young, I spent a year on coffee freighters in the South American trade. I've been writing full time for about ten years.

I have no hobbies, really, unrelated to my work. My particular interest is in building up a library of early American roguery and vagabondage—the sleights and speech of wandering pack-men, doctors, dentists, fire-eaters and so on (our hinterland highways and wilderness trails were literally jammed with them for many years). There's not to much contemporary record along this line, I'm sorry to say, but now and then you uncover something, and when you add it to what you've already got, the picture grows. And it's a pretty stirring picture.

www.ingramcontent.com/pod-product-compliance
Lightning Source LLC
Chambersburg PA
CBHW060414030726

47495CB00003B/571